Dragon's Breath:
Black Flame

Kenla Nelson

Dreamsphere Books
Winnipeg, Canada

Published February 2023 by Dreamsphere Books, an imprint of Story Perfect Inc.

Dreamsphere Books
PO Box 51053 Tyndall Park
Winnipeg, Manitoba R2X 3B0
Canada

Visit http://www.dreamspherebooks.com to find out more.

THE DRAGONS

The Weavers
Nihility the Harbinger
Frety the Reaper
Apryl the Relinquisher
Raravarra the Siren
Ygi the Screecher
Bendre the Ghosteater
Terghelm the Redeemer
Jaydum the Soulbreaker
Sako the Specter
Ivylth the Trickster
Pimo the Mender
Niore "Fireball" Firewind
Paxtiya the Red*
Bysi the Mad*
Otunte*
Livy the Sightstealer*

The Walkers
Destined the Farseer
Sia the Mindbreaker
Tuzys the Mindhunter
Arsu the Savvy
Mica
Ergodi the Wise
Kuri the Beleaguer
Ellot*
Lazarus the Gold*
Cimbu*

The Watchers
Endrir the Broken
Olvess the Beast Tamer
Zennar the Hidden
Shegur the Quick
Britir the Tranquil
Uzzod the Beastmaster
Iros the Blender*

The Council of Elders
Ergodi, Elder of Patience
Kuri, Elder of Frugality
Ivylth, Elder of Kindness
Pimo, Elder of Diligence
Shegur, Elder of Virtuosity
Britir, Elder of Humility
Uzzod, Elder of Giving

The Old Ones
Jezzar Brightflame
Rona Brightscales*
Lar Hardscales*
Iris the Melancholy*
Verganeau the Wild*
Sye*
Thena*

Deceased

Dragon's Breath:
Black Flame

PROLOGUE

Terg, a little green and gold dragon, climbed over his father's back, counting the old dragon's spines as he made his way down to the great spikes of his tail. A tiny blue spark of light fluttered around his head. His giggles echoed off the deep red and black rocks around them as he marveled at the spots where his father's spines had been chipped and broken.

His father was a great grand purple dragon, easily five times his current size. Thick black lines of scales marked him from his snout, over his eyes, and down his sides. He loved the time he got to spend with him because he knew his father was special. He was Lar Hardscales of Petrall. The only dragon without a link to the Great Dream Tree, Aconi, allowed to come and go as he pleased from the Dreaming. Other than his twin brother, Aerrad.

Aerrad did not have a link to Aconi as Terg did. He was not a Weaver like Terg either. But like Terg, Aerrad had never been to Sathea. They had spent all their lives in the Dreaming under the protection of Great Mother Gilliphae.

"Terg," Lar called as Terg hopped in between his spines back towards his head. "Terg."

"Yes, father."

"Come sit, youngling. It is time for your lesson."

Terg groaned. "I want to play," he whined.

"Terghelm! Down, now!" Lar snapped.

"Yes, father," he said gliding down. He sat down before his father's head. His large brown eyes were on him. He tried to stifle his giggles as the light danced between his father's horns.

"Get that thing off of me, Terghlem the Redeemer," Lar said. He clicked his tongue lightly and the light flew back towards the grove where the Great Tree of the Dreaming, Aconi, thrived. "What are you calling those beings?"

"Tree Sprites!" he said excitedly.

"Another of your creations?" his father asked narrowing his eyes at him.

"Aerrad made them," he said quickly.

"It is my understanding Aerrad created them to deal with the dream mites you made." Terg groaned and rolled his eyes. "Great Mother was very unhappy when she came to see me about them, Terg."

"I didn't know they would infest the trees! I only meant for them to annoy Great Mother. She was going on and on about how special the trees were. On and on about how her dryads were fallen trees on Sathea given new life in Dreaming. I was bored."

"Your boredom with your lessons has caused a bigger problem. The sprites build borrows in her trees."

"They eat the dream mites though! I don't know why she fusses. She said all things must find their harmony here in the Dreaming. The dream mites eat the leaves, and the tree sprites eat the dream mites. The sprites burrow to build homes in the trees. They cause no harm! Great Mother's precious trees are protected now."

"You should use caution in your creations, Terg. They are infused with your emotions and thoughts. You give them life and will here in the Dreaming."

"I know, father. I will apologize to Great Mother...again," he said rolling his eyes. "I want to play not be lectured."

"I swear you are more stubborn than a jerboa during mating season, youngling. There will be time for play later. You should take your lessons with enthusiasm like your brother."

"I am not Aerrad, father," he said turning circles in the grass.

"Sathea wept, do you ever sit still?"

"If you want Aerrad instead of me, then just say so," he huffed.

Lar sighed. "I want you, Terg. I know you are not your

brother, but it does not hurt for you to take some pointers in behavior from him now and then."

"Why can't you take me to Sathea? That can be our lesson today."

"You are safer here. Sathea is safer with you here."

"It is not fair! I am tired of being trapped here in the Dreaming!"

"It is not safe, Terghelm!" Lar roared. Terg cowered, backing away a few steps. Lar sighed again sending a waft of smoke into the air. "You are so much like me," he said shaking his head.

"Really?" Terg asked.

"Oh yes. Stubborn, willful, and determined. I swear when your mother had your egg she did it to vex me. Two dragons behaving in every way I did when I was younger. Ways, I might add, your mother claimed infuriated her to no end, and here I am taking my own behavior on the snout," Lar chuckled. "You more so than Aerrad. Your brother inherited my moodiness and love of silence. You got everything else."

The fact that he was like his father made him feel warm. He raised his head and stuck his chest out. "Did you get lectured too?" he asked.

"No lectures were had in my time, my youngling. When I annoyed my father, he would grab me by my tail and hang me over pools of liquid fire threatening to throw me in if I did not stop."

"Seems a big excessive, father," he said, giving Lar a look. He glanced around to make sure there was nowhere Lar could dangle him over something as his father laughed.

"Things were different then. I know it is difficult for you. You are curious, and I encourage your curiosity, Terghelm. However, I need you to remain here in the Dreaming to keep it safe. It is the greatest gift we have been given," Lar said. Terg nodded. "Do you know where we sit, my youngling?"

He nodded. "Near the Berc Mountains on Sathea. Here in the Dreaming, they are the Blackhold Mountains. The place you now call home."

"Do you know why?" Lar asked.

He frowned. "You did not give me that lesson."

"Correct. The lesson was for Aerrad. However, you are twins, and the information should have been shared."

He panicked for a moment, wracking his mind for an answer. He heard his brother's voice faintly in the back of his mind say "hide."

"To hide from Brightscales!" he shouted, louder than he intended.

"Thank your brother for saving your hide again, Terghelm. Yes, I came here to hide you and your brother. I came here to keep the time I spend with each of you a secret from Brightscales."

"Brightscales says not nice things to the Nightmare. She thinks Aerrad and I are the Nightmare. Well one of us anyway. She doesn't seem to realize we are two."

"You pay her no mind, Terg. She has been enthralled with her own being for a very long time. A dragoness with an ego that big leaves very little room for nice things," Lar said.

He nodded. He did not care for Rona Brightscales. She was his mother's twin, but he saw her as a monster of cruelty. He could not believe his mother would be the twin to a creature so foul and full of hate. As soon as they hatched from the egg, they could hear her curse their existence, even if she believed she was speaking to the Nightmare. She called them the spawn of the betrayer.

"What is my lesson today?" he asked, shaking himself.

"Normally, I share the stories with your brother, but today I want to test not only your ability to share thoughts with your twin, but also keep the memories I will give you."

"Like the ones you gave me of Mother?"

"Aye," Lar said quietly. Any mention of his mother always made him sad and withdrawn.

"Will it be a new story, father?" he asked, trying to bring life back into his father's eyes.

"Aye. The story of Sathea and her great protectors, dragons," Lar said. Terg sat up attentively. "A tale I heard from a Great Tree named Magnus, and one that ends with your creation."

"Wait! Do not begin yet!" Terg said excitedly. He closed his eyes for a moment and a bright yellow flower bloomed before Lar with its petals closed tight.

"What is this?" Lar asked.

"A Ciel flower! It will hold the memory of the story if you touch it. You have to be gentle though!"

Lar chuckled. "Great Mother teach you that bit of magic?" he asked.

Terg nodded. "I got the idea from the red ones behind the grove that bloom when a great dream has been had. Go ahead and try it!"

His father lightly flicked the flower with his tongue. The petals opened and Lar began his tale.

Before Sathea found her name, she was a dark place. A place of chaos and corruption. A place of death and destruction. Nothing grew. Nothing flourished beyond fetid decay and putrid fire. It remained so until a bright warm light bloomed in the sky and seven beings stepped forth. Seven sisters saw the land and wept at what was.

The seventh of the sisters looked around and told the others, "There is a balance here. Though there is naught but darkness and death, there is balance."

"Nay sister, there is no balance in darkness and death. How can anything hope to flourish and grow without light and life?" the first sister asked. Then she raised her arms to the sky and the light became the sun. It shined all across Sathea. "Now there is light to balance the darkness," the first sister said.

The seventh sister shook her head. "There is no balance in the light, sister," she said. "The light keeps the darkness away, but without the darkness the land merely burns."

"I can help," the second sister said. She touched the ground where their tears had fell. There was rumbling and groaning until the sound of water rushed through. The fires were extinguished where the water touched.

"There is no balance, sisters," the seventh sister said. "The water washes away the land until the heat of the sun burns it away."

"I can help," said the third sister. She picked up a handful of mud and formed it into a ball. She rolled it and the valleys and hills were created channeling the water into rivers, streams.

"There is no balance," the seventh sister said again. "The land still burns, and the water disappears. You have solved nothing, and you have missed what is for what could be."

"I can help," the fourth sister said. She touched the land and lush grass sprouted, coating the land. It flourished with the water in the soil. Swaths of dry dirt were transformed into tall green grass.

"There is no balance," the seventh sister said. "The grass withers and dies, the land dries, and the water disappears. Where is the balance for what is here?"

"I can help," the fifth sister said. The fifth sister dug in the ground. She pulled at the roots of the grass twining them together. When she was done, trees began to sprout and grow. Shadows loomed under thick branches filled with great leaves. There was a cooling in the areas where the trees blocked the light of the sun.

"There is no balance," the seventh sister sighed. "The trees burn, the grass withers, the land dries, and the water disappears. The shadows cannot move, and where does it leave what was?"

"I can help," the sixth sister said. She took a boulder from the ground and threw it at the sun. The force of her throw created winds and clouds. Before the boulder could reach the sun, it stopped, blocking part of the sun's light. Darkness and light held space upon the land.

"There is no balance," the seventh sister said with tears in her eyes.

"Then you show us the balance you see that we do not," the first sister said.

"Nay," the seventh sister said, shaking her head. "I will wait. I will watch."

The Seven Sisters watched as life blossomed across the land, but what they did not know is this land was home to something else before they arrived. Something the seventh sister acknowledged in the darkness and death. Something that thrived in the dark and the chaos. The great beast called the Prem. Seen and unseen, it hid deep in the land, watching and waiting, as the Seven Sisters went about their work. It lingered in the dark, and while the sisters watched, the Prem emerged, and chaos followed.

The sisters argued with each other. The land changed with their disagreement as the Prem fed on the chaos. The harmony between the Seven Sisters was lost as fires erupted from the land, burning all in its path. The creatures that were beginning their new lives were consumed by the Prem's insatiable hunger. The Prem thrived on the chaos, growing bolder. It's belly grew fat from fear and its happiness exacerbated by misery.

The Seventh Sister pleaded with her sisters to hear her. She pleaded with them to see the destruction and the chaos. She wept as her sisters fought violently with one another, choosing sides and plotting against each other. She wept until her sadness turned to anguish, and her anguish to anger.

It was then the Prem decided to attack the sisters. Even in her anger and sadness, the seventh sister stood before the others to protect them. The beast, once hidden in shadows and darkness, stood before the light of the seventh sister. Her fury threw the shadows away, exposing the truth of the Prem. A great beast covered in black and green fur. Its eyes pulsed with an eerie green fire as a putrid grey slime dripped from its jaws lined with long sharp teeth. It walked on four legs but raised itself to stand before the seventh sister.

The Prem lunged at her, snapping at her as it growled deep in its throat. The seventh sister sent the wind created by her sister at the beast pushing it back. She brought her fist down into the ground splitting the land open. She took hold of the beast and pushed the Prem down into the gaping hole. She closed it on the sounds of the Prem's howls. The land bulged and groaned unable to contain the Prem. Where the Prem fought for freedom became mountains. Where the Prem were cast to their fate rose a great one of black stone.

The Seventh Sister was not done. She took a stone from the land, and threw it at the moon, cracking it into five pieces. Four pieces remained high in the sky, but the fifth fell to the land. The six sisters raged against the seventh sister. They shouted and berated her for daring to destroy their work. The mountains had changed the land, pushing the water and directing the growth of the trees and grass.

The Seventh Sister picked up the piece of the moon that fell and brought it to her lips. "You will hold the Great Balance," she whispered. She sat it down into a patch of land where light, wind, fire, and shadows met. She looked at her sisters and spoke to them with tears in her eyes. "You ignored the one here before. You ignored their place in balance. I cannot mend what you have done. I can only try to protect what remains while you watch what your blindness has wrought," she said.

Each of them turned into a tree with roots deep in the soil. As the Seventh Sister gave up her will to become the grandest tree of them all, the piece of the moon she left cracked open and two full-grown dragons emerged. Their names were Sye and

Thena. They flourished across the land, and more dragons appeared. The land they lived on would come to be called Sathea where they and their progeny were the protectors of the Great Balance, and guided by the Seven Great Trees.

"That can't be all of it!? There must be more to the tale, father," Terg said, frowning.

"Why do you believe it is not the end of the tale, Terghelm?"

"Well, what happened to the Great Balance? What happened to dragons?" Terg asked, thinking of the foul things Rona would whisper to the Nightmare.

"Dragons flourished, and the Prem waited. The Prem was a being very good at waiting. Sometimes it had to wait many years for a meal. Sometimes it had to allow life to grow before devouring it. The Prem realized it could not defeat these great beasts as they were. Their numbers had grown. The Prem had to grow too. The Prem had to change. It split itself into many pieces and began infecting the land slowly. Each piece destroyed, would return to the whole with knowledge of the land until the Prem had its prize. Dragons," Lar said.

"Dragons were not immune to the corruption?" Terg asked.

"Why would they be, my youngling? Why would dragons be immune from the corruption that is said to have infected even great beings like the seven sisters?" Lar asked. Terg shook his head without answer. "Once peaceful dragons began to fight one another for space, mates, and dominance. They ravaged the land with their fury. Those that did not want to participate in such behavior were forced to hide or fight."

"This was during your time!" Terg said realizing what his father was saying. "You are really old."

Lar chuckled. "Aye, dragons live very long lives, my youngling. We age with the trees. At the time, I was a very young dragon. Barely out of the egg, but forced to fight to survive or be killed," Lar explained.

"What happened, father? You survived! Something must have saved you!"

"The Great Trees," Lar said with a slight smile. "They watched, speaking in a way only they could understand. A rustle of leaves and a creaking of branches showed their disquiet. They stored their magic, protecting themselves as best as they could from the dragons that no longer heeded their calls. They did so until they could no longer. The Seventh Sister, now the Great Tree Eovus, spoke to them all and promised to ease the suffering of Sathea and the dragons. Eovus knew the cause of the chaos, its roots ran deep. It was the Prem."

"Eovus took a cutting of itself and planted it in a space now filled with wonder. A place that would be called the Dreaming. It was a place of silence and peace at first. Then the cutting took root, and as the sapling grew and burst forth with its first flowers, all the beings on Sathea fell into a deep slumber. In that slumber Aconi grew and the Dreaming blossomed. The Dream Grove appeared, rivers ran, and mountains burst forth from the land. The Great Sleep of those on Sathea added power to the growing sapling, Aconi. Some dreamed of living peacefully without fear of being consumed. Others dreamed of a place where dragons lived in harmony. Even Eovus dreamed, but their dreams were powerful. Eovus dreamed of all the things that would and could be on Sathea. The Prem was dragged into slumber as well. Eovus had locked them away, fearful of their insatiable hunger. As Eovus slept, so would the Prem in a place they would later call Bishamyr."

"Dragons did not wake until they heard the call of two young dragonesses, Rona Brightscales and Jezzar Brightflame. One a prophet, and the other what would be called a Weaver because of her link to the Great Dream Tree, Aconi. They amassed an army of young dragons who longed for peace and together brought the Great Balance back to center on Sathea."

"You were one of those dragons," Terg said in awe.

"Aye. I was older than them by some years. I had grown tired of fighting and hiding, so I hid deep in one of the forests of Sathea. I hid near a tree bigger than any I had ever seen."

"Did the Prem sleep too?"

"Aye, for many years until it woke. When it did, I believe it was nearing the end of its years. To save itself, it split into pieces, beings that had their own minds and will but were still tied to one another. Eight of them, but only seven remain."

"What you call demons?"

"Aye, we have no other name for what the pieces of the Prem became. Those pieces have given rise to countless others. All of them we call demons. Some have more power than others, but they are all the same. They are all pieces of the beast that was the Prem."

"How do you know this?" Terg asked suddenly. He heard the whisper from his twin asking the question that burst from his snout.

"Your brother's question, or your own, Terghelm?" Lar asked.

"Aerrad, father, but I am curious as well."

"You have heard the things Rona says to the Nightmare, Terg, but have you truly listened? Have you realized the deal that was made yet unfulfilled?" Lar asked. Terg frowned not sure of what his father meant. He touched his link with Aerrad hoping his brother would help him, but Aerrad remained silent. "When you find the answer, you will find the reason we know of the pieces of the Prem, my youngling."

"I ignore her," Terg mumbled.

"As you should, but sometimes you should listen with the absence of feeling. The truth lies in the words spoken and unspoken," Lar said.

"Did you…" Terg started to speak and stopped.

"Ask your question, my youngling."

"Did you love mother or Rona?"

"I believed in Rona's cause. We had a bond forged in agreement. We needed more dragons like us. We were no longer mindless beasts. We had magic we could grasp and wield at will, and we had dreams. We needed more dragons like that on Sathea. Dragons who would care for her, and place her needs above their own."

"And mother?"

"I fell in love with your mother, Terghelm. I fell in love with her the moment I saw her. She was a beautiful dragoness the color of the grass of the Dreaming with eyes as blue as the sunlit sky. You and Aerrad are a testament to that love."

"Did Great Mother really protect them in their egg?"

"Aye. It was Eovus's wish. Great Mother and Aconi would control the Dreaming, and watch over the egg until it hatched. She protected your mother just as she does you and your brother. The only difference was she did not know there were two in your mother's egg. She did not see Rona when she tethered Jezzar to Aconi and gave your mother the gift of a link to the Dreaming. Great Mother believes it allowed Rona to become a prophet instead."

"She can see the past and future?" Terg asked.

"So she says, and I have no reason not to believe her. However, I think she is only seeing a piece of it."

"Like how she cannot see Aerrad and I?"

"Just like that, my youngling. It is also why I brought your egg to Great Mother at your mother's request. She believed you would be safe."

"You brought us to her to protect us, but I don't know why Rona hates mother so much. I don't know why you won't speak of her, or allow us to see Sathea. It was her home!"

"Terg," Lar sighed. "Rona is a lesson. Chaos will always find a way, youngling. We must balance it as we do everything else. We must balance the good and the bad. Jezzar, your mother, gave the Dreaming form, Terg. All around us, there are things she brought forth in a space that was once empty. If she loved the sight of it upon Sathea, then it appeared here in the Dreaming."

"There are dark things here, not just beauty," Terg said frowning. "Dangerous things."

"Aye, your mother saw the beauty in both. She saw the need for both to create a balance in the Dreaming, just as we do on Sathea. Jezzar Brightflame was the balance of the Dreaming. She carried it on her wings. She could create here in the Dreaming just as you and Aerrad do. I know you do not understand, but what she was is lost, Terghelm. All I can give you are memories of her. The Dreaming was her home more than Sathea."

"She created these places in the Dreaming? These creatures?"

"Aye, just as you have done with your Ciel flowers and dream mites. The Weavers flitter about in what the first of them gave form. It was Jezzar's insistence, Great Mother grant a link to other dragonesses. It was Jezzar who called those with a link to Aconi, Weavers, dragons responsible for tending to the dreams of those on Sathea. She made a home for herself and her Weavers. A home for you. A home you add to just as the other Weavers do. You know Tirk the Arkuth?"

"The old bird that is always around Great Mother?" Terg asked. His father nodded. "Aye, Great Mother has assigned him to the dark place in the Dreaming beyond the Nightmare."

"His kind exists because of your mother, Terg. Beings tied to the Dreaming and Sathea. They even see her as their mother. Mother Brightflame is what they call her."

"I did not know that!" he said shocked.

Lar nodded his great head. "Your mother was strong, loving, and kind, Terghelm. She loved the Dreaming, Sathea, and you before you were even hatched. You must take solace in the fact that she loved you, but the being who loved you is lost forever."

"No, she isn't! I hear her!"

"What?"

"I hear her calling to me!"

"You must not listen. That is not your mother, Terg!"

"Yes, it is! She speaks and I see her in my mind."

"It is not your mother, Terghelm! Your mother is gone! She is lost to darkness! The being you hear is not her. It will never be her again. You must grieve as I grieve," Lar hissed. Terg turned his head away as tears stung his eyes. "If I could, I would take you and Aerrad to Sathea, but I cannot. The risk to Sathea is too high. You and your brother are all there is to hold the chaos of the Prem, and the whispers you hear of demons at bay. You are the only thing keeping the shade of your mother in her place."

"Yes, father," he mumbled.

"Terghelm, I am giving you a task. It is why I brought you here today and not your brother. You must remember. You must guide. You must hold on to our history to save our future. You can do those things here in the Dreaming," Lar said. He nuzzled Terg gently as the little dragon cried softly.

"In her place," Terg said to himself as he looked around the hidden cave he sat in.

Magnus, the same great tree that sheltered his father so long ago, created this space for him using his thick roots to cover the entrance. It was the place where he kept his memories. A place full of history. They sat around him intertwined in vines along the walls of the cave. So many Ciel flowers. So many memories. So much history. He was much bigger than he was the day his father told him the tale of Sathea, the size his father was then. He did not learn from the tale or take heed when he should have.

He did not remember the history, but he tried to make the future better.

He sighed sending smoke wafting into the air to hover around him as it fought for release from the cave. He stood up and made his way out. He needed fresh air. He needed the sky. As his snout touched the roots to allow him passage, one of the vines slipped down, touching the top of his head, and pulling him into a memory he both cherished and wished to forget.

CHAPTER ONE

"You called me way out here, Pax? Why? The air feels like I'm trapped in a cave with half of Petrall, and I can smell that damn fairy Womriel!" Terg said as he walked into the meadow to meet her. It was an area where the trees were sparse but abundant with grass and bright yellow and white flowers. She sat in the middle of them, enjoying the heat of the sun.

"You smell him because this is the place that borders Wom from the forest I named for my Verg," Pax said. "Besides, it was you who cursed Womriel to become the Forest of Wom where the Fairy Folk thrive."

"That was Magnus, not me."

"Magnus asked you to punish Womriel. If my memory serves me correctly, and I believe it does, it was you who decided to turn him into a forest," Pax said grinning at him.

"It needs more trees," he said with a huff. "Ones that do not stink of treachery."

"Do you ever stop complaining, you old grumpy dragon?" she asked. "It is a beautiful day."

"No. Character flaw that I will not apologize for. I am old, and I am entitled to my aches and complaints."

"You are not old, Terg. You cannot be old and get around among the dragonesses as you do."

"I am old, but not where it counts," he said, winking at her.

"Never change, Terg," she said, laughing.

"I have no plans to. Although, I would if the right dragoness came around. A dragoness that could sedate the fire in my loins and make me quiver with desire. One that would have me crawl on my belly until it is raw," Terg said, with a sly smile.

"I am not that dragoness, Terg," she said, rolling her eyes. "I told you, it is unnerving to even think about. What is wrong with Ygi?"

"Nothing, but she is not my dragoness. Not in that way, anyway. The only dragons crawling on their belly for her are the Pillars," he said, laughing.

"Yet you still go to her," she said, smirking at him.

"Well, of course. I have needs, Pax! Needs you will not fulfill!"

"You were my brother's mate, Terghelm the Redeemer."

"But you were twins! Twins share everything!"

"For Sathea's sake, Terg! That is not how that works!" she hissed.

He laughed as she huffed smoke at him. "I know Paxxy, but I cannot pass on the opportunity to ruffle your scales. You are glorious when you are agitated with me," he said, nuzzling her lightly.

She sighed at him and hummed at his touch. "I need a favor, Terg."

"Anything, beautiful, but what do I get?" he asked.

"To keep your life," she hissed.

"You older dragonesses become surly with age, you know. There is no fun. No banter. No wagers. No flirting!" Terg said, sitting down. "Otunte threatened to eat me yesterday! Can you believe that?"

"I can. Otunte is weak, but she is still a dragoness. You should spare yourself and stick to the younger ones."

"Perhaps I will. The younger ones find me pleasing. You should hear the things they say about me and my size," Terg said, grooming his claws.

"I am sure Ygi hears well enough for the both of us."

"Pax, unnecessary," he said, trying to hide his grin.

"What does Jaydum say about all these young dragonesses flocking around you?" Pax asked.

"Pax!"

"Do not play coy, Terg. I have known for years he wanted you. I am pleased you found your way to him. You should not have to spend your life alone regardless of my twin," she chuckled.

"He is not Lazarus, but he is mine. He is a beautiful dragon, and he cares for me," he said thoughtfully.

"I know, Terg. I am an Empath, my dear friend."

"And a wonderful source of information about one's feelings. How long has Jaydum desired my company?" he asked, laying his head at her feet.

"Most would ask their mate that question, Terg. Not an Empath," she said, rolling her eyes.

"You are an Empath, and my best friend, now tell me," he said, nudging her.

"I am not sure. I only noticed after Laz was gone to us. You be good to him, Terghelm," she said.

"I promise, Pax."

"Lazarus would want you to be happy, and so would Bysi. Now, the favor I need," she said, shifting her position.

"No," he said, rolling his eyes.

"No?"

"Aye. You will remain with me. I am not ready to say goodbye to you yet. My heart is not ready. However, we can enjoy this meadow and the silence. I could entertain you by burning small pieces of bark from Womriel. He screeches when I do that."

"Terg, please," she whispered.

"No! Damn it, Pax! No!" he shouted.

"I am hurting badly. Every day is harder than the last. Please," she begged.

"Fly off Paxtyia of the Depths!" he said, turning his head away from her.

"Terg! Really? That was unkind."

"But warranted," he said, huffing smoke at her.

"How did you know that is what I wanted?" she asked him after a moment.

"You never leave Petrall anymore, Pax. Not unless you must. You have been gone for many moons. I knew something was wrong."

"I do not want to return," she said.

"Then don't. We can find a forest for the two of us. We can live out our days as the handsome dragon and his grumpy dragoness companion. Well, three of us. I will not leave Jaydum. I cannot leave Jaydum. The moans on that dragon, Pax, they set my scales to shiver."

"Terg."

He sighed. "What is the favor? I will hear you, but I agree to nothing yet."

"I need an image of myself left here in this place where eyes can see," she said.

"See what?" he asked, confused.

"My decision to give up and go to the Dreaming. I do not want to be found or sought after."

"My previous words still stand; fly off Pax."

"Terg, why can I not go? I miss them. I miss Iros. I miss Laz. I miss Verg."

"Yeah, and I miss Laz and Bysi, but you do not see me giving up my life, do you?"

She looked off across the meadow towards Wom. The sound of the forest moving drifted on the breeze. "You are stronger than I am," Pax finally said.

"Lies and jeroba shit, dragoness. Neither suit you," he scoffed.

"You are the most foul-mouthed dragon I have ever known, Terg!" she hissed.

"You want me to aid you in your endeavors to snuff yourself out with that kind of fire still in your belly," he said, raising his eyes at her.

"Stop baiting me!"

"Never, Pax. I take great pleasure in it. It is how I know the dragoness I love still lives as her mate asked her to."

"Not fair, Terg."

"And it was fair for Laz to burden you with taking care of me, Pax of the Depths? Was it fair for him to do the same with Iros for you? Nothing is ever fair, but we do what we have to ease the pain of our absence from the hearts of those we leave behind. You and I have a luxury most do not, Pax. We still have each other without the complication that being mated brings. We are still here! We are family!" he retorted.

"I am afraid, Terg! Do you hear me! I am afraid," she said, trying to control her tears.

"Afraid? You are afraid of nothing, Paxxy. What is going on?" he asked, shocked.

"I saw something in a dream thread. I have seen it before, but I cannot remember clearly. I have been out here trying to figure it out, but I cannot focus."

"Tell me."

"I saw a serpent. A serpent that was as green as the vibrant leaves on the Dreaming's trees. Like all the greens of the Dreaming manifested on its body. Those of short lives, they adored it, Terg. It was almost like they worshipped it. I do not know, but it felt strange."

"Short-lifers are strange, Paxxy. They smell too. I guess they would have to, or I'd eat the lot of them," he said, bobbing his head.

"Be serious, Terg," she snickered.

"Why does the serpent disturb you? Is it the serpent or the behavior of the short-lifers in their dreams?"

"Both. I cannot weave those dreams, Terg," she whispered. "I can only view them as if some other Weaver has control over them."

"What? That is not possible, Pax. You have consumed dream essence! You are the only Weaver capable of exercising control over the dream and the dreamer. No other Weaver could," he said. He stopped and looked at her closely for a moment. "What are you not telling me, dragoness?"

"Why must you be so damn inquisitive, Terg!? Can you not just be a good friend for once?"

"This is not friendship, Paxxy. This smells of secrets and half-truths. You suddenly call me here when half of Petrall is upset over your absence. You tell me you tire of living this life when you are the talk of the Dreaming. It has been forty-thousand years since the Culling of the Warida, but the mere thought of the wrath of the Black Flame brings obedience to the Depths. Now you say you are afraid of a serpent in dreams that you cannot weave. Enough, Pax. I would have what lies between the words you say."

"Laz left himself in that place to keep demons away from Sathea. He made himself a barrier."

"To guard against those great demons, the Seven," he said, nodding his head.

"Aye. I think Laz suffers without me, Terg. I feel like my twin is in extreme pain and cannot hold the void without me, but more. The serpent I saw is connected, I am sure of it, but I cannot gather how."

"Nonsense Pax. You cannot feel any of that. You are only grieving."

"It is not nonsense!" she shouted. "Terg, I need you to believe me, please."

"Pax, you have told me about this barrier. You cried under my head as you told me what Laz had done. I felt him leave, but I have felt nothing since. Just emptiness where his heart once was. I have felt no pain."

"I know you have not, but I have, Terg!" she said, exasperated. "Pain like I have never imagined. I know it is him. I feel him pulling at me."

"You have done as he asked. You have organized Petrall to

ward against them. The Weavers thrive, and the Watchers and Walkers grow. You do not need to hold on to this sense of duty you have to Lazarus! You break my heart with this. What else do you think you could do?"

"Protect him!" she shouted with tears in her eyes. "Protect my twin as I always have!"

He took a deep breath. "This serpent you have seen, is it what made you feel the urgency to do this?"

She nodded. "Lazarus left me a message, Terg. I thought he was mad, but he was not. I think the serpent is what he was perturbed about, but I cannot grasp it all. He worried about the Seven, but this serpent...it felt wrong."

"Because you spend too much time on Petrall," he said as a matter of fact.

"Aye, but that is not all. The serpent felt familiar. It almost felt like us, like a Weaver, I mean."

"I have never heard a tale of anything like that, Pax. Even Hynro cannot touch dreams as we do. No other creature on Sathea is born with a link to the Dreaming as we are. Not even the Arkuth or the Serbsut are linked. We have guided them there, but we feel the Dreaming as we feel Sathea. No other can. Have you talked to the Great Mother about it?"

"Aye, but she was vague as usual. She said the serpent has lurked for time untold and that with its movements, the Nightmare grows."

"You know her words hold meaning, Pax. You just have to find it. Have you visited the Nightmare?"

"No," she said, making a face. "Why would I? I have no need for that thing," she said. She squinted her eyes, reading him. "Why do you feel like that?"

"Stop reading me, dragoness! For Sathea's sake!" Terg said, sighing. "You said Laz left a message. Did he mention anything about it?"

"No. Only about the first Matron."

"Jezzar?" Terg asked, frowning.

"Aye, Jezzar and some creature called a Mooza. He did not mention these things to you?"

"I was his mate, not his pair. As his mate, I shared Laz's heart and his nest. Iros was his pair, his best friend, and who he shared his mischief with. Those little details, codes, and ideas, he only shared with Iros."

"They kept too many secrets," she said with a huff.

"Of course they did. It was all a part of the game Laz and Iros played. The thrill of the hunt," he said, rolling his eyes.

"He said he left pieces. Have you found them?" Pax asked.

"I have not even bothered to look, Pax. You know I find those games annoying. I would rather have the information forthright, but I will speak to Magnus if you give me time to do so."

"I have no time left," she whispered.

"You have plenty of time, dragoness. Stop this now."

"Terg, do you ever have the feeling like your time has run? A feeling like you are in the way of something bigger?"

"No, but that is probably because my ego is considerable."

"More than considerable, I would say," she mumbled. "I have that feeling. I feel like what I plan to do, is the right thing. That it is meant to be now. I cannot explain it better than that."

"Pax, I… Tell me your plan," he said, defeated.

"I mean to go in as he did. I am going to reunite myself with my half and seal the Black Flame with me."

"You want the illusion, so no one comes to look for you," he said.

"Aye. I need you to sustain the image of me here. I want them to believe I decided to fade away into the Dreaming forever. I need to be back with Lazarus. The Twin Stars of Petrall must be whole again.

"The Black Flame, is this why you created it?"

"I needed to. I know you do not understand, but as Empath, I needed to," she said.

"Why did you really call me here, Paxxy? You do not need me for that illusion. You can sustain it yourself."

"I...I wanted to say goodbye, and I wanted to let you know where I truly went. That I went to my twin and half of your heart," she said. He nodded and turned his head, trying to hide his tears. "Terg, another will come. Another like me, I mean. An Empath. If you are still around, and I hope you are, protect them. Empaths are... The burden is heavy, Terg. Make sure they have more than I did. They need more than the love of a mate to see them through. They need more to protect them from..."

"The serpent you saw?" he asked.

"Aye. It felt like it could devour me. Like it could devour the Dreaming. Like..." she stopped huffing smoke.

"The Nightmare," he said. Pax nodded. "Can I change your mind? Can I promise you that if you stay with me, we can work it out together?"

"No. This feels right. It always has since the idea occurred to me before I lost Iros. I belong with my twin. He needs me. I feel it deep in my heart," she said. He nodded. "Take this, Terg. It is for you."

A memory orb floated over to him. It was a deep red orb with silver and white striations in it, the color of the aura of Pax of the Depths. It disappeared as it touched his snout. "Paxxy!" he sobbed. He rested his head on hers. "You have not been whole in a long time. Why did you not tell me! I could rend him in two for forcing you to that!"

"I promised I would keep him safe, but I am tired. I am almost 400,000 years old, and I am tired, Terg. The pain consumes me now. You are the only one I have left. Do not let them mourn me. Tell the Pillars..."

"I will tell them."

"And let my sweet Ygi know..."

"I will, Pax."

"I know, and you will not forget because we are not on Petrall. Now go on. I will not have you linger in grief. Go spend time with Jaydum."

"Nay. We will see it done together. You can play the stubborn dragoness with your twin. Tell him I said hello, and that he is missed and loved as you will be."

"Terg…"

"If you insist on doing this, I am going with you, Pax, discussion over. I know you know where the place is, so lead us there, dragoness. Today, I am the dragon who soars under the power of your wings."

She smiled at him. "I love you, Terghelm the Redeemer.

"I love you too, Pax. Now come on before I come to my senses. Great Mother is going to have my scales for this."

"No, I think…I think she knew it would come to this," she said.

The cries of pain echoed off the rocks where he lay in the Dreaming. He looked around, wondering what poor animal could make such a sound. Nothing lived in this part of the Dreaming. This forest was sacred, a shared place between the Dreaming and Sathea he named Xtyia Forest in both areas. It was the same place where he met her that long-ago day, one-hundred and fifty thousand years ago. It was his gift to her life that he watched bloom from a single seed as he counted the days she had been gone.

"What on Sathea is going on," he said, rising with a huff.

He followed the sound but could not pinpoint where it was coming from. He opened his eyes and emerged from his cave on Sathea. The cries were deafening here. "Whoever is trespassing is going to regret it," he said, swinging his head around. This was *his* place.

"Be still, whelp! This is for your own good," a female voice said. He recognized it immediately. "Hold her still, Ergodi."

"Hurry, Ivy. I am already bored with this, and I have work to do with the Farseer."

He made his way into the forest. It lay before his cave, a sprawling expanse of greens, yellows, and deep browns. He crept through the trees, trying not to give away his presence. Although his scales allowed him to blend well in the coverage, it was still harder than it looked, given his size. As he pushed through the trees into the same clearing Pax once spoke with him in, he saw them; Ergodi, Ivylth, and Pimo. He frowned as he saw the little fledgling before them. Ergodi held her down while Ivylth raked her claw down the little fledgling's neck and side, drawing blood. The little one gasped for air, struggling against Ergodi's grip. Pimo was sending waves of healing aura at the wounds Ivylth inflicted with her claws.

"I said, be still! Worthless dragoness! You are no Weaver! You are a monstrous stain on all Petrall stands for. You brought us destruction with your hatching!" Ivylth hissed. The little dragoness cried out again in agony. "Stop it, you foul beast! I do not care to feel your pain! Your pain is nothing compared to what I have endured! You will learn that you exist to do as I say and no more!"

Bones snapped. He flinched as he felt the fledgling's pain flow over him. He realized, horrorstruck, she was an Empath.

He rushed through the trees, bashing Ergodi with his tail and knocking him down as he pinned Ivylth to the ground. "What on Sathea do you think you are doing!?" he shouted as fire licked his jaws.

"Terg!" Ergodi said, shocked.

"Master Terg to you, coward," he said, narrowing his eyes at Ergodi.

"I am no coward!" Ergodi said, trying to right himself. He bashed him again with his tail, sending a tree crashing down.

"You will always be the coward who hid while others died," he said. "Now, do you want to explain yourselves, or should I just kill you all and spare myself the lies?"

"Teaching! We were just teaching," Pimo squeaked.

"Lies!" he shouted, sending her cowering against the trees. "You lying useless dragoness! I expected more from you, Pimo the Mender! Is this how you use the magic gifted to you?!"

"This is not your concern, Master Terg," Ergodi said, standing himself up.

"I have made it my concern, coward," he said, backing away from Ivylth. "If you move, Ivy, I will kill you," he said. She whimpered and looked at Ergodi. "He cannot save you. He cannot even save himself today. He only tries to look brave, but I can smell his fear. Try me, Ergodi. I want you to, dragon!" he shouted. "I will take your hide and line my cave with it."

"Ter...Master Terg, this is just a misunderstanding. We were well on our way back to Petrall," Ergodi stammered.

"Were you? Was that before or after you tortured this little Weaver?"

"She is no Weaver!" Ivylth screeched.

"Moving your snout counts, Ivylth," he said with a grin. His eyes glowed and pulsed as she fell to the ground, writhing in agony. "I should have snapped your neck when I found that pool of death, but she would not let me," he said as he dug through her mind. "It surprises you it was the Grand Lady who spared your pitiful life? I'm not surprised. In fact, I was annoyed at her interference. But she is not here to save you this time. There is no one here to save you," he whispered as her screams filled the air. "What is this?" he said as he found a part of her mind she had locked away. "Shall we have a peak, Ivylth the Trickster?"

"Stop it!" Ergodi shouted. "Stop it, please! I will take her and Pimo back to Petrall. Just stop!"

"Your heart only gives you common sense when it comes to this poor excuse for a dragoness, Ergodi. Go back to Petrall and remain there. If you think to escape my wrath, know that there is nowhere you can run on Sathea from me. I will set your punishment when I return."

"Who do you think you are to punish us?" Ivylth said, righting herself.

"You see, Ergodi, she is so daft that she does not realize that she has escaped death yet again," he said.

He spit fire at her, hitting her on the more rigid scales on her back. She screeched and lunged at him. The roots of the trees wrapped themselves around her, pinning her to the ground. A thin branch whipped her across the snout, slashing her open. Her screams were cut off as the roots found her throat and squeezed while the smaller branches swung across her side hard enough to remove scales.

"How does it feel, Ivylth? Do you think I have come close to the pain that little dragoness felt?" he asked as the branches continued their assault.

"Master Terg, please. Please. I am begging you," Ergodi said near tears. "Please do not kill her. We will go back and wait. I swear on Mother Rona!"

"Another useless dragoness," he snapped, releasing Ivylth. "Go. Now!" he shouted. It tempted him to kill all three of them, but that was not the way. It would make him no better than them, and he wanted all of Petrall to know what they were doing to one of their own.

Once they cleared the trees, he turned to look at the little dragoness in the grass. She had not moved but was alive. She was black from tip to tail. Even her tiny horns and spikes were black. He had never seen a dragoness painted in such a way. Even the new generations of Watchers were various hues of the same color. This little one was as black as a cave that goes deep under the mountains.

As he approached, she cowed and cried out, hiding her head under her wing. He moved away from her, giving her space to see him. He laid down and stretched himself out, exposing his belly to her. "What is your name, little dragoness?"

She moved her wing just enough for him to see deep brown eyes peek out at him. "Harbinger," she whispered. Her voice was soft, but there was strength in it.

"Do you know who I am, little Harbinger?"

"Terg the Redeemer," she whispered. "The Matron tells me stories of you."

"Have you been taken to Weaver Circle yet?" he asked. She shook her head. "Why not? Do you wish to stay with the Matron? You are too big to be there now. You must have at least a thousand years to the sky."

"Three thousand, and I am not welcome there," she said.

"Says who?!" he hissed. She whimpered and cringed. He took a moment to calm himself. How easily he had forgotten how to navigate around an Empath, beings who could read, transfer, and manipulate emotions "Do they do that often to you, Harbinger?" She remained hidden under her wing. He could see where patches of scales were missing from her side, exposing the soft pink flesh underneath. "I will not hurt you. Did the Matron not tell you I was harmless? Well harmless to beautiful young dragonesses anyway," he said, chuckling.

"They hurt me all the time because of what I know and what I am," she said from under her wing. "They all hurt me."

"What would one as young as you know that would cause them to do such things to you?" he asked.

"How they truly feel. The things they wish to hide in the dark," she said, peeking out at him again.

"Their emotions, you mean?" he asked, shocked. The echo of Pax's words hit him with force. She had warned him there would be another like her. An Empath he would need to care for. He stood in the last place he shared with Pax with the manifestation of her words before him.

"Aye," she said, shaking. "I do not feel well."

"Are you hurt? I should have checked you first. I am sorry, little one," he said, rising.

"My belly. Ivylth made me eat the blue flowers again, and now my belly hurts badly."

He watched as she shimmered and returned. He was struck silent, watching her. She was trying to heal herself on instinct by carrying herself to the Dreaming. "The flowers that grow near Weaver Circle?" he asked. She nodded and whimpered. "Never eat those, little one. They are not for you," he said. He closed his eyes, and a few small purple berries appeared in front of her. "Eat those. You will feel better."

She stuck her snout out and sniffed them, nudging them around. "What are these?" she asked, looking up at him. Her eyes made his heartbreak for what Ivylth had done to her.

"Abscella. They only grow on the bushes in the Dreaming. It will heal what ails you."

"These grow where the one that sings to me lives," she said, sniffing them again.

"Great Mother Gilliphae," he said. "She sings to you?"

"Aye, when I am sad," she said, taking a berry. "Thank you."

"Harbinger, I must decide what to do with you. Is there a place you would like to go? I need to return to Petrall and deal with those three."

"You should not punish them. They are afraid of me. Fear makes them do what they do," she said. "If you punish them, they will only find someone else to hurt or fresh ways to hurt me."

"Wise words for one so young. What if I take you somewhere safe? There are those on Petrall that I am very close to that would look after you."

"Are they nice?" she asked.

She moved towards him, limping on her back leg. She sniffed him near his front leg, making his scales tingle. "I believe so. They are my family," he said, trying to keep his emotions balanced.

"You do not have to hide your feelings from me. I feel them anyway," she said, sitting down in front of him. "Sometimes I wish I didn't, but I do. Even now, the land speaks to me, sharing how it feels."

"I am sorry they hurt you," he said. She was already using her magic naturally. He could see it in the way she tilted her head as if she was listening to something only she could hear.

"I do not need pity. The only reason Ivylth and Ergodi do what they do is because I am little, but I will not be a little dragoness forever."

He smiled at her. "No, you will not be. I can already see the great dragoness you will become. However, until then, I must keep you safe."

"You can't unless you stay at my side. They will find me. They always do. I will not have them harm anyone else because of me."

"I promise you, I will always be there to protect you. They will never harm you or anyone else again, Harbinger," he said. He paused. "Do you have no other name?"

"I am the Harbinger. I am death on black wings."

"You are beauty on black wings. If you bring death, it is because they deserve it," he said with a tone. "Has another dragoness has given you a proper name?"

"Aye, she was nice, but I have not seen her since that day," she said.

"Do you remember her name?"

"No. She came to the nursery to speak to the Matron and saw me. She was like the sunset in color. She had an odd voice that tickled my ears. She said my name was Nihility, but no one calls me that. Well, no one except Endrir and Destined."

He chuckled at the circle he had found himself in. The dragoness he wanted to take the Harbinger to was who named her; Ygi the Screecher. "It is a pleasure to meet you, Nihility," he said. She nodded her head at him but looked away. "Who are Endrir and Destined? Can they protect you?"

"No, they can't!" she said. There was worry in her voice. "I must protect them."

"You are their dragoness?" he asked with a slight smile.

"We are bound together no matter how hard they try to keep us apart," she said. "But I am no dragon's dragoness."

"Yet," he mumbled. "Come on, little dragoness. I know exactly who can keep you safe until you grow as big as you desire," he said. For the first time in one hundredthousand years, he was eager to get back to Petrall.

"I cannot fly all the way back to Petrall. I hurt all over," she said.

"Then you can ride," he said, smiling at her. He lowered himself and nudged her with his snout. She carefully glided up to his neck and sat in between the first of his spines. "You must hold on tight. I do not wish for you to fall. If you did, you would shatter my heart. That would be a travesty after you captured it so easily."

"You do not have a dragoness to protect you?" she asked.

"I do now. A little black dragoness called Nihility has captured the heart of the Great Terg the All-Powerful Redeemer," he said, blowing fire and making her giggle. He had not heard a sound so sweet in a long time.

Terg roared and pushed himself through the roots, tearing himself away from the vines.

"Damn you, Magnus," he shouted to the empty forest before him. The trees of Xtiya Forest rustled in response to his curse. He huffed smoke. "You could speak, Magnus, instead of using my magic against me!" he said as he dug his claws into the ground in frustration. He stopped as the silence grew thick. The trees went still until a soft breeze caressed his snout. "Ygi," he whispered as he caught her scent.

His ears tickled, and there was the faint sound of birdsong and the hiss of fire. Ygi was calling for him. There was an urgency in her message he had not heard before. He took flight. Ygi was calling him to Petrall with a whisper of Nihility, the hatchling he saved, on the wind.

Terg made his way high into the sky, flying high enough the air thinned. His lungs ached as if Sathea gripped them tight to keep him from flying too far from her. He wanted to be away.

The memories were vivid and fresh. They led to other thoughts. Thoughts of his betrayal of his twin, Aerrad, the life of lies he had built around himself on Sathea, the loss of those he loved, and the sacrifices of the Twin Stars of Petrall to keep his mother locked away.

"Shit," he mumbled to himself.

There was a sinking feeling that his own history was catching up to him. It placed a pit of dread in his belly. He knew the danger of demons, the Prem, and his mother Jezzar. He knew even when Pax did not. He understood what Laz didn't. The serpent was his mother, Jezzar, and she was awake, but contained. "Nihility," he thought to himself. The image of the little black dragoness filled his mind. Dread disappeared, replaced by a strong urgency to fly faster.

CHAPTER TWO

The Mother Moon hung bright in the sky, painting everything a blueish hue. The Mother's two children were away with the Maiden Moon this night and three nights before. Only the Mother Moon and the stars held the sky. Nihility lay in the cool soft green grass before a sea of short lifers those in the cities called the Dark Ones for the depth of brown in their skin. They were the Daughters of Ote, nomads who roamed Sathea using her landscape as their home.

They were over a hundred thousand strong, and she sat as the only dragoness among them. They did not fear her presence. Instead, they welcomed her and believed her presence blessed them and their dreams. She did not dissuade their beliefs. If there were any short lifers on Sathea she respected, it was the Daughters of Ote and their nomadic ways.

In her borrowed form, she appeared as one of them, and they honored her as a Sister of the Aether, the fire wielder. However, tonight she was not here to walk among them and revel in their festivals, partaking in their ways. She was here to bring them into the Dreaming and to offer them a seat with the Council of Dreaming. For that, she needed her proper form. She needed to be dragoness. The black dragoness of Petrall they named the Harbinger.

Their leader, Mother Tangi, had raked the dream sand into the pit so the Dreaming could send its message for their next journey. They had doused their fires and laid out their soft pallets of woven grass to sleep. She could hear the murmurs from the fathers who were calming their children while the mothers suckled those who still needed the strength of their milk.

This was her night to gather their threads to her and tie them to the grove where the Great Dream Tree Aconi stood with his keeper Gilliphae, the Great Mother. Great Mother had chosen her to honor the Daughters of Ote. "Nihility the Harbinger, it is your duty to guide them to the Dreaming," Gilliphae had said to her. She felt pride at the request. Lady Ygi could have come, but Great Mother chose her.

She was Lead Weaver of Weaver Circle on Petrall. She was chosen because they believed she could harness the Crystal of the Depths and the dreamers it watched, as no other Weaver could. She did not feel she had earned the position yet, but she worked hard to make the other Weavers that followed her proud. It was her duty to tend to the dreamers of Sathea, but it was an honor to offer the Daughters a seat on the council. They would become one with the Dreaming, allowing it to grow and flourish.

The Daughters of Ote could already touch the Aether, the place where the elements of the Dreaming existed. Their ability to interact with those elements would add to the power of the Dreaming. She had asked Gilliphae about allowing them on the Dream Council, and the Great Mother concurred, but only after she had learned their ways. She accepted the task with enthusiasm, spending the better part of the last fifteen thousand years among them. She had seen the death and birth of many of the Daughters over those years. The love and respect she had for them as short lifers ran deep. They were part of her family.

The Daughters were also Dream Readers. They believed that the images in the dreams held significant meaning in their lives. They were part of the many other short lifers of Sathea that placed weight on the importance of their dreams. Dreams were where great thoughts were born. She agreed but saw no merit in it for her own personal use.

It was her duty to see that the dreamer's dreams were fruitful and safe. She was a Weaver. You would always know if a Weaver touched your thread to weave your dreams. It could be in a scent that can be smelled even in the dream or one that brings memories while awake, for example. If a Weaver was present in your dream, you would know as well. It would be a face that should not be or cannot be remembered. A shadow glimpsed and felt but not really seen.

She loved being a Weaver. She was hatched with a link to the Dreaming. The Dreaming itself was her home. It mirrored Sathea before the short lifers spread across the land. Sathea changed faster than the Dreaming landscape, but some places remained the same; those linked directly to the Dreaming. She laid in one of those places now, an area the Daughters of Ote called Blackhold Acropolis.

On Sathea, Blackholdsat in open land bordered by the desert, the last peaks of the Berc Mountains, and the Berestague Gulf. The Acropolis was nothing more than the edge of the mountain that had withered away and stood alone. Alcoves littered the rock where the nomads came to birth their young or die in the peace. It was a place where the Silent Sisters worked their magic to ferry their dead from this life to the next and where Lady Shi founded the Sisters of the Aether before her death.

In the Dreaming, it was a border place between the brightness of the upper levels and the Depths where the Nightmare lived. The place where the Shadow Mist swirled. She knew it as the Borderland, the area in the Dreaming between life and death. It was also the place where the Great Lady Pax of the Depths ended her journey through the Depths of the Dreaming.

She languished in the moonlight of the Mother Moon, waiting for them all to sleep. The light of the moon made her scales shine, even though she was the deepest black from snout to tail. Her spines, the two horns curled from her head, and the cluster of eight deadly spikes on her tail, all the deepest black. Only her eyes held a different color, brown. She hummed, lulling them to sleep with her song. She closed her eyes and entered the Dreaming. Her body shimmered as she held her presence on both Sathea and the Dreaming. She was gathering their threads when she heard someone call to her.

"My Harbinger," a voice whispered, startling her out of the Dreaming. She opened her eyes and saw a tiny orange bird sitting before her. At the sight of it, her sadness and longing threatened to claim her. She pushed it back down quickly.

"Sia?" she asked, confused.

The bird flew towards the pit of dream sand Tangi had placed earlier in the day. She saw one nomad stand. Vivian was a Sister of the Aether who wielded the land. She was tall. Her skin was the color of the red sand of the Acropolis with a yellow tint. Her long black hair was braided down her back with coils of green woven through, the color of the Aether that marked her.

Vivian walked over to the sand and bent down, placing her palm in it. She could hear the sand shift at Vivian's touch. She moved slowly over to Vivian to see and gasped as the sand moved and took on color, revealing a picture. A figure dressed in white stood with a staff, and a jade serpent surrounded him.

"Destined," she whispered. Her heart was pounding. She looked at Vivian. Her eyes were closed, her face slack. "Vivian?"

"Nihility the Harbinger, Sister of Fire," Vivian said in a sleepy voice. "The one who sees you as his world sends you a message. His mind and his heart call to you."

It startled her. Vivian had done nothing like this before. "What is the message, Vivian?"

"Come home, my little dragoness. Come home, my world," Vivian said. "Come home. The Farseer needs you."

"Come home," she said, shocked. Sia was warning her that something had happened to Destined. She spread her wings and took flight, sending the picture away. "Destined," she said to herself. Something was wrong. She touched the link they shared, but it was faint. She felt a slight ache in her heart of hearts. "Fool!" she swore, pushing herself to fly faster with little care if anyone saw her.

Petrall was two days away on wings, but she would have to make it sooner. "Destined," she said again with panic pulling at her belly. She did not know what had happened, but it had to be something with that place. She knew she should have never left him. If he was in trouble, she would not know until it was too late. "Endrir, come home. I need you," she said over and over, hoping he would hear her. She was afraid of what she would find when she returned to Petrall.

CHAPTER THREE

"Endrir, come home. I need you."

Endrir sat up in his bed covered in sweat. His heart was racing, and his breathing heavy as he tilted his head to the side, listening. Something had jarred him from the terrible dream that had been haunting him lately. He was thankful but nervous. He sat there waiting, his blanket a tangle around him. He was sure he heard someone call his name, but only the sounds of the city surrounded him. Tresai was a constant barrage of noise. Even at night, the city did not sleep. The short lifers he watched were always busy.

"Endrir, come home. I need you."

His heart skipped a beat. "Nihility," he said to himself. He got up from his bed, yanking the blanket from around his legs as he stumbled to his window. Dawn would come soon; he could tell how the Mother Moon faded as the sun made its appearance.

"Endrir, come home. I need you."

He could feel her fear and worry. Something was wrong. He grabbed his pack from the floor beside his bed and quickly gathered his things for the journey home. He dressed as he went, making the wood floorboards creak and groan as he ran back and forth from room to room, gathering his possessions. It would take him four days regardless of how fast he moved. He could not fly the entire way; short lifers would see him, but he could fly swiftly and make some distance if he used the sun to hide himself.

"Endrir, come home. I need you."

"I'm coming! I'm coming!" he said, frazzled.

He threw open the wooden hatch that led underneath his home. It is where he slept as dragon if he needed to, a deep underground cavern he had dug himself from outside of Tresai. It went all the way to the valley before the Kassok Peaks, the mountains that loomed behind the great city. He stopped and sighed as he came to the small alcove where he had hidden the egg he helped create. He touched the pendant that hung around his neck. He could not leave it here, but he could not return to her, to his Nihility, with it.

"Endrir, come home. I need you."

He groaned. "Sathea, help me," he said as he threw his pack down and gathered leather to fashion a harness to transport it back with him. "She will not forgive me this. This is too much even for her. I am so screwed," he whined to himself.

"Endrir, come home. I need you."

He wiped tears from his eyes as he tied knots in the leather around the egg. "I am coming, my goddess of the moon."

He shifted out of his borrowed form and took off out the tunnel that led him far away from the city. He needed to make some distance as quickly as possible while carrying the egg before the light of the day forced him back to his short life form. "Fool of a Watcher! She finally calls you after all these years, and you return to her with a symbol of your betrayal of her heart," he thought to himself. He did not know if even Destined could help him out of this mess, or if he even would.

"Destined," he said to himself. He felt a strange ache in his heart of hearts. He frowned as he made his way high into the sky. He was sure the Destined was safe. He felt no danger, but he felt the Farseer strongly. "Odd," he said to himself. He had been dreaming of Destined, he was sure of it, but as sleep faded, he could recall nothing more than bright white light and a strange sense of both comfort and fear.

The clouds were thin, but he glided through them, creating shadows on the land beneath him. He was always a shadow, blending in until he wished to be noticed. It was a byproduct of his calling. His iridescent scales shimmered in the growing light of the rising sun. Most of the dragons on Petrall were one or two colors, but he was shades of one, purple. His scales changed and shifted as the light hit him.

He and others like him were born Watchers; duty to watch the world and those in it, a warning bell for calamity and catastrophe, and those put in place to warn of any disturbance to the Great Balance. All the Watchers had different duties, but all were required to change their form for more extended periods than any other dragons. Their scales were a telltale sign of what they were. Like the Weavers who were born linked to the Dreaming, the iridescent scales of a dragon linked Watchers to Sathea.

The others on Petrall had labeled them "Lost Ones," as they rarely returned to Petrall. While they were active on Sathea, they blended in with those they watched. Most arrived randomly in the day to make reports or warn of a pending crisis and then quickly return to their duties. Others remained away using the communication system he created called the Watcher Way. It allowed them to communicate with each other without arousing suspicion of what they really were; dragons.

Watchers were respected amongst the other races on Sathea that worked in the shadows, but it was hard for some of those on Petrall to understand those who could live as something else as Watchers had to do. There were very few others who used a borrowed form that were not Watchers. For them, there was a risk; too long in a borrowed form could cause irreparable damage to their bodies, and their magic They had to revert to their dragon forms far more often than a Watcher. Watchers could sustain their shape for many days before secreting away to shift to dragon.

It had been almost two years since he had last returned to Petrall. At first, he had convinced himself he could no longer deal with the pain of living without Nihility while Destined enjoyed her openly. It became something else when he met Ena, and she had this egg; his egg. He returned now with dread in his belly and an ache in his heart.

"Endrir, come home. I need you."

"Nihility is going to remove all my scales one by one, set me on fire, and use my bones to clean her claws," he mumbled.

CHAPTER FOUR

Destined stood in the darkness of the Between, deciding which way he would go next and trying to keep his frustration under control. The Between was a place of lost and lingering souls. Not all those who lived lives on Sathea passed peacefully. Some of them ended up here in this place; a place that did not have a sense of organization until your mind created one. The minds of those who entered created their own landscape to navigate. For him, it was always the same endless pathways lined with doors. Every door could lead to something else. The doors only changed to accommodate his form; dragon or short-lifer.

He had projected himself into the space in his borrowed short-life form and not as a dragon. He was dressed in white from head to toe. The hood of his cloak covered his bald head. His skin was pale. No matter how hard he tried, he could not change it. It was as if his white scales shined through regardless of his form. The only color on him came from the blue trim on his clothing, the blue crystal embedded in his staff, and his hazel eyes. They shifted sometimes. The others believed it to be a gift of his sight. He was the Farseer, Destined, the Great White Prophet of Petrall. Truthfully, they changed depending on the use of his power; if he was Destined, they were hazel. If the colors separated, swirling around one another, as they were now, the Farseer had emerged from his cage.

The crack of his knuckles broke the silence as he gripped his staff tightly. The ache in his body was imposing itself on his mind. He had been gone too long. He did not know how long, but if Nihility returned from the nomads to find his body empty and his mind too deep in the Between to contact, she would come for him. That is the last thing he wanted. This was not the place he wanted her to be. He had not prepared her to travel this deep.

"She is going to have my head," he said to himself. The last of his words echoed down the hall before him.

It was supposed to be a quick walk. He only needed to find out what had caused a disturbance in the ranks of the Walkers. Two of his best had not returned to their bodies after three days. The healers were keeping their bodies alive, the six before them, and were likely doing now for him. He promised her he would wait until she returned, but when Ellot stopped sending him messages and Mica returned raving, he had no choice. It was his duty, but he did not feel good about it.

"You are breaking all the rules now, Destined," he said to himself. He heard the word 'rules'n echo, mocking him. He should not have come in alone. Tuzys or Master Sia should have come with him. The Order of Walkers existed with rules he created or altered to keep them safe from those creatures in the Between who would prey on the walking mind. One of those rules was to travel in pairs.

Only he, Tuzys, and Master Sia could walk the Between without a second It was an edict given to him by the elder Walker and one he followed without question. He believed it was because he could go places the others could not and see things they could not see. Even now, he could see the aura of the creatures circling around him but not daring to come closer. Even though they feared him, they could not control their desire for him. However, he felt like this time he should have stowed away his ego in the name of safety. He should not have come alone. "Fool," he mumbled. It echoed, making him roll his eyes.

It had been over six months since the first pair had gone missing. Walkers had been lost before in his time as the Order's lead. After four thousand years, the count stood at four. Four novices, in four thousand years, that had wandered off lost in the Between. He was proud of his odds. Unlike Kuri before him, whose count was twelve, and Ergodi, his mentor, who stood at thirty-five, he had kept the casualties of the Walkers to a minimum.

The Between held things that would drive others out of their minds with madness. It was a place of breaking and a place for the broken. He could walk and find the doors necessary to the places he wanted with ease. He could avoid the madness, and he knew nothing here could break him unless he allowed it to happen. It is what made him a celebrated Walker on Petrall. The only reason he led the Order of Walkers was because of his mentor Ergodi's insatiable need to control his power.

He did not feel like much of a leader now. Guilt ate at him. He did not see that something was amiss sooner. He knew in his heart that something was preying on the Walkers of the Order, but he could not fathom what would have the power to do so. When one half of the last pair, Mica, returned half-mad, rambling about a presence, doors, and darkness and his partner had not, he was leery. He wanted to investigate Mica's mind before he ventured into the Between to search, but Ergodi and Kuri insisted he go at once. He would have held firm but for his worry over Ellot. He would rather die than leave any of his Walkers in danger. The four he lost before, he searched for endlessly. He knew he had waited too long this time. He had left the search to Ergodi and Kuri when he should not have. When he finally arrived himself, he knew something was wrong.

Under normal circumstances, when he entered, there were whispers like a light wind rustling the leaves of trees. They would always call his name softly, "Farseer," over and over as he walked. He always felt a presence, one of enormous power that lurked around him. It watched him but never showed itself. It was the only thing he feared in the Between because he could feel the size of its power, and it seemed to know the halls even better than he. Now there was an unusual silence.

He could see traces of the auras of the ones that were lost. They were faint, but there. It was apparent they had gone much farther into the Between than they should have. The question he had was why. Why had Kuri and Ergodi not seen them? He saw their aura's trail off in a different direction from the missing. Was this the reason for Mica's madness? The danger in walking too far in the Between was becoming lost, not madness. Madness only came when something assaulted the mind-body. He had placed wards, warning them of danger, projections of himself leading them away from the things that lurked, ready to devour the unaware. He did not think any of them had been disturbed. He tried to search his memory for the ones he had passed and stopped himself.

The Between was a place where inner balance was mandatory. Doubt, fear, prayer, and even passion could mean trouble in the Between. All emotions had to be balanced when walking. If not, things could find you and take hold of the mind in its temporary weakness or distraction. He took a deep breath, sat on the ground with his legs crossed, his hands clasped around his staff, and closed his eyes. He needed to sense the things around him much farther than he had ever dared. He could not waste any more time wandering. His body was hurting, sending waves of pain through his mind.

The presence of the souls that lingered in the Between swirled around him. He reached beyond them and felt those hungrier things lurking, afraid to show themselves. Then he felt the more significant presence. It surrounded him, causing his heartbeat to quicken. Panic gripped him, closing his throat and making him clench up. Just as quickly, it vanished, as if it only needed his attention for a moment. He frowned. It never left him so quickly when he felt it. It would follow him as he traveled the Between like a predator, waiting before it pounced.

He focused his concentration on the point where the presence had gone. He wanted it to believe that he searched for it instead; he sought the surrounding places. Then he felt it, a flicker of familiarity quickly fading. He sprang to his feet, the crystal in his staff glowing and the air shifting around him. A door appeared. This was his secret in the Between, creating entries in the Between to get to places quickly. All the others that walked the Between had to find the hidden spaces, searching endlessly. He only needed to command them into existence. He stopped himself before he opened it.

It was an ordinary door, no different from the ones you would see in the homes of the short lifers that lived below the mountain. He touched it lightly, feeling only wood beneath his fingertips, but he knew this door. He knew it well. It was the door he had only seen in the visions that had been plaguing him the last year, and Ellot lay behind it. In his visions, he stood before it but never entered. A soft voice, not his own, cautioned him against it. Except in the last vision, the door was open to him, but he could only see darkness beyond it.

Standing before it now, he could feel the power behind it. A force that he felt even in his visions. It sat there as if it had been waiting for him. He opened it and stepped into the darkness. He turned briefly and made sure his aura left a trail behind him. "Just in case," he said to himself. He turned back around to face the darkness, and the door slammed behind him.

The cries of countless voices assaulted him. Some were screaming in agony, others in a fury. It was paralyzing to hear so many at once. He quickly cast a pale blue barrier around himself and breathed a sigh of relief. He could still hear them, but the sound was manageable. The voices had dulled to whispers in the darkness that surrounded him. He waited to see if his eyes would adjust, making the deep black grayer. Then he saw it, a tiny pinpoint of white.

"Ellot!" he shouted. The darkness seemed to swallow his voice; there was no echo. He probed with his mind, feeling things hiding in the dark. He could feel them, but he did not know what they were. Usually, curiosity would get the better of him, but he stood in a space that felt both right and wrong at the same time. He sensed something in the darkness that was familiar.

"Well, that is why I am here," he said. He shook his head and chuckled. He was talking to himself. Nihility would have called him a fool and told him to calm down. He was nervous. He had never been this deep in the Between. He sensed danger, but he could not pinpoint where it was coming from. He looked at the point of light before him and sighed as he began walking towards it, hoping to find Ellot safe.

The voices diminished the closer he walked to the light. Only one seemed to grow louder. Part of him screamed to stop, but he pushed it aside. He was the Farseer and would not succumb to fear, not here. He knew a presence strong enough to project its thoughts so clearly was dangerous, but he was curious. It was not screaming in agony but speaking calmly, seeking a way out of the darkness. He wondered if it was the same thing Mica raved about. He would find it, and Ellot. If it had Ellot, he would lock it away where it could cause no further harm. He would find out what it was and what it knew if it did not.

He focused on figuring out what it was while keeping track of the light before him when he stumbled over something in the darkness and landed on his belly. "Damn it!" he swore. He summoned an orb of light and gasped. It was Ellot. Something had drained the essence of his mind-body, leaving only a dried husk behind. He had fought against something powerful, judging by the way his snout was locked in a snarl. There was a scream that froze his heart.

"Nihility!" he shouted.

CHAPTER FIVE

She crested the peaks of the Petrall at top speed, headed directly for the rotunda that was the home she shared with Destined between the Order of the Walkers and Weaver Circle. Her wing joints were burning from the strain of the speed of her flight. The closer she came to Petrall, the heavier the feeling of something wrong became. She entered the rotunda and saw Destined's prone form lying in the center of the bedding they shared. Her glorious white dragon looked as if he was peacefully asleep. Healers were scrambling around him and sustaining the soft pink healing orb that surrounded him.

"How long has he been in there?" she asked the healer tending to him. The young dragoness looked at her with enormous eyes. The young one's fear rolled over her, agitating her. "I have no patience for your silly little fears, dragoness. I asked you a question, now speak!" she roared.

"Nine days, Lady Nihility," a voice answered. She turned her head to see an elder of the council and former Walker, Kuri. He was a long, lithe, crimson dragon with black spines. He had a presence about him that made her always feel like he was secretive and dishonest.

"Nine days!" she hissed. "Destined has been in there nine days, and you did not think to go after him?"

"He is being cared for," Kuri said, rolling his eyes at her. "Obviously, as his mate, I mean, if you did not feel it, then he is in no real danger. You have your own to attend to in the Dreaming, Lady Nihility. Your dramatics are unnecessary here."

She hissed and lunged at him. He retreated a few steps with his head lowered. His fear was thick and ripe enough to taste. "Tread carefully, Elder Kuri, before I show you just how dramatic I can become," she hissed as her tail swayed back and forth, and she flexed her wings as her scales made a soft scraping sound. "They say a dragoness's wrath is fearsome when her mate is threatened," she said in a silky tone. "I wonder just how fearsome I would be? More than what you already believe, I wager," she said, bashing her tail once on the ground.

"My apologies, Lady Nihility. I meant no disrespect. The situation is distressing for us all. My tongue has got the better of me in my worry over Lord Farseer," Kuri said, backing away.

The color of his emotions betrayed his words. Kuri was not concerned about Destined at all. He was only afraid of her, the Harbinger. They were all afraid of her on Petrall. Long ago, his reaction to her would hurt. Now she used it to her advantage.

She touched her snout to Destined's. She could feel him through their mental link. He was balanced as he usually was when he walked the Between, but she felt fear as well. "Where are you, Destined, and what do you think you are doing?" she asked quietly. "Nine days is too long. You know this, Kuri. He risks becoming lost to that place," she said, turning back to him.

"Aye. Ergodi and I were preparing to retrieve him, but something prevents us from entering. We do not know if it is Destined or something else. Ergodi is trying to figure that out now."

"How long were the last two gone before he ventured in?"

"Three days, of which you were here for. When they did not return, Elder Ergodi and I decided it would be prudent if the Farseer followed them with haste."

"He would not have gone just for that reason alone, Kuri. Ellot and Mica are skilled Walkers. What happened?"

"Mica returned, Lady Nihility," a reddish-orange dragon with bold black lines running down his sides said as he entered.

"Tuzys," she said, nodding at him. He was Destined's first and a close friend.

"There is no need to give her false hope, Tuzys Mindhunter," Kuri hissed.

"I do no such thing, Elder Kuri. She asked what happened that caused Destined to go despite his desire to wait for her return," Tuzys said. "Lady Nihility, Mica returned hours after you left, but he was not himself. He is with the healers now, at the Circle of Healing. Lady Frety tends to him. Destined entered shortly after his return."

"Thank you, Tuzys. I would have you remain here with Destined," she said, readying herself to leave.

"Of course, Lady Nihility," Tuzys said, making himself comfortable near Destined.

"Lady Nihility," Kuri called. "How did you know to come here?"

"You said yourself, I am his mate. Regardless of how you see me, there is no mysterious power at work beyond the exchange of our heart of hearts," she said, looking at him. "What is it you all whisper about me when you think I cannot hear you, Elder Kuri?" she asked. Kuri did not respond to her. "The Harbinger brings death on black wings. You can correct me if I am mistaken, but I believe that is the sentiment you all share."

"I believe you have the right of it, Lady Nihility," Tuzys said, chuckling.

"I will make sure those are the truest words that have ever been uttered on this peak if he does not return before I do," she said as she spread her wings and took flight.

She needed to go to her safe space to enter the Between and find Destined. She was not meant to walk the Between as Weaver, but that did not mean she could not do so. Destined had taught her to enter, but the mental state required to do so she learned long before even he realized. Sia had taught her much about herself, her mind, and controlling her powers.

She flew over the Burning Waste of Petrall even though fatigue pulled at her. She had a place deep in the peak's heart, beyond the one that still spewed fire. She entered quickly and laid down to close her eyes and empty her mind. The place had belonged to another dragon before her, but she never knew who. All she knew is that it was abandoned but provided her the space she needed from those on Petrall.

There was a pull that made her feel as if she had been moved. She opened her eyes and saw the murky pathways of the Between before her. It always looked like this to her here. An ever-present haze existed, like a forest where the sun could not penetrate through the leaves. Her first few trips here, she found it unnerving. It was not like the Dreaming that mirrored Sathea with sunshine, the Maiden and Mother Moons, and life. The Between was a void of whispers shrouded in a cloudy haze. It was emptiness. She could never truly feel grounded as she did in the Dreaming. She felt absent from herself. She stood still, trying to sense any and everything. She could feel the countless emotions of the spirits here threatening to overwhelm her.

Suddenly screams filled the air, making her tuck her head under her wing. It was as if the spirits of the Between wanted her to hear them. The sound unnerved her. This was a place of whispers and secrets. She did not want them to take more notice of her than they already had. She moved quickly, searching for him.

Sia had taught her long ago to keep her mental barrier strong and empty herself of anything that weighed on her. He was a powerful telepath, just as Destined was, but they were not the only ones on Petrall who were. Some harmed her long ago and would continue to do so if she allowed them. She refused to have her thoughts infiltrated and poisoned again. She carried enough weight without someone else trying to cloud her mind or make her feel less than she should.

Destined warned her of the dangers of the Between. He said it was vital for her to understand, as his mate, what he faced every time he entered the space. There were things here that looked to manipulate and abuse the mind-body out of spite for the life they no longer had. Bored things that relished pleasure and pain.

More dangerous than anything else was the threat of demons dragon kind had been warned about.

Demons were believed to have come from the Between long ago when Rona Brightscales stood against them. She had never seen one, and according to Destined, neither had he. However, the souls here had warned him of the danger. Demons were beasts who preyed on the mind-body for sustenance and control. Once they conquered the mind, they could manipulate the body for their own and walk Sathea again.

She swung her head back and forth, searching for a trace of him in the gloom. As his image crossed her mind, the thick foggy cover that swirled at her feet cleared, and she saw it; a pale-yellow line so bright it was almost as white as his scales. She pursued it. It would lead her to him and keep her from becoming lost in the maze of the Between.

Time passed differently in the Between, just as it did in the Dreaming, but being here worried her. The Dreaming slowed time. The days were longer, as were the nights. In the Between, time ran faster. She could feel her fatigue overwhelming her. She knew hours or days could have passed already since she arrived here. There was no one to watch her body as they did Destined's. If gone too long, she could die alone where no one would find her. She shook her head, fighting back her worry.

A door appeared before her. Destined's aura coated it. It pulsed with it slowly, like the breathing of one who is deep in their sleep. She touched it with her snout, and a strange look came over her face. His magic was potent as if he wanted to keep something in.

It was too small for her to fit through as dragoness. "What exactly did you think you were doing, my foolish light?" she asked, confused. Destined had not walked as a dragon but in his borrowed form. He never came to the Between in his borrowed form. Especially if he walked deep. He said he felt more in tune with himself in his proper form. "What on Sathea are you doing, Destined?"

She had no choice but to shift. She would not fit through the door as dragoness. Her black scales fell away to dark brown skin that favored the Daughters of Ote. She was tall for one of their kind, with thin arms, an ample chest, and wide hips. The bulk of her height came from her muscular and thick legs. She wore brown leather shorts slung low on her hips that hugged her bottom and laced on the sides with soft black cloth, a vest that only covered her breasts and the top of her back tied the same, and soft-soled boots that came to her knees, like the hunters of the Daughters of Ote.

Her horns became long black hair that hung down to the small of her back in tiny twisted loc. Strands of bright red ran through the coils at her temples, braided and tied with a red string to hold it back from her face. She had high cheeks and full lips that hid fangs that were slightly larger than the average short lifers. Her deep brown eyes were the only thing to give away what she really was if one looked closely. The dragoness never left her eyes, from their subtle tilt to the way the pupils moved. She always had the eyes of a dragoness, even in borrowed flesh.

Across her shoulders, down her left arm and side, were thin tendrils of black that resembled the roots of a tree. They all led from the Weaver mark on her back, a black butterfly sitting on the hilt of a sword laid between her shoulders. Her Weaver mark distinguished her from all other Weavers and connected her to the Dreaming. All dragons bore a symbol when they shifted. It was a symbol of not only their calling but what they stood for as dragons. She tightened down the black fingerless gloves she wore on her hands and touched the door.

"Destined," she called. The moment she pushed, agonizing pain consumed her mind.

"Silly little dragoness," a voice she did not recognize said.

She glimpsed a tendril of green aura before she screamed in agony.

"Destined," she cried out. She could feel him surround her for a moment. He was trying to speak to her, but another was interfering with his presence. She tried to focus on his voice, but the other presence would not ease. It made a sound like a thousand insects buzzing in her ears.

She shook her head, trying to fight back and push the noise away. She pushed herself forward into the door. She had to get to him. "Destined," she said through gritted teeth. She had the door open a crack. The buzzing abated a bit, and the pain with it. It was enough for her to hear him clearly. "Fight my love! Fight Nihility! Do not succumb!" he shouted at her. It played over and over in her head.

She screamed again, fighting against the buzzing in her mind. She tried to surge forward through the door, but the pain dropped her to her knees. Tears streamed down her cheeks. She struggled to hold on to the cadence of Destined's voice over the buzzing. She placed her head against the door. "Destined," she said again before closing her eyes.

"You are a dragoness. We do not fall. We soar and leave naught but the ash of our enemies in our wake," a voice said.

She opened her eyes. She was no longer in the Between, but she knew she was. She could feel it around her, but she could also feel her body in her sanctuary. "My mind turns against me now," she said as she looked around. She was in the place she came to within herself before accessing the Dreaming, a space in her own mind. She had never done so while in the Between.

"You are in danger, young dragoness," the voice said again. "The Between is not a place for one such as you who weaves the dreams of dreamers." Fear gripped her as she turned, searching for the source. "It is not me you should fear, but what lurks in the place your mind has gone," the voice said.

Out of the shadows of her mind appeared a large dragoness,

one easily three times her size. Her scales were black except for her chest, where there was a small patch of white shaped like a star. Her spines were a deep red except for her silver horns and tail spikes. Familiarity pulled at her, but she could not say why. "Who are you? How are you in my mind? What is happening?"

"You must calm yourself, young one. Fear causes a disturbance in your inner balance. Any disturbance in this place will mean more danger for you. Especially beyond the door, you opened. I am one of the Twin Stars of Petrall, Pax of the Depths, the Herald of Change," the dragoness said.

Shock ripped through her. "No way on Sathea!" she said in awe. "There is no way. You cannot be…Lady Pax of the Depths, Champion of the Dreaming?! Impossible," she said. Pax was a legend. She had been told tales over and over by her own teachers. Pax of the Depths was the red and black dragoness who had carved the Depths of the Dreaming with flame.

"You are indeed a Weaver if you have heard of me by such a title," Pax said with a chuckle. "It is I, but I am champion no more. I am merely a shade that has not fulfilled its purpose."

"Shade? Purpose? What purpose? Why are you here in this place?"

"I left a piece of my being like a spell in this place. Something has happened to the barrier I left the spell on deep beyond where you sit. Something has triggered the magic I used to provide protection," Pax said calmly.

"I do not understand. You cannot be here! I cannot be here if I linger in the Between! The mind is not capable of such. This is madness!" she said, confused.

"Your mind has created its own safety for you. To relieve yourself of the pain, you are here. It seems you have shielded not only your mind but that part of you connected to your heart of hearts. Look there," Pax said, nodding behind Nihility. She turned and saw herself on her knees in front of the open door.

"How are you here in my mind? Are you a dream?"

"Weavers do not dream, young one. The one who sought to aid you, the one you called Destined, has come to this place. I do not know how he found it. Perhaps he sensed the threat, or he must be one who can walk the Between. Only a dragon who could travel this place could find the barrier. He now stands before that barrier, and he cannot close it. He cannot close it once it has been breached," Pax said.

"How do you know all of this?"

"I am linked to it, and it is the only way I could be here now. Someone or something has found the barrier and tried to open it. It is the one you call Destined who seeks to close the barrier again, but he cannot. What has been done cannot be undone. Your Destined has walked into danger, and he must turn away before he is lost."

"How do I help him?"

"You must first help yourself. I am here because something crossed the barrier but did not perish at the hands of the spell I left on it. It has latched on to you and brought me with it."

"What?" she asked nervously.

"There," Pax said, swinging her head in the opposite direction.

How she envisioned her mind was nothing like how Destined saw his own. He often teased her about its simplicity because, in his own words, she was far from simple. Her mind was a cave big enough for her and two others. It held trappings of both life below and dragons. Pax sat on the large nest tucked neatly beside one of the cave walls. A small table and three chairs sat beneath an opening in the cave adorned like a window. A wall painted with three dragons' images hid the place where she stored her memories. In a dark corner, next to the painted wall, was a creature struggling and covered in a red and black aura. She could not tell what it was. "What is that?" she said, squinting. "What on Sathea is that!"

"It is a demon, but not, young one," Pax said. "There is

something more to it. It is contained for now, but you must aid yourself before it breaks free."

"It is what caused the buzzing and the pain," she said.

"Aye."

She thought she would be appalled if something like this ever happened, but she was angry at the intrusion. "For Sathea's sake!" she swore.

Destined had explained what she needed to do if another ever forced itself into her mind to control her. He attacked her mind repeatedly until he was satisfied with her skill. He did not tell her about the pain she would experience, though. "Yes, leave that part out, Farseer," she hissed. "When I get him out of here, I am going to set him on fire," she mumbled.

She thought of the containment orbs they used in the Dreaming with beings hostile to dreamers, and it appeared around the demon. She could not make out exactly what it looked like as it remained surrounded by darkness. She could feel it pounding, but she could no longer hear the loud buzzing. She would need his help to expel the vile thing, but for now, it was held. "Lots of fire," she said, turning back to Pax.

"Perfect young one. Now, what do they call you dragoness? Beyond Weaver, that is," Pax asked.

She stood tall. "I am the Harbinger, Nihility, Lead Weaver of Weaver Circle."

"Well, Nihility the Harbinger, let us retrieve your Destined. You must place your attention back on the door and continue through. There will no longer be any pain; however, you must be cautious," Pax said. Her mind swirled with questions. "They must wait, youngling. For now, we go to your mate," Pax said, seeming to read her mind.

She focused her mind on the door and found herself back on her knees before it. She took a deep breath, found her feet, and stepped through the door. She felt Destined engulfing the room.

He was using tremendous power, but she could not see him. "Where are you?" she asked as she stepped forward.

The door slammed shut behind her. Her instincts were sending her waves of danger. As her eyes adjusted, she saw a minor point of light a great distance away. She walked towards it and stopped. At first, she had not noticed, but something was lurking in the darkness. She closed her eyes. She did not need to see or hear; she only needed to feel. She opened her eyes quickly. There were thousands upon thousands lurking in the dark. She could feel them all; their need, hunger, and desire to kill.

"You are an Empath!" Pax exclaimed. "Feel where they are and go quickly, youngling!"

Two blades appeared strapped to her back. She ran towards the light with whatever lurked in the dark at her heels.

CHAPTER SIX

"Nihility!" he shouted again as her screams echoed in the darkness. He tried to send a part of himself to her, but he could not. Something was pulling at him. He realized he had an intruder in his own mind. With his stumble and her scream, he had erred and allowed his defenses to drop. "Damn it!" he swore. He would have to leave her to her own strength. He sent a thought to her across their link before closing himself to her. He had to expel the presence before it was too late.

"Parasites!" he hissed. "Fucking parasites, all of you!" he shouted. His temporary loss of concentration was just the opening the presence needed. He had to calm himself down. He took deep, slow breaths and tried to assess where the spirit had gone in his mind. He frowned when he realized it was not trying to overwhelm him, as others in the Between had tried to do. Instead, it went for those areas of his being it thought would be weak. There was no way this was what happened to Ellot.

"No dragon, that weakling cowered before everything I am," the presence said with a hint of laughter.

Visions of his heart's desire assaulted him. What any being on Sathea wanted the most above anything else was their heart's desire. Even the smallest insect had something they cherished above all, food, love, shelter, and countless other things that gave a being the will to live and thrive.

The heart's desire was a place in the mind and the hardest for Walkers to control because it was the one place that connected the mind and the body; the heart. This was no mere lost soul lingering in the Between. This was what he had heard tales of from the others. This was a demon.

"What is happening?" the demon asked in a panic.

He laughed hysterically. He was sure he looked like madness

had consumed him in the darkness as laughter shook his body and tears streamed down his cheeks. He had conquered his heart's desire long ago. He was Destined the Farseer, and his greatest weakness was also his greatest strength; Nihility. His heart's desire was her, preserving her safety and keeping her love. The deeper the demon dug into the place he devoted to her, the bolder he felt. He saw memories flash of himself lying at her feet. He saw her naked shifted form beneath him and the face she made the moment he pushed inside of her; the pleasure she felt manifested on her delicate features. He could feel her surround him. He could smell her, the smell of wildflowers and fire. He heard her hums as dragoness and her moans of pleasure in her short life form. He gathered himself together and slowed his breathing as he turned inward.

The mind could hold layers upon layers of one's being. It was infinite in its depth if you allowed yourself to see them. His body was in his home on Petrall, his mind-body was in the Between, and now, his consciousness stood before a being he had no reference. It did not resemble any creature he had seen in all his twenty thousand years on Sathea. There were parts he could compare but nothing to match precisely. He studied it for a moment, trying to get his mind to understand what it was seeing.

It was built like the short lifers; two arms and two legs, but with clawed hands and feet. The black horns on its head curled around the sides like the mountain jerboa they often hunted. Its skin was not skin like the short lifers that lived below the mountain peaks but appeared like that of the Quag, the beast of great venom that roamed the land, grey and smooth. It appeared coated in a substance that glimmered in patches of black and green. Its eyes were like the river serpents, slanted and pale green like the aura that pulsed around it. Its face was like those of the short lifers, except for the jaw. It protruded with sharp teeth, making the nose and ears nothing more than mere holes. It wore nothing but a dirty grey cloth tied over its midsection, leaving its narrow chest bare. It was toned but had very little mass.

"I have seen nothing like you," he said in awe. "You are a demon, are you not?" he asked.

"I am (buzzing) dragon! I will have your form!" the demon said.

He shook his head. He could not hear what the creature called itself. It sounded as if buzzing insects had invaded his head at part of the demon's words. His voice sounded male, but he was still not sure. It piqued his curiosity. "Did you do that to Ellot?"

"That weak one was not a proper vessel, but his essence made a fine meal. You are a far better host," the demon said.

A smirk crossed his face. "You can stop struggling. You will not get free."

"We will see about that," the demon spat, continuing to press on his mind.

"I am no demon's host. However, you are my prisoner since it seems I cannot expel you as I have others who have tried to prey on my mind."

"I am no prisoner!" the demon shouted.

He spread his arms wide, "considering your current situation, I would say the prisoner is exactly what you are." A bright white light tinged in the deepest black had surrounded the demon. It noticed too late and tried to break free. The light coalesced into an orb around it and decreased in size, restricting its movements. "It seems in your eagerness to exploit a perceived weakness; you have allowed yourself to become a real predator's prey."

"Release me now, dragon!"

"No. I am Destined the Farseer, Long Walker of the Between, and I am far from just a mere dragon. Now I have questions, and you will give me answers."

"Just because you believe you have contained me here does not mean I will do your bidding!" the demon spat.

"Then I will crush you into nothing but a passing thought," he said calmly as the orb grew smaller.

"Wait!"

He looked at the demon and smiled. "What is this place?"

"I thought you were the great Long Walker of this place you call the Between, yet you do not know this space?" it asked. He waved a hand as the orb shrank again. "Stop!" the demon shouted. "It is a space. I do not know what it is. It held the door that kept us from here!"

"What door?" he asked.

"The door placed here long ago. It is no more. It is opened now, and we are free!"

"There was nothing beyond the door but darkness," he said, frowning.

"You look the wrong way, dragon," the demon said with a laugh.

Destined wondered if it meant the door was the light he was heading towards. "Think of it, so I see it," he said with an air of command.

The demon looked surprised. "You hold such power?" it asked. He shrugged. The demon kept his eyes on him as a picture formed. A wall of magic that pulsed both white and gold.

"Who opened it?"

"I do not know. I only know the companion to the other there touched it," the demon answered. "He screamed such wonderful sounds of terror and then disappeared after touching it. The other tried to run, but we were too many," it said with delight.

Mica flashed in his mind. "Why he went mad?" he asked himself. "I need to see this door."

The demon spread his arms in the same way Destined had earlier, "you only need to ask," it said with a smile.

He grinned at him. Fool he may be for Nihility the Harbinger, but he was not so foolish about other things.

Invitations or requests made to any creature in the Between were dangerous. "I no longer need you now. For the time being, be still until I decide what to do with you."

"Free me!"

"I said, be still!" he snapped. He waved a hand, and the orb went completely black. He studied it for a moment to make sure his binding was secure. The last thing he needed was a demon running free in his mind. He was not even sure if he could rid himself of the damn thing. He had tried all the usual techniques, but they did not work. Things were not going according to plan.

He had another problem to deal with as well. The demon said they were many, too many for Ellot to overcome. He did not sense any others in the room held the power of the one he had trapped, but the numbers he felt were significant. However, they did not seek escape from the space.

"Shit! Nihility," he said, realizing he had forgotten about her. Her screams had stopped, but he was not sure when. He opened his link with her cautiously, sensing her presence but no danger. He felt something else with her but was not sure what. He had taught her how to protect herself, so he was not too concerned. She was strong, but he had a choice before him. He could return to the door and Nihility or move to the light. He knew there was danger in the direction of the light, but if the feelings he gathered from his visions were correct, then there was a greater danger to Nihility, Petrall, and Sathea if he did not close the door. He gripped his staff and moved towards the light.

"She is going to set me on fire. I can feel the heat of it already," he said as the light drew closer. "Why did you not go to her, you fool of a dragon?" he asked himself. "It is like you ask for trouble from that dragoness. You better…"

He stopped in his tracks as he stood in front of the light. It was a barrier, and it was alive. He stood breathless, trying to make sense of what he was seeing. It was not just a barrier; it was a dragon. A beautiful dragon coiled upon itself with white scales and gold spines. "How?" he asked.

His right arm bore marks that signified that he was not only a dragon but also Walker and Prophet in his borrowed form. The dragon that made the barrier was curled around itself, much like his markings. He felt the aura. It was weak and growing weaker. He reached out with his mind to touch it, and the dragon's head moved, exposing one vibrant blue eye. "You must not!" a deep voice shouted into his mind, making him recoil.

He fell to his knees, gasping for breath as the truth of who the dragon was invaded his mind. He had found the door of legend. The door the Walkers had been created to protect but never look for. The door his mentor Ergodi and later Kuri wasted many years searching for. A door forbidden to be thought about while in the Between unless destruction be brought down on the world.

"Laz of the Between," he said in awe. One of the Twin Stars of Petrall had discovered the Between over two-hundred and fifty thousand years ago. In doing so, he had also found demons. Many years later, he disappeared into the Between, never to be seen again. It was believed that he sealed himself and the danger of demons away to save Petrall and Sathea behind a great door deep in the Between. Master Sia had told him that Laz only left behind a warning, that should anyone find and open the door, they would find great power and destruction, darkness and madness, the serpent and beast. They believed demons to lurk beyond it, waiting and ready to consume Sathea.

Those warnings, primarily delivered by Master Sia, were more than enough to keep his normal curiosity at bay. He had never thought to find it, despite Ergodi's persistence that knowing would better serve the Walkers. The eye continued to stare at him. "You made yourself into the barrier," he breathed. He could see the breach. He could also see where something else had placed another spell on top of the barrier. He reached out a hand to touch it and pulled back. "A curse," he said in awe. He looked at his hand and saw blood. "You are dying!" he said, shocked. "No!" he shouted. He could hear the demon laughing in his mind.

Something had inflicted a mortal wound. He sat back on his knees, overcome with worry. There was no open door, Laz was the barrier, and he was dying. He shook his head. He could heal this; he knew he could. It was a life barrier, and it required a soul to create. Perhaps that meant it could be like the other souls who came here damaged from their life and heal, but he would at least give it a chance to do so.

His hands glowed as he slowly worked the spell; Flare of Deep Healing. It was a spell that took tremendous energy that he found in a book long ago. He could not close the barrier, but perhaps he could heal the wound and save it. He had to. He could feel the beginning and the end of something swirl around him. It thrummed through his entire body. He was standing on the edge of something far beyond his sight and control, but he had to try.

He sent the spell at the barrier, and a vision met him. He saw the great white and gold dragon Laz encased in an orb. Laz's brilliant blue eyes locked with his own. A tear fell, and a bright light blinded him. "They come," Laz's deep voice said. The vision shifted, and he saw a sea of monsters before him as he hung suspended in the air. He turned to see what held him and screamed. He was Laz, and Laz was he. He could feel his life ending and beginning. He felt pain like he had never experienced in his life consume him.

The spell faded, and he looked down at his hands in shock. "Why?" he asked, looking at the barrier. "Why would you do that to yourself, Laz?"

"Find the Watcher's Cypher. It holds the truth. Find it before the serpent strikes!" Laz shouted at him. He locked eyes with the dragon who had given himself to save Petrall. In them, he saw a jade serpent lunge forward. The image took his breath away. "Warn the Guardian," Laz whispered as his voice faded away.

CHAPTER SEVEN

Destined's scream echoed to her through the darkness. She ran, resisting the urge to call out to him, but she could feel him. She tripped on something and rolled. She bounded back to her feet with her swords drawn. She was tense and ready for an attack until she realized her pursuers had ceased the chase. She no longer felt their hunger, but their fear was thick. She tucked her swords away and summoned an orb of light.

"What on Sathea has happened to him?" she thought to herself as she saw the body of Ellot. She had stumbled over his corpse.

"They have fed on his mind, youngling. There is nothing you can do. You must go quickly," Pax said.

She was confused about what was happening, but she did not want to waste time questioning with Destined so near. He was using tremendous energy. She continued quickly. It was not long before she came to him, sitting in front of a brilliant white and gold barrier.

"What is this?" she asked, grabbing at her chest. She felt intense pain and sadness overcome her, but they were not her own. She saw the blood spilling from a hole in the barrier. "It is alive!" she said in shock.

"Lazarus, your light fades," Pax said sadly in her mind.

"Nihility," Destined said. "You should not have come."

His voice was strange, as if he was present but still far away. "You were gone too long, Destined Farseer! What has happened?" she asked. He tried to stand and stumbled. She caught him and felt his pain at their touch. "Are you hurt? Where? Tell me now!" she said. His emotions were erratic and overwhelming.

He shook his head. "Come, we cannot stay here, and I do not know how much longer we have."

She looked at the barrier. There was sadness and grief, but she also felt a sense of danger to it. "Can you make it on your own?" she asked.

"Aye. I just want to move away from here. I can bring the door to me, but I do not want to do it so close to Laz," he said.

She looked at him closely to make sure he was indeed okay. He smiled at her sadly as she touched his face. "Do not fall behind, my fool. I will not come for you twice in one day, or days by now," she said as she turned and set off at a run.

They ran until they came back to the light she left on Ellot's body. "What do you want to do with him?" she asked.

"Nothing. What we see is just how the mind sees in this place. This is Ellot's mind. His body lies empty on Petrall and now a danger to the rest of the peak," he said, looking back at the barrier.

"Destined?"

"I will explain after, my love. I think we are far enough," he said, raising his hands. The door she came through appeared before them. He opened it and gestured for her to step through. He hesitated at the threshold and placed his palm on the ground next to Ellot, where a large rune appeared. It pulsed across the floor. He nodded, satisfied with his work, and followed her through the door, closing it after him. He had a curious look on his face.

"What is wrong?" she asked.

"I cannot send the door away. I must send it away. We cannot leave it here. No one else can find it!" he said, slightly panicked.

"I can help," she heard Pax say in a sad voice. "Tell him to return to himself, and you will follow."

"Return Destined. You have been gone too long. Your body cannot sustain much more."

"Are you mad, dragoness?! I will not go without you," he said, frowning at her.

"You can be angry at me later. I will be there shortly after you wake. I am not with you, but I am close," she said. She used his own spell against him.

His eyes went wide when he realized what she was doing as she touched his face. "Nihil…"

"Lady Pax, what do I need to do?" she asked. "And can we do it quickly? I do not feel safe." There was a green aura that lurked around the door. She could almost hear laughter, but she felt nothing.

"Aye, youngling. Place your hand on the door. I will do the rest," Pax said.

She did as Pax asked, and a black lotus appeared etched in flames. "Your Weaver mark!"

"Aye. It will allow me to know if anyone enters here. Now return youngling. Something sets my scales to rise even here inside your mind."

She removed her hand from the door, and the door disappeared. She returned to herself with a sigh of relief.

CHAPTER EIGHT

He opened his eyes slowly. He could barely feel his own body. His legs felt like sharp pins had taken them over. His belly was cramped with hunger, and his throat burned from thirst. He knew he was gone far longer than a few days. Otherwise, Nihility would not have come. She did not worry easily. He tried to look around for his healers, but his neck was stiff. He tried to speak and could not. He pushed air through his throat to emit fire and only made a hissing sound. He heard someone gasp.

"The Farseer is awake! He is awake!" they shouted.

Others quickly surrounded him. Wings flashed around him. The fuss that usually annoyed him, he suddenly found comfort in. He was back in his body whole. As soon as they brought him water, he took long slow drinks. "How long?" he asked when he felt his throat loosen. It came out a whisper. He cleared his throat and tried again. "How long was I gone?"

"Thirteen days, Destined," a voice said. He looked over and saw Tuzys.

"Tuzys," he said with a sigh of relief. "Did you say thirteen days?"

"Aye," Tuzys said with a pause, "we were afraid you would not return."

He watched him for a moment. Tuzys was one of his oldest friends and hatch mate, but he sounded odd. Tuzys did not avert his gaze but shifted his brown eyes slightly to the left. He frowned. He could sense something at work but did not know what. "Where is Elder Ergodi?" he asked calmly. One attendant froze. "Get him now," he said.

The reaction of the young one bothered him. The question caused the novice to close his mind. He watched him quickly exit

Walker Tower before he turned back to Tuzys. "We will speak later. Tell me then," he said.

Tuzys nodded. "I am going to find Master Sia and let him know you have returned. Then I will head to the Circle of Healing. I suggest you do the same as soon as you can," he said, leaving the rotunda.

"Understood," he said, watching Tuzys leave. Something was wrong if even Tuzys acted as if he had made an ordinary trip to the Between. His mind was sluggish, but he knew something was not right. Before he could have time to sort out his thoughts, he was interrupted.

"Lord Farseer! I am glad you are back with us. We have all worried for you and your safety," Kuri said as he entered the rotunda.

He had to suppress his groan. The very last dragon he wanted to speak with right now was Kuri. "Elder Kuri, where is Master Ergodi?" he asked. He did not trust Kuri. He never did. Anytime he opened his mouth, he made him feel like he was not speaking the entire truth. It always scratched at his mind, but he stowed his distrust the best he could. Kuri was older than him by eight hatchings and almost a hundred thousand years old. He made no secret of his animosity towards Destined. He was the only one that could make Lord Farseer sound like a curse instead of a title.

"He is coming, but you know how slow he moves as he ages. It is like he has forgotten that time moves. I suppose that is the way when you are over two-hundred thousand years old. He was preparing to enter the Between to find you. However, it seems that will no longer be necessary," Kuri said.

"The Mindhunter said it has been thirteen days. How do the others fair?" he asked. He was slowly flexing his muscles and wings. He needed to move. Kuri made him feel uneasy and almost vulnerable in his current state.

"Aye, thirteen days. Mother's Moon has passed her time

back to the Maiden. The condition of the others is still unchanged, I am afraid to say," Kuri said, making himself comfortable.

"Who tends to them?"

"Lady Arsu, Lady Frety, and some other healers. Speaking of Weavers, that mate of yours, Lady Nihility, was here some four days ago. She was in one of her rages," Kuri said, looking at him and smiling. "You know the kind that makes a dragon wish to wrap himself around the raw power of the dragoness she is and drag himself across the rocks until he is raw," Kuri said. "But I have not seen her since."

He glared at him. "Mind your tongue, Kuri," he said through gritted teeth.

Kuri bobbed his head. "My apologies, Lord Farseer. The Lady Nihility is sometimes hard to resist."

"Try harder. Nihility is a mated dragoness."

"Your mated dragoness. Yes, I know. Though it does not change the fact that Lady Nihility is one dragoness that can arouse longings in a dragon," Kuri said. "Besides, Lord Farseer, need I remind you, you do not own that dragoness. You merely share her heart of hearts. She can take on as many mates as she desires."

"Kuri!" he snapped.

"What happened that kept you for so long, Lord Farseer?" Kuri asked.

He took a deep breath to settle his aggravation. "I was deep in the Between. As you know, time moves differently there. I returned as soon as I could."

"What cause did you have to travel so far, and without proper preparation? Arsu and the healers have overtaxed themselves tending to you," Ergodi asked.

The great bronze had finally arrived. Ergodi was an enormous dragon. It would take two more of him to match his mentor's size. Ergodi was the oldest on the Council of Elders but not the oldest dragon on the peaks of Petrall. His spines were a deep brown, a brown that used to match the patch of hair that grew from his jaw. It had long since gone white over the years.

"Elder Ergodi," Destined said, nodding.

"Destined, you, better than most, know the danger," Ergodi said.

"Aye, I do. I owe the healers great thanks for their work. I did not intend to be gone for so long. I found a trail as you suggested I should and thought I would see it to the end."

"Did you find them?" Ergodi asked.

"No. I found no trace of them except Ellot," he said. He did not let on that he saw the traces of the paths the others had taken, as well as his mentor's and Kuri's. He had a feeling something was wrong.

"Ellot? He has not returned to himself. I was just at the Circle of Healing," Kuri said. "Mica has not woken again either."

"Ellot's mind-body is gone. What lies with the healers is just an empty shell," he said.

"You saw no trace of Mica?" Ergodi asked.

"No."

"Where did you find Ellot?"

He looked at Ergodi for a moment. It was a curious question from the old dragon. Curious that he would ask where, before the more considerable concern of what could consume the mind-body of a dragon. "In a hall I had mapped previously for exploration with Master Sia," he said.

"Did you not sense any danger there, or did Ellot not heed the warnings?" Ergodi asked.

"I do not know. I may be able to search Mica's mind to find out. When I arrived, Ellot was already gone."

"That is not wise after you have just returned, Lord Farseer," Kuri said.

"I agree with Kuri, Destined. You should rest first. After you have, make it a priority to check Mica. I would also like to speak to you at greater length on what you saw," Ergodi said.

"Aye," he said, nodding. Ergodi was not putting him at ease. He was far too relaxed over the little he had shared, almost like he already knew.

"Very well. You are of little use to yourself after such a long time away. We will leave you with the healers to tend to your needs. Come, Kuri, we need to see about the others," Ergodi said, turning to leave.

He called over one of the novice Walkers. "The Mindhunter and Arsu are with the missing. Please go to them and inform them that no Walker under my command is to enter the Between until they are told otherwise directly from me," he said.

"Yes, Lord Farseer!" the novice said, taking flight quickly.

He did not need to send the messenger. He could have easily contacted both his first and second telepathically; however, his message was for the two lurking elders.

"Please provide the Lord Farseer with food and drink at once. He does not need to worry about hunting right now," Ergodi told one healer.

"For two," he said, interjecting. "Lady Nihility will be joining me."

CHAPTER NINE

Nihility landed quietly on the open rim of the rotunda that Destined called home. Although it was their home, she rarely spent time here. It was not her true home. It never was. It was nothing more than an extension of the Order of Walkers. There was no peace, no safety, no comfort for her. When they were here, others constantly pulled them to their duties or watched. Destined enjoyed her presence here, so she often came to rest at his side for short periods to appease him.

It was one of those times she would have made sure she was somewhere else. Both Ergodi and Kuri spoke with Destined and questioned him about his absence. She was not fond of these two or the Elder Council that guided them. Ergodi made no secret that her pairing with Destined was against his desires for him. He had done so painfully and repeatedly in her youth with Ivylth at his side. Kuri used her to antagonize Destined endlessly. She could tell by his emotions he was also in no mood to deal with either of them.

The healers fussed over him and flittered about. None of them had noticed her presence. She was large for a dragoness her age. At twenty thousand years to the sky, she should have been smaller, but she was the size of some dragonesses twice her age, maybe three depending on who they compared her to. No dragoness that hatched with her matched her size. However, her size did not give credit to her agility or speed. She was one of the fastest flyers on Petrall and lethal on the ground and in the air.

She perched on the lip of the rotunda spread low as if ready to pounce with her wings tucked tight. She was watching and waiting. The only one to notice her presence was Destined. He looked up at her with his sweet hazel eyes and commanded they bring food for them both. She watched until they got his meal before gliding down. "Leave now," she commanded. The healers were startled but gathered themselves to go.

"Lady Nihility, he should be tended to. He was gone for many days," Ergodi said.

"I am sure a dragoness such as Lady Nihility can care for the Lord Farseer, Master Ergodi. It should be no more difficult than the Matron wrangling hatchlings," Kuri said as he left.

"Please go," she said, ignoring Kuri's remarks.

She moved around Destined slowly, looking him over carefully. Unlike the Watchers of their kind, who tended to be slender and long, Destined was a bulky dragon. She was bigger than he was, but that was not abnormal. A dragoness was always larger than the dragons who equaled her in age. Destined would catch up and possibly even surpass her at some stage.

Destined was unique for a different reason. He was the only wholly white dragon on Petrall. His scales and spines held no other color, making him white from snout to tail. Even his spikes were white. Only his black claws and hazel eyes gave him color. His face was wide set with two horns that curved back from his head to a point. He was agile once he found his momentum in the sky, but his mind was the real danger.

"I only need to move about, my love," he said.

"What were you thinking going in alone knowing what has been happening to the others, Destined Farseer!?" she said with a growl. "I should set you on fire!"

"Nihility, my love, I could not ignore it forever. There is no one else that can walk as deep as I can. You know this."

She glared at him. "Do not feed me your foolish bravado, Destined. I know that Master Sia is just as capable as you are in that place. What I know is that you could have provided directions to one of those other two and sent them in instead, or even Master Sia. What I know is you allowed yourself to be pushed before you were adequately prepared," she hissed.

He gave her a look and spoke to her mind. "No, Nihility, I

could not. Not those two anyway," he said. She gave him a look, and he grinned at her. "But yes, I could have found Master Sia first."

"You know I hate when you are reckless!" she said.

"I know, my love, but I did not intend to be," he said, nuzzling her. "Eat, please. You are hungry." She pressed herself against him, and he sighed heavily. The rotunda offered little privacy, but the peak of Petrall was no better. It was why, when they were hatchlings, Destined forged a link with not only her but Endrir. They could speak freely without worry through their minds.

He watched as she ate. He laid his tail over hers, "you risked too much walking on your own, my love."

"And you did not?" she asked, not stopping her meal. No one knew she could enter the Between. He had sworn her to secrecy. It was forbidden for any other than Walkers to enter.

"You know what I mean, Nihility. Ergodi and Kuri have been lurking."

"I am not so foolish as you. I know Ergodi and Kuri well, Destined. I made sure I entered alone and unobserved. Besides, they were not lurking anywhere but here. Kuri told me he and Ergodi were being prevented from entering the Between."

"That was his exact words, my love? Prevented?"

She took a minute to think back on the conversation. "Aye prevented, and that Ergodi saw to it as Kuri spoke with me. Tuzys arrived, and I asked him to stay at your side. You are lost in your thoughts. What did I say?" she asked.

"Nothing, my love. I just worry about your safety. I felt your distress," he whispered.

"Yet you did not come for me, dragon," she said with a smirk.

"I knew you would be fine. You are strong," he said, looking away.

"You still could have come to see to your dragoness, Destined."

"I was…distracted."

"You said we would speak later after you have rested, Destined. I would hold you to that and do the same. For now, you are safe, as am I. However, I do not know how many days I have lost," she said, smiling at him. She knew he had sensed the difference in her. There was no way she could hide Pax and the other from him.

"Thirteen for me and four for you."

"Thirteen! Destined Farseer!" she said, shocked.

"I know. I know," he said, shaking his head.

"My light, please do not do that again. Take Master Sia with you or Tuzys if you must go, but please do not go alone again."

"I will not go alone again, my love. I promise. You must promise me you will not go in again. It is dangerous, Nihility. Actual danger."

"I will not make that promise, Destined. I may have to be the one to go with you. Also, I do not think I can keep my ability to do so a secret anymore."

"Nihility!"

"I have to tell Ygi, Destined. I…"

"What is it?"

"I did not finish the ritual with the Daughters of Ote. I have not connected them to the Dreaming. I left when…I came back when I felt something was wrong with you."

"I am sorry, Nihility. Will it cause problems with the Great Mother?"

She felt his guilt cascade around her. "It is not your fault, Destined. I have a duty to you as your dragoness as well. Great Mother will understand. Master Bendre will rend me in two, though," she said with a weak laugh.

He winced. "Can I talk to him and explain for you? It is my fault, Nihility. You are right. I should have used more caution."

"No, but thank you, my light. I will speak to Master Bendre, but I will need to explain myself. Especially if it has been four days," she said, finishing her meal and looking at him. He thrashed his tail, making her giggle. "What has got into you," she asked as he shivered.

"I missed you," he said, nuzzling her again. Her body vibrated beside him. He looked up at the Maiden Moon that hung alone in the sky, casting white light in the darkness. "Shall we go explore what remains of the night? The Maiden sits high for a while longer," he asked.

"Are you sure? You should not overtax yourself," she said. She felt cramped and wanted to spread her wings and flex her muscles, but she knew he had not been truthful in saying he was well. She could tell by his grimace and feel his pain. Her four days were nothing to his thirteen.

He smiled and flicked his tongue at her. "I think a flight will do me good. I have been down too long."

She stood and nuzzled his side. A small blue light glowed briefly and circled his entire body. "That should help some," she said. She had used a rejuvenation spell on him. Her strength was not healing, but she could perform the more minor necessary spells.

He sighed with relief and swept his tail around her, caressing her lightly. He lifted himself to his feet and flexed his massive wings. His scales shimmered in the Maiden's moonlight like glass, making him appear a silver hue. He took to the air in a slow leap. She waited for him to crest the opening before she followed. Where he glimmered in the moonlight, she drank it in. She appeared even darker than usual. Only sharp eyes could spot her against the night sky.

They flew together, slow at first before they picked up their pace. Once Destined's muscles worked more freely, the dance began. He always let her lead. While she guided their direction, he would weave around her, barely touching. He circled around her, caressing a different part of her with his tail. At that moment, they were lovers, dancing as dragons who have shared their heart of hearts.

She hummed softly, filling the air around them with music. He brushed her lightly with his wings. She rolled to her side, and as he flew around her, he trailed his snout down her belly. She rolled to the other side, and he repeated. Her hums grew louder. Suddenly, they both shot straight up as if headed for the stars, intertwining around one another as they climbed higher. A white light silhouetted in black glowed between them as their bodies locked around one another. They descended back towards the middle of the rotunda, still tightly wrapped together. Their bodies changed from dragon and dragoness to their borrowed short-life forms as they fell. Her arms were wrapped around his neck. As he hugged her waist, their feet came to rest on the stone.

"I am glad you are okay," she whispered to him.

"More than okay right now, my love," he said.

She smiled, running her hands down the back of his head and neck as he pulled her close to him. His hands slid up her back as he kissed her neck. "I missed you," he murmured against her ear. "I love you, and I want you, Nihility," he whispered.

She pulled away to see his face. She saw a flicker of a shade of green that she had never seen before in his hazel eyes. His face, for the briefest moment, changed. She felt anger and annoyance. Then it was gone. She stared at him longer, "Dest…" she tried to say before he kissed her.

It was a long kiss that started slow and then grew in intensity as his desire for her overcame him. His hands moved down her sides and around to her bottom. She moaned through the kiss as he lifted her up, placing her down on the soft nesting on the floor. Her hands roamed over him, removing his thin white shirt. She slowly moved her hands over his chest as if she was memorizing his form. He grinned at her and giggled. "What is so funny, Destined Farseer?"

"Nothing, my love," he said, kissing her quickly. "I am just enjoying the sight of you," he said with a devious grin. He thought she was probably checking him for wounds, which made him giggle more.

"And if I am?" she asked, pinching him.

She playfully tried to roll away, and he grabbed her, pinning her arms above her head. He hovered over her, placing himself between her legs. He took one hand and ran his fingertips down her wrist and arm. He touched her neck briefly before continuing down over her breasts. He stopped long enough to run his fingers around her nipples through her top. When she gasped in pleasure, turning her head, he kissed the side of her neck.

He unlaced her top and pushed it aside, freeing her breasts as he kissed down her chest. He smirked as he kissed her stomach, moving his hands down her legs. He unlaced her shorts and slid them off, kissing down each leg. He brought himself back up, pushing against her so she could feel his desire for her. She wrapped her arms around him and whispered his name.

He moved down between her legs and kissed the inside of her thighs, pushing them apart and lifting them gently to rest on his shoulders. He placed his lips against her and kissed her, quickly sliding his tongue inside. She put her hands on his head, rubbing it and pushing him deeper. He tasted her until her back arched off the floor, and her thighs squeezed him. When she shook, he relented. He moved back up to her and kissed her.

She tugged at his pants until she had him free of them. As her hand caressed him to guide him inside of her, his breath caught, making him pause and close his eyes. They began a new dance, one that was sensual and deep as she wrapped her legs around his waist, locking him inside her. At the height of her passion, she moaned with her face buried in his neck. He whisperedher name over and over as he squeezed her tightly.

They held each other until their breathing slowed. He rolled over onto his back, and she snuggled up to him, laying her head on his chest. He ran his hand through her hair, twisting the tiny locs in his fingers.

"Do you want to sleep?" she asked.

"After thirteen days, I do not think I could even if I wanted to, my love."

"I can help if you would like," she said, kissing his chest. Being a Weaver allowed her to grant any creature sleep and peaceful dreams.

"Nay, my love. I would stay awake here with you," he said, trailing his fingers down her back. "I realize why Endrir gives me such grief about the Between now."

"What do you mean?"

"I lost thirteen days at your side, and I can never get them back," he said, kissing the top of her head.

"I am here, my light. We are together, and that is all that matters."

"Nihility, you sound strange. What is wrong?"

"Nothing, my light," she said, sitting up and kissing him. "If you will not sleep, then we should discuss what has happened. I have questions that need answers and things I need to tell you."

"Aye, but not here," he said. He got up and dressed, as she did the same. He watched her intently.

"Are you sure talking is what you wish to do, Destined Farseer?" she asked, laughing. She could feel his desire.

"Other things tempt my tongue," he said, biting his lip.

"Would you have it now or later?" she asked, standing before him, holding her shorts in her hand.

He grinned at her. "Later, when nothing else can fill my head but you. However, I am not sure I can help myself," he said, moving to her and kissing her again.

"I could always let you watch while you tell me what it is you have to say," she said with a wicked grin.

"Nihility Harbinger!" he said as the image appeared in his

head of her touching herself. He groaned. "That image will be stuck in my head for days, Nihility!"

"Good," she said, pulling on her shorts.

"We are doing that. I mean it, dragoness. I want that! Not now. Wait…. No, I must be serious now," he said, frowning.

"What if you read me those stories you like from the short lifers while I do?" she asked, trying to keep a straight face.

"Yes!" he said with excitement. "Yes! I am going to get a new one just for that occasion. You are a brilliant dragoness!"

"Come on, my fool, where are we going?" she said, laughing.

He took her by the hand and spoke over their link. "Secret place. Do not be mad, please. It was not a secret from you, I just…"

"Needed a place for your tinkering Ergodi does not know about?" she asked.

"Aye," he said, leading her over to the far wall.

"You should tell the old dragon to fly off or find a hole and crawl into it or something. Preferably something painful," she said with a tone.

"Nihility," he said with a sigh.

He reached down to the floor and touched a square panel of stone. It glowed in the pattern of his hand. A section of the floor disappeared, revealing an opening. They would have to descend single file, and even then, it was a tight fit.

He descended first, motioning her to follow down steps that went deep into the ground, into complete darkness. After a while, he tapped her leg twice. A signal Endrir taught them to stop when they traveled silently. She heard him moving around and could feel his magic. A light glowed beneath her, and she saw she was almost at the bottom. She dropped gracefully into a crouch and stood as she heard the opening close above her.

He sent the orb of light to her. "Extend your hand, my love. I must do this in your short life form," he said. She looked at him curiously but did as he asked. The orb touched down to her palm and encased it in light. It pulsed before growing dim. "Now you can come and go from here as you please without triggering my traps," he said with a grin.

She looked around in awe. It was a large space that almost matched the rotunda above. It was littered with scrolls, books, and magical artifacts. There were tables covered with vials of liquids and powders. It was also a mess, which made her smile. Destined appeared ordered and neat, but when it came to his dabbling in the magic and knowledge of those below the mountain peak of Petrall, he was far from both. "You should really tidy up before you bring any more dragonesses down here, Destined."

"Aye, but you know I work best in my mess," he said with a wink.

"Oh, you have learned their poetry too! I am in love!" she shouted. He laughed and smiled at her.

"I am sorry I did not tell you about it. I finished it a few months ago."

"We have both been busy, my light. Besides, I do not demand you tell me everything you do. I only care that you are safe."

"I know, but I pride myself on the fact that we tell each other everything Nihility. You are my mate, but you are also my best friend."

"Aye," she said, looking away.

"We have a problem, my love," he said after a moment. "What I sensed in that space in the Between, behind that barrier was indescribable chaos, Nihility. I could sense the malignant desire to rip the world apart. I am sure you did too. I do not know how to protect the Walkers, so I have banned them from entering the Between until I can decide a course of action. Kuri and Ergodi are hiding something from me. Something is not right. I have missed something. Something that may have cost the lives of eight Walkers."

"What happened after I left to see to the Daughters of Ote, Destined?"

He sighed heavily. "It started before then, but I ignored it as poor training."

"What? Destined!" she said, shocked. It was not like him to ignore any problems concerning the Between.

"I know," he said with a grimace. "I have no clue why I did either. I know I was tired for a while, but you granted me dream space, and I felt much better. I trusted in Ergodi's assurances he would search for the missing, which I should not have. Even saying that, though, hindsight does not make my behavior clearer. I feel like I was purposely blinded to seeing what else is at work, and that thought makes me nervous. Whatever is happening, I am blind to it."

"You have had no visions of this?"

"No. I mean, yes, but they make little sense. The word 'betrayer' haunts me in them and fills me with dread."

"How long has it been this way?" she asked, concerned. She had never seen him so distraught.

"Over a year now. All of this," he motioned around the room, "are my failed attempts to bring clarity to my visions. I cannot see his face Nihility. I only see this being through that word. Nothing surrounds that word 'betrayer!' The times it appears in my visions of events are random. However, I think it connects the fallen Walkers. Something is coming, Nihility. I can feel it," he said with a look of distress.

She understood his frustration, but she also felt his anger and fear and could not make sense of his feelings with his words. He was off somehow. "Why can you not see the connection? I can understand this betrayer's ability to hide from other Walkers, but you are no ordinary Walker, my light. Could he be a prophet like you, and that is why you cannot see him?"

"No. I know the other prophets Nihility. We stand around one another and instinctively know to stay away from another prophet's path. I can see the past and future. I cannot see around the corners of time. It is in these corners where he hides his presence. I feel as if they know my abilities. I feel like I have been studied and watched. 'Betrayer,' a word is all I gleam because it is all I am supposed to see. I am a prophet, but I cannot see what comes!" he shouted. The force of his words rattled the glass on the table.

She went to him and wrapped her arms around him. His fury was high. She could feel the heat in his form and the color surge around him. "You must calm yourself. Anger and frustration will not lead to answers," she said, trying to soothe him. She could feel his breathing change. He was trying to control himself. "You have lost eight walkers, correct?"

He nodded. "Only one has come back, Mica, and he returned screaming of doors and darkness."

"Did you check his mind before you ventured in?"

"No. I agreed with Ergodi and Kuri that time was of the essence. Once Mica returned raving, and without Ellot, Ergodi believed the trail of their auras would be fresh. I should have waited and checked on him first," he said with a scowl.

"Did you speak to Master Sia about it?" she asked quietly.

"No. I will, though. I should have, but you know how Master Sia is, Nihility. He is not always in the best of moods," he said. She did not reply. She knew Sia well, better than even Destined realized. "Something holds them somewhere in the Between. I do not know where and I do not know what. What I know is that their bodies are empty of mind. I cannot leave them as they are. It is dangerous."

"Destined, what are you thinking of doing?"

He turned to look at her. He had a distasteful look on his face. "The proper thing to do would be to kill what remains, so nothing else enters, but I am not sure I can bring myself to do such a thing."

"Is there no other way?" she asked. "A barrier perhaps to

protect their bodies from anything else entering. Something like the stasis orbs I have at Weaver Circle?"

"It would take tremendous energy, and they would need to be monitored at all times. Your orbs sustain themselves with the Weaver's crystal and the Crystal of the Depths, my love. They are genius, but I have nothing but the mind of the Walker to work with. If there is no mind present, then there is nothing. Has anything strange been happening in the Dreaming?"

"No, my light. If there have been, the information is being kept from me or disregarded. I have sensed nothing unusual myself, but the Dreaming is vast."

"Did you feel anything in the Between when you entered?"

"You would know better than I. I only followed your path as you taught me to," she said. He gave her a look. "Yes, I know I roam! I did not this time!"

He grinned. "Tell me what you saw and felt, please," he said, kissing her forehead.

"It was murky as usual like a cloud had descended on everything. I felt heavy, which differed from the other times. It was also not as quiet as it usually is. The whispers were screams, and I could feel fear and eagerness."

"You heard voices?" he asked, genuinely surprised.

"Aye. I could not understand them. It was the sound of a crowded space," she said. He had a look of deep thought on his face. "What is it, Destined?"

"Nothing important at the moment," he said, shaking his head. He took her hand and led her to the center of the room where he had cushions on the floor. He motioned for her to sit. "You did not come back from the Between alone. I know you know this," he said, taking a seat in front of her.

"Aye."

"I could feel one when you perched on the rock earlier. She is powerful or was. I sense only what remains of her inside you like a mist after the rain, but I can feel her power coursing through you. She handled your protection when I could not?" he asked. She nodded again. "She feels old. She does not hide her presence from me like a demon. Are you not afraid of her?"

"I have no reason to fear," she said with a smile.

"Why? What is that grin for Nihility?"

"Who you sense is Lady Pax of the Depths, Destined! The Lady Pax of the Depths!" she said excitedly.

"How? That is not possible!"

"My words exactly," she said, laughing.

"Are you sure it is not some trick?" he asked. She did not have time to answer. "No, it cannot be a trick. I can sense the similarity between the two of you. I sense the dragoness. Her aura is strong, but does not overpower your own" he said, frowning.

"I am sure it is her. I spoke with her myself. She saved me and helped me reach you. Besides, she looks just as Master Bendre and Master Jaydum described her."

"Well, that explains the mark. Your scales will hide it while you are in your proper form. You will need to exercise care while in this one, though. Keep your hair down if you walk around Petrall."

"What mark?" she asked, looking at him confused.

"I thought it might have been a spell you placed on yourself," he said, moving behind her. He moved her hair off to one side. "You know, like what happens when you summon the fire from the Aether with the Sisters. When I looked closer, I realized it was a magical burn. Only a potent spell, or transfer of power, could have done that," he said, tracing it with his hand to show where the mark was. On the back of her neck was a burn in the form of a closed lotus in black flames; the flames trailed down the top of her shoulders. She winced as he touched it.

"Ouch, Destined. That stings."

"I am sorry, my love. I have read about them, though, and I know Master Sia knows about them. He is where I got the book," he said with a laugh. "It will remain sore until the transfer is complete. Does it pain you when you fly?"

"Not too much. I just assumed I was sore from my lack of movement for four days. Plus, I did not stop when I flew back here from Blackhold."

"Nihility! That is a two-day flight!"

"Do not start with me, Destined. You were the fool who went and got yourself lost in the Between."

"I was not lost," he mumbled. He moved back to his seat in front of her. "Now I think it is time I met Lady Pax for myself."

She gave him a look. He felt wrong. "How do you plan to do that?"

"I am going to project my mind into yours. Do not worry. It will be just like when I speak to you through our link except, I will go deeper. You will feel me much more, but you know this. It is not the first time I have done it. Just give me a moment."

She frowned. Destined was not giving her a choice or asking her permission. It was like he did not trust her judgment. She wondered briefly if he sensed something else. She knew he would not hurt her, but there was that look from earlier; his eyes, a green that was not his. It happened again when he was angry, his eyes, but not his eyes.

"Destined, wai…" she said.

He touched her head and sent his consciousness into her mind before she could finish.

CHAPTER TEN

Nihility's emotions overwhelmed Destined. Her annoyance was choking. "I will not be long, my love," he whispered. The annoyance abated, but he knew she had just shut her emotions off from him. He would have to explain himself quickly after this.

He stood in her mind. It was not the first time, but it was the first in this kind of circumstance. It had not changed. It was still the bare cave he did not understand. She was far too complex for something so simplistic in her mind. It was a large cave, but it only contained a large nest and a small table. There was nothing else that gave away who she was.

He moved directly towards the dark corner, where he sensed the demon inside her. He wanted to make sure it was secure. He could feel the other, but he could not see her. She encased the demon in a black orb. Red ripples of aura coursed through it. It impressed him that Nihility could produce such a powerful barrier. His pride surged at the power of his dragoness. He figured the traces of red belonged to the other. He touched it, adding his own to it. The orb now hosted ripples of white and red.

"My addition was a precaution. The young Lady Nihility's barrier is more than sufficient and impressive for something done with little understanding of the depths of her own mind. However, Empaths carry enough weight that the breadth of their own mind is often consumed by the needs of others," a stern voice said. "You must be the one she was so desperate to reach. I am Pax of the Depths, Twin Star of Petrall, and sister to Lazarus of the Between."

Destined turned to face the voice. There was an enormous form sitting on the nest that occupied Nihility's mind. She seemed comfortable as if this was her space all along. "If you are

Lady Pax, how do you even exist? You have latched yourself on to my Nihility like a parasitic demon. How can one who has been long gone from this world remain? How do you still have enough consciousness to do what you have done? How did you even come to be in the Between? Stories say the Lady Pax met her death deep in the forest near Wom," he said. His voice dripped with doubt as he readied himself to attack to free Nihility if this proved to be a trap.

"Control yourself, Destined the Farseer," she said, laughing. "I have no desire to harm her. If you must know who I am, I can show you."

"I have no time for tricks."

"I have no tricks to play, youngling. Your time grows short. The one you care so much for grows impatient. Impatience for an Empath, and dragoness, does not leave one in the best situation. Especially one that calls himself mate," she said with a slight laugh. "Pity to be you once this is done."

He winced. He knew she was right. Nihility had no patience for vagueness, and he had not adequately explained himself before he intruded into her mind. "Fool," he mumbled to himself.

"All you need to do is place a hand on my snout. I can show you and provide the information you seek," Pax said, rising out of the darkness.

He could finally see her entire form. A large black dragoness with a red ridge of spikes and silver horns appeared from the darkness. "I am in so much shit," he said. He sighed and walked forward, placing a hand on her lowered snout.

Her memories flowed into him. "This way is much faster. I shared this ability with my twin, though he was much more adept at it than I. You may access my memories as your own when you are ready. I only need to tell you one thing that will not be there," Pax said. He nodded. "That barrier was never meant to be found. Someone who had knowledge of its location led the one you found there. For me to be here now, something made its way through. Something far more dangerous than that demon there," she said, nodding at the demon in the corner.

An image appeared of her seal she placed on the door. "Is that how you made the door disappear?" he asked.

"Aye. It will not hold the dead space or anything that comes through. It is nothing more than a warning. You have my memories and may reconcile them to what you know. I am sure after you have done so, no doubt will remain as to who I am. Now, I think it is wise that you go back to Nihility."

Nihility's anger was rising, which was not an emotion he wanted to be this deep in her consciousness to see. Not when he had seen its wrath from the outside. "One last thing, Lady Pax. What power does she now possess?"

"That, Destined the Farseer, is not your concern. Once she knows, you may know. If she chooses," Pax said with a tone.

He felt Pax's agitation with him; it melded with Nihility's seamlessly. She had no more tolerance for his intrusion than Nihility did. They were so similar in their emotions they could have passed for twins themselves. He took a deep breath and exited her mind. "I am sorry, Nihility. I just wanted to be sure you were safe," he said in a rush.

"You could have asked me before taking it upon yourself to intrude on my mind!" she hissed angrily. It was an odd sound in her short-life form.

He could see the fire in her eyes. "I am sorry, my love. I just wanted to check. Demons play tricks!" he said, speaking faster. He was trying to explain himself and diffuse her anger.

"She is not my enemy, Destined. She aided me when I was afraid I could not reach you. She has control of the demon inside me, and I am grateful for her help. I did not wish to lose myself battling the creature."

"But you did..."

"You should have asked!" she said, interrupting him.

It shocked him she did not realize that she was holding the

demon all on her own. "Aye. I should have. I apologize. I added my own just to be safe, my love."

"However," she said, raising her voice. "I did not ask for your help. If you wanted to check, you could have asked without treating me like a novice. Especially after we have spent time together."

"My love, I only wanted to…"

"I know what you wanted, but your method was wrong, Destined Farseer," she mumbled.

"I am sorry," he said, ashamed. He had let her annoyance turn to anger. Now all he could do was let her calm down. These situations always made him feel trapped with her. If he remained quiet with just a simple apology, she would get angry. If he spoke, he feared he would put himself in worse trouble. "I would speak to her again after I process what she has shown me if that is okay with you," he said. The look she gave him froze his heart for a beat.

"You spoke to her and gathered your own information before I have even processed her presence?!" she said. She was shouting by the end.

"Shit," he mumbled under his breath. He did not think about it. He should have. He knew she had come straight to him after they left the Between. "Fuck," he said with a deep sigh.

"I need to stretch my wings. I feel cramped down there," she said, getting up to leave.

He could see the tears standing in her eyes. "Nihility," he called to her softly. She stopped. "I am sorry. I did not think when I should have. I was worried and acted rashly."

"And I was worried about you," she said as she left.

He did not enjoy upsetting her. She was angry, but she was more hurt by what he had done. "I do not know why she tolerates me," he sighed, defeated. "I truly do not know."

He loved her immensely, and sometimes he doubted if he showed it enough. His failings with her were always his second guesses, even though he could read her well. She was the only thing he ever doubted himself about. Loving her was easy, but feeling deserving of her love was different. He never did. His greatest fear was losing her. She could take as many mates as she wanted, but at twenty-thousand years to the sky, she still only had him at her side. She cared for him more than he felt he deserved, and that made the last words she spoke sting even more.

However, she was safe, and that is all that mattered to him. He needed to process what Pax had shown him. He also knew that Nihility would be angry when she found out he had his own demon to deal with. He tried to hide his discomfort from the thing's presence, but he was unsure if she had noticed or not. He sighed. "I would gladly take the fire at this point because she is going to fucking kill me when she finds out," he groaned, falling back on the cushion.

CHAPTER ELEVEN

Nihility flew in lazy circles in the eye of the rising Sun. She was angry at Destined's intrusion into her mind. That space was hers. She invited him willingly, but not like that. Not in how he had done it. She took her anger and hurt out in flight. She soared high over Petrall. She had no destination in mind but needed to let the sky take her mind away. Flying always gave her a sense of peace.

Empaths held magic that cut both ways. She could easily read others' emotions, but they also plagued her. She could not wield her magic on command like so many others. It always existed. The sky gave her distance and peace. The only place that came close to the sky was the arms of Sia, but she could not even have that anymore. Destined was not only her mate but her friend. She would have stayed and spoken to him, but she was so shocked by his behavior.

"Fool!" she said to herself. Her flight faltered when she heard laughter from her mind. It felt like when she laid in the grass with Ygi whispering to one another. Lady Ygi could manipulate sound. In the game they would play, Ygi would whisper softly using different tones in her voice that created a funny warble in her ears. "Lady Pax?"

"Yes, youngling," Pax said. Nihility could feel her mirth.

"I cannot get used to this, Pax. I mean, really. I have a whole dragoness just sitting around in my mind."

"I know it is unsettling, young one. Imagine how it is for me. I am only a spectator to another's thoughts with no real physical form."

"I am sure that whole dying thing was probably a bit unsettling too," she said.

"Not as much as you would think," she said with a chuckle.

"I hope you enjoyed your brief reprieve with your mate, young Lady Nihility."

"I…" she stammered, flustered.

"Rest easy, young dragoness. I did not spy on your time. However, although I am only a guest in your mind, some of my abilities still function. Probably because we share them. I was an Empath as well. I felt your emotions strongly."

"I thought it would last longer, but the fool had to show himself again. Destined is lucky I adore him; otherwise, he would have been ash by now."

"Long lives we may live, but our happiness always seems shorter than our years," Pax said. "I only interrupted your thoughts because we must speak. I do not know how long that seal I placed upon the door will last."

"Is that not what we are doing?" she asked.

"Yes, that it is, but I would rather see you, and there is the matter of our prisoner. We need privacy. It seems some things have not changed since my time. The rocks of Petrall still have eyes and ears. How long would it take you to return to the place you were before?"

"That is an understatement, Lady Pax. It will not take me long. I fly fast," she said with pride.

She circled Petrall a few moments longer before taking an indirect approach to her place deep in the Hidden Oasis. It was in the Burning Wastes of Petrall. It was not a wasteland; however, it was one of the most dangerous parts of the mountain. It was an area where one of the mountain peaks was constantly in flux. Randomly it would erupt fire, almost as if a dragon lay in its belly. The result was a large pool of fire rock that divided Petrall from what laid beyond the Burning Wastes.

The peak that spewed forth its fire burned most of the surrounding area, except for a small swath of land a short distance below, where the fire rock had cooled, creating a natural barrier around the area that was fertile and pregnant with life. Vibrant greens, yellows, blues, pinks, and purples covered the rich black soil as far as the eye could see. Only those familiar with the area could find the Hidden Oasis.

The other dragons of Petrall did not come here. It was warm, secluded, and had natural barriers, making it a perfect spot for dragon eggs until the Shattering destroyed it and many eggs. The elders of Petrall believed the area cursed. It was not cursed or dangerous. Truthfully, she was the only real danger in this part of the mountain. She was the largest predator, and the others that inhabited the Hidden Oasis knew it. They also knew she never hunted here. The place was sacred to her for many reasons. She felt like she was its guardian and protector. The area had its own water source, so those that dwelt there rarely left.

"Have they always lived here?" Pax asked.

"Aye. Well, they have for as long as I have known, and beyond from what Sia has told me," she said as she crested over the Burning Peak. The landscape changed from a charred black to a lush green. "I call them friends and share their fires when I can."

"How?" Pax asked.

"What do you mean, Lady Pax? It has always been this way." She could feel Pax's concern and confusion. "What is it, Lady Pax?"

"I know this place. I feel I know this place, but through your eyes, it looks different. I had a sort of home here. A place where I would come to be away from everyone and rest from the endless emotions. If I am correct, you may go there. The entrance, however, would be behind you."

"That explains why it seemed like it had already had some use before I found it. I did not realize that it had once belonged to you, Lady Pax."

"You know the place I speak of? It's well hidden!" Pax said excitedly.

"Aye, and it still is. I have used it for almost three thousand years since I lost my home. The entrance you spoke of is no longer in use. The Shattering collapsed that part of the mountain on itself. Now there are only two. One I head for now, and one other, but it is more properly used as an exit. It can be a tight fit for one my size," she said, laughing.

"Curious," Pax said.

"What is curious?"

"It can wait. Show me where you enter. I would know more of how the world has changed since my death."

Descending deeper into the canopy, she pressed herself between the foliage and gracefully glided down to the oasis. The water was a clear blue, and you could see the fish swimming in some places. Large white objects were floating on the surface, a sign that one of the groups who lived here were fishing the waters. The center was the only place where the water changed. It spiraled down into darker shades of blue until it was almost black. There was a waterfall running from a small rock outcropping. A river flowed into it from inside the mountain. She made her way to the top of the waterfall and launched herself into the air as fast as she could. She glided until she was right over the top of the middle of the pool. Then she tucked her wings tight to her body and dove into the center. She entered the water without a splash. Only ripples gave a hint to her disturbance of the water's surface.

She let the momentum of her body break through the force of the water before kicking her legs, swimming towards where the light appeared. She angled towards it, surfacing into a beautiful white crystal-filled cavern. She pulled herself up and onto the rocky surface, shaking water from her scales. She walked up to a wall of solid crystal and gently used her claw to touch one of them, making a soft chime. The wall split apart, exposing a deep cave.

"This is wondrous! I did not know it was here!" Pax exclaimed.

"I am sure the Shattering exposed much of the hidden treasures of the mountain," she said. The path that lay exposed could accommodate two of her side by side. As soon as her tail crossed the threshold, the wall slid back into place. She could feel Lady Pax's awe at the magic of the door. "It responds to only me. As you know, each of us resonates differently with our magic. It permeates our entire bodies. Only a chime from my claw will open the door, and the brush of my tail closes the opening."

"Brilliant, Nihility," Pax said.

There was darkness as the wall closed behind them, but she did not slow her pace. Instead, she released a gentle stream of fire from her belly—the path filled with a soft orange glow. The rock walls appeared on fire, shimmering in the heat.

"You are cautious as well!"

"I have to be," she said. After a while, the path opened into a room large enough for several dragons to sit comfortably. Empty holes where glowing orbs sat lined the walls. Some were glowing brightly, others were dim and some no longer glowed at all.

"You did not remove them!" Pax said excitedly. "Oh, my sweet Sathea, you kept them all!"

"I did not know who the memory magic belonged to. Some memories have long since faded. Some were damaged from the Shattering or time. The ones that glow brightly still did not hold clues to whose memories I watched. I had no clue they belonged to you, Lady Pax. Honestly, I thought they belonged to some dragoness that had a lust for Master Terg. He is in most of the memories I have seen."

Pax laughed until she had tears. "Of course, those are the ones that suffer no damage. Tell me, Lady Nihility, is that old dragon still alive?"

"Aye, but I have not seen him in several years," she said.

"I am glad you were the one to find them, Nihility, and I

hope they helped you even if all you had were my memories of Terghelm the Redeemer."

"Terghelm? That is his name?!"

"Aye. I see that fool still finds shame in it. It is a noble name and suits him. The dragon named by the Great Mother herself!"

"He said she named him Terg the Powerful, but the other Weavers fussed, so she called him Redeemer instead."

"For Sathea's sake," Pax groaned. "At least some things have not changed. You know, the memories of others can hold great knowledge. Does your mate know of this place?"

"No. I have not kept it a secret on purpose. The time is just never right to bring Destined here. I am sure had I done so earlier, he could have easily told me they were your memories. He adores the history of our kind. He knows I retire somewhere in my solitary moments, but he does not pry," she said.

"If you don't mind, I would like to revisit one of my memories," Pax said quietly.

"Of course, Lady Pax. Do you know which one?"

"Nay. Why don't you decide," Pax said. Her emotions were hard to read. Nihility felt fear mixed with happiness as she looked around the room at the glowing memory orbs. She picked one that was black and red with bright purple and gold lines streaking through it. She touched the orb gently with her snout and was engulfed in the memories of Lady Pax of the Depths.

CHAPTER TWELVE

Pax lay in the small meadow beside Weaver Circle, the depression where one of the mountain peaks had fallen long ago, trying to find her peace before her day began.

Bright blue Dreamflowers bloomed around her in the light of the rising sun. Their stems tilted as their petals peeled back, exposing deep yellow centers waiting patiently for the sun to make its way above the mountain peaks. It was early in the Season of Calm; soft breezes still brought a slight chill to the air of the hot peaks of the Petrall Mountains. These were the mountains of Sathea where the cold could never settle, but the Season of Sun would be on them soon when the days were long and brutally hot.

For now, it was the time she liked best. When flowers bloomed, the breeze brought sweet smells with its calming embrace, and memories of her lover filled her mind. This was their place. He often came here to see to her before she entered the cavern under Weaver Circle to tend to her duties as lead Weaver. Every morning he would bring her a meal, clean her scales, and give her the most beautiful laments.

"I must always begin my day surrounded by beauty," he would say to her. "And you, Pax, are a being of pure beauty. My eyes see little else but you, my dragoness."

She sighed, allowing a small tendril of smoke to escape her nostrils. She hunted for her own meals now, and the only laments to her beauty were phantom memories brought on by the breeze. She missed him, but she could no longer cry. Her tears had dried with his fire. All she felt now was emptiness. It was a hollow feeling, laced with dark whispers telling her to let go of it all, that she had nothing left in this world to hold her. "I miss you, Iros," she whispered to herself as the memory of their last time here together rolled over her.

• • •

"Pax," he called.

"Yes, my love," she said as he laid his head beside hers. He was a beautiful deep purple dragon laced with patches of gold. The spine of spikes along his back was a magnificent gold that shimmered in the sunlight. His large bright brown eyes met her blue ones. All she felt was love for this dragon, her dragon that she had given the ultimate promise of protection; her Iros.

"Promise me you will not sacrifice yourself for me."

"No," she said calmly.

"My fiery dragoness, this is important."

"I hear you, Iros, but my answer remains. Just as I have said the last thousand times you have asked me," she said as she groomed her claws. He had been trying to get her to agree to this madness for weeks now.

"Paxtiya!" he shouted.

She looked at him sharply. "Do not shout at me, Iros the Blender," she said as smoke wafted from her nostrils. "I will not cower to you or any other dragon on this peak," she snapped and then sighed. "What has got into you lately? Where is my sweet dragon that cared for his dragoness's heart?"

"Pax, I need you to feel me, please," he said.

She nodded and closed her eyes. She was Empath, but she could not read him without focusing. For him to ask, she knew it was important to him. "I am ready, my love," she said.

"I love you," he said. "I have for many years. I have longed for you for many years. I have dreamed of you since before I left my egg. I made a promise to Laz to love you for not only myself but him as well. I agreed without question or hesitation, even though it is a heavy weight to carry. Love always is, Pax. Your grand dragon, Verganeau, batted that lesson into me with his wings when I carried my foolish self to challenge him for your heart. It takes more than laments and hunting to love your dragoness. It takes time. It takes understanding. I am asking you to understand me now."

She opened her eyes, shocked at the emotions she felt from him. "Iros," she whispered.

"Please do not use the magic that binds us as mates to save me. No matter what, Pax of the Depths, and Twin Star of Petrall."

She blinked, trying to clear the tears from her eyes. "You would ask me to break a promise I made to you, a promise bound in my heart, so you may keep the one you made to my twin?"

"Aye," he said, nuzzling her under her chin.

"Iros, you would break what remains of my heart," she mumbled. "How is that keeping your promise?"

"I would not do so by choice, my fire, but," he shook his head. "Something is not right, and I do not know what. I feel danger lurking around me. It seeps under my scales and grows stronger. I only say this to you just in case."

"Speaking of it will only bring it about!" she said, crying. "I have lost enough, Iros."

"We both have, but Paxxy, you are special," Iros said as she rolled her eyes He nudged her playfully. "You are. You always have been. I would protect you, and that means asking you as my dragoness, as the dragoness that holds my heart of hearts and I hers, not to use that magic should something happen to me."

"Iros, I cannot do that! I cannot! I will not! I could not save Laz, and I could not save Verganeau, but you I can save! I am tired of death! I am tired of loss!"

"Please, Paxxy. You may never have to make that choice, but if you do, do not choose to spare me. Allow my death to come, as you did Verg's. Live and find peace on Sathea."

"That is not living, Iros the Blender! It is loneliness. There is no peace in loneliness. I would have nothing. All of you dead and gone while I linger here in agony."

"Nay. It is living. It is living knowing that you carry a piece of me forever no matter what. You have lived all this time just knowing that Verganeau loved you deeply. That he was your dragon. I know it's hard, and I know you are afraid, but those pieces and those memories carry a promise that will bring us back together. Besides, you always have Terg to keep you company," he said with a chuckle.

"Yes, I have Terg," she said, rolling her eyes. "We would be the perfect pair. I could fill my remaining years playing a game with him to see which of us will eat the other first."

"He would win," he said, grinning.

"Iros!"

"He would, my dragoness. If only to say he tasted the Grand Lady Pax," Iros said, collapsing into laughter.

"Pax."

A voice called, ripping her from her memory. She opened her eyes to see Terg before her, a large dark green dragon with streaks of gold running down his side from each of his matching spines. His eyes were a gray so light they almost appeared silver if the light struck them just right. They were of the same age, hatched together. He was also the only dragon on Petrall she considered a friend; her best friend. She was not close to many, and of those, she had lost all but Terg.

"What is it, Terg? I swear you have some kind of sixth sense," she said.

"I do, but that is not what brings me to you today," he said, winking at her.

"That is a relief," she said, smiling. "What is wrong? Why do you feel like that?"

"Stop reading me, dragoness. It is rude."

"Then do not be so easy to read."

"Great Mother asked me to find you. The Warida have

started an uprising in the Depths of the Dreaming. They have taken the lives of a few hundred deep dreamers."

"Are you sure?" she asked.

"Aye, I checked the Crystal of the Depths myself before disturbing you. Their leader, Zenam, tries to force them into the grove. He leads a march now."

She sighed and stood. "They will never leave me to grieve," she mumbled to herself.

"We never are Pax," Terg whispered.

She looked at him as she felt his sadness. "Are you feeling sorry for me, Terg the Redeemer?"

"Nay. You do enough of that yourself," he said. "Probably why you sensed nothing in the Dreaming."

"Your tongue has grown dangerous, Terg," she hissed.

"Really? Has it? I haven't noticed."

"I will have to speak to Livy and Ygi about you. Make sure they know when to punish a dragon for his manners in the presence of a dragoness like myself," she said with a smirk.

He winced. "Unnecessary Pax, and slightly cruel."

She chuckled. "But rightfully earned. Just because she is no longer here does not mean she no longer has power. Livy has taken hold of the Pool of Spirits, and yours might pay if you do not behave Terg."

"Livy would not dare! She adores me," he said, grinning. "However, do not tell Ygi."

"Why not?" she asked coyly as they walked towards Weaver Circle.

"Pax, she has a temper. Do not tell her. I am begging you. You know how she gets. I need my hearing, dragoness!"

"Then you should mind your tongue, dragon."

"I will, but if I cannot hear her moans of pleasure, it will be for nothing!"

"Crude, Terg!" she said, laughing. "Go see to the young Weavers. I will handle the Warida."

"Do you want me to send the Pillars to aid you?"

"No, they must go see the Serpent of the River, Hynro. I need an exact count of those dreamers we have lost. Send those other two, Pimo and Ivylth. Pimo can tend to the wounded. Ivylth needs a lesson," Pax said as they walked to the edge of Weaver Circle. The big water stretched as far as the eye could see. You could hear the water crashing into the rocks far below even over the sound of dragons moving about the peak.

"Pimo tends to Otunte," Terg said.

"Otunte needs no one to tend to her. She will be weak for her remaining days, so Pimo can stop hiding behind her. Send her to me. They should tend to their duties in the Dreaming for once. How on Sathea do you call yourself a Weaver, but you do not weave dreams?" she said, frowning. Terg nodded and looked away from her. "What is it?"

"I do not trust them," he hissed. "Pax, I think…"

"Nor do I," she said, interrupting him. "The most we can do is watch them. We cannot accuse without proof. I will not accuse without proof. I do not have it, and I have not found it. Only suspicions and glimmered feelings."

"Ergodi leading the Walkers worries me, Pax. The Elders should have named someone else."

"I know, Terg, but we can do nothing about it. All we can do is wait and watch. The Elders made their choice."

"Then have those four Watchers do so. They are good, Pax. Iros and Laz trained them well."

"I do not want them involved, especially with Little Red still grieving for Iros. Besides, if something happened to them, I would not forgive myself. I will find another way."

"Aye, I will send them to you," Terg said, sighing. "Pax, be ready to fight. I do not think Zenam will reason this time."

She nodded at him and took flight. She flew around Weaver Circle before dipping down below the side of the mountain to enter the belly of Weaver Circle. She made herself comfortable on one of the large empty nests. As she closed her eyes, she shimmered, a sign she had entered the Dreaming.

The Dreaming was a place where the dreams of those who slept thrived. All things dreamed. All things except Weavers. They were the conscious beings of the Dreaming, tasked with guarding and protecting the dreamers. The Dreaming itself was an interpretation f Sathea, where time moved slower, but the senses were sharper. Colors were vibrant, smells thick, and feelings heightened. Places on Sathea existed in the Dreaming, but the landscape changed and shifted frequently. For Weavers like her, it was home, even more so than the soil of Sathea.

She flew directly to the edge of the Depths. She was one of the largest dragonesses on Petrall and appeared even more prominent in the Dreaming, with her black scales and red spine. Both of her horns and her tail spikes were silver. A swirling aura wafted around them, the mark of the Weaver who has consumed the Dream Essence granted by the Great Tree Aconi.

She landed in the scrub that laced the ground. Blueish green lush grass from the grove flourished in the Dreaming, except here. Where the Depths began, it was hard-packed, weather-beaten dirt. Grey clouds that held no storm hung over the area, casting it in perpetual dusk. It was gloomy here, even though it had plenty of life, like those that stood before her now.

Smoke wafted from her nostrils as she took in the thousands of Warida amassed in front of her. They were creatures who walked on two legs like the short-lifers that proliferated across Sathea now. Their jaws jutted forward, exposing fanged teeth. Their eyes were black unless they had fed recently. Then they took on the blue of dream essence. The males were armed for battle with nothing more than sticks they had sharpened to points. The females were tethered by their necks to the males that owned them with thick blue chains. They all had gray skin lined with deep black marks specific to their tribes covering their thin bodies. They wore no armor, only dirty white cloth. The males were bald with deep black lines on their heads. The females wore their hair in long braids down their back, a sign they were owned by a male of their clan. They were all tiny creatures that smelled of dream fruit and ash from the wood they burned in their fires. She could smell fear on some and bloodlust on others.

"You called for me, Lady Pax?" a small light blue dragoness with brown spines and two brown streaks on her snout said as she landed beside her.

Pax was three times the young dragoness in length and width. She towered over her, throwing her in shadow. "Yes, Ivylth. You will watch and no more. I need no help. I would have you learn how to deal with those in the Depths of the Dreaming. They are not all reasonable or fearful of a dragoness."

"Yes, Lady Pax," Ivylth answered.

Ivylth set her teeth on edge and had since the moment she hatched. Sometimes when a hatchling comes from its egg, you can feel a connection. It is how they pick those they will mentor. With Ivylth, she felt dread in her belly. She gave her lessons, but she could not find a connection with her as she did so many other young Weavers. She turned her attention back to the Warida.

Their leader had stepped forward unarmed but confident. They chose only one male to direct the eight clans. Once selected, they marked him with a large glowing blue eye that sat in the middle of his forehead, the Mark of the Deep Dreamer.

"Go home or die, Zenam!" she shouted.

The Warida were a reclusive folk. They were not creatures of Sathea. They lived only in the Dreaming, feeding off the essence of dreamers. They were the things that lured you into a place in your dreams where you felt as if you could not wake, or you believed you did, only to find out you remained in the dream. It seemed they had been flourishing in the Depths of the Dreaming unnoticed. Their numbers were far more significant than they should be.

"You cannot take us all, Weaver," Zenam said.

"I am in no mood for your plans and plots, Zenam. Go home now and take your people with you. Terg and I will speak to you later about the overabundance of your numbers. We will sustain you all, but there must be changes."

"The clans are done with the rules of the Great Mother! We need sustenance! We need the grove of the Great Tree of Dreaming, Aconi!" Zenam shouted.

"Zenam, I must tell you that this was not the best day for your little uprising. I am in a mood, and a dragoness in a mood is dangerous. Go home or become nothing but ashes to ride the winds of the Dreaming."

He laughed at her as a sizable brown clay jar appeared at his feet. It came to his waist, its contents concealed by a blue waxy substance. He took his hand and peeled the wax away. A blue mist rolled out of the jar surrounding Zenam.

"Lady Pax, that is the essence of the dreamers," Ivylth said beside her. She looked at her sharply as she felt Ivylth's delight at the sight.

"Death essence, Zenam? Have you lost all your wits?" she asked, looking back at him.

The essence of the dreamers he had killed consumed those around him. He was not feeding on them but storing them to fuel his warriors. Their eyes and the marks on their skin glowed a bright blue and pulsed with power. The females dropped to the ground as the males siphoned their magic away.

"Stop this now, Zenam! They should not be treated so!" she hissed.

"They have served their purpose. They exist only to provide us power in times of war, and this Pax of the Depths, is war," Zenam shouted.

"No, this is a fool on a mission to meet his death," she said.

"And you think you will be the one to stop us, Pax? I hold no fear of dragons. You are nothing but pets for the trees," Zenam said, laughing.

"You stand there with sticks against a warrior of the Dreaming, you little pest," she spat. "There is no war, only your half-brained delusions. It is a shame you are a terrible leader for your people, Zenam," she said.

She filled her chest, letting the fire build. Then she let her anger flow as she opened her jaws, allowing the Black Flame to pour forth. It engulfed Zenam instantly. His screams ripped through the air. He flailed, and those he touched ignited as well. She watched as the army before her crumbled.

"If you wish to live, go home. The flames will not follow you. However, those touched by it will die and exist no more. Hynro will feast on all that remains. There will be no rebirth for those touched by the Black Flame. Only agony and darkness," she said, drained. She could not let them see the effects of the magic of the flames. She had created them, but at a cost.

"What have you done?! That is not Dragonfire!" Ivylth asked, gasping at the carnage the Black Flame caused. The Warida had been halved in number.

"Ivylth; that is the Black Flame. It will burn anything and everything it touches until it exists no more, or I stop it."

"Stop them, or there will be no Warida left! There is no balance in that, Lady Pax!"

"No. There will be survivors who remember this day," she said, watching the Warida run away from the flames back into the rocks behind them.

"It does not burn the ground!" Ivylth said in awe.

"It burns what I will it to. This is a culling. It is a lesson for you and the Warida, Ivylth. They have grown too large, fed without thought, and acted without thought. They followed foolishly. Now they will use caution, and those that have succumbed to my Black Flame will be the reminder of the lesson they learned today. They will have to rebuild themselves and find their place. They will have to do so in a way that respects the balance of the Dreaming, and they will need our help."

"Why should we lower ourselves to deal with those filthy creatures," Ivylth said.

"Because it is your duty, Weaver. That link was not given to you to reign supreme here. It was given to you as a gift. We must protect the creatures of the Dreaming and the dreamers, Ivylth!"

"Can you teach me to use the flame, Lady Pax?" Ivylth asked.

"No," she said, frustrated.

"Why not?!" Ivylth shouted. "How is that fair? Why would you ask me to come then? What kind of teacher taunts their students with a power they cannot have?!"

She gave Ivylth a looked coated in fire. "You were sent here to learn how those of the Dreaming live. You were sent here to see how they must be treated when conflicts arise, dragoness!" she hissed. "Only an Empath can wield the Black Flame, and you are no Empath."

"But my illusionary magic is the best on Petrall!" Ivylth said with defiance.

"Illusions do not make you an Empath. Ivylth, you are gifted. Your talents will lead you elsewhere," she said. Ivylth was frowning at her. She could read her emotions easily. "Find what makes you unique, Ivylth, and you will find your purpose in the Dreaming. The self-professed best at something is not a purpose. It is ambition. Dangerous ambition," she said, narrowing her eyes at the little dragoness.

A pale green dragoness with deep blue spines landed beside them. "Lady Pax, you called for me?"

"You are late, Pimo the Mender!" she snapped.

"I beg your forgiveness, Lady Pax!" Pimo said, lowering her head.

"Do not beg for forgiveness, dragoness. Own your mistakes! You have a duty to the Dreaming, not Otunte. Your duty lies here!"

"Yes, Lady Pax."

She eyed Pimo for a long time. She could feel the guilt rolling from the young dragoness as she cowered under her gaze. The echoes of Terg's feelings of suspicion thrummed through her body. "Pimo, go tend to their wounded. After that, I want you to find the remaining females in each of the eight tribes. I want to know who has been sacrificed, who has not, and the un-mated that remain."

"Yes, Lady Pax.

Pimo did not move right away. She looked at Ivylth as if she was seeking permission. "Now, Pimo!" she shouted.

"Pimo is afraid of the flames, Great Lady. I will go with her," Ivylth said in a silky voice. Pax felt Ivylth's magic trying to take hold in her mind. Ivylth was gifted with mind manipulation and illusions. She could make you spill your secrets if you were not careful, or believe things that never happened. It was why she was given the title Trickster.

Pax bashed Ivylth with the side of her tail, sending her falling to her side. She was on her within seconds, her front claw on Ivylth's throat. Pimo whined and flattened herself low to the ground. "How dare you try to use your tricks on me, whelp!" Pax roared. "I should burn you where you lay!"

Ivylth gasped for air beneath her. "Lady Pax, you are hurting her!" Pimo screeched.

"Leave now, Pimo, or share her fate," she hissed. "You have used up what little patience I had today, Ivylth. Who do you think you are?" she asked as flames licked her jaws.

"My darling, Pax," a melodious voice called. "What has this young Weaver done to anger you in such a way?"

A female appeared beside them, wearing a long flowing green dress the color of grass. She was tall but still tiny compared to a dragoness, with sun-kissed skin and lips red like the flowers that bloomed around the grove of the Great Tree. Her long brown hair hung down her back, pinned at the sides by flowers with blue petals that went black at their tips; they matched her eyes.

"Great Mother Gilliphae, go mind the grove," she said without taking her eyes from Ivylth.

"Calm, my beautiful dragoness," Gilliphae said. A light wind blew over her, making her sigh. "Tend to her with a calm mind."

Pax took a long slow deep breath before she tried to speak to Ivylth. She had tried to gather information from her mind by tricking her into believing she had agreed to tell her about the Black Flame and the Well of Infinite Emotions. "I am the Twin Star of Petrall, twin to Lazarus of the Between, Master of Memories, who could do more with them than you could ever achieve in all your years, Ivylth. If you try to glamour me again, it will be the last thing you ever do," she breathed as she released her. Ivylth whimpered and move away.

"What do you say, Ivylth the Trickster?" Gilliphae asked.

"My apologies, Great Lady Pax. I...I only wanted to know why you do not teach us all we should know. You show off this great flame, but you say that my lesson is to find what makes me unique. I do not understand. You are only an Empath. I wanted to know why you hide lessons from me."

"Pax is more than an Empath. She is the Herald, a sign of what is coming in the Dreaming," Gilliphae said. "Some would say even on Sathea. If you believe her only talent is a flame, then you have missed the message she has brought you and Petrall."

Ivylth rolled her eyes. "Your manners, dragoness!" Pax hissed.

"Yes, Great Mother," Ivylth mumbled.

"The Well of Infinite Emotions that you tried to pull from my mind is not a place for you, Weaver. It will never be a place for you. Go find Master Terg. Our lesson is done."

"Why? Why can I not learn it too?" Ivylth asked.

"Because you are not an Empath. You have no ability to

understand and control the emotions of another. You cannot feel them as I do. You cannot control them as I do. They do not cause you pain as they do me. You show no control over yourself or your emotions. You are not worthy!"

"But you took Ygi and her mate," Ivylth said with distaste.

"Pity Livy is not the one standing before me instead of you, but I guess I have that coward of a dragon you favor to thank for that," she said. Ivylth glared at her. "Ivylth, enough! You are not an Empath…"

"Neither is Ygi!" Ivylth said, interrupting her.

"Hold your tongue, dragoness, before I rip it out of that silly head of yours!" she snapped, with fire in her jaws. "You are not an Empath. There are no other Empaths on Petrall except for me. However, there are others with abilities that use emotions. Ygi has mastered the ability to detect the emotional base of sounds, and Livy could see the color of emotions with ease. Your illusionary magic may someday manifest in a way that shows it uses emotions, like Britir, but as of now, it has not. Instead, you use it to pry into places you have no business and commit deeds you should not!"

Ivylth looked away quickly, trying to compose her shock. "He is a Watcher."

"And you are a Weaver. Focus on what makes you unique. Hone your skills and stop trying to take steps away from hard work. There are no shortcuts, Ivylth! We accomplish nothing with shortcuts. You must work and work hard. That is the essence of the Great Balance."

"Lady Ivylth, please help Terg," Gilliphae said. She now sat quietly in the grass, listening. Ivylth nodded and took flight. "Paxtyia."

"Do not start, Gilliphae. I am tired, and my heart hurts," she said. "Call the Pillars, Bendre and Jaydum, to see to the rest. Hynro will wonder where the souls have come from."

"Paxtyia," Gilliphae called again.

"Yes, Great Mother," she said, sighing.

"Do not let the darkness consume you, my darling. There is no relief there, not for you. However, you may find peace in the light of your half."

"I know, Gilliphae," she said as she took flight. She did not spare a glance at the carnage, even though the screams of the Warida followed her. Pax had doused the Black Flame, but the smoldering remains of the rebellious Warida lay strewn in the grass in piles of ash where they once stood. The cries of those injured carried, but it paled compared to the pain she felt in her own heart.

CHAPTER THIRTEEN

Nihility released the memory, moved to the center of the room and laid down. It seemed like hours, not days, she laid in the same spot to walk the Between. She sat comfortably and closed her eyes as if to sleep. She turned inward into her own mind. The demon inside assaulted her, all its emotions raging at her.

"Turn here, youngling. It can wait," Pax said.

She stood in the cave of her mind and moved over to Lady Pax. She was a glorious dragoness and a legend among Weavers. They still spoke her name with reverence in the Dreaming. She sat down in front of her and looked into warm blue eyes that told her age. She had a slight smirk upon her face.

"You used the Black Flame against Zenam that day," she said quietly.

"I did. It was the first time I used that power, but not the last."

"You were sad and angry."

"I was grieving, yes. My anger and grief were strong that day," Pax answered.

"I should have picked a different memory," she mumbled.

"Or you picked the perfect one, youngling. Your disquiet grows from questions. You should not be afraid to ask them. It is how you learn."

"You knew how they were long before," she said.

"Who?" Pax asked with a frown.

"Ivylth."

"Ah, yes. I had a feeling," Pax said with a slight chuckle. "Never good ones, but I could not punish her simply because she gave me a bad feeling."

"She's done plenty to be punished for," Nihility snapped.

"Judging from what I feel from you now, I'd say so," Pax said eyeing her carefully.

She turned her head away. She did not want to talk about Ivylth or the things she did. "Did you know Master Terg well, Lady Pax?"

"Yes. Terg was my closest friend on Petrall Tell me, Lady Nihility, why do you take the form of the short-life creatures that live so far below the mountain?"

"Our Watchers who wander Sathea take the form of others to blend in. Destined and I learned to harness the ability from a friend, Endrir," she said.

"He is a Watcher?" Pax asked.

"Aye."

"So why did you choose your form, the form of Ote's people?"

She shrugged. "They are kind, and the way they live appeals to me. They are warriors. I feel like they are dragonesses, but they are not dragonesses," she said.

"I would see it here if you can do so without disturbing your resting form," Pax said.

She closed her eyes and thought about her form. The dragoness disappeared into the more diminutive form of the nomad women she favored. "It took me a few years to finally feel comfortable in it and how it looks. But now I feel no different in either unless I am hungry," she said sheepishly.

"That is because a dragoness's belly is much bigger," Pax said, laughing. She was silent as she inspected Nihility's form. "Interesting. I can see your borrowed form clearly, but you now have a shadow that is your true form that lingers behind you."

Pax's sadness crashed around her, making her gasp. "Lady Pax, are you well?"

"Aye. You resemble someone I used to know long ago. You would not remember her, but her name was Shi. She was one of Ote's daughters, her last daughter."

"I have been told that I favor the Lady Shi by a few. She passed during your time."

"Aye, she did," Pax whispered. "She brought powers to her people even I failed to understand, but I know they were tied to the Dreaming and Sathea."

"The Aether. Lady Shi created the Sisters of the Aether. I stand with them now, but their numbers have never been as they were when Shi lived. At least, that is what Lady Ygi tells me. She is where I learned about it. She stands with them as well. Or she did. She has not in a long time. She leaves the duty to me."

"Have they been given a seat on the Council of Dreamers?" Pax asked.

She winced. "I was supposed to be doing that before I came back to see about Destined," she said. She groaned. "Master Bendre is going to kill me."

"He will do no such thing. You had a duty to your mate. It cannot be helped. We will go speak to him after this," Pax said with authority.

"Lady Pax, Master Bendre will not care if you are with me. He demands I fulfill my duties as Lead Weaver," she said with a whine.

"I know Bendre well. He will be fine. How many years to the sky do you have Nihility?"

"A little over twenty-thousand," she said.

"So young and already Lead Weaver. If he pushes you, it is because he sees greatness in you. How long has it been since my passing, Lady Nihility?"

She looked at Pax, hesitant to answer. She could feel anxiousness and a bit of fear from the old dragoness. "Are you sure you wish to know Lady Pax?" she asked. Pax nodded. "I believe it has been around 150,000 years since your passing and my birth."

Pax looked crestfallen. "Such a long time. So much has changed, yet so much has not."

"I am sorry, Lady Pax," she said, placing a hand on her. She felt a surge of anger and removed her hand quickly before realizing it did not come from Pax. She turned her head towards the demon. "What are we to do with that thing? Its presence in my mind is unsettling," she asked.

"For now, nothing. The barrier will hold. When you are ready, we will deal with it. For now, we must speak of other matters," Pax said. "I shared the information with Destined through my memories. However, you are Weaver, so tell me Nihility the Harbinger, Lead Weaver of Weaver Circle, what do you know of me?"

"You are the Great Lady of the Depths, Pax! The black dragoness who stormed the Depths of the Dreaming bringing balance on your wings and with your fire!"

Pax laughed. "Is that what tales they are sharing about me these days?"

"It is no tale! I have seen your work with my own eyes. Master Bendre and Lady Ygi had me learn all about you. You...you are who I aspired to be," she said, embarrassed.

Pax hummed happily. "I think you have done that already, youngling. Especially if you are already Lead Weaver of Weaver Circle. Do you know the tale of my twin and me?"

"Not much. My lessons were always focused on your work in the Dreaming."

"That is because you are Weaver and Empath. I suppose it is best if you hear the tale from me. The only one that could tell it with any real accuracy would be Terg, and I am sure he has not lost his uncontrollable need to embellish every tale that leaves his snout," Pax said with a tone.

"No, he has not," she said, giggling. "But I find it charming, and he knows it."

"You should not encourage him," Pax said.

"That is what Lady Ygi says," she said, laughing harder.

"I am surprised he has not attempted to make himself your

dragon," Pax sighed. "Terg the Redeemer should have been named Terg of Uncontrollable Loins...Nihility? No!"

"I cannot help it. Master Terg is charming, and I owe him more than he will ever know."

"Yet he has not taken your advances? Are you sure he is well?"

"I am sure he knows, Lady Pax. I mean, I have not told him. I have no need to. Every dragoness has the first dragon they ever notice. He is mine," she said with a shrug.

"I agree, and I also agree that it is unnecessary to pursue every whim a dragoness may have. However, if you noticed Terg, then it means he has noticed you," Pax said with a chuckle. "I am surprised you cannot read his emotions. Terg was never very good at hiding them."

"I can, but he is not Destined. Master Terg is older and wise. I will not throw myself at him like some young dragoness who has finally realized dragons exist," she said, making a face. "Not that I need to. We have a bond. That bond is enough for me."

Pax laughed and smiled at her. "That is right, youngling, a dragoness does not chase. If Terg the Redeemer wants you, he will come for you. When he does, it will be your decision to make," Pax said. "I would not worry. Terg the Redeemer is the sweetest dragon I have ever known, and I am sure that has not changed regardless of time. Now, while we are about foolish dragons, I must tell you about another one I knew, my twin Lazarus."

CHAPTER FOURTEEN

The last thing Destined wanted was for Nihility to see him and renew her frustrations with him. He gave her a few minutes before he followed her out. Sometimes it was best to let the dragoness rest in her own emotions. He could see her flying, which made him feel even worse for his actions.

She was always guarded, even in their youth. The Elders feared her power and abilities because of a prophecy no one really understood. They saddled her with the stigma that she would be the reason for the downfall of dragon kind moments after she hatched from her egg when it was only the mountain shaking.

The quiet black dragoness, Nihility the Harbinger, was nothing like the rest of Petrall believed. She hid the truth of who she was behind a mask of toughness and emotional detachment. However, she was not cold or cursed. She was the brightest light of them all. She cared about others and did things without expecting a return for her efforts. She was an Empath and understood what emotions really were. She led with not just her heart but her mind as well. She could feel deeper, longer, and more complex than anyone he had ever met. She was never angry for long, but she would not forget those who harmed her. She placed value in a being by their actions because she always told him words can be delivered in an empty mouth, but actions cannot.

Nihility was his best friend on Petrall. She cared about him and not his abilities. Where everyone else placed him on a pedestal, she saw no pedestal. He was Destined the Farseer, Great White Hope of Petrall. To her, he was just Destined the Fool, Great White Dragon of Petrall, who used to roll around in the dirt to dull his scales.

He adored her. He could spend hours talking to her about

anything. When he did not understand how he felt, she guided him. She always appeared mysterious in her quietness or ability to speak but not talk about herself or her feelings. However, if she allowed you access to who she really was and allowed you to bask in the emotions she had, then it was the greatest gift you could ever receive. It was the greatest gift he had ever received. He had become so accustomed to her admitting him to her thoughts that he had violated her without thinking. He watched her turn towards the Burning Wastes and made a note to himself to make up for his latest foolish act.

He shifted out of his short life form and spread his wings, taking flight out of the rotunda. He flew in large circles around Petrall. Petrall was the name of the mountain range they lived on. The Petrall Mountains stretched as far as the eye could see, though not all the mountain was used by dragons. The time when dragons spread their wings across the whole of the Petrall Mountains was long gone. They had cloistered themselves into a small section of the mountain between the Burning Wastes and the Apex.

The Durming Sea surrounded the backside of Petrall. Near the sheer cliffs, where the mountain had crumbled so long ago no one remembered, was the Apex. Nothing lived there except Ostidas, lightning, and thunder. Ostidas were large birds that resemble storm clouds with their white and grey feathers. They spewed lightning at their enemies and were believed to be a warning of an oncoming storm. Storms continually raged above the Apex, churning the surrounding waters. The risk of being struck was far too high for dragons to use the peak, but he knew Endrir had trained there.

On the opposite side of Petrall lay the Burning Wastes. It was the direction he had seen Nihility go. It was once the nesting ground for dragons, but the last eggs to hatch from there was the generation that included himself and Nihility. The Shattering had taken the peak, leaving only an inferno in its place. Only seventeen hatchlings survived that day; Nihility, Endrir, Tuzys, and he were but four. He knew other creatures lived beyond the Burning Wastes, but they did not come near the main dragon roost of Petrall.

Sprawled beneath him was the place where they called home. Watcher Hold was nestled on the side nearest the Apex. It was built deep into the mountain and cast in constant shadow. Rumors and tales had always surrounded the Hold. It was a series of rooms and tunnels that supposedly spanned the entire mountain range, said to have been created by a dragon called Lar of Petrall. He did not know if the stories held any truth; the Hold held many secrets. There was never much activity there. Those that came and went did so with complete secrecy, as was the Watcher calling; never to been seen or heard, but to watch. He once spent an entire day on top of the Tower watching the Hold. It was not until the Maiden Moon rose with her soft white light that you could see the Watchers come and go in various forms.

Weaver Circle was where Nihility now guided the Weavers as the lead. He was so proud of her. She had turned it from a place of gloom and ever-present sadness to one of happiness and life. Even though they carried the Dreaming with them, the dragons, mostly dragonesses, connected to it were full of life. They flew in and out of Weaver Circle, filling the air with hums. You could see the shimmer from the ones inside, a sign they were in the Dreaming about their duties. Weaver Circle was a depression that went deep into the rock, but the opening allowed them exposure to all the elements of Sathea. They had space under as well, but he had never been inside. Only a dragon with a link to the Dreaming could enter the rock face that blocked the entrance to what lay under Weaver Circle.

He turned himself and climbed. He was headed for the top of the Order of Walkers, Walker Tower. It was built from one of the peaks of Petrall. It spiraled high into the sky. He did not know how it was created, but it remained well used. Down below, he could see dragons basking in the sunlight of the grassy area in front of the Tower. They were meditating and centering themselves. You could see others stretching and flexing their wings with smaller dragons. There was a bright spot of orange and yellow giving orders to the novice Walkers. It was Master Sia. He winced, thinking of the lessons he endured with the old dragon. If you were not linked to the Dreaming or had the iridescent scales of a Watcher, then you were a Walker of the Between.

He positioned himself on the top of the tower. He perched, letting his thoughts roll over him. Everyone knew that if he was atop the Tower, he wished to be alone, and right now, that is precisely what he wanted. He was frustrated. He felt like he held the pieces to a puzzle, but not all of them, so he could not complete the picture. For many months visions had assaulted him. The frequency of them had increased, and he did not know why. Then the Walkers started going missing from the Between. Not all at once, but set in a way that did not raise his alarm. He trained them well, but all his training could not account for the folly of pride. He had rescued many that had gone farther than their abilities.

"Betrayer," he said to himself. He turned the word over in his mind. He thought about all the times it would appear in his visions. It was not the first time words had replaced individuals in his visions. When he was preparing to start the dance to win Nihility's heart of hearts, the words "mate and love" plagued him. However, they were connected to visions of Endrir. This word, this "betrayer," had no direct connection to his visions. Images of a door, images of a round of sickness that plagued the fledglings, pictures of various places on Sathea, and visions of the whole of Petrall are what he saw when the word would appear. Never a face, just a word. It could have been anyone.

He did not even know how the betrayer was to betray him. It was like something trapped him in an endless circle. He could feel the connection like an itch he could not scratch under his scales. He let his mind fall empty. Suddenly he saw the word flash in his mind again. This time someone shouting 'no', and a scream of pain accompanied it. He knew the voice; it was Ellot.

He followed the path of thought his mind had latched on to. He thought about the pairs of Walkers he had sent into the Between. One after the other, like fledglings playing a game of air chase. The three pairs of Walkers went missing before he thought there may be a problem. He shook his head. Three pairs of Walkers went missing before he knew, not thought, there was a problem. He was lulled by Kuri and Ergodi's assurances they would look after the missing. It was not until Tuzys alerted him that none had returned that he acted.

"I let them lead me like a hatchling," he said to himself.

Neither Ergodi nor Kuri could have walked that far into the Between without aid. They could not have even done so together. Ability limited their interactions with the Between. The only one with the power to go that deep into the Between alone and unaided was Master Sia and himself. He shook his head again. He knew Sia would risk none of the Walkers. He was more inclined to keep them out and had insisted that Destined do so countless times. Master Sia was the only Walker he knew that acted as if he did not want to go to the Between.

Ergodi's image appeared in his mind. He sighed heavily. They had chosen him first to leave the nursery to become Ergodi's student. He had barely reached his third year out of the egg. No hatchlings had ever left the nursery before their fifth year, but Ergodi had insisted. The old bronze told Destined he saw great potential in him and that he could teach him to bend the Between to his will. Ergodi had pushed him to find what he believed was the great door, but Destined resisted, and he had a convenient escape in Master Sia, who urged him against following Ergodi's lead. He knew the old bronze had not found it, so he wondered how Ellot and Mica had discovered it so quickly?

Pax's memory invaded his mind. She was right. Someone or something had to have led them there. Someone that knew where it was all along. 'Betrayer' flashed in his mind again. This time he saw himself in the Courtyard of the Moon, standing before the Elder Council of Petrall. All of them were present.

"I ask you to hear me now! Petrall, no, Sathea is in trouble!" he heard himself say. "One of my kind?" he asked himself. If the betrayer was indeed one here on Petrall, why would they want to unleash demons on Sathea? Ergodi appeared in his mind again. "For Sathea's sake," he said. He knew the old bronze was greedy for power, but unleashing demons was madness. "But she said Kuri told her something was keeping him and Ergodi out," he mumbled. It was not possible. Nothing kept anyone from the Between. If you could find the balance in your own consciousness to carry you there, then you went.

Something was different about the Between when he entered. Nihility had confirmed his suspicions. She spoke of the screaming and wailing of spirits within, and he heard no such screams. He heard nothing when he had entered. The Between is a void, but one can hear whispers in the silence. Whispers like a soft breeze. Something must have been happening when he entered, and the climax at Nihility's, to agitate those that dwelled there.

He saw the barrier in his mind. The story of Laz and his discovery of the Between had always fascinated him. "Two to make. Two to break," he said aloud but did not know where the words came from. He was growing frustrated with the lack of answers. He did not see how any of this fit. Where were these demons? Did they exist in a space linked to the Between? How had Laz come to know a demon? The image of the serpent flashed in his mind, and he cringed. He did not know what it was or what it meant. It seemed there were more questions than he had answers for. All he knew for sure was that somehow it involved his old master.

Although, none of this mattered in the face of the task he had in front of him. He had to decide what to do with the bodies of the missing Walkers. With their minds lost, they were empty vessels. Should anything in the Between find the link and follow it, they would have a shell perfect for a new host. He did not want to destroy their bodies. Doing so made him feel like he had given up hope of their return. "It is not my decision to make anyway," he said to himself. Ergodi and Kuri were hovering over the fallen like the Matron hovered over the fledglings. It was time he went to the Circle of Healing himself. If they were involved, then they could clean up the mess.

CHAPTER FIFTEEN

"Long ago, I guess it would be almost 500,000 years ago from what you have told me," Pax began. "My twin brother and I hatched. The Elders believed we fulfilled the Prophecy of Black and White, Light and Dark. Do you know of the prophecy?"

"Aye," Nihility said, rolling her eyes.

"It still holds then," she said sadly, reading Nihility's emotions. "I do not know if we did or not. I do not know if it refers to you and Destined. Judging from your emotions, I would say that they have marked you for doom and Destined the savior. Would that be correct?" she asked.

"Aye. I am the Harbinger sent to signal doom for Petrall," Nihility mumbled.

She sighed and shifted positions. "It was not that way for Laz and me. I was the savior, but only because I was Weaver."

"Because the other callings did not exist," Nihility said.

"That is right. It was my brother who discovered the Between. Before then, our kind, particularly the dragonesses, were only Weavers linked directly to the Dreaming before we hatched from our eggs. Those of us who could weave brought the dreams of peace to those that needed it. I, as you know, was a Weaver. My brother was not, and it was he and his curiosity that stumbled upon the Between."

"There were dragons that are Weavers, Lady Pax."

"Of course! There were three great dragon Weavers, males of considerable power in the Dreaming during my time. You have spoken of two, Terghelm the Redeemer who seems to invoke feelings of respect and affection in you, and Bendre the Ghosteater," she said, looking at Nihility. She felt her embarrassment plainly and chuckled. "Who is the third, Lady Nihility?"

"Master Jaydum the Soulbreaker. He and Master Bendre stand as the Pillars of the Path of Sprits in the Dreaming."

"Remind me to tell Lady Ygi what a wonderful job she has done in her lessons. However, even though this Weaver's tale merges with my brother's, it is not the heart of what I must tell you. That place, the Between, have you spent time there?"

"With Destined occasionally. At first, I did not. It was not until we paired that my trips became more frequent."

"I know Laz spent a great deal of time there before he took me into that place, he called the Between. Together, he and I spent many moons exploring. We spoke to those that had come long before us and those who had been long forgotten. Those conversations with dragons long gone allowed us to rediscover things once lost to us, namely our magic. We brought back our knowledge to Petrall, and soon others were learning to wield various types of magic we thought we could not before."

"Weaver healing magic," Nihility said.

"Aye. Specifically, our healing chants and songs, but many other things were specific to us as dragons. Magic that no other on Sathea could wield. Magic that brought us closer to Sathea herself. You spoke to the heart of it when you told me how your entrance to this place opened and closed. The magic in our bodies resonates with us individually and collectively," she said.

"Master Bendre says we are linked to Sathea through the trees and the land," Nihility said.

"He is right. Laz believed the same and wanted to use the magic to bring us down from the peaks of Petrall. He wanted us to flourish across Sathea, not just sequestered on the peak of one mountain. Laz wanted us to interact and discover those that lived below the mountain. Those like the form you have now. It was as if he was preparing for something and wanted all dragon kind to be prepared as well."

"Did you not believe the same, Lady Pax?" Nihility asked. "You speak as if it was only Laz who believed these things, but I have heard Master Bendre and my Sia... I mean, Master Sia, speak of it in such a way. That we should not be here on Petrall."

She sighed heavily. "My brother was not like your Destined. He did not speak loudly or command such a presence. Laz was quiet, almost withdrawn except with those he was close to, and me, his twin. He would desperately try to explain what he was sensing, but I was stubborn. I was always stubborn. I am a Weaver. As a Weaver, I know dreams are interpretations of reality. They can bring hope, sorrow, confusion, happiness, ecstasy, and pain. Weavers must always remember reality, so as not to become trapped in the sweet seduction of their desires or the dreams of others. It is why we are linked, or tethered, in such a way to the Dreaming. We are the physical proof of the Dreaming's existence. The Between had no such proof because there was no link. The mind simply drifted there and required the traveler to return of their own accord."

"The lack of a link makes you nervous as it does me," Nihility said.

"Aye, but I cannot say why for certain. That place... That place leaves me uneasy for reasons I do not understand. Those were reasons I could not articulate to my twin. Reasons that frustrated the both of us," she said.

"Lady Pax, what happened? Something must have for you to feel as you do. I feel your sadness and grief heavily."

"I drifted apart from my twin, and I did not know why, youngling. I blamed that place, the Between. He spent so much time there, blocking his thoughts from me. I know you are not a twin and do not understand how difficult that is, but he managed it. He only seemed to return to me out of necessity. Each time I would see him, he would seem like less of himself. I did not realize, Nihility, that my brother had spent countless years with a demon inside him. They grappled for power constantly. Laz was trying to control the demon, while the demon was trying to control him. I believe the reason he avoided me is because he knew I would see."

"Lady Pax, the fight between the two of you!" Nihility gasped and covered her mouth as tears stood in her eyes.

Pax nodded her head slowly. "I grew tired of his avoidance one day. I demanded that he talk to me. I do not even know why I picked that day. All I know is my anger was high, and the fire in my belly raged. I was heartbroken that it seemed like my twin no longer wished to be my twin. Regardless, we fought, and I was badly hurt. Terg placed me in a dream sleep while Otunte and the Great Mother worked to repair the damage," she said.

"After the battle, Laz disappeared. No one would tell me where, but I had my suspicions. When I woke, my brother was there beside me and asked me to come to the Between with him. He took me to the space you found Destined in. He called it a dead space. It was a place in the Between where he said he had created emptiness. A trap, he said, but that the trap was not good enough. He told me of demons and the Seven great demons that led them. He told me they wanted to bring destruction, control, and chaos to Sathea and destroy the Great Balance. He said he had battled one just as powerful as the Seven, but not one of the Seven for days since its attack on me."

"I do not understand Lady Pax."

"Neither did I at first. I thought my twin had lost himself to madness, but then I saw it. I saw it through the link we shared. I saw what Laz spoke of, and I saw his plan. While I was healing from my wounds, Laz was fighting for his own life with the demon he held. I still cannot imagine how my brother managed, knowing that he still suffered from the wounds I inflicted on him myself, but he did. He won, but barely, and he had brought me to the dead space to finish his battle."

"He was the barrier I saw. I felt the life in it and the pain, Lady Pax."

"Aye. Lazarus cast a spell. I do not know where he learned

it from, but he made himself a barrier. Laz gave up what remained of himself to be the barrier against the demon horde he believed was waiting to tear the world apart. He said the dead space was created around a place where the demons had come before. Because they had come before, it had thinned, allowing them to come again if they had enough power. He did not know how to stop them if they gained a foothold on Sathea, but he knew he could prevent them from accessing this place of thinning again. He brought me there to tell me goodbye and ask for my help. He needed me to sever the link we shared as twins; to sever part of my heart and soul."

"How is something like that even possible, Lady Pax? I..." Nihility stopped, overcome by Pax's pain.

"Laz told me he could not stay because it would mean the demon inside him would stay. He told me the demon was strong, far stronger than he expected. The demon had already attacked me, and he did not want him to hurt anyone else he cared for. He believed he needed to protect everyone from these demons, because more were coming. The Seven were coming, and they were powerful enough to destroy Sathea."

"The barrier was his soul," Nihility said, sniffling.

"He fed his entire life force into its creation; body and soul. I severed my link with him through great pain. I was now without my twin, empty of his presence. When I placed my snout on it, I felt his heartbeat, and it gave me a memory. It showed a great host of demons and the Seven that led them. I decided at that moment to imbue the barrier with a bit of my own life force. Something I believe he knew I would do. We were twins, after all. If he was to leave this world, he would leave the way he entered, with me."

She lifted her large head to expose her chest. There was a patch of scales that were white in the shape of a star. "That is how you got your names," Nihility said with wide eyes. "The Twin Stars."

"Aye, but the brightest star had fallen from the sky to save dragon kind," she said sadly. "I returned from the Between deep in mourning for my lost twin. I threw myself into collecting all I knew about the Between, his travels, and demons. No one could tell me where demons had come from. Those that knew the word spoke as if they were always here. I tried to protect our kind from them instead."

"That's why you created the Three Great Callings of Petrall," Nihility said.

"That was something Laz, and I started before. We were always Weavers linked to the Dreaming, but I was the one who convinced the Elders we needed more. They never listened to Laz or Iros, but they listened to me. To honor the last wishes of my twin, I created safeguards so my brothers' fate and sacrifice would remain intact. I forced the Elders to understand that we must put rules in place; dragon kind must remain pure of heart and spirit; a balance must remain within and without, dragon kind must watch the world for these intruders and their magic, and the Between must be guarded."

"Weavers, Watchers, and Walkers," Nihility said, grinning. "The three of you gave us purpose, Lady Pax. You changed Petrall and the Dreaming."

"We did, or we tried to," she said, smiling at her. "I continued to collect knowledge and store it here in this place. I continued for years until I lost Iros. When the time came that my sorrow was heavier than my desire for life, I cast a spell while standing before the barrier that was once my twin. If the door should be opened and the barrier breached, the bit of my life force would awaken and attack the intruder. Just as my twin before me, I faded away."

There was silence between them for a moment before Nihility spoke. "I am sorry about your brother, Lady Pax. I can tell you he loved you just as deeply as you love him. I felt that love standing before the barrier."

"Thank you, youngling," she said.

Nihility looked over her shoulder at the presence in the darkness. "Why is this thing inside of me and not consumed by the spell you left on the barrier? Can I not rid myself of it? It does not belong here, especially here."

"I do not know, Nihility," she said. "From what I gathered in my search, demons gain entry through emotions. That is why, for a Walker of the Between, it is important to keep a balanced mind and heart. This is the opposite for Weavers who need emotions; the stronger, the better. The demon attacked you in a time when you were vulnerable, unsure in your search for Destined. I think in attacking you, she was trying to escape me."

"Destined believes I can go to the Between because I am an Empath and understand how to control my own emotions."

"He may be right. I could go easily with Laz, but I believe that was more because we were twins. Understanding emotions will not keep a demon from attacking, however. They seek your heart's desire. The heart, especially in a dragon, is connected to the mind. What you want the most is what the demon preys on. I believe your desire to find Destined was so strong it pulled the demon to you, although I do not know how that was enough for it to invade your mind. To my knowledge, which I will admit is not complete, some demons are easier to rid than others. I am sure my brother knew there was no way to expel his demon. We will have to see if yours is as stubborn as the one inside Destined."

Nihility flinched as if slapped with the spikes of her own tail. "Destined!? There is no way there is a demon inside of him! Pax, what are you talking about? He is a Walker. He would know how to handle a demon trying to invade his mind!"

"Calm yourself, youngling!" Pax shouted over her. "There is indeed a demon inside him, and it has become his prisoner. You have seen it yourself, or at least glimpsed it. I saw it the moment he touched me to take on my memories. Did you dismiss your glimpse? Perhaps you thought it was simply a trick of the light?"

"A trick of the light," Nihility said aloud. "His eyes," she said, looking at Pax with worry.

"I did not sense any danger to him, Nihility. He is in control of himself and his mind. If he was not, you would have noticed. You know him well, and you hold his heart of hearts."

"I do. I feel him more than I normally do. Destined is always…torn mentally," Nihility said. "I feel his consciousness more than normal. I will speak to him. I will need his help to deal with my own."

"You do, but first we need to find out what it knows," she said.

"I do not want to connect with that thing. It feels horrible, like a sore spot under my scales," Nihility said with a frown.

"You must detach from your feelings, Weaver!" she snapped. Nihility's head whipped around quickly. "Seek only its feelings, not your own, just as you would a dreamer."

"Yes, Lady Pax," Nihility said.

"Breathe deeply and process your feelings about it and push them away. Then feel for the being inside the darkness."

Nihility walked over to the orb that was deep in the corner. "It is female, Lady Pax. She knows we've trapped her. She is angry about it, but your presence also causes her great fear; overwhelming fear."

"Tell me how you know, Nihility."

"She speaks to me, or at least she speaks aloud to herself. I can hear. She has heard tales of you in the Depths and seen your wrath," Nihility said. She paused and turned to look at her. "I do not understand. There are no demons in the Depths."

"What else does she say?" she asked, ignoring Nihility's confusion.

"She was not prepared for me. She was seeking the other Walker that ran away. She had to find refuge quickly from the flame. She knew the minute she entered me that my power was more than she could handle. She speaks of another as well, one whose name I do not understand. She says he betrayed her. That he used her to feed the flame. Speaking of him makes her angry."

"Keep listening, youngling. I would know what the demon is after."

Nihility stood with her head tilted to the side for a long while, listening. "Even though she is trapped, she says she does not wish to leave here. She has no desire to die, and she believes that she will perish if she does so. She speaks of an injury and how her power has been greatly diminished."

"Do you sense her injury? The pain should lead you to the source."

"She feels foreign to me, but I do not sense death. Injury, yes, but not a grievous one. There is something familiar. Wait," Nihility gasped. "It is you I sense, Lady Pax! A piece of you is lodged deep inside her. Burned inside this purple," she paused. "It is her heart! It is burned into her heart!"

Pax did not respond to her. She watched Nihility, waiting to see if this little dragoness was as perceptive as she believed. The moment their minds touched, Pax felt great strength and power in the one they called Harbinger. She also felt dread—two Empaths housed in one mind and one far more substantial than the other. Nihility could swallow her whole with her ability with ease, but it seemed she did not realize it.

"Lady Pax, you did not just seal away a part of yourself in the barrier with Laz. You sealed away the fabled flame. The flame said to burn any and everything if you unleashed its wrath. The creatures that live in the Depths are still kept in line from the fear of those flames. You sealed away the Black Flame," Nihility said with wide eyes.

"Aye. A trap for any demon that dared to destroy the life barrier," Pax said with a slight smile.

"The Black Flame burns her heart but does not kill her. Why? She should be ash now!"

"That I do not know, youngling. It seems it bound that

demon to me through it, but because I am bound to you, so is that demon."

"I do not understand. Why are you bound to me? Why have you not faded away with the breaking of the barrier?"

"The Black Flame still burns," she said, eyeing Nihility closely. She knew why she was bound to Nihility. The Black Flame needed pure emotional power to wield. It required an Empath. Something had come through that barrier that she did not have enough strength to deal with, but the flame wanted to grow. It had found an Empath to do so as if she was fated to be there.

Nihility moved her shoulders and rotated her neck where she was sore. "It has become mine. That is why you are bound to me. This is not a mark from the use of magic. It is a mark because the Black Flame has passed to me," Nihility said.

"It was not my intention, youngling. I believe it was because you were in the right place at the right time. You had the power to bind the demon and the emotions to fuel the Black Flame. Yes, it is yours now, and I believe I will only exist until the transfer is complete. I hope when that happens, I take the demon with me, but until then, we must find out what she knows."

"How long?" Nihility asked quietly.

"What?"

"How long will I have you to guide me, Lady Pax?"

The young dragoness's need for her made her pause. "I am not sure, Nihility. For a dragoness of your skill, it could be merely a few moons. You will have to harness the flame before you can use it. Maybe you have until you are in control before I fade away. We do not know, so I suggest we act as if our time is short."

"With my luck, you will go before I am ready," Nihility mumbled, turning back to the orb.

Pax watched her. She could feel Nihility's eagerness to learn. The little dragoness had grown excited at the idea of her presence in her mind. She was not afraid but seemed delighted. She did not want to pry, but she knew she must have suffered in her twenty-thousand years. She carried herself in a way that spoke of pain and heartbreak. "And still so young," Pax thought to herself. She liked her very much. Nihility had determination, drive, and thirst for knowledge, but she also had a fierceness about her that was both wild and free. She had been watching Nihility closely since she touched her mind. She watched the young dragoness's hesitancy change to fearlessness with ease. "I hope you kept your promise, Terg," she thought as she watched Nihility prepare to deal with her demon.

CHAPTER SIXTEEN

The Circle of Healing was a space on Petrall marked only by overhanging rocks that created a natural shelter over a sizable barren area. There were eight dragons surrounded by glowing pale pink light. It was how they were keeping the eight missing Walkers alive. They could not feed themselves or move. He could see where patches of scales had fallen away from those that first went missing. They were slowly dying.

"Destined."

"Tuzys. We need to talk," he said.

"Aye, but not here," Tuzys said, nodding towards the back of the Circle of Healing.

He could see Elders Pimo and Ivylth sitting with the mate of Mica as she cried beside him. He nodded and walked with Tuzys away from the circle. "How long have they been here?"

"Since you woke. They relieved me of my duty," Tuzys said.

"Who the fuck ordered that?! I said you were to remain and to keep the others out of the Between."

"Lady Ivylth, of course. With the full weight of the old bronze behind her."

He huffed smoke from his nostrils. Ergodi kept creeping around the edges. "Tell me what happened while I was gone."

"Destined, do not walk alone anymore," Tuzys whispered.

"Tuzys, you are not my dragoness," he said with a tone.

"As if dragonesses are the only thing you fancy, Farseer," Tuzys said, rolling his eyes.

"Fair enough, Mindhunter, but you are not my dragon either," he said, laughing.

"Thank Sathea for that! I'd end up feeding you and your dragoness."

"I feed her!"

"With food I hunt for you, Destined. Besides, that is not an order from me. It was a message I was told to give you."

"From who? I know I upset her, but really? Is she not speaking to me now?"

Tuzys gave him a look and shook his head. "One day, I need you to tell me how you can make love to a dragoness and then piss her off so quickly."

"It is a talent, my friend. Nothing more than pure talent. The Great White Hope of Petrall strikes again," he said, grinning.

"The Great White Fool you mean."

"I aspire to live up to the title she has given me," he said, chuckling.

"Anyway, the message is from Master Sia, not Nihility. Although, the pain of ignoring a command from either of them could prove painful for you."

He groaned. "I will talk to him. Now tell me what happened."

"You were gone too long; that's what happened, Farseer. You know those eight are lost to us. I told you as much. We need to let them go because keeping them like this is cruel. Galen is decaying before our eyes!"

"I know Tuzys, but…"

"But nothing, Destined. You are Lead Walker, and I'll honor your decisions, but I urge you to end it. They tax the healers. Leaving them empty is asking for trouble."

"I know, Tuzys!" he said, exasperated. Tuzys huffed smoke at him. "I will, Tuzys. I promise. After what I saw in there, I agree with you and Master Sia, actually."

"He will find the utmost enjoyment hearing those words," Tuzys said.

"Do me a favor and find another way to express my agreement with him," he said, rolling his eyes. "I already sent the messenger drake to Ergodi. I have called a meeting of the Council of Elders."

"Is that how you upset Nihility?" Tuzys asked with a grin.

"She does not know yet," he said, wincing.

"Fire, Farseer, can you feel the heat? I can. It carries the smell of the charred remains of your corpse."

"Yeah, yeah. You should tell her for me! She adores you," he said, grinning at Tuzys.

"She adores me because I know how to mind myself around a dragoness. That means I also know when a duty should be left to her mate. That, my friend, is you," Tuzys said.

"Come on! I would consider it a personal favor," he said, winking.

"As many times as I have hunted for you over the last three thousand years, you owe me," Tuzys said. "She might as well be my mate at this stage."

"You know she and I share everything," he said, grinning.

"Then I'd just have two dragonesses to hunt for," Tuzys said.

"The sting, Mindhunter. I can feel it deep in my chest."

"That is your ass, not your chest, Destined. Seriously, I am not telling Nihility."

He groaned. "I will tell her when it's closer to time. There's less chance of me being burned to a crisp where I stand that way. Speaking of Nihility, she said something curious to me when I returned. She said that Kuri told her something kept him and Ergodi from entering the Between and following me."

"Aye, but it was nothing abnormal, so rest easy. Ergodi and Kuri both seemed reluctant to go after Master Sia arrived," Tuzys said.

"What do you mean?"

"I mean, when you did not return right away, I went to get Master Sia. When he arrived, they seemed hesitant to go," Tuzys said. He gave Tuzys a look. "I am only reporting what I saw,

Destined. I can assure you I had no problem accessing the Between myself when Kuri claimed they could not enter."

"Then what was Ergodi doing?"

"I do not know, but he went back to his alcove once Master Sia arrived. Lady Nihility arrived a little over a day later ready to have your head."

"You are adamant about reminding me of how much trouble I am in."

"It is my job as your first," Tuzys said with a grin.

"Stay here at the circle until the meeting," he said, looking at Ivylth. "Have Master Sia come and check their minds with you once the Elders assemble. I will delay my arrival to give you time."

"Arsu should come here and help."

"Where is she?" he asked, frowning. "I swear that dragoness is useless."

"With the fledglings."

"Tell her I said her duty is here, not the nursery," he said. "Here with her fallen brethren. Honestly, I do not know why Nihility thinks she's so capable."

"Lady Nihility has her reasons," Tuzys said, looking away. "Where are you going?"

He looked at Tuzys and grinned. "Endrir is close. I want to speak with him before the Elders know he has returned."

"Do not get yourself in more trouble, Destined. I have my wings full now. The last thing I need is Lady Nihility out for your heads. I will not cover for you!"

"No need. I won't be long, and I will behave," he said, making room to take flight.

"You two should really tell her," Tuzys said.

"Not my call. You know how the Watcher is," he said, taking off.

CHAPTER SEVENTEEN

Nihility examined the orb. It was solid black with white and red lines of aura coursing through it. "Lady Pax, could you drop your barrier, please? I want to look at this demon," she asked. Pax did not answer her, but the red vanished. She frowned, unable to see inside; the black was too deep. "Lady Pax, could you please remove your barrier?" she asked again.

"I have, youngling. The only thing that remains is Destined and yourself."

She laughed slightly in embarrassment. She did not realize it was her barrier. She was unaccustomed to seeing her own magic as an outside observer. She honestly did not know how she could have produced such a thing without willfully trying. It never looked like this when she practiced with Destined. His presence would vanish, leaving her mind as her own again. When she used it on the creatures in the Dreaming, it appeared as glass.

She took her hand and touched it to the barrier. Immediately she felt her own feelings—raw and powerful emotions coursed through her, all of them surrounding Destined. The demon was trapped by the core of her feelings for Destined. There was something else. Not just her feelings for him, but also his. But only one, his desire. She wanted to laugh and blush at the same time. It was so much like Destined. Only he would leave an emotion such as that behind; lewd, direct, brutally honest, raw desire.

The demon did not seem to notice her presence. She tried to probe the orb to no avail, stepping back to observe it. She did not know how she had created it to manipulate it. She had practiced with Destined to keep her mind strong, but they had never practiced her ability to hold a creature like this.

"Find the heart of it. Once you find the heart of it, you can understand any emotion before you." She tensed as the words echoed in her mind. "Sia," she whispered. The sound of his voice made her heart race. It was a memory, but it was the memory she needed.

The orb was black, the deepest black like her. The depth of the darkness kept her from seeing through it. She could see the white of Destined course through, but that was all. "The heart of it," she said to herself. She adjusted her emotions tied to the orb. She pulled back on her thoughts of Destined; the black faded. She thought of her desire for him and fed it into his desire for her. The orb transformed. It was no longer deep black with white striations. It was now a darker shade of grey, marbled with white.

The demon crouched. When the orb changed, allowing a view, she stood, and Nihility came face to face with her. Nihility was shocked by her but did not let her thoughts or body language betray her. The demon was not like anything she had ever seen before, but it had qualities of something she was familiar with but could not put her snout on. She studied her, and it seemed the demon was doing the same.

The demon was tall, lean, and her skin a dark shade of gray. Nihility's short-life form was not small. She was tall by the nomad's standards, but the demon was at least half a head taller. Her skin appeared made of tough hide. There were no scales present. It was smooth except for where scars had prickled her flesh. They covered her. She was muscular but thin and wore green armor covering her chest and legs. The chest plate was damaged, a hole burned through, and a lavender light flickered in a steady rhythm. She had long black hair wrapped in a single braid that hung at her waist. Two small horns protruded from her forehead. She had an angular face with a pointed nose. She could almost pass for a short-lifer, especially with her eyes. They were a vibrant green that showed years of living. She saw fear, hurt, pain, and even hope in those eyes.

"What is your name?" she asked.

"How can you speak to me?" the demon asked.

She read her shock plainly. "How am I supposed to know? I asked your name. If we are to communicate, then we should at least be cordial and proper."

"Names have power," the demon said.

"Indeed, they do. However, here in my mind, you have no power. That is something else we can agree on. See, we are off to an impressive start! Now demon, what is your name?" she asked with a tone.

"You may call me Ana."

"Very well, Ana. Do you know who I am?" she asked.

"I know the one back there is Pax. The Grand Lady Pax, the Dragoness of the Depths," Ana said with disgust rife in her voice

"I am," Pax said coolly.

With a sneer, the demon turned back to Nihility, "but you, I do not know."

She tilted her head to the side. It was a quirk that carried over regardless of her form. She did it when she read someone or something. The demon had malice in her words. She spoke to her as if she were a creature beneath her. She looked at Ana and grinned. With a dismissive wave, she made the orb darker again. Before the barrier was complete, the grin left her face, replaced by a look of complete seriousness, "death on black wings," she said. She heard Ana scream as she walked away and back to Pax.

"Did you learn anything from that youngling?" Pax asked, raising her eyes.

"I gathered what I needed for now, but she is not unlike a fledgling who must learn a lesson quickly and early so as not to repeat their mistakes," she said with a touch of annoyance.

Pax chuckled. "Well, tell me what it is you have gathered so far."

"I do not know what demons are in perhaps the way that Destined does. I would need his help to make sense of what else I have gathered. I know the Dreaming and the creatures who dwell there. I know those deep in the Depths, in the place of the deepest dreams. Dreams, within dreams, within dreams, the place where death comes. She reminds me of the dream feeders that live there, the Warida."

Pax looked at the orb and frowned, "what else do you know of the Warida?"

"They take the dreamer deeper than just the dream. They take them below the dream within a dream where dreams begin to feel like reality. We Weavers call that place the Divide. The dreamer feels as if they are living their greatest wish or desire. Once the dreamer enters that place, they cannot leave of their own free will. We must awaken them from within the dream. That is the job of the Weaver. If we do not awaken them, the Warida feed until the host dies," she answered. "But Lady Pax, you know all this. You culled their numbers long ago during their uprising."

"I did, and I agree she gives off the look of their kind, but not completely. However, it raises an interesting theory. If they take the dreamer to the Divide, what would happen if the dreamer was in fact taken by a demon first?"

She made a face of disgust. "You do not mean to say that demons are here already roaming around Sathea?!"

"It is a possibility, Nihility, and one my brother warned me of. Someone had to get those Walkers to the barrier. I do not believe they could have stumbled upon it accidentally. Perhaps if it was your Destined, yes, but..."

"What is it?"

"I am not sure, youngling. I just had a sense of disquiet. A sense of familiarity, but I do not know why. You should continue trying to speak to her."

"She can wait a bit longer. I have more questions for you first. I would like to know if you sensed the same as I," she said. Pax nodded at her. "Did you see her hesitation and fear over her name?"

"I did, youngling. When she was raving about her betrayer, did the name come to you?"

"No. It was strange. I have no problem understanding her. However, each time she said his name, I could not grasp it. The buzzing I heard in the Between invaded my head."

"I cannot remember the name of the demon who held my brother either. I know he told me, or I at least think he did. It falls through my mind when I try to remember. This may be of importance," Pax said.

"I have a feeling she might be more receptive to my questions now," she said when Ana's screaming stopped. "She does not like the dark. She also does not realize that Empaths can do far more than feel," she said, turning back to the orb. She pulled back on the barrier again. "Shall we try this again, Ana?" The demon looked at her, and for the first time, there was a hint of fear in her eyes. She nodded. "Do you know who I am?"

"I do not know your name, dragoness, but I know you from the Depths. You have taken the lives of many of my kind there. You are the shadow. You are what we believe to be the shade of the one behind you," Ana answered quietly.

"Your kind? I have never run across one like you in the Dreaming," she said.

"There are no others in the Dreaming like me, but the Warida are my clan."

"Let me clarify for you. I am no shade or shadow. I am Nihility the Harbinger. I am the darkness you see in the Depths and the fire that follows those that prey on helpless dreamers. You're in my mind, a place sacred to me. I am not your puppet, nor am I beneath you. Think anything of the sort again, and you will spend the rest of eternity trapped with the fear the darkness brings for you with only the hope of your thoughts to keep you company."

"Aye," Ana said.

"How were you betrayed?" she asked.

Ana looked as if someone had struck her. "How do you know I was betrayed?"

"The same way I know you cared about the one who betrayed you. Remember where you are."

"He left me to the darkness. He did not tell me what the barrier was or what it would do to me. He left me to die no different from the rest."

She felt Ana's hurt and anger. "I sense no desire to leave from you. Why is that?"

"If I leave, I will not survive. My heart burns; it will consume me in time. The minute the flame touched, my body burned."

"How are you both demon and Warida?" Pax asked.

"My father is a demon. My mother Warida," Ana answered.

"How did you come to be in the Between?" she asked.

"Through the barrier."

She laughed. "Thank you. That is all for now, Ana," she said, moving to darken the barrier.

"Please," Ana said. "Could you leave it?"

She left the barrier down but took care to adjust it so Ana could not sense her presence. "That was a kindness, youngling," Pax said.

"Kindness is necessary. She will be here for an undetermined amount of time, and we may need her. It is best to remember that. She wants to talk, but she does not trust yet. She spoke to me like Sia used to, answering the questions put to her plainly and as simple as possible."

"You have mentioned him a few times, Nihility. Who is he?"

"What? Who?"

"Sia," Pax said with a tone.

"I should go speak to Master Bendre and Lady Ygi. They will want an explanation for my lapse in duties," she said, avoiding Pax's question.

"Excellent idea. It will be good to see those two again," Pax said.

CHAPTER EIGHTEEN

Endrir had been near Petrall for a few days. He had quickly hidden the egg and come to the small cottage he and Destined had built a few hours flight from the peak. He sat at their small wooden table, agonizing over what to do. He closed his link to Nihility, afraid she would feel his emotions. After hours of debating, he had opened himself to Destined to let him know he was near. There was a soft tap on the door followed by two more before it opened. He stood quickly, full of nerves. It had been almost two years since he had last seen him, and it had not ended well.

"Endrir! I'm home!" Destined said with a grin as he came through the door. He had a smile that brightened the world. His hazel eyes were alive with happiness.

They were of an equal height. While Destined was bald, he had long black hair that hung just past his neck streaked with deep violet. He often wore it neat and tied back. They were both average builds, but he was heavily muscular, while Destined was toned and firm. You could tell he spent his life swinging a sword. He had violet eyes and a beard he kept trimmed low and neat. He was handsome for a short-lifer, and he knew it. It took pride in his appearance because it was part of how he blended in.

"It is good to see you, Farseer," he said. Destined came over and hugged him tightly. He pulled back and looked at him, frowning.

"What is wrong? What has happened?"

"Both questions I should ask you," he said.

"What? Why?"

"Nihility called me back here, Destined."

Destined laughed and grinned. "I might have been in the Between a smidge too long."

"How long is a smidge?" he asked, giving him a look.

"Thirteen days, give or take," Destined said, wincing.

"Farseer!"

"I have already been thoroughly admonished, my treasure," he said, taking a seat at the table. Endrir rolled his eyes at him. "Your mind is in turmoil, Endrir."

"Stop it, Destined."

Destined raised his arms in surrender. "Then tell me, or did you just call me all the way out here to tell me we are over? I mean, you come back when Nihility calls, but not to see me."

"No. It's not like that. I just needed time to sort myself out before I go up there," he said, sitting down again. Destined took his hand and squeezed.

"What have you done, Endrir?" Destined asked, frowning.

He winced. "I told you to stop!"

"That was not me. It was you. Control yourself better. I can't turn this shit off. If the thought is powerful enough, I will see it. We are linked mind, body, and soul. Besides, be more worried about how you are going to keep yourself that pretty purple and not a charred mass of black when she burns the scales off you," Destined said, laughing.

"Wait! What?"

"I saw her, Endrir, and I hope you do not think you are in love with that short-lifer," Destined said, making a face.

"If I am?" he said with a tone.

"You will suffer, and she will die," Destined said with a shrug. "There will be no place that you nor she can hide on Sathea, or in your dreams, for that matter. You are playing with fire, Endrir the Broken."

"Help me then. I do not want Nihility to be angry."

"I can't, Watcher. I am in enough trouble myself."

"She is never angry at you. Even when she is, she is not. She would be all over you right now, after thirteen days. I am surprised you even came here and are not lying naked with her somewhere."

"First," Destined said, holding up one finger, "I would drop everything to come to you. I always have. Second," he continued counting them off, "she was. Third, then she was not."

"For Sathea's sake, Farseer. How do you screw up that fast?!"

"It is a gift. Not a great gift, mind you, but a gift nonetheless," Destined said, sitting back in the chair and lacing his fingers behind his head.

He groaned and laid his head on the table. "I am so screwed."

"You can be if you wish," Destined said, grinning.

"Destined, really? Now? Can you not see I am in agony?"

"Yes, but it has been almost two years. I would see that agony turn to ecstasy."

"Not now, Farseer."

"Fine, but I suggest you put a smile on your snout and some pep in your step before you go up to Petrall. I have called a meeting with the Elders."

"You tell me now?!"

"How was I supposed to know you were coming back? You close yourself to me constantly. What difference does it make, anyway? You are here now. It is not like I called the meeting because I knew you were down here hiding. I have duties of my own."

"I was not hiding. I was preparing."

"For what? To come home? Odd unless you want to avoid those you love and who love you."

"I am not avoiding you," he said, defeated.

"You could have fooled me. You sit here with images of some fucking short-life female in your head when your dragoness sits on that peak. You ignore me, your mate, whom you cannot even greet like it has been as long as it has."

"She is not my dragoness. She is yours."

"She is ours, and you might want to remember that before you go up there," Destined said, rising and heading for the door. "I have to get back."

"Destined, wait," he said, grabbing his hand. "It is not you or us. I mean, there is no problem between us. Destined, these last few months…"

"After the meeting with the Council of Elders, we will talk," Destined said, smiling. He nodded. "Endrir."

"Aye."

"This short-life female, is it over between the two of you?"

"Aye."

"Then I will speak to Nihility."

"Thank you, my Sun."

Destined kissed him. He grabbed onto his cloak, not wanting him to stop, but he pulled away. "Get yourself together and come home, my treasure. I need you around, and so does Nihility. Things are not okay, Endrir."

"I know," he said as he watched Destined walk out of the door.

He did not fly across Petrall even though it would have been faster. He walked as a dragon. He hummed a tune in his head from a song he heard at a tavern he bedded at on his way back to the mountain. He was happy to be back, even if he was nervous. He still had not opened his link to her, but he and Destined agreed he should act as if he had just returned conveniently in time for the meeting with the Council of Elders.

When a formal meeting with the Elders was called, it meant the leaders of the three callings and their first and seconds had to be in attendance. He was neither but held a position of honor with the Watchers. He was constantly pushed to lead them, but he could not. He could not stand the Elders and their endless schemes. He could not handle dealing with them and how they treated Nihility. He'd had enough of that in the nursery. He did not understand how the Farseer tolerated it.

That led him to Tresai. It was one of the most challenging assignments a Watcher could take; short-lifers in the great cities. They were always involved in something that might disrupt the Great Balance, usually several things at once. He enjoyed the work and the time away from Petrall. The time away from the raging ache in his heart her presence brought him.

"Endrir! You have returned to us again, and it seems in good spirits!" Destined said as he landed in front of him.

Endrir rolled his eyes. Destined knew he would be here. "Aye, Destined, I have. How are you?" he asked as if they had not seen each other a few hours before. However, he had to control himself. It was the first time he had seen Destined as a dragon in a long time; he had grown.

"Taxed, but better now. You received notice of the meeting, yes?"

"Aye. Zennar sent it to me through the Watcher Way. I was on my way back, anyway."

"Good. I will see you at the meeting. I have a few things to do before the time comes. Do not be so hasty with your departure, Watcher!" Destined said, retaking flight.

He nodded and watched him go. He never could understand why everyone fell all over themselves for the Farseer. He was brilliant, but he ended up in trouble most of the time.

"I see some things will never change between you two. Time flows, but you two find your rhythm with ease," she said. He looked up in the direction of her voice, startled. He cursed himself for not sensing her presence. "Do not worry, the dragonesses will still fly into jagged rocks to know that either of you noticed they existed. The younger ones still follow him around and fall over themselves at the mere mention of his name. You have become the mysterious, handsome dragon in your absence. I cannot wait to see what they will do now. I fear the peak will be littered with dragonesses who have injured themselves trying to appease the Broken Watcher."

"Nihility! Beautiful dragoness of my heart! I see you received your summons as well," he said.

She had stretched out on top of the rock wall that lined part of the Great Path of Petrall. Her head rested on one of the higher, smooth pieces. Her eyes were closed, and she did not even move as she spoke. "You know full well I have no choice but to be here even if I have no desire to be."

"Elders are still up to their same games, I see. You should have become a Watcher. Then you could have avoided their nonsense altogether."

She opened her eyes to see him. "Give up the Dreaming? If you believe I could do that, you are a bigger fool than Destined. I am where I am meant to be."

"I may be," he mumbled. "I will see you at the circle, beautiful, where the Maiden Moon will hold nothing on your beauty," he said with a smile.

She rolled her eyes at his lament and closed them again. "Always the charmer, Endrir." He walked away. He needed to place distance between them. "Endrir," she called.

"Aye, glorious one."

"Thank you for coming back."

"Of course, Nihility. I will always return for the two of you," he said, continuing on his way. He glanced back at her and saw that she was, once again, well hidden in the shade. He really needed to get himself together. His lack of noticing her showed he was not his usual self.

Nihility was always his weakness. He supposed she was Destined's too, but for different reasons. He was Endrir the Broken. For a while, he was Endrir the Unnamed. He was one of those lost in the Shattering that claimed so many eggs, including his twin. His egg was behind a rock, hidden from view. The stone had cracked his egg, injuring him, and killing his twin. He lay there, unable to break free, wishing someone would save him. He was trapped in his egg with the dead body of his twin sister in agony.

He had heard the story of his rescue from the Elder Watchers. Nihility and Destined had continued to escape the nursery where the newly hatched fledglings were kept, returning to the place where their eggs had been. For days they continued, Nihility labeled defiant and Destined the savior. She and Destined devised a plan and got him out from behind the rock. He asked Nihility once about it, and she told him Destined saved him. He believed it was her.

For a long time, it was always the three of them together. In their own time, each of them took up the mantles of their callings. The Farseer became a Walker, the Harbinger a Weaver, and the Broken a Watcher. He truly cherished the memories of their youth, and he loved them both. However, it was history, and the time for games was over. He just hoped that he would not come out more broken than he went in once they learned what he had done.

CHAPTER NINETEEN

Weaver Circle was alive with activity when Nihility arrived. There was no fanfare at her appearance. There were no cries of the Harbinger's return, only nods of an acknowledgment as the other Weavers went about their duties. She was on her way to the grassy area beside Weaver Circle, where the Dreamflowers grew. She could see the three of them lounging in the last rays of the sun with their snouts touching.

"This is the place I would often come to sit," Pax said happily. "I would give lessons here as well."

"Lady Ygi is often found lounging here with Master Bendre when they are not at their home below Petrall," she said.

"She has grown more beautiful than I could have imagined," Pax said of the orange and red dragoness with the long swirling lines of yellow and lavender streaked through her scales. Lady Ygi the Screecher always reminded Nihility of the sunset. She could emit sounds that could rend the mind to nothing. "Is that the Specter?!" Pax asked about the red dragoness beside her with the deep blue belly and spines. "She was such a tiny thing the last time I saw her!"

"Aye. Lady Sako the Specter," she answered.

"My little dragonesses have blossomed!" Pax crooned. "And look at Ghost," Pax said as Bendre looked up at her with his deep brown eyes. He was a giant dark blue dragon with black spines and spikes. There was a black stripe that ran down the center of his belly. "Now that is a dragon!" Pax said.

"I am so dead," she groaned. She was hoping to speak to Lady Ygi alone, but her hopes were quickly dashed when she saw the three teachers lying together. She landed quickly and walked over to them. "Lady Ygi, Lady Sako," she said, nodding. Ygi looked up at her but did not speak. "Master Bendre," she mumbled.

"Nihility! My sweet dragoness! You have returned. I missed you!" Sako said with delight.

"Lady Sako," she said, dipping her head.

"Raise your head, dragoness! Pride is our right," Sako said. "To think you could challenge me and then show submission. You shame me, Nihility Harbinger!"

She looked up at her, trying to hold back her tears. She was frustrated with herself for letting them down. "Yes, Lady Sako," she mumbled.

"Will you ever tire of that moment, Sako," Ygi said, chuckling.

"Never," Sako said, giggling. "That fierce dragoness that showed herself that day still gives me the shivers!"

"How are you, Lady Sako?" she asked.

Sako stretched her head out and nuzzled her. "I am well, Nihility. How are you?"

"I am okay."

"I am sure you are relieved the Farseer has returned, though."

"Aye, I am, I guess," she said, huffing smoke.

"He returns and finds himself in more trouble than when he went in," Ygi said, laughing. "Why have you come to see us, my little butterfly?" Ygi asked. She looked down at the grass and did not answer. She was ashamed of her actions, even if they were justified. They expected more from her. "Sako, my fiery love, would you go to the nursery in my place? I believe Nihility wishes to speak with me."

"Aye. The Fireball is due for her lesson. I cannot chastise her for her tardiness if I am tardy myself. Come as soon as you are done here. I want to go see Jay," Sako said, rising. She nuzzled Nihility again and took flight.

"I am interrupting your duties, Lady Ygi," she said, wishing she could find a cave to hide in.

"You are not. Sako wanted to go anyway, and she is always impatient, as you know," Ygi said.

"I would have an explanation on why you returned when you were to prepare the Daughters of Ote to be accepted by the Dreaming," Bendre finally said. "As Lead Weaver, you have a duty, Nihility Harbinger."

She whined low in her throat and stepped back away from Bendre. "Ben," Ygi hissed. "He is her mate."

"He has a duty too. Why did you return, Nihility?" Bendre asked.

"I was aiding them, gathering their threads when I heard someone call to me. Then I saw his bird," she said, trying not to cry.

"Sia's?" Bendre asked, frowning. She nodded. "I am going to rend him in two," he mumbled.

"What happened, Nihility?" Ygi asked.

"I saw the bird and then Vivian, one of the Sisters, she threw the dream sand in her sleep Lady Ygi, and it showed Destined! My Destined! A green serpent surrounded him! I felt..."

"Danger," Bendre finished for her.

"Aye. Then Vivian spoke and told me what he used to say all the time when I would not return right away from my lessons," she said, crying.

"Come home, my world," Ygi sighed.

"So I came back as fast as I could. I was going to tell you, but..."

"Nihility, it has been almost five days. The time for the ritual has passed them. What took you so long? Why did you not come straight to us?" Bendre asked.

She shifted her wings, wanting to run away. "You must tell them, youngling," Pax said.

"I went into that place to get Destined. I lost time. Four days, I think."

"It is forbidden, Nihility Harbinger!" Ygi hissed.

"I know Ygi, but it had already been nine days when I returned, and Ergodi and Kuri lie, and no one was there to help Destined!"

"So, the Mindbreaker calls you home but was not there to meet you?" Bendre asked.

"Nay. Only Kuri and Tuzys. Tuzys is a great Walker, but…"

"There is no way he could retrieve the Farseer on his own, and keep an eye on Ergodi and Kuri," Ygi said.

"Master Bendre, please do not be angry at him. He… Things are complicated," she said, looking away.

"My little brother does not need you to defend him, Nihility," Bendre said.

"The only complication is he is an ass of a dragon, Nihility Harbinger. He disrespects his dragoness over two other fools, and it is unnecessary. You are dragoness! A dragoness does as she pleases! She mates with who she pleases!" Ygi hissed.

"I know Lady Ygi," she said, defeated.

Bendre looked at Ygi and sighed. "Lovebug, send a message to Terg, please. Tell him I need to speak to him, but not here. I will meet him below Petrall at our usual place."

"What do you want me to do?" Ygi asked.

"Go talk to Sia. Find out if he knows what is going on. If I go, I will hurt him."

"Ben," Ygi said.

"I know. That is why I am sending you," Bendre said, grinning. "You are my self-control."

Ygi rolled her eyes at him. "Do you want to come with me to see him, little butterfly?" Ygi asked softly.

"No."

"Nihility," Ygi said with a tone.

"Ygi I… Please do not make me."

"I would not dream of it, Nihility. You are dragoness. He has to come to you. I only thought you would want to see him. It has been a very long time."

"I do, but I cannot right now. Destined has called a meeting with the Elders. I need to prepare myself."

"Nihility," Bendre called. "I heard a tale that the Grand Lady lingered in that place protecting the half of herself that was lost. Is that why I feel her with you now?"

"Aye. She protected me and helped me save Destined."

Bendre smiled at her as his eyes glowed slightly. "She is not like you, Grand Lady. She is delicate, but the cocoon protects her, his cocoon. He protected her from the tricks that can be played. She slumbers there, safe inside, until she decides she is ready. However, the butterfly has yet to emerge and spread its wings."

"What?" she asked, confused.

"The message was for me, youngling. Please tell Bendre I understand," Pax said.

"Lady Pax said she understands," she said, frowning.

"We will all speak soon," Bendre said. "Go to the meeting and mind yourself, Nihility Harbinger. Remember, you are no longer that little hatchling anymore. You are dragoness!" he said.

"Master Bendre?" she called.

"Yes, Little Butterfly?"

She sighed with relief at his use of her pet name. "Will they be able to see her?"

"Nay. Neither of those Weavers has the skill, and those two Walkers could not find their own snouts if Sia gave them directions and left a trail of jerboa meat. Waste of dragons, the both of them," Bendre said.

She was exhausted and needed to connect with the Dreaming to recharge. She had planned to do so after speaking with Master

Bendre and Lady Ygi, but she would not have time with the meeting starting soon. The last place she wanted to be was in the Courtyard of the Moon in front of the Elders. She just wanted to be home.

"Is your home the place you were with Destined, Nihility?" Pax asked.

"No. It is Destined's home. I do not have one anymore," she said.

"What do you mean anymore?"

She sighed. "Where you sit in my mind, that place is real. It was my home, but I cannot go there. I can't go home until he calls."

"The one Ygi spoke of, Sia."

"Aye."

"How well do you know Ivylth the Trickster?" Pax asked.

"Better than I would like," she snapped.

"She has not changed."

"If she was how she was with me while you were around, you should have killed her and saved Sathea from her existence," she said as she landed on the Great Path. She chose a spot along the wall shaded by a large tree and rested herself on it. "You should have set the Black Flame on her while she stood beside you in the Dreaming that day!"

"Perhaps I should have," Pax mumbled.

Once upon a time, she would have been small enough to sit in the tree itself. She lay there going through the events of the last few days. Sia was heavy on her mind, but he was not the problem. He only muddled her ability to feel what was wrong with Sathea, to hear her voice in the leaves. He was a Son of Sathea, and Sathea worried for him as well, making it hard for her to distinguish what ailed the land. There was a shift, but she could not find the source. She had been feeling it for months. She had not talked to Destined about it because she did not want to burden him with something else. His load was already significant.

He was consistently divided in his thoughts. Only when they shared themselves with one another could she feel more of him, but not all of him.

Her thoughts were interrupted when she sensed him coming near. He was on his way to the meeting. He did not speak to her over their link. He seemed preoccupied in his thoughts. She watched him fly over her and land on the path. Others saw him as regal with his gleaming white scales. All she saw was a fool. A fool she loved, but still a fool. She watched him stop to speak with Endrir and was hit with a flurry of emotions. Love, jealousy, envy, confusion, anger, and fear. She closed her eyes to get a better reading, but it was gone. "What was that?" she thought to herself.

Endrir and Destined were as close as brothers, if not closer. She felt nothing from either of them other than love. Sometimes she felt jealousy from Destined, but she knew that was because he knew how she felt about Endrir. He called it natural jealousy because he told her who would not want her to themselves. "What is going on?" she asked herself. She felt like her life was coming undone overnight with the number of strange things happening.

She spoke before Endrir could pass her resting place. She sensed an odd happiness about him. Then again, he was never easy to read. He was Watcher, and they were trained to control their emotions. He often did so with her. It frustrated her to no end, but she allowed him whatever brought him peace. He loved her deeply. She knew it. He had loved her for so long she could not remember when it began. When the dance started to win her heart of hearts, the only two to engage were Destined and Endrir. She loved them both. Endrir almost at once, but Destined was a slow build.

"Nihility," Pax called.

"Aye, Lady Pax."

"Does he hold your heart of hearts?"

"No, Lady Pax. I choose Destined. I lost Endrir a long time ago."

"What do you mean, youngling? Another dragoness holds his heart of hearts?"

She sighed. "Endrir's heart is his own, but he has Destined. I am not much of a dragoness in that respect. I lost my dragon to another dragon," she said with a laugh.

"Is he a Watcher?"

"Aye. He takes assignments that are the furthest away from Petrall. He always has, but he used to return more," she said.

Endrir made her sad in a way she could not express. She never wanted to hurt him. Endrir of all held a special place in her heart and always would. In fact, the three shared a mental link that had never been severed since they were fledglings. Endrir closed his connection to her when he needed to, but she kept hers open to him just in case he needed her. She tried to reread his emotions, but there was nothing.

"What of this Sia? Ygi said he is your dragon."

"Lady Pax, Sia is…he is hard for me to talk about right now. Yes, he is my dragon, but he is not."

Destined interrupted her thoughts with a gentle call through their link. "Nihility," he breathed. He did not know saying her name in such a way made her anger fade away.

"Yes, fool."

He sent an image of the Courtyard of the Moon where the Circle of Elders was. They were all in their respective places. She could feel his agitation through the link. "I am sorry, my love, but we only wait for you."

She let out another long sigh. She really hated this part of her duties. "I am on my way. You can tell them to rest easy for the doomsayer comes," she said, taking flight. She could feel his lack of amusement at her quip.

The Circle of Elders in the Courtyard of the Moon was a depression between two of Petrall's peaks. It was said to be the place where Rona, the Mother of Dragons, made her nest. It was the part of Petrall that sat against the Durming Sea. If you stood with your back to the water, you could see all of Petrall spread out before you. The council which guided them made this their meeting place to honor her.

She made her way to the rock appointed for her as head of the Weavers, feeling like a complete fool with the pageantry the elders insisted upon for these meetings. "How on Sathea do you actually make something like this worse," Pax groaned. "It is a meeting, not some Fairy Folk festival!" Pax hissed.

"Beauty has finally arrived! Glad you could join us, Lady Nihility," Elder Kuri said. She nodded her acknowledgment of his words, then looked at Endrir confused when she felt his anger surge for just a moment before it disappeared. He grinned at her and winked.

The Circle of Elders was composed of seven raised rock platforms fanning out into a half-circle, one for each of the elders that formed the council. The other half of the circle was made up of a lower set of stone platforms. There was one for each of the three callings; Walker, Weaver, and Watcher. Each of them had to have both their first and second present.

Destined was Lead Walker of the Order of Walkers, and beside him stood his first Tuzys the Mindhunter and Arsu the Savvy. Endrir was not lead of Watcher Hold by his own choice, but he kept a position of honor among them. The head of the Hold was Olvess the Beast Tamer, with his first Zennar the Hidden. No second had been chosen. She led the Weavers with her first Raravarra the Siren and second Frety the Reaper.

"The two beside you are deeply tied to the Dreaming in unique ways, almost like Ghost for the yellow one. The red and green one reminds me a little of Ygi," Pax said.

"Aye. Frety is a Pillar to the Path of Death. Her pair is Apyrl the Relinquisher. She was my first for a long time, but she stepped away to allow Raravarra a chance to learn. Apyrl despises all the fuss. Raravarra can craft illusions and manipulate sounds."

"I recognize most of those who call themselves Elders now, Nihility. I will need an explanation for some of those I see on the council soon."

"You are troubled and angry, Lady Pax. Why?"

"We will speak about it later," Pax said. "I would have you pay close attention now."

There were seven titles as elders besides the ones they carried through their lives. The aged bronze with a white beard and brown spine was Ergodi the Wise, Elder of Patience. The crimson with the black spine was Kuri the Beleaguer, Elder of Frugality. He was the youngest of the council members. His ascension to elder came with Destined's acceptance of the leadership of the Walkers.

The Weavers on the council were the pale green dragoness Pimo the Mender, Elder of Diligence. Pimo was a skilled healer or used to be before Nihility became the lead of Weaver Circle. The other Weaver was Ivylth the Trickster, Elder of Kindness. Ivylth was skilled with illusions that worked well in pulling dreamers from the grasp of beasts in the Dreaming, but kindness was the furthest thing she was. Nihility loathed her. She could not look at Ivylth without remembering all the vile things she had done to her with Ergodi at her side.

The Watchers boasted three members. This would change once an elder stepped down. They called this the Rotation of the Three. It kept the balance on the council between the three callings. For the last three thousand years, the Watchers held the rotated position.

Uzzod the Beastmaster, the Elder of Giving, held the rotation. He was a medium-sized iridescent green dragon. He was part of the Poisoned Four. Great tales were told of him and his experiments with the bile from the Quag, poisonous dragon-sized lizard-like creatures who roamed Sathea. Uzzod was the only dragon to withstand their bite. Next was Britir the Tranquil, Elder of Humility, pair to Uzzod, and mentor to Endrir. He was an iridescent blue dragon. Of all the Elders, he was the surliest.

The last to round out the council of seven was the iridescent red, Shegur the Quick, Elder of Virtuosity. She was the former Lead of the Watchers. Together, she, Uzzod, Britir, and Azzi composed the Poisoned Four of Petrall, and she alone was the Great Red of Watcher Hold. She had spent years grooming Endrir to take over and angry at his refusal. Once, long ago, she was at the side of Lady Azzi the Devourer, training Nihility in the art of dragoness. Now she treated her as an annoyance.

With the exclusion of Uzzod, Britir, and Shegur, the council members made her angry. They were relentless in their mistreatment of her. When the physical torture stopped, the whispers never did. "Death on black wings," is what they said around her. She took a deep breath, and then another. She needed to control her anger and bitterness. Suddenly she felt love wash over her and turned her head to see Destined watching her. He smiled at her and nodded.

There was a gentle nudge in her thoughts. "Do not let them under your scales, beautiful. You shine brighter than anything here tonight. So bright that even Mother Moon weeps at your beauty," Endrir said. He had opened his connection with her once again. She hummed at his lament and settled herself down, waiting for the meeting to begin.

"Endrir must have said something pleasing to you," Raravarra said, smiling.

"And how do you know it was Endrir and not Destined?" she asked her.

"Destined's laments are worse than the smell of jerboa shit, Nihility," Frety whispered.

She laughed and tried to cover it by huffing smoke. "That is why he steals them from Endrir," she said, making them laugh.

CHAPTER TWENTY

Sia had just come back from seeing the fallen Walkers at the Circle of Healing with Tuzys. The whole damn place smelled rotten. The Farseer had sent word through Tuzys to check Mica's mind. There were traces of something, but it was faint. Someone had tried to wipe his mind. He told Tuzys to inform Destined. He could have done it himself, but he avoided direct interactions with Destined when he knew Nihility would be around.

Lately, she was always around him, and the chance of him having to speak to her was too high. He could not risk it. He knew the minute he was near her, his words to her would be simple, "I miss you. I love you. I'm sorry. Please come home, my world." Calling her back was a risk he took. He did not know if the serpent was after Destined, and he could not risk searching with Ergodi and Kuri lurking. He had placed his hope in her to call him back, and it worked.

He laid down in his alcove for a much-needed nap. It had been days since he last slept because his dreams brought her, his world, his Nihility. He shook himself and huffed smoke. He looked over at the empty nest beside him and sighed. He had made space for her here before they found a place to make their home together. He missed her. He had missed her every day for the last three thousand years.

A shadow covered the moonlight that shined down in the front of his alcove. "What on Sathea did you think you were doing calling her back here?" Ygi hissed at him as she entered.

"Hello, Ygi."

"Do not 'hello Ygi' me, Sia Mindbreaker! What have you done?!"

He sighed. "Destined needed to return. I thought Nihility

could call him back, and she did. He has returned, and all is well on Petrall again."

"She went into the Between to get him!" Ygi said with venom in her voice.

"What?"

"Nihility went into that place. That is how Destined returned, Mindbreaker! You fool of a damn dragon! Why did you not tell us she could go there? Bendre is beside himself with worry for her. He has gone to speak with Terg, and Sathea knows what he will do to you when he finds out. Sia, you should not have taught her to do that!"

"I did not know she could, Ygi! I did not teach her that!" he hissed. He frowned. "Fucking Farseer!" he spat.

"Oh, do not start with your anger toward Destined."

"You don't like him either, Ygi!"

"Correction, Mindbreaker, I think he is charming. It is that damn Watcher that sets my teeth on edge. However, I don't like any of you right now. Destined is foolish, and he is young, Sia. You are neither of those things. You are bitter at him for what you have done to yourself!"

"I have a damn good reason. Do not belittle me, Ygi."

"I am not belittling you, Sia. I don't understand why you would subject yourself and Nihility to unnecessary pain. She is a dragoness. She can hold every dragon on Petrall to her if she chooses!"

"I know!" he shouted.

"Yet you send her away from you. Cast her away like she has not had enough of that in her life."

"They love her, Ygi, especially Destined. I cannot hurt either of them when they care for her as much as they do. They need her."

"And so do you," Ygi said.

"I feel guilty, Ygi! I taught them both, but Destined," he sighed. "I did not mean to fall in love with her."

"Then talk to him and tell him that!" she snapped.

"I'm trying to figure out how without making a bigger mess of things for her, Ygi. I'm trying! I know you do not understand, but Nihility needs him in her life too. Destined is rash and impulsive. I don't need him doing something he will regret when it comes to Nihility."

She took a deep breath. "Bendre said she carries the Grand Lady with her and that strange Warida you told me about from the Depths."

"What?"

"Sia Mindbreaker, I should turn your mind to mush for this!"

"Ygi, stop blaming me. I did not know. If I had known she would do something so dangerous, I would have never called her back. He must have shown her how. Nihility has always been bright, and entering the Between requires only intense meditation. She does that just as you do."

"It is dangerous for her! She even said the Grand Lady protected her."

"That means he found it," he said to himself. "Why on Sathea would he go looking? I warned him!"

"Found what? What do you mean?"

"It does not matter, Ygi. I have to go see about something," he said, rising.

"Where are you going?"

"Home. I mean my home with her, where I can enter safely," he said. "Keep an eye on her."

"That is your job! You are her dragon."

"Destined is her dragon now, Ygi."

"Tell that to her heart, Mindbreaker, you ass."

"Ygi, she will forget about me in time."

"In time?" Ygi hissed. "You haven't forgotten about her, and I can assure you she has not forgotten about you!" Ygi spat, coming within inches of his face. "She only came back because you sent that damn bird. A bird you could not have sent had she still not carried that token with her. A warning and a test, right, Sia? A test to see if she still belonged to you?" Ygi snapped. He looked away from her. Ygi always read him easily. "I know what you did and why you did it. However, that does not give you the right to toy with her heart after three thousand years. She is your dragoness, and you are her dragon. Act like it," she said.

"Is she okay?"

"Yes, Sia. Well, she seems okay. Bendre was harsh with her as usual, but she knows he did not mean it," Ygi said, sighing at him. "I wish you would stop this, Sia, and just call to her. Together, the two of you can speak to Destined. She needs you," she said before turning and leaving.

He sighed and moved off his nest. He took flight from his alcove, headed for the Burning Waste. It was time for him to go home.

CHAPTER TWENTY-ONE

"As the sun begins its descent into the land, and the two children of the Mother Moon stand beside her, we meet here at this most special place for our kind. The place of our rebirth. The place where She of Many Colors and Mother to us all made her nesting ground. It is here where we guide our kind. Here, we ask our future leaders to discuss with the Council their issues, concerns, hopes, and ideas. It is here where the elders give their knowledge and advice. Let us open with homage to our Mother, as we pay heed to her words of wisdom and caution," Ergodi said, opening the meeting.

Elder Shegur stood and spread her wings. She tilted her head up to the sky and spouted a stream of flame that glowed red against the fading orange sky. "These are the words spoken by Rona Brightscales, She of Many Colors and Mother to us all."

The sun will rise red.
The brilliant light it once was, given to the scales of a fledgling born.
Then the red shall bloom upon the land, casting shadows of bruised shades.
Where two were, only one shall be.
The bond will break.
Broken in darkness, the shadows weep.
The Maiden Moon will rise.
The two eggs of the Mother's Moon will hide.
The stars will not shine.
One of the deepest black shall fly upon the dream to wake the beast.
As they breathe, so shall they see.
As they fly, so shall they dream.
As they live, so shall we prosper.
As they break, so shall we all.

White to open the space between the three. Sathea will weep.
Black to close the space between the three. Petrall will fall.
Death holds the key to the Shadow's salvation.
The Prophet screams in agony while fear grips tight.
As the Serpent moves, it brings damnation.
Spread your wings, oh sweet fiend.
Unleash the pain, oh sweet redeemer.
Lest the Balance will fall!
Death. Dreams. Darkness.

"The Lord Farseer has returned to us from the Between. Thirteen days he spent searching for our lost. We are happy to have you back, Lord Farseer," Lady Pimo said. "You have asked the council to appear here to address a concern you believe goes far beyond just the Order of Walkers. Please, Lord Farseer, tell us what you have learned and what affects us all."

Destined resisted the urge to roll his eyes at the unnecessary show the Council of Elders insisted upon with these meetings as Pimo spoke to him. He stood, the fading light making his scales shimmer. He was not suppressing his link with Nihility or Endrir. He had no intention of telling the elders anything about the barrier, but the threat the empty bodies of the fallen Walkers posed was too significant for him to keep hidden.

"As you know, the Order of Walkers has lost eight of its members over the last year. When the last two, Mica and Ellot, traveled to the Between and did not return, I heeded the words of Elders Ergodi and Kuri and went in search of the missing. What I found left me concerned. I believe us to be in danger, and we must decide how to protect ourselves," he said.

"Danger? You spoke nothing of danger, Destined. You said that you found Ellot's mind-body," Ergodi said.

"I would have thought hearing him say he found a body would have been alarming enough," Britir said, rolling his eyes. Endrir snickered.

"Finding Ellot's body is the reason I say there is danger, Elder Ergodi," he said before Ergodi could bite back at Britir. "I found Ellot, but not his actual body. It lies in the Circle of Healing, Elder Britir. I found his mind-body."

"It is still a body, Farseer. Mind-body or physical body. One cannot work without the other, and we should have been told sooner," Uzzod said, looking at Ergodi. "What was the state of the body?" he asked, looking back at Destined.

"Something consumed the essence of Ellot," he answered.

"You do not know what could have been the cause?" Elder Uzzod asked.

"I believe it to be the work of demons," he said simply. They met his words with hisses and gasps. He saw Endrir's head snap towards Nihility with big eyes.

"Jokes are not like you, Lord Farseer, and neither are exaggerations. You mentioned nothing of demons when you spoke to Ergodi and me," Kuri said.

"You did not ask," he said with a smile.

"I should not have to, Lord Farseer. You are Lead Walker," Kuri hissed. "Regardless, I have walked the Between long before you, and I have never seen even the slightest presence of a demon."

"Perhaps you looked in the wrong place," he said.

"Perhaps, in your time away, you have confused the bed tales told by Weavers with reality. Not that I blame you. Lady Nihility could muddle the senses of any dragon with eyes," Kuri said.

He knew Kuri and Ergodi would dismiss his words. It involved them. He just had not figured out how yet. The word betrayer flashed in his mind again. This time it appeared on the backdrop of the sky overlooking Petrall. He could see them all where they stood now, even himself. He shook his head and blinked, trying to clear his vision. "Destined," Endrir said over their link.

"Not now, Endrir. I will explain later," he said. He turned

his attention back to Kuri. "You're right, Kuri, she could, but only for a dragon worth it. I am not sure you are packing enough to please my dragoness. You would need to find a better use for your tongue first. I could give you lessons, but my mind is muddled by her magnificent tail. Excuse me, her magnificent Weaver tales," Destined said. Uzzod and Britir laughed and huffed smoke to compose themselves. He heard her hum beside him. He was done taking their shit. The dragon roared from his cage, and he did not stop him.

"Destined!" Ergodi hissed.

"He earned that one, Ergodi," Uzzod said with a chuckle. "Magnificent tail," he said under his breath, making Britir snicker again.

"Over the years, I have done what you asked without question. I have gone days without rest to see for our kind. I have done my part in keeping us safe. I have taken the words and knowledge of this council like a good student, even when my own studies proved your words false. I came to you today to tell you of a threat. Not just any threat, but the great threat of demons," he said with his voice growing louder and more profound. His hazel eyes separated in color. The brown, green, and blue circled each other perfectly. His anger was increasing. "But what do I get? Jabs and a sorry excuse for a dragon questioning my abilities. You doubt me? Me! You accuse me of jokes and foolery? Me, Destined the Farseer, the one who can see the very minute of your demise should I choose to do so!"

The Courtyard had fallen in shocked silence—everyone except Endrir. "Farseer, control yourself," Endrir said over their link.

"I am in complete control, my treasure," he said. He turned his attention back to the elders. "I come to you because there is a threat. A genuine threat. One that I caution you to prepare for. We must take steps. I ask you to hear me now, Petrall, no Sathea is in trouble!"

"Well, that is how you liven one of these things up!" Britir exclaimed, breaking the silence.

"Shut up, you old drunk dragon," Shegur hissed.

"Fly off, Shegur. I am not drunk. Not yet anyway," Britir said, yawning. He looked around at the others. "Well, I am not apologizing to him. You two were the ones who did not believe him. Ask him what he needs," he said, looking at Kuri.

"I will not insult you by asking if you are sure, Destined. What steps are you asking the council to take?" Ergodi asked. "What is it you require of the council?"

"Now, now Ergodi. We all know your fondness for the Farseer, but I do not think we should just agree because he showed a little backbone. We need proof of this threat," Elder Ivylth said.

"At least he has a backbone, sneaky miserable old dragoness," Nihility mumbled from behind him.

"Yes, Ivylth, I am fond and proud of my former student. He has surpassed me in more ways than I could have imagined," Ergodi said.

"He said he found a body" Britir said, annoyed. "That little trip you took to the Dreaming must have affected your hearing as well, Ivylth. You should have that checked with the healers."

"Where is this body? I do not see it," she snapped at Britir. "You should really mind your manners with a dragoness, Elder Britir."

"I am afraid that skill died with Azzi. Wait, you know that, though. You were there," Britir said, looking at Ivylth. His blue eyes blazing.

Uzzod gave Britir a look and shook his head. "Destined, what facts do you have of this threat? It is not that we do not know of the existence of demons. It has been told and untold for years gone. We have been told the threat looms, but what has caused you to attribute the current crisis of the Walkers to demons?" Uzzod asked.

"I have no physical proof, Elder Uzzod. I have only what I have seen in the Between."

"Then we are to prepare on your words alone?" Ivylth asked.

"You do everything else based on the words of a dead dragoness. I figured mine would carry more weight since I am breathing and standing here before you," he said with a tone.

"Your tongue Destined," Ergodi hissed.

"Right, I forget your fondness for weakness," Destined snapped. Nihility laughed, and he could see Ivylth give her a look coated in rage.

"Problem with his backbone, Elder Ivylth?" Nihility asked, flexing her wings.

"She'll have a bigger problem with yours, Lady Nihility, if she keeps it up," Uzzod said, smirking.

"Your proof, Destined?" Britir said, smiling at him as Ivylth huffed smoke.

"I have no proof for you tonight. Just my words and this," he said. He saw all the elders flinch at his contact. None of them were prepared for his ability to project images directly into their minds so easily. He saw Ergodi take a sharp look at him. He had even surprised his teacher. He projected the image he had of Ellot's mind body. His body a husk of scales left unnaturally twisted, and his jaw locked in a snarl of pain.

"That is definitely a body," Britir said with a huff.

"I'm going to need a Weaver to remove that image from my dreams," Uzzod said, shaking his head.

"That is Ellot!" Elder Shegur shouted.

"No shit, Shegur," Britir said, rolling his eyes.

"What on Sathea did that!?" Pimo asked in shock.

"That is all that remained of him when I found him. Nothing but a dried shell of himself like the skin shed by a growing fledgling," he said.

"You think a demon did this?" Britir asked. He nodded. "Destined, I mean no insult, but I could name several creatures with the ability to do something like that here on Sathea. Why do you think it is the work of a demon?"

"Yes, you know of creatures here on Sathea capable of such. However, that is not the physical body of Ellot, Elder Britir. This is just the body of his mind. I showed you proof that his mind will never return to his body again. What our healer's care for is only an empty vessel."

"Are there no creatures in the Between capable of such?" Britir asked.

"I am sure there are, but it is not the way for any I have met. The goal is to keep the mind-body intact because it allows them a passage out of the Between. The mind of a Walker becomes their way to freedom. Ellot suffered destruction, a severing of the mind. Something consumed him. Something fed on him."

"Uzzod," Britir said.

"I know, Britir," Uzzod said.

"You know what?" Shegur asked them both.

"Nothing you would need to concern yourself with, Red Lady," Uzzod said, smiling. "Britir only wants to know if I have seen anything on Sathea."

"Well, have you?" she snapped.

"He cannot check if you keep flapping your jaws, dragoness," Britir said.

"What do you propose, Destined?" Pimo asked, ignoring the three Watchers.

"We must first deal with the fallen Walkers, Lady Pimo. Leaving their bodies empty of their minds invites danger to Petrall," he said.

"You would have us kill them?!" Pimo asked, shocked.

"Elders, if I may?" Nihility interrupted. He looked at her, frowning; something was off.

"What would you have to add to this matter, Lady Nihility? You are a Weaver, not a Walker," Ergodi snapped.

"You should mind the Dreaming," Ivylth said.

"Shut your snouts and let her speak," Uzzod hissed. "Have there been disturbances in the Dreaming Lady Nihility?" he asked.

"I have not thoroughly investigated yet, Elder Uzzod. Things have been chaotic. However, I informed Master Bendre and Lady Ygi. I only wish to say that yes, the threat is real. It is as real as Laz of the Between believed it to be. It is as real as the Grand Lady Pax of the Depths believed it to be when she took steps to ensure that you, the council, and the leaders of the Walkers, Watchers, and Weavers, be prepared should the threat arise."

Something changed in her; Destined could feel it. Her words changed, like the sound of an echo. Lady Pax was speaking with her. It was as if Pax stood beside Nihility, speaking the words simultaneously. Energy pulsed from the both of them, strong enough to cause a shift in the breeze.

"The Between has suffered a great breach; treachery, betrayal, and collusion have paved the way. The time has come to prepare the spirit, body, and mind. Long gone are your days of meetings and councils. Gone are the days of sitting upon your pedestals like you are some higher power on Petrall. They come, and chaos, destruction, and sorrow will follow. We must preserve the Great Balance. We must protect Sathea. You wanted proof from the one you named Farseer, then let my presence be your proof and my fire burn you into action. Cast your doubts aside!" Nihility and Pax said.

She spread her great wings. From deep inside her, she let out a furious roar; with it followed flame, but not just any flame, the Black Flame. The flame said to burn for eternity. The flame that could burn the dreams of those it touched. Flames that were created and used by only one dragoness, Lady Pax. When she closed her maw to cut off the fire, she looked at the council not with the brown eyes of Nihility the Harbinger, but the blue of the Grand Lady, Pax of the Depths.

"You who sit upon the council! Know me! See me! Name me! For I see you well," Pax shouted.

"Mother of Watchers," Britir and Uzzod said, rising quickly.

"Lady Pax," Shegur said in awe as Pimo cowered and whined.

"You have a duty. See to it," Pax said calmly as she closed her eyes.

CHAPTER TWENTY-TWO

Endrir saw what was happening before Destined could pull himself from his shock. He leaped over to her and let her collapse against him. He quickly laid her down with a hiss. The grass beneath her burned away. He looked at Destined with panic in his eyes. "She is burning, Destined!" he shouted. "Nihility," he whispered. "Nihility, can you hear me? Hurry, Farseer!"

Destined rushed over to him. He touched his snout to her head and pulled back quickly from the heat. He touched her mind instead and looked at Endrir. "She is okay, Endrir, but we need to cool her off quickly."

He relaxed and then turned to the other Watchers. "Olvess, get water immediately for Lady Nihility!"

"Thank you, Endrir."

"I do not need thanks caring for our dragoness, Destined. What I need is an explanation. What on Sathea was that?"

"The Black Flame."

"How?"

"Not here, Endrir," Destined said, shifting his eyes.

He saw the Elders composing themselves behind him. "I will wait with her if you can have a place prepared for her to rest," he said. Destined nodded and was about to speak to Tuzys when Endrir stopped him with a nudge from his snout. "Farseer, a quiet place. I do not want them bothering her until she wakes. Send me a message in the usual fashion when you are ready."

"Aye. Thank you for watching over Nihility and for being here."

"As it should be," he said.

"As it always will be," Destined said, taking off.

He watched him go, feeling an overwhelming surge of love for him. He was growing impatient with Olvess while he waited for water. It was his nerves. Nihility had set them on edge. He wondered how much she knew and how she had channeled the Mother of Watchers. He was sure he was the only one that noticed, but there was another who lurked behind the two voices. He had questions and no answers. When Destined shared the image of Ellot's mind-body, he wanted to run far away from Petrall. He had seen that place in his dreams.

"You still care for her a great deal," Olvess said, pulling him from his thoughts. He had organized the Watchers to bring water. They were carrying great orbs filled with water and releasing them over Nihility, the water hissing and steaming as it touched her.

"Both of them. We have always been close, but you know this well, Olvess. You were always my little shadow."

"Zennar was more your shadow than I. I was the little shadow of Destined, but yes. I also know that you have had multiple opportunities to take over and lead Watcher Hold. All of us know you are the most qualified. You trained those of us that remain. If you took over, at least you could see them more often. The council torments Lady Nihility."

He looked at Olvess. The younger dragon was more than capable of leading Watcher Hold, but he let his lack of confidence get the better of him. "That is why I do not, Little Shadow. Then it would be three for their torment instead of two. At least this way, you can maintain a middle ground and watch where I could not."

"Wise choice, Endrir. One I am not sure I could make. I wish I could consider the wellbeing of those I care for," Olvess said with a weak smile. He turned back to supervising the other Watchers.

He frowned as Olvess walked away. There was something off about the exchange, but he could not grasp it. He laid himself down where his head was as close to Nihility's as he could get without burning his snout. "I am here, beautiful," he whispered.

"I see the prodigy of the Poisoned Four has returned to us again. You spend too long among those with short lives youngling," she said.

"Hello, Lady Shegur. You look well."

"As do you, Endrir. Quick as ever with your observations as well. I heard your exchange with Olvess. Your reasons for not succeeding me are still the same, I see. Still surrounding her. So much contempt for the elders, even with me among their ranks," she said.

"It is not contempt, Lady Shegur. It is a difference of opinion. One that I see has not changed. I will not hide the fact that if I stood beside her, I would not stand idly by while you trade insults and disregard her."

"I sense the truth in what you say, as I know you can sense mine when I say you would make a valuable contribution as leader of the Watchers, Endrir."

He turned his head to gaze up at her. She was using her truth-seeker ability on him. She always had high hopes for him. They just did not share the same view on how those hopes would come to fruition. "Aye, I do, Lady Shegur, but as you know, the actual truth is always somewhere in between."

"Indeed, it is. Just as it is with Nihility, whom you seem to hold out for when she has made her choice of dragon obvious," she said, rolling her eyes. "I will leave you to care for Lady Nihility. Destined has asked the council to wait for his return. He does well in seeing to the needs of his mate first," she said as she turned and made her way back to the other elders.

He watched her walk away and sighed. "Some shit never changes," he mumbled to himself. He gave a slight nod to Elder Britir, the old blue nodded in return with a smile. Britir was his mentor and taught him much. Shegur he knew well to watch and learn. She taught him as well for a time, and they shared the truth seer ability, although it seemed she had grown lax in her power.

Destined spoke the truth to them, but he was not telling the entire truth. He gathered the same from Nihility. They were both hiding something, but no one else seemed to notice. Shegur was only looking for truth in Destined's words, and that was there. The truth in between was missing. He wondered what they were up to. He did not doubt why his friends were hiding something; the council was an awful mess. Besides, he had his own secrets. As the thought crossed his mind, Destined contacted him. He sighed at himself for forgetting again. He had been gone too long.

"I am ready, Endrir. Do you need me to help you bring her here?" Destined asked, sending him an image of the place.

He chuckled; it was one of their old hiding places. "Are you sure the three of us will fit? We are no longer fledglings," he said, trying to control his laughter.

"Well, you and I will have to shift to our other forms until she wakes, but yes, she should be comfortable here," Destined said, laughing.

"I will be along with her shortly," he said, standing up to prepare to leave. Shegur approached him again.

"The Farseer has sent a message to Elder Ergodi that he will return shortly. We would have you stay as well, Endrir."

He glanced past her at Britir, who gave him a slight shake of his head. He looked at Shegur and frowned. She wanted him to truth-see Destined's words. "I must decline with my apologies to the council, Lady Shegur. Please have Olvess remain in my place as he should. I have made a promise to care for Lady Nihility while the Farseer speaks with you, and it is one I intend to keep," he said. She glared at him before turning to leave.

He spread his wings and positioned himself over Nihility before gently lifting her in his claws. She was a lot wider and heavier than the last time he did this. He got a sudden flash of her battering him with her tail for that thought. He lapsed into giggles again and almost dropped her. "I am asking to be set on fire," he chuckled to himself.

CHAPTER TWENTY-THREE

The council had never questioned Destined when he told them of a threat. It appalled him they would do so now, especially when the danger was significant. It was not something trivial like the storms that raged over Petrall for a week. Even when the sickness took most of the hatchlings a few thousand years ago, they listened to him without question. Ergodi and Kuri were up to something, but he also realized that so were Shegur, Ivylth, and Pimo. The only two that seemed genuinely concerned by his words were Britir and Uzzod.

Then there was Nihility channeling Lady Pax. The manifestation was magnificent but startling. He felt the two bonding, and he did not know if Nihility realized it. Pax had somehow given her the Black Flame. Those flames were legend, and now they were being wielded by Nihility. The one the elders he suspected saw as their doom. It did nothing but place Nihility in danger. He also felt the demon at the edge of her, which bothered him. It did not feel like the one he had trapped.

He shook his head. He had to find a place to keep her safe until she woke. Endrir had aroused his suspicions even more by insisting Nihility stay away from the council. He trusted Endrir's judgment more than anyone else, even Nihility. The Watcher had sharp eyes and ears; he was a truth seer. He could tell if the words spoken by another were truth or lies. Endrir had fine-tuned his craft where he could tell if something was missing from the truth in the sound of the words. It was what he called the truth in between. Thinking of Endrir made him realize he knew exactly where he wanted to go.

There was an area of Petrall that buffeted the forest far below, called the Jagged Cliffs. The sharp points of rock that jutted out of the mountainside and dangerous crosswinds gave it its name. A dragon could impale themselves on the large pointed rocks if they did not know how to manage the winds. Many dragons had injured themselves here. The Council of Elders declared it unsafe long ago. That fact alone made it a perfect spot for Destined and Endrir to explore.

They had done so one day while they were waiting for Nihility to finish one of her mysterious training sessions. They figured out the breaks in the wind that would allow them to float down to the grasslands below if timed right. It had been a long time since they had come here, but he did not doubt his memory. He landed on soft, lush grass with a grin on his snout. Pink wildflowers called Pewhas stretched to where the trees became thick. Nihility loved those flowers.

He went to an area just below the last line of jagged rock. The cave they had found long ago was still there. Memories of the time they spent here poured through his mind. It was here they created the telepathic link they still shared. It was here they would tell their secrets and explore their feelings. It was their place, and by the looks of things, no one else had discovered it since.

The dishes Endrir had brought back to teach them the ways of short lifers were still here, covered in a layer of dust. The scars of magic gone awry still littered the cave walls, and the grass mats where they slept still lay where they last left them. He looked around to make sure it was secluded. He could smell the jerboa deep in the forest and other game. He did not know how long she would sleep. He wanted to speak with Pax and warn her about how the council treated Nihility, but he dared not while she was asleep.

He also did not want Endrir to know more than he should. Something was off about his treasure. He did not understand why. He knew that short-lifer in his mind worried him, but that was not enough to make him behave with such secrecy. Usually, he would be ready to tell Destined everything after being gone for so long, but now he seemed distant. Painfully distant. He knew it was not Nihility. She could and would choose a mate that suited her. He never took that for granted. She loved them both and believed they lived far too long and loved too profoundly to behave like the younger species and their ideas of love and mating. If she wanted another mate, she would take one.

She chose him over Endrir, and he knew it caused Endrir great pain. It caused her great pain, but she hid it well. He caused that pain. He pushed the dance upon them all with a lie, and he carried that guilt for three thousand years. Endrir stayed away from Petrall for more extended periods. It was how he coped with her choice. He had won Nihility's heart of hearts, but he had lost the frequent presence of his treasure in exchange.

Destined frowned as he realized he was hesitant to trust Endrir for the first time in his life, but he could not say why. He was mentally exhausted. He decided he would deal with Endrir with Nihility's help. He made his way back up to the plateau. Endrir would need help to bring her down.

CHAPTER TWENTY-FOUR

Endrir was struggling with Nihility's limp body. He laid her down on the ground and sat down beside her, panting. "I," he paused, catching his breath, "I don't remember her being this heavy."

"She has grown," Destined said, struggling not to laugh.

"You are asking for us both to burn," he said. They both started laughing.

"Has she changed?" Destined asked.

"Nay. She still sleeps, but she is no longer too hot to touch. I have never seen her like this, Destined."

"I think she exhausted her powers. I know she rarely ever does it, but it can happen even to an Empath," he said, nuzzling her. "Let's get her down before someone sees where we are going."

They lifted her, Destined cradling her head while holding her lower half. Together they floated her to the bottom, allowing the wind currents to do the work for them. "I have to go finish with the council. I will be back soon. Will you wait here with her?" Destined asked once she was safely nestled at the entrance of the cave.

"You do not need to ask, Destined," he said, nodding. He turned to leave. "Farseer," he called.

"Aye."

"Watch yourself and watch them. I do not know what is happening, and I will wait until we can speak, but do not allow the council more than needed."

"Aye," Destined said, taking flight.

Endrir watched him disappear over the plateau. He turned to survey what was before him. The grasslands below the Jagged Cliffs were still the same after all these years. He flicked his tongue, tasting the air. The forest was ripe with game they could hunt. He could hear the stream that flowed through where they would often swim. This was a place filled with memories for him.

He turned his attention back to Nihility, laying himself down next to her and feeling everything around him. He loved the way the moonlight made her almost shimmer as her scales drank in the light. He tried to keep his focus on her, but it had been days since he last slept. His eyes grew heavier as he thought of her. It was not long before he dozed.

He was back in Tresai, the largest and oldest city of short lifers on Sathea. It sprawled across the land, once nothing but a cluster of grass huts, now an expansive town filled with stone and wooden homes. Farms settled around the area, but inside the city's unscalable stone walls, there was the hustle and bustle of life. Merchants peddling goods, taverns where one could drink the intoxicating brew the short lifers crafted, and various vendors selling meat they cooked with fire littered the pathways through Tresai.

He had been in this city for a long time. He knew it as well as he knew Petrall. In the heart of it lay a tower. It spiraled high into the sky. The official name was the Tower of Piety, but it was the Tower of the Lost to those who knew its history.

Over the years, the short lifers found their own means of belief beyond the Great Balance. They prayed to deities Endrir never understood. For him, all things served the Great Balance. In Tresai and other places, they worshipped the Seven Gods of Bishamyr. Seven deities said to perform various miracles around Sathea. The Temple of the Gods of Bishamyr was constructed around the Tower of Piety some years ago. Together with the tower, it made up the center of Tresai. All the other great cities each held a tower dedicated to one of the seven. Only the temple in Tresai paid homage to them all.

The one believed to watch over the seven, and Sathea was called Mother. The Gods of Bishamyr were her disciples, sent by her to care for her children on Sathea. They only worshipped her at a temple near the mountain that stood behind Tresai. They raised a magnificent monument to her there as a jade serpent. The short lifers would make journeys across Sathea to pay homage to her image. They left tokens and trinkets in her honor. The Farmarks, the family who controlled Tresai, raised an area beside her statute where they buried their dead and those of the other six noble families. They were the only ones allowed to do so. He had seen the thing for himself at one of these burials. Looking at it made his scales itch.

He was walking in an area where the other short lifers laid their dead outside the city walls when he noticed her. She was crying uncontrollably. She had long black hair set in a single braid. She was tall for a female short-lifer but attractive for their kind. "Why are you crying? Did you lose someone?" he asked. She looked up at him but did not speak. She reached up and touched the side of his head near his eye with a single finger.

Suddenly, he was back in his egg with his sister's lifeless form. He could not scream. He flailed until it cracked, and like a newly hatched fledgling, he was free, covered in the egg's ambrosia. However, he was not a fledgling; he was himself as he was now, twenty thousand years to the sky. He found his feet and stood ready to fight. He was in a space of complete darkness, not just dark but also emptiness.

"Endrir come to me," he heard someone call out to him. He could not make out the voice, but it sounded almost like Nihility. His heart raced. "Endrir, I need you," the voice said. He turned, trying to determine where it was coming from. He walked and stopped; he was no longer a dragon. Somehow, he had shifted to his short life form. When he raised his eyes from his own self-inspection, he gasped. The girl he saw crying was standing before him. Her eyes blazed green.

"You have come, champion of my tears," she said.

"Who are you?"

"I am who you wish me to be. I am what you want me to be. I am yours to do as you wish. What is it you desire more than anything in this world?" she asked.

He could not stop himself. It was as if something had control of his tongue. "Nihility," he said.

She turned away from him. He wanted to reach out to stop her, but something diverted his attention. Beyond where she stood was a door marked with his name. "Open the door, and your desire will be a reality," she said. Her voice was growing faint. He walked to the door. Part of him rebelled, but he could not stop. He saw the husk of a dragon on the ground as he passed. He placed his hand on the door and opened it.

"Endrir! Some Watcher you are!"

He was jerked from his dream; the Farseer had returned.

CHAPTER TWENTY-FIVE

The elders lay on the ground enjoying a meal when he arrived. "Farseer! I hope you do not mind. We have more if you are hungry as well," Uzzod said.

"No, thank you, Elder Uzzod. Shall I wait until you finish to continue?" he asked.

"If you do, I will probably set you on fire, Destined," Britir said with a tone. "It is long past my time to be at home."

"I do not mind if we speak while we eat if the others have no objection," Uzzod said.

"I do not care if they do. There is no reason to linger on the subject. What do you need of the council, Farseer?" Britir asked.

"You must decide the fate of the fallen Walkers. That is why I called on the council. I believe the decision to be yours," he said.

"Are you not the Lead Walker of the Order, Destined? Why should the decision be ours?" Shegur asked.

"I am. However, my duties do not extend to deciding the lives of others of our kind regardless of the situation."

"He is right. Eight Walkers are lost and have not returned, some for many moons. Our healers work day and night to care for their bodies to ensure they do not decay, but it is a losing battle. It is not the Farseer's place to determine their fates. It is ours," Pimo said.

"Do you have a suggestion, Lady Pimo?" Uzzod asked.

"Not yet. I do have questions. I am no Walker, Farseer. What is the threat that these eight bring to our kind that may involve demons?" she asked.

"Those eight that we have lost are without mind to anchor to their bodies. If their minds are not anchored, then the risk of something else picking up the thread that leads to their bodies is great. The greatest threat being a demon who could then control the body even if the owner's mind is not present," Ergodi said before he could answer.

"Is there no hope of their return?" Ivylth asked.

"I only located Ellot, Lady Ivylth. He was the image I shared with you. Of the others, I saw no sign."

"Then they could very well return to their bodies at some point," she said.

"Perhaps," he answered. "I hope they do."

"All except Ellot, of course," Kuri said. "There is no hope he will return to his body if the image the Farseer shared is indeed true."

"For Sathea's sake," he said, rolling his eyes.

"Now, Lord Farseer, there is no need for that. I am not saying that what you saw is not the truth. I am only speculating for the council."

"Ass," Britir mumbled.

"Tir, behave," Uzzod mumbled.

"Fly off, Zod," Britir said with a grin.

"I am not comfortable taking the life of a sleeping form if there is a possibility of life," Pimo said. There were several grumbles of agreement with Lady Pimo's sentiment.

"I am not comfortable overusing our healers and resources on what is essentially a corpse. If we speak in terms of balance, then those eight lives for the safety of the rest of Petrall is balance," Britir said.

"You are always so harsh, Britir. How will you explain those actions to the rest of Petrall?" Shegur asked.

"In the same way it was just explained to us, but with smaller words that are easy to follow so you can keep up," he snapped. "It is a threat. One that I believe we should take seriously."

"I agree with Britir," Uzzod said.

"Of course you do," Shegur said, yawning.

"There is still much we do not understand," Ergodi said. "I

would know more of what did that to Ellot. I would know without a doubt that it is demons that lurk in the Between."

"There is not much more to understand regarding eight bodies that could cause havoc on Petrall if something were to creep up inside them, Ergodi," Britir said.

"You have been dying to say that, haven't you," Uzzod said, chuckling.

"Perhaps," Britir said, grinning. "It alludes to so many other things. I could not help myself."

"Knock it off, you two," Shegur hissed.

"Yes, Great Matron of the Hold," Britir said, making Uzzod choke.

"What do you propose, Ergodi?" Ivylth asked, glaring at Britir.

"It is dangerous to send anyone into the Between. I agree with Destined on this, but we must know what hunts there," Ergodi said.

"Then perhaps a middle ground would be more effective here," Shegur said.

"Go on, Shegur," Ergodi said.

"Of the eight that have fallen, there is one we know for sure will not return to his body. Is that correct, Destined?" Shegur asked.

"Aye."

"Then I propose we hold a Ritual of Return for Ellot. The others should remain in the Circle of Healing for a while longer, but not forever. We will tend to them until we can further investigate the Between. I suggest you do that with haste."

"We are not sending the Farseer back in there. Thirteen days he was gone last time," Uzzod said.

"I think we can leave that for later discussion. I would like to give Destined time to think. He knows the Between well. I am sure he can find some means to investigate without putting himself or any other Walkers at risk," Ergodi said.

"I believe the hold you put on any Walkers entering the Between should remain in effect until you have determined a course of action," Kuri said. "Perhaps they can put their minds to aiding you in that endeavor in the meantime."

"I am sure they would be happy to help if it means the chance of saving the others," he said.

"We have an agreement on the matter then Destined. I suggest you take it back to Lady Nihility, once she is herself again, and Olvess. We will determine the day of Ellot's glory and inform you, so you may prepare the Walkers," Ergodi said.

"Go tend to your dragoness, Farseer," Uzzod said, smiling at him.

"And your mate," Britir whispered.

He looked at Britir, surprised, and nodded. He gave his thanks and took flight. He was eager to be away from them. There was something wrong, but he still could not put claws on the problem. He needed to speak with Endrir. He felt like a pawn in a game he did not know he was playing.

CHAPTER TWENTY-SIX

"Endrir, wake up!" Destined said as he nudged him. "Endrir! Some Watcher you are!" he said, laughing. He had startled him. "Are you okay, Endrir?"

"Aye. I did not realize how tired I was from my journey here is all. I am okay, Destined."

"Are you sure? Endrir, you…"

"I am sure Destined," Endrir said, cutting him off.

"Come on, let's get inside before the cold comes. Nihility will keep us warm for now. We can start a fire later," he said, shifting and walking around Nihility and into the cave. Endrir followed behind him.

Destined stood in all white. He took the hood of his cloak down, exposing his bald head, and grinned at Endrir. His skin was sun-kissed but still pale compared to most. It was a stark contrast next to Nihility's mahogany skin in her form. He removed his cloak and laid it on the ground before sitting with his back against Nihility's side. He wore the sleeveless white tunic and pants the monks below Petrall wore. His entire left arm bore the mark that named him Walker and prophet; three dragons nestled in concentric circles, one brown, one green, one blue, each devouring their own tails. In the center of the third was the all-seeing Dragon's eye. Below that were thick black lines that covered his forearm to his wrist. He was taller than Nihility by a head and almost the same height as Endrir. In his proper form, he was a bulky dragon. He was average size in his short life form but tone and lean.

Where he was bulky as a dragon, Endrir was not. He was lean, long, and a beautiful cascade of purple hues. In his short life form, he was magnificent. He was firm and rippled with muscle. His broad chest and shoulders could not be hidden beneath the form-fitting clothing he favored. He always wore the same black leather vest buckled across his chest with nothing underneath and pants that fit his form. Thin black lines covered both his arms and chest except for one spot over his heart, markings that he was Watcher. They always reminded him of the roads he could see sprawled across Sathea as he flew the sky. The lines became thicker down his left arm, like the tree branches with purple flowers sprouting from various spots. His hair was neatly pulled back. His violet eyes looked tired, a difference from their typical luster. His black beard was neatly trimmed as usual. His skin was a few shades lighter than Nihility, brown the color of gold sand.

He smirked at Destined as he sat down next to him. "Enjoying the show, Farseer?"

"When do I not enjoy the show?" he said, grinning.

"Do you really believe we are in danger?" Endrir asked.

"Aye. A lot more than we have ever been in before."

"How long do you plan to stay here?"

"At least until she wakes. I will sort the rest out after that. We all need to talk."

They were silent, sorting through their own thoughts. They had known each other for a long time. In some respects, they knew each other better than Nihility knew either. They shared a deep bond.

"It truly is good to see you. You were gone far too long this time. I missed you," Destined said, placing his hand on Endrir's leg.

"I know. I missed you too, Destined," Endrir said, placing his hand over Destined's and squeezing. "As long as we are here, and all we can do is wait on her to wake, would you humor my nostalgia more?"

He laughed. "This place brings back memories."

"It does. Some I thought I had forgotten. Others I still remember like they happened yesterday."

"What would you have me do?" he asked.

"I would like to hear the story of my egg," Endrir whispered.

"In all this time, you have never asked me to tell you this story. I never questioned it because I figured Nihility had told you long ago. You two were always together after I left the nursery," he said, shocked.

"No. Nihility told me you saved me. I heard the story from Lady Shegur. I assumed her words were true because here I am, and both of you are always with me."

"I suppose now is as good a time as any," he said, chuckling. "Especially here in this place where our mischief really began. I can tell you and show you," he said, smiling. "Nihility will have to recount what I cannot, though. I do not have her memories."

"I will ask her when she wakes," Endrir said.

"Well then, Watcher, prepare yourself for the story of your birth. Which is really the story of our birth," he said.

He turned his hand over where a small yellow orb appeared. It was a memory projector. It allowed one to show their memories to another without transfer. He extended his hand, so it rested between Endrir and himself. Endrir touched the orb, and it flashed purple. Now he could see the memories as Destined recalled them.

"As you know, the three of us and fourteen others were the surviving hatchlings of the Great Shattering. Those that tried to hatch during the Shattering perished. The survivors were moved to a new nursery until we had the basic skills to care for ourselves and be assigned into one of the three. Most of us were none the worse for wear. Our eggs kept us safe."

"Our first night in the nursery, the older fledglings that were on their way out of the nursery told us a story. It was about the ghosts that didn't hatch and how their spirits wandered at night looking to take vengeance on the living. All of them foolish stories designed to keep young ones from wandering away at night."

"Do they still tell those stories?" Endrir asked.

"Yes, unless the Fireball is around," he said, laughing. "Niore 'Fireball' Firewind loathes those stories. Anyway. That night I woke to the sound of Nihility crying. I thought she was afraid because of the stories we heard. When I asked her why she was crying, all she would say was, 'he is so sad.' The next night I found her in the same way, but she stood at the entrance to the nursery. She was gazing out towards the cave where the remains were with her head titled. I asked her again if she was okay, and she said, 'I promised.' It was not until the third night that she ventured out, and I followed her."

"What are you saying to her?" Endrir asked, looking at the memory.

"I asked her where she was going. I told her the Matron was going to be mad if we left. She said, 'he calls for help, and I must keep my promise.'"

"What promise?"

"I do not know, Endrir. You would have to ask her. She has never told me, and I have never asked. Some things…there are some things she keeps to herself," he said. Endrir nodded. "We reached the cave, but before we could explore, they caught us and sent us back to the nursery. She fought as you can see," Destined chuckled.

"Destined, that is Uzzod!"

"So it is," he said, laughing. "I never realized. All I remember is Shegur. It was she who carried me back. I remember her, Nihility's cries, and thrashing, trying to break free. I am sure Uzzod received some nasty scratches for that. Nihility was beside herself, but it was the same every night for five nights after. We would leave, and they would bring us back. It was not until the sixth night that we could get inside. I do not know if Shegur and Uzzod had just given up the chase or hoped she would find what she was looking for so desperately. On that sixth night, once we stepped in, I received a vision of two. One was trapped, and the other gone. I told Nihility what I saw, and she said, 'that is why he is sad. He cries because he wishes to live, yet he does not know how to do so without her. I promised.'

The memory shifted to a vision of a very young Nihility crying and speaking, but you could not hear her words. "What did she say, Destined?" Endrir asked.

He sighed. "Nihility said she could not find you, but she could feel you. She was distraught. I could not get her to stop crying. She said her chest hurt badly, and she just wanted to find you. Looking at it now, my first vision was mere days after my hatching, and it was of you. Nihility's abilities as an Empath came into power at the same time. She was crying because you were. She was hurting because you were. It was your pain she felt."

"Why are you touching the eggs? I thought you could sense life just by standing in a room," Endrir said, nudging him with his elbow.

"Yeah, yeah," he said, laughing. "I can now, but I was little then. Instinct guided me. Each time I touched a lifeless egg, it was distressing. There, you see! I found you!" he said happily.

"You look confused."

"I was. I was sensing life and death in your egg. I did not understand how that could be. Nihility helped me. She told me you were two in there; twins. She said she had seen your twin in the Dreaming."

"You are having a vision, Destined!" Endrir said, shocked. "At least I know you have always had that glazed look when they come on you."

"A past vision, and not one I really care to think about much," he said, wincing.

"You saw it, didn't you," Endrir whispered.

"Aye, I saw what happened to you. The rock had smashed your egg on her side," he said his voice breaking. He could see tears filling Endrir's eyes. "Would you like me to stop?"

"No. Please finish."

"It took us another two days before we figured out a way to

free you because no one would listen. The Matron would dissolve into tears anytime we mentioned the eggs there. The others thought we were mad, but Nihility was who they took it out on. Ergodi said she was mad and should be put down. Ivylth agreed. He thought her continuous escapes were proof of her madness. She was actually coming to see you. She would sit in front of your egg with her snout touching, whispering that we would save you."

"Destined," Endrir whispered as his memory showed three dragons berating a very frightened Nihility who cowered between the Matron's front legs.

"Aye, I know, but what could I do, Endrir! We had no one to listen to us! Not at first anyway," he said, laughing. "Britir."

"What about him?"

"You know that tree she likes on the Great Path?"

"Aye."

"We were sitting in it, and one day, Britir came by the tree. He had just returned from an assignment with Lady Azzi. He must have heard the tales or sensed our distress because he showed us a trick to cheer us up. He shifted for us into the form of that cloaked wanderer he likes."

"First time you had ever seen a dragon change forms?"

"Aye! It was amazing, but that is not all. He told us about the folk who look like mountain cats. He had been with them in their home. He told us of how they lived. He said they hunted the water like we hunt the land, and they prepared their food with fire and spice. As you can see, he promptly fed our dragoness."

"It is his fault she eats so much. He started it," Endrir said, laughing.

"Agreed, but do not tell her that. I asked Britir how they hunted the water, and he took a net woven from blades of grass and string. He said it tricked the fish that lived in the water and allowed them to be pulled out with ease."

"Why is she excited?" Endrir asked.

He grinned at Endrir. "She asked him if we could keep the

net, and Britir agreed. I think he knew what she had planned. I did not. However, just as all the nights before, I followed her. We took the net and placed it around one side of your egg. Together we pulled until we had your egg away from the danger of the rock bearing down on it. Once we did, I removed your sister first and placed her on an empty nest. Then Nihility and I freed you. You would not wake, though, so we carried you back to the nursery between us. You can see the shock on the Matron's face; they did not expect us to return with you."

"They saw she was right. Why did they not stop their torment of her?" Endrir asked as the memory played. He could see her cowering again as Ergodi and Ivylth stood with the Matron.

"They blamed her. They did not thank her. They blamed her for all of it, Endrir. They blamed her for the Shattering, and the hatchlings lost, not the Matron, but Ivylth and Ergodi. The Matron was relieved. Ergodi told everyone it was my keen sight that saw the truth. That I was the light to guide us through the destruction the Harbinger would bring us," he said, wiping his eyes.

"They know nothing about her. They never did," Endrir said.

"No, they do not," he said. He moved to close the orb, but Endrir stayed his hand.

"What are you doing there?" Endrir asked about the memory he could now see.

He wiped his eyes. He had not forgotten this part; it stuck in his memory more than others. "You lay in the Circle of Healing for some days after we rescued you. Nihility refused to leave your side. I, however, had another matter to attend to. I went back to the cave. I went back for the other half of you," he said, falling silent and letting his memories tell the rest.

He was just a hatchling, but he used his abilities like he could now. He pulled the net alone from around Endrir's broken egg.

He tugged at it in frustration until he had it where he wanted it. Then he laid down on the ground, staring at the nest where her lifeless body lay, a little unnamed dragoness with lavender scales and white stripes. Suddenly, the soft grass and straw that made the nest moved, and the dragoness with it. It floated onto the net. He gathered the ends in his claws and flew slowly out of the cave. He took her to a grassy area near the new nursery. He willed the land to open, and he placed the little dragoness inside with the net. He covered her with dirt with his own claws.

The memory changed, and he was back at the cave again. He was searching for something. He picked up two pieces of shell from Endrir's egg. He studied them outside in the sunlight. He touched his snout to them both, and the two pieces changed shape, forming twin dragons. One was the same purple as Endrir, the other lavender.

"Hers," he said. His voice broke, and he cleared his throat. "Hers I left on the rock I used to mark her place. Once the tree sprouted, Nihility moved it to hang from the branches. The other, well, I gave it to you," he said. The memory showed him placing the trinket next to a sleeping Endrir as Nihility watched. He had whispered in his ear before the orb went black.

"What did you say?"

"I said rest, join us, and we will love and care for you as she would have. That we would be your half to the whole. If we were not enough, then I hope this would be a comfort and a reminder of the time you shared with her, however brief," he said. Endrir stared at his hands with tears in his eyes. "I am sorry, Endrir. I am tired. Will the Watcher stand watch for a bit?"

"Yes, this Watcher will do his duty to protect the two he loves the most. Rest Destined. I will hunt while you do. Our dragoness will need to eat when she wakes, and so will you," Endrir said, standing.

Destined moved himself to the spot between Nihility's front leg and neck. He curled up next to her, resting his head on the soft part near her jaw. "Thank you, and I really missed you, my treasure," he said. He was asleep before he could say anymore.

CHAPTER TWENTY-SEVEN

"Do you believe the Farseer has told us everything?" Pimo asked.

"I believe he told us what he wished for us to know. Do you think you could find where he was, Ergodi?" Kuri asked.

"He hides his paths well, Kuri. You know this. I believe we may have another way."

"Are you going to enlighten us, old dragon?" Shegur asked.

"I thought it might be obvious, Shegur. The Farseer found the others by tracking their auras in the Between. It is a method taught to him by Master Sia, but Kuri can do it. Destined's presence in the Between lingers, as it always has. We did not know who to follow, but it seems the Farseer has answered that question for us," Ergodi explained.

"That is true, but I think the Farseer will be watching to see who comes and goes from the Between," Kuri said.

"Of course he will, Kuri. He would not be Destined if he did not. However, we are elders, and he knows we will be there searching for the others. I suspect he will venture in himself as well. While he seeks the other six, we will look for the mind-body of Ellot. It will have to wait until after the Ritual of Return, however. I should be able to find it using his remains. It must lie before the door of legend," Ergodi said.

"I am not sure if searching for this door of yours is the best course of action given Lady Nihility's display," Shegur said. "We should stick to the plan I gave you. We are close to finding the magic we need to mend Ivy and Pimo and solidify Petrall's existence. You wanted to show Sathea our true power, and I have provided us a way to do that without even using the Between."

Ergodi groaned. "I have no patience for the fits of emotional outbursts that the Harbinger is prone to," he said. "There is power in the Between, and we would do well to have it at our disposal before we march on those that ruin Sathea with their misguided beliefs."

"She is a Weaver and an Empath, two things we have not seen together in some time. Emotions are a part of everything she is. If you doubt that after what she displayed here, you are all fools," Ivylth said. "Maybe we are all the fools she believes us to be."

"You seem sure of that, Ivylth. Maybe the only fool is you for entertaining that spectacle of hers," Kuri said.

"Watch your tone, Kuri," Ergodi hissed.

"Sorry, Master Ergodi."

"That was no false show, Kuri," Shegur said. "She did indeed channel the Grand Lady Pax. I would know her voice anywhere. I am sure Ivylth and Pimo will agree. Also, let us not forget the appearance of the Black Flame. I know you were not hatched during her time, but those flames perished with her. There is no other dragon that can wield them. She was their creator."

"How did she learn such a thing when countless others before her have failed?" Pimo asked.

"It is curious, but I do not think it matters or interferes with our business," Ergodi said.

"I would not be so sure of that," Ivylth said.

"Ivy, do not start. Leave the fear of ghosts to Pimo," Ergodi said.

"I am not afraid of ghosts. I am afraid of vengeful spirits. Spirits who know the truth of the things we have done," Pimo hissed. "You should be too!"

"Shegur, what of Uzzod and Britir?" Ergodi asked, ignoring Pimo.

"What about them?" she asked with a yawn.

"Shegur."

"Uzzod does as I say. He will always do as I say. Britir grieves and couldn't care less about anything other than his precious Azzi."

"And Endrir?" Kuri asked.

"He will not remain here long. He never does," Shegur said. "Will you be able to continue collecting those things for me, Ivylth?"

"Nihility is none the wiser, and I would have her remain that way. As long as she does, then yes. If that should change, then no."

"A very non-answer, answer Ivy," Shegur said with a sigh.

"Regardless, it is an answer and the only one you will receive. If Nihility finds out about Pimo or me, there is no telling what she will do," Ivylth said. "She controls the Crystal of the Depths now, and that means I must tread carefully."

"Were you at least able to procure the other item I asked you for?" Shegur asked.

"Aye, and another to make sure Destined remains unaware of our movements. I will give it to you later," Ivylth said.

"What is this?" Ergodi asked.

"Our guarantee that things go according to our plan, Ergodi," Shegur said. "You do not need to worry."

Ergodi gave her a long look. "I see no need for us to change anything. Just be cautious in your movements. Ivy, I would have you see to the bodies of the fallen Walkers. We will hold vigil for Ellot's body. If any of the others should return, hold them and contact me. I would have them dealt with before the Farseer finds out," Ergodi said.

"The Farseer is distracted by the Harbinger, Ergodi. We would do well to scrub Mica's mind thoroughly before he returns. Arsu can keep watch," Kuri said.

"Does she obey you still?" Ergodi asked.

"Aye. Arsu is my obedient little pet."

"Make sure your pet keeps her affection for the Farseer in check. The last thing we need is her causing a scene with the Harbinger," Ergodi said. "And tell her to stop hiding from her duties at the Tower. Destined has noticed."

CHAPTER TWENTY-EIGHT

Iros had left him to guard this place so long ago he could no longer remember. For years it stood silent despite Ergodi's meddling. The spirits spoke, but there was quiet. There was peace. Then the Shattering occurred, and the serpent woke from her slumber. He could feel her lurking, not showing herself. He did not seek her out. He only kept watching the Between. Sia the Mindbreaker, the Watcher of the Between, left to do his duty by his master, Iros the Blender.

The Farseer thought he knew the pathways of the Between, but he knew them better. He knew what it really was, not what the mind wanted to see. A place of lingering. A place of illusions. The place where the lost dwelled in the serpent's belly. The true visage of the Between was Sathea. Old Sathea, before the short lifers, appeared from the mountain, and the trees spoke.

He walked as Destined had before him in his borrowed form. He had spent years among the trees in Emberwood Thicket, and his form paid homage to the Greenbark Elves that dwelled there among the leaves. He was a Son of Sathea, the Hidden Sun of Thyene and Magnus. He stood on the dirt pathway in his green and brown leathers designed to camouflage him among the trees. His amber eyes were alert, assessing the shadows that lay before him. His hair, once braided neatly and tied with red and black ribbons, sat hastily pulled on top of his head.

He sent a small orange bird before him as he entered. A yellow one perched on his shoulder. He walked deep into darkness until he could see the orange bird flittering in front of a door that hung from nothingness. He ran his hand over the wood. Burned into it was a closed lotus. The yellow bird on his shoulder chirped softly. "Lady Pax, you say. Is this her Weaver mark, Livy?" The bird chirped again. His hand moved to open it and the orange bird flittered madly in front of his face. He removed his hand. He could feel others lurking behind, but he also felt Ellot. "Well, sister, if I cannot go in, what do you expect me to do?" he said to the yellow bird. It chirped rapidly and loudly. "Do not yell at me, Livy Sightstealer! Stop treating me like I am still a fledgling. I'm a grown dragon!"

He stepped back and opened his hand. A small green bud sat in his palm. He tossed it, letting it fall in front of the door where it bloomed into an enormous orange flower with black lines streaming across its petals. He could see traces of Destined's aura all over the door and the path he had taken. The image of the Farseer appeared, hesitating in front of the door before opening it. "Damn it, Farseer," he mumbled. "Do you ever fucking listen to me!?" he said as he watched the image of Destined fade into nothing. He thought that was all there was to see until he saw Nihility.

"My world!" he gasped as he saw her. The little yellow bird chirped happily. "I know she is beautiful; back off, Livy. You have your own damn dragoness!" he hissed. The bird pecked at his ear, making him flinch. "You are a shit," he said, rubbing his ear. He watched as Nihility shifted into the beauty of her borrowed form. The bird chirped again, and he rolled his eyes. "I will not answer that. We are twins, but that does not mean we share everything. Seriously Livy?" he said.

Nihility touched the door and fell to her knees. He instinctively moved to her and stopped when his hand met air. The yellow bird chirped again. "Just don't, Livy. I do not want to hear it," he said. He heard her scream as a green orb linked to a red one swirled around her. He frowned. "Pieces of their minds, not their spirits," he mumbled. "Odd."

"Did you go inside my little dragoness?" he asked as he watched her on her knees. She went from shaking to calm. She stood and went through the door. "Oh Nihility, no," he said sadly. He was ready to turn away when he saw a purple flicker from the corner of his eye. He turned back and saw the image of Endrir, but the door had changed. Endrir's name stood out on it in bright green flames. The yellow bird ruffled its feathers and chirped again.

"You have got to be fucking kidding me," he said with a sigh as he watched Endrir open the door and fade away. "I could kill the both of you! What have you dragged my dragoness into now?!" he snapped. He turned to leave when the yellow bird on his shoulder shrieked and disappeared. A green aura surrounded him.

"You again," a silky female voice said. "You come here often, but you never speak. You can walk this place better than the Farseer does. Tell me, why does the Farseer not speak to me?"

"I do not know. Ask the Farseer yourself."

"I am asking you," she hissed. "You should not be rude. This is our first meeting."

"This is just the first time you have found the courage to speak, and I am not the Farseer's damn keeper."

"But she is," the voice said with laughter. A vague image of Nihility formed in the aura. "Who is she?"

"None of your business. Now fly off," he snapped.

"Everything in this place is my business, even you, dragon. Whoever she is, she is a foolish dragoness. So quick to enter places she has no business. Touching things she has no business touching. She should be more careful," she said.

"Was your ego always so fucking massive, or is this new? Is this what happens when your dragon sees your madness and locks you away?" he asked, grinning.

"Foul-mouthed dragon!"

He heard the hiss and felt her power build. "I see you," he whispered, releasing a flock of orange birds at her before pulling away and back to himself. He laughed nervously as he sat up in his home. "My mouth is going to get me killed one day."

"Only if Ygi does not kill you first," a voice beside him said. It was Jaydum, a dark blue dragon streaked with violet.

"How long was I gone, Jay?"

"Almost a day. She sent me to check on you."

"You mean she sent you here to yell at me," he said, shifting and stretching his legs.

"Glad you could save me the trouble by knowing you are in trouble," Jaydum said.

"I aim to please," he said sarcastically.

"Your foolishness has upset Ygi, Mindbreaker."

"I did not know she would go in there, Jaydum. I would not put her in danger, you know that."

"Aye, so does Ygi. She is more upset that you have not rushed your ass to see about your dragoness," Jaydum said, rising.

"I know. I know! It is complicated, Jay. Destined does not know. I am sure she has not told him. If she has not told him, then what am I to do? March in and declare she is mine."

"Why not? She is."

"No!" he shouted.

"Why? Help me understand so I can make the family understand, Sia," Jaydum said.

"Jay," he sighed.

"No, Sia. We have spent long enough watching the two of you float through life on a cloud of sadness and pain. Explain now!"

He took a deep breath. "I am Destined's teacher, Jay. He calls me Master with honor, and I have done nothing but take his dragoness."

"You don't really believe that jerboa shit, do you?" Jaydum asked, laughing.

"It's not jerboa shit," he mumbled.

"It most certainly is," Jaydum said, composing himself. "Destined and that Watcher can declare all they want she is theirs, but do they feel it? Did they feel it then? She did, you know."

"What do you mean?" he asked, frowning.

"I forgot you had stopped coming to the family fires by then," Jaydum said absently.

"Don't be cruel, Jay. They reminded me too much of what I lost."

"It was no jab, Mindbreaker. I said it because Nihility came and enjoyed them. She brought you back to them. It is why Terg lingered here on Petrall again for a time. I was there at that fire when those two broke her heart. Well, when the Watcher did, anyway."

"I don't understand."

"They left on some adventure, but before they did, the Watcher had his hands all over her, and she wanted him. He pushed her away for the Farseer," Jaydum said.

"Did she tell you this?" he asked. Nihility had never told him about it.

"Nay. She does not talk to me about such things. That is what she saves for Terg and Bendre. However, she was so heartbroken she sang into the big water in front of Ben's place. The flames of the fire showed us what happened. Azzi was alive then and beside herself with fury for what her Watcher had done. Ygi confirmed, of course. Did she not tell you?"

"No," he said.

"I can tell you that is the reason she does not like that Watcher. He should be worried. You know how Ygi gets," Jaydum said, chuckling. "Those two did not seem to want her as you did. They did not notice her, but you did, Sia. I'd say that makes her your dragoness."

"It still does not change the fact that I will not compete with them for her. I will not cause her suffering because of their anger that they did not know," he said.

"Nihility never hid the fact that she was your dragoness,

Mindbreaker. The only dragon she has ever kept a secret was Uzzod, and you both did that for a time. She has never hidden her love for you, Sia," Jaydum said, laughing. "Every Weaver that knows her knows you are her dragon. They still whisper about you even now. So why don't Destined and Endrir know already? Why have they not known for thirteen thousand years?"

"Because," he stopped and frowned. "I don't know."

"The only foolish dragon competing with other foolish dragons is you. I feel sorry for Nihility. That poor dragoness has done a better job of surrounding herself with fools than Ygi."

"Are you including yourself in that, Jay?"

"Do you not remember the shit Ben and I did to get Ygi's attention?" Jaydum asked.

He smiled and shook his head. "Vividly," he said. "Jay, I do not know how to fix what I've done."

"Simple, call her back to you."

"I fucked up, Jaydum! I can't just call her back after three-thousand years. I promised I would not hurt her, and I have!"

"Then face it and make up for it, Sia. Be a dragon!" Jaydum snapped. "I see why Livy and Ygi gave you so much shit over the years."

"Ouch."

Jaydum sighed. "I am sorry. That was cruel, but Sia, so is what you are doing to that sweet little dragoness."

"I know, but Destined and Endrir are family. I am trying to keep them together," he said, looking away.

"Family is not always easy, but we always find our way back to each other. You should know that. You were away from us for a long time, but you found your way back."

"Aye."

"I understand your feelings better than you think. I love Terg. I loved him for many years, but he was Lady Bysi's mate, and I, her student. I struggled with the respect I held for her and the love I hold for Terg."

"You have been with him a long time."

"I have, and I still question myself sometimes. However, I do not hurt him with my insecurities."

"I will speak to Nihility," he said.

"Good," Jaydum said, bobbing his head.

"Come on, we need to see Terg."

"What has happened?"

"The serpent moves freely in the Between, and I just pissed her off," he said, grinning.

"For Sathea's sake, Sia. You are as bad as Terg!" Jaydum said, rolling his eyes.

"Now that is a compliment! The nicest thing I have heard in a while, in fact. Come on. He will want to know what is going on."

They flew down the mountain into the forest beneath the Burning Wastes. It was a secret space they often met at when they wanted to share information away from Petrall. It was buffered by the fire flow from the mountain above and hidden deep in thick cloud cover formed when the heat from the fire flow met the small lake at the bottom of the Mountain.

"Mindbreaker, I should rend you in two!" Bendre snapped at him as he landed.

"Do it later, Ben. Where's Terg?" he asked.

"I am here," Terg said, appearing from the large cave at the base of the mountain. "You went into the Between?"

"Aye. The barrier has been found," he said.

"Not funny, Mindbreaker," Terg said, rolling his eyes.

"I am serious, Terg," he said.

"Who found him?" Terg asked with a sigh.

"The Farseer," he mumbled.

"What happened to you fucking watching him, Mindbreaker? For Sathea's sake! I told you to be cautious when he got the damn journal from those short lifers that live at the base of the mountain, the Order of Zal. Does anyone listen to me?" Terg shouted.

"I was cautious. Destined asked, and I told him the basics, that the barrier protects us against demons. He does not search for it. More so because Ergodi wants him too. Destined is cautious Terg; foolish, but cautious," he said.

"Just the door or the barrier?" Terg asked.

"I believe both. I did not enter to see for myself."

"Why not?"

"I saw something," he said, looking away.

"You saw Nihility," Bendre said.

"Aye. I saw Nihility. She must have forced him back to himself," he said.

"So, what Ben said was true. The Harbinger can enter that place?" Terg asked.

"Aye, but I did not teach her! If I had known, I would have told her it was not wise."

"Of course, you did not teach her," Bendre snapped. "The Farseer did. I knew the minute she said it. However, she would have known the danger had her dragon been at her side."

"Bendre, please," he said. "Regardless of who I am to her, she is a damn dragoness. She does as she pleases."

"But she would heed the words of her first mate, Sia!" Bendre said.

"Shut up the both of you!" Terg shouted. "The Harbinger went into the Between to bring the Farseer back because he was gone too long. Is that the right of it?"

"Aye," he said.

"Why?" Terg asked quietly as he stared at him.

"What?" he asked, looking down at the ground.

"Why, Mindbreaker!?" Terg shouted. "Why did she go, and not you!?"

"I called her back," he said, barely above a whisper.

Terg huffed; smoke wafted from his nostrils. "You called her back to retrieve her mate but did not go get him yourself. Sia…" he said, shaking his head.

"I know. I know I fucked up Terg! I was trying to keep an eye on Ergodi and Kuri as well. Something was off about everything. I did not want to leave any others vulnerable with the Farseer in that place or risk telling him more than he should know."

"You wanted to test Nihility to see if she would come back if you called her," Bendre said. "Stop your damn lies."

"It is not a lie! Well, not all of it. Yes, I knew she would return, but I also had to keep an eye on those two," he said, frustrated. "Not everything I do is about her. I have a duty!"

"What have they done that has made you suspicious of them, Sia," Jaydum asked.

"They've been in the Between far more often than they should, as of late with Shegur," he said.

"Little Red?" Terg asked, frowning.

"I think she prefers 'Red Lady' now, Terg," Jaydum corrected. Terg rolled his eyes at him.

"Aye," he said. "I was trying to find out what they were doing when Destined decided he would go see for himself. I did not even realize he was in there until the Mindhunter came to get me."

"Send a bird to Ygi and have her listen. I want to know what they are plotting this time," Terg said. Sia quickly closed his eyes, and a yellow bird flittered away quickly towards the top of Petrall. "Now, the Farseer, why did he need to find a door he has never searched for?" Terg asked.

"Walkers have been going missing in the Between over the last year," he said. "I saw no pattern. It appeared random. Sometimes it would be novices. Others trained Walkers. All of them spaced in odd intervals."

"You found nothing, Sia?" Jaydum asked, frowning.

"No. I followed their auras, but the Farseer does not know.

I did not want to give him false hope that he could find them because I knew he would do something foolish like spend too long in that fucking place. I followed them, and they all just ended abruptly into nothingness."

"Ergodi did not search?" Jaydum asked.

"He went in with Kuri. They claimed to have searched, but they were not searching for the missing they were looking for something else. I thought it may have been the door. You know those two have wasted themselves on that endeavor, but now I am not sure."

"Explain, Sia," Bendre said.

"Their paths seemed too constant to be searching. They knew where they were going."

"But what of the door? How did the Farseer find it?" Terg asked.

"The last two to go in, Ellot and Mica, both from the hatch of the Shattering. They found the door, or the door found them. Terg, something was strange."

"Strange how?"

"I saw Destined and Nihility enter, but just before I was about to leave, I saw the Watcher too, but the door had changed. It held his name."

"What damn Watcher?" Terg asked, exasperated.

"Endrir," Bendre said with a sigh. "Endrir the Broken. What on Sathea have they got her into this time?"

"The Watcher who lost his twin?" Terg asked, frowning.

"Aye."

"And Nihility carries Pax with her?" Terg asked, looking at Bendre.

"Aye, I saw her clearly," Bendre said. "She speaks to Nihility, but Terg they are almost one in their existence."

"Truly!?" Jaydum asked, shocked.

"She is still magnificent, Jay," Bendre said, grinning. "I do not know how, but it is almost as if she has found her twin spirit in Nihility."

"Not her spirit. Part of her mind. I saw it clearly while I was in there," he said.

"I think you have all lost your fucking minds," Terg said, laughing.

"Terg, this is not the time for jokes, my dragon," Jaydum said.

"But it is. Ygi calls to me after not hearing from her in years! Then these two show up to tell me that the Farseer has found my mate in that horrible place he left me for, and my best friend now rides around as some spirit in the body of a dragoness I did a shit job of protecting! If this is not a joke, Jay, I do not know what is."

"I would not joke about something like that to you, Terg. It is cruel," he said.

Terg looked at him with tears in his eyes. "You do not understand Mindbreaker." He sighed and laid himself down. "I was there the day she disappeared, you know."

"Who?" he asked.

"Lady Pax," Jaydum said, laying down next to Terg. He nudged him until Terg raised his head, allowing Jay to lie his head on his feet.

"But you said…"

"Be still, Sia. Give him a moment," Bendre mumbled.

"She called me to the meadow outside of Wom. Xtyia Forest, the one I created for her. She asked me to help her create an illusion of herself, but it was jerboa shit. She could have done that herself. She called me out there to say goodbye. She was tired of living. Losing Iros was just too much, and she had nothing but me to fill the gap. Me, the dragon grieving for Laz, Bysi, and Livy. I should have fought harder to get her to stay, but I…I wanted to join her. I was going to until I thought of Jay and the rest of you. How much pain you would have if I was gone too."

"What did she do?" he asked.

"Laz is the barrier Sia. His body, his mind, his soul, is that barrier. But something was missing from him when I went in with Pax. I do not know what, but a part of him was gone. I could feel it. Pax cursed that barrier. She said, 'Terg, it took two to make it, it will take two to break it,' and she did just that, but she took that flame with her."

"What does that mean, two to make it, two to break it?" he asked.

"They were twins, Sia," Bendre said. "That is what she did, right Terg? To break that barrier, it would take a set of twins to do so."

"Aye, but whoever did would be consumed by the Black Flame. Pax had no intention of letting anyone destroy that barrier and walk away with their lives. You know how she was," Terg said.

"Then why is she with Nihility?" he asked.

"Laz is dying," Terg said. "I realized when I stood there in that space that what I felt when he left me to that place was not his death, but his absence. He still lived. This last time when the Maiden Moon went into hiding, I felt pain. It was not excruciating pain but a deep ache. I felt drained as if something was pulling at me."

"You feel him still," he said in awe. "He shared himself with you!"

"Aye. Laz is dying. If the Farseer has found him, it means she knows where it is now. The most we can hope for is that she stays in the Between. Someone or something knew not only how to find that barrier but also how to break it. Sia, Iros charged you with watching the whole of the Between because he never knew where that door was. Only Laz, Pax, and I knew its location. I shared that information with you the moment I found out what Iros had done in charging you as the Watcher of the Between," Terg said.

"I never said anything, Terg," he said. "I never even told Nihility the truth of it. She knows I watch, but nothing more."

"I know, Sia," Terg said with a sigh. "I know, but what you do not know is I am the one who helped both twins work their magic. Pax did not know what I had done. Laz made me promise not to tell her, so she would not take her grief out on me. I helped him with the spell work for that barrier and to hide the space."

"From demons. Iros told me that is why he did it," he said.

"He was not hiding that space from demons, Sia Mindbreaker. He hid that space from her!" Terg shouted.

"But we were always told demons were a threat," he said, frowning.

"They are a threat to Sathea only regarding the Great Balance," Terg said. "She is a threat to all of us. She is a creature seeking dominion over Sathea with the power to do so, the one who would truly be the mother to us all. Laz did not tell me; I figured it out because of Pax. She was afraid before she left us. She told me about a serpent in the dreams of some short lifers. Dreams she could not weave. I know you do not understand what that means, Sia, but for a Weaver who has consumed the essence of the dream tree Aconi, no dream is untouchable."

"Terg! Nihility said she saw the serpent surrounding Destined in the dream sand of the Daughters of Ote!" Bendre said.

"A warning then, for both Nihility and the Farseer. Sia, has she shown any interest in the Farseer when he travels that place?"

"I would have said no, but she spoke to me for the first time while I was just there. She asked about the Farseer," he said, frowning. "Why would she be interested in Destined?"

"He is a prophet, Sia, just as Rona was," Jaydum said.

"So what? I still do not see why she would care, especially if he does not even acknowledge her in that place," he said.

"Jezzar," Terg said with a look of disgust, "has waited for years untold to return to Sathea. She has plotted and schemed. I do not know how, but she calls those who worship her in their dreams. She still weaves, you see. Pax saw it, and it frightened her. Instead of discovering the truth, she gave up. I do not blame her. Her grief was strong. However, it left the task to me to find out what I could about the first Weaver; tales I have shared with all of you," Terg said. "The door is connected to her, and I believe she is connected to the demons Laz tried to keep away."

He frowned, trying to see the connection. "She was there when I went to check on the door. I did not feel her at all; Livy did, though," he said, thinking about the confrontation.

"What did she say?" Terg asked.

"She wanted to know why the Farseer did not acknowledge her, and she wanted to know who Nihility was," he said with a chuckle. "My mouth may have upset her."

"Good. Keep Nihility out of that place, Mindbreaker. Any interest Jezzar shows in that dragoness cannot be good," Terg said. "She knew of Pax as well but showed no interest in her to my knowledge. Strange she would be concerned with Nihility's presence there, but if Pax has found Nihility, it is my fault," Terg said. "I made a promise, but…"

"Terg, what happened to Nihility is not your fault. You do not live on Petrall. How would you have known what she was or what Ivylth would do?" Bendre asked. "The fault lies with me."

"I promised Pax that if another Empath like her ever showed up on Petrall, I would care for them. I would give them everything she never had. Surround them in love so they would not feel so lost in darkness, but I found Nihility too late."

"Wait, just wait. What are you two going on about?" Sia asked.

"Ivylth abused Nihility for years before Terg found out," Bendre said. "He heard Nihility crying in the Dreaming and followed."

"I found Ivylth and Ergodi…Savagery like you have never seen to one so tiny," Terg said. "I asked her if it had happened before, and she said that was her lessons with Ivylth to curb the 'fragility of the empath' and keep her free from madness."

"Show me," he said.

"Sia," Bendre said.

"Show me now!" he snapped. Terg lowered his snout to him, and they touched briefly. He pulled back with a hiss. "You said they were cruel to her, Terg! You did not tell me all of that! She did not tell me that!" he shouted. "Why would you keep that from me? Why would she not tell me?!"

"Because she believes she is stronger than her past, Sia. You did that. You saw her," Terg said. "You did not pity her or see her as weak. All you saw was a beautiful dragoness."

"Fuck!" he shouted in anguish. "Why did Nihility save Ivylth then? Why did she not just let that miserable old dragoness die in the Dreaming?"

"Because Nihility is kind," Jaydum said. "Jessa...the Matron said the same. She is kind despite the unkindness they show her. She is a mark of their failures and their guilt."

"She is everything Ivylth wanted to be and more," Bendre said.

"That is why the Shadow Wraiths exist. That is the darkness she keeps locked away!" he realized.

"Aye. After Nihility saved Ivylth, Terg and I agreed she needed to be pushed in her abilities," Ben said. "She needed to protect herself without depending on us."

"How long did they torture her?" he asked.

"Three-thousand years," Terg whispered.

"She met you, and I knew it was time. I tried to teach her to use that darkness as a weapon with her fire. Pax did it, and she did not have the advantage of flame control as Nihility does. However, I underestimated the damage Ivylth had caused," Bendre said.

"You underestimated?!" he said, huffing smoke at Bendre. "Saying you underestimated is a fucking understatement. I saw that darkness with my own eyes. It was not just the physical wounds Ben! Ergodi rifled around in her mind with little care for the damage he caused. The only thing keeping it from consuming her is us! She uses the fucking Farseer to keep it locked away!" he screeched.

"That is why you do not fight for her!" Jaydum exclaimed.

"No! Yes. Well, it's part of it," Sia sighed. "It took me days to fix the damage Ergodi had caused," he said, looking up at Bendre with sadness in his eyes. "Days, Ben. I had to repair and then teach her to keep those defenses strong."

"When you kept her from Weaver Circle," Bendre said. "I didn't realize, Sia."

"Because you did not ask. Nihility was my dragoness. She was mine to protect, and you and Terg made your plans without even speaking to me first. You did not even explain your intentions to her. She tried to tell you, and when you would not listen, she reacted. Those hounds were her reaction," he explained. "Her heart and her mind screamed for you to not make her confront the darkness."

"You trained her and them," Terg said.

"Of course! My dragoness hungers for knowledge!" he said with pride.

Terg smirked at him. "Yes, she does, and that fact alone leaves her in constant danger."

"Do you know where she is, Ben?" he asked.

"She is with Destined and Endrir at that cave they used to hide in when they were younger. The one under the Jagged Cliffs," Sako said, emerging from the trees. "Ygi is speaking with Great Mother, Bendre."

"What has happened?" Bendre asked.

"Nihility channeled the Grand Lady at the Council Meeting, and she used the Black Flame. She exhausted herself, though."

"Did you tell them to keep her safe, Sako?" he asked.

"I did no such thing. If those two cannot keep Nihility safe, it is not my problem," she said.

"Sako!"

"You keep her safe, Mindbreaker!" she shouted at him, huffing smoke. "Ben, those other two were lurking in the Dreaming. Raravarra found them near Hynro. Great Mother asks that you speak to him."

"It just keeps getting better," Terg mumbled.

"Why Hynro?" he asked, frowning.

"I suppose that is what Great Mother wishes me to find out, Mindbreaker," Ben said.

"Is the Between secure, Sia?" Terg asked.

"No. I have already told the Farseer to not walk alone, but I will hammer the point home now that I know she is far more interested in him than she should be."

"Something smells on the peak," Jaydum said.

"I could not agree more," Bendre said.

"It is not a smell. It is what Laz believed would happen. If Jezzar lurks freely, then someone has called to her. You said Ergodi and Kuri were in the Between searching for something, find out what Sia, and keep an eye on your dragoness, please. I am going to go speak with Magnus," Terg said, rising.

"She is not…"

"Finish that sentence, and I will kill you where you stand, whelp. You will need more than Livy to keep my jaws from your throat. She is, and she will always be. Enough with your shit, Mindbreaker!" Terg snapped.

"Aye," he mumbled.

"While you're at it, Sia, talk to your other mate, Stormbringer," Terg said.

"Terg!" he hissed.

"None of us here give a shit, Mindbreaker," Terg said, rolling his eyes. "I would have him using keener eyes on that council from now on. I am sure Magus will be waiting to hear from him as well. Jaydum, you go with Bendre. You know how Hynro can be," Terg said.

"And leave you alone with Magnus?" Jaydum asked, giving Terg a look.

"This is not a trip for play, my jealous dragon. I will be back as soon as I can. Stay with Ben, please. Lady Sako, darling, go to Weaver Circle. Collect Ygi and make your presence known. I would know what Ivylth and Ergodi are up to," Terg finished.

CHAPTER TWENTY-NINE

Endrir covered Destined with his cloak and stood watching him for a moment. He had rocked him more than he had let on. Why had he asked him to tell him that story after all these years? He was chasing something that lingered just out of his reach and believed Destined, and Nihility held the answer. He left Petrall to find space and time to think. It's what he felt he needed to quell the frustration and anger gnawing at him. He removed his vest, folding it neatly, before heading out of the cave. Cold air caressed his bare chest as he extended his arm, a bow appearing and the arrows strapped to his back. He would hunt as a short-lifer, not a dragon.

The night was cloudless with the moon high above. He had smelled a pack of jerboa earlier that would do for a fine meal. He stood for a time, sniffing the air and feeling the path of the wind. He reached up and absently played with the necklace he wore; it held the trinket Destined had given him that day. He toyed with it endlessly in this form when he was sorting through his thoughts. He made his way towards the tree line that hid the mouth of the river the jerboa often came to drink from.

He believed that Nihility had given it to him. She was the first he saw when he woke sometime later. She was curled around him with her head resting beside his. He was disoriented and consumed by a feeling of emptiness. The only comfort he found was the black dragoness around him. He believed her to be his twin in his confusion. It was not until he calmed down that she explained that his twin had died and was alone. He fell in love with her at that moment. He believed she was his dragoness, even if they did not share their heart of hearts, but there was a strain between them.

He knew the reason for that strain, but he denied it

vehemently to himself and to Destined. He did not have the spine to admit the truth. He chose Destined over Nihility. His choice hurt her, and then he had spent years rubbing that hurt raw with his actions. Nihility was never easy for him. He could never find his words to tell her how he felt about her. She did not help him either, which frustrated him more. She was an Empath. She should know how he felt. She was his dragoness, and he didn't need a damn dance to prove it. He frowned as he came to the river. He had spent a day here with her long ago.

She had refined her form and asked him for his approval. He more than approved. His whole body ached to touch her. He had already planned to kiss her that day. He had finally worked up the courage to tell her how he felt. He kissed her, and that kiss blossomed into more. He could still close his eyes and feel the heat of her against him. He could smell the scent of wildflowers and fire that always surrounded her. Her arms around his neck and in his hair as he touched her body. He could hear the sounds of her moans and the breathless way she called his name. Then Destined called to him. Destined called, and he left her there. He remembered the sadness on her face. A sadness in her eyes that remained every time she looked at him.

She didn't understand. Destined was his mate. They had done as mates do for thousands of years by that time. He loved Destined because he was there for him, more so than Nihility. Destined endured his tears and fears, and for two years, he had neglected their relationship. He had been a shit mate for two years. He left his dragon, his Sun, to Petrall and the burden of his position without a second thought.

He had convinced himself that he did not need them anymore. He had kept this last assignment long for that reason. Usually, he would leave for three months, always returning. This time he remained in Tresai for almost two years. He was trying to break away from them. The pain of not having Nihility as mate and his relationship with Destined drowned him. He had to get away. He was coping, trying to live without them by throwing himself into his work. He believed he was fine until he heard her call him. Then something in his mind shattered. All the feelings he had for her crashed down around him. He felt a need for her and Destined. Coming back had done nothing but make him more confused. He sighed and calmed himself. He would focus on the meal he needed to return with for them both.

CHAPTER THIRTY

"Youngling, you must wake!" Pax shouted.

She stirred slowly, then sat up with a gasp. "Where am I?" she asked, looking around. "Sia!" she called as their home appeared around her.

"Nihility focus!" Pax shouted.

She shook her head and turned. She was in her mind again. "Why am I here? What has happened?"

"You used too much power channeling me! Hurry and place your barrier back on this one!" Pax shouted.

She sprang up and forced her barrier back into place. Ana was angry and screaming. "Pax, what is going on?" Pax was huffing smoke on the nest in her mind. She must have been using what she could to hold Ana. "I exhausted myself again," she said with a sigh.

"We are in no danger that I can sense," Pax said.

"Aye, I sense nothing, but I cannot rouse myself either. What happened?"

"I was ill-prepared for your feelings towards the council. It was like fuel for that one," Pax said, nodding towards Ana. "When you accessed my power, instead of just pulling for my spirit, you brought forth the Black Flame too. The message was passed, but it drained you. That one exploited your anger."

"I have never channeled anything before Lady Pax. I do not have that kind of power."

"I am sure my presence here made it easy for you. However, you did not need to use the Black Flame. It was dangerous, youngling."

"I did not mean to. I only meant to show your form in my flames. Something shifted at the last minute and," she trailed off, struggling to remember.

"Your anger with the council grew, and the Black Flame blossomed. That is the nature of the flame you now wield, Nihility. Ana was able to gain a foothold and come forward for a moment before you fell unconscious."

"The Black Flame feeds off anger?" she asked.

"You said you know Terg. He never told you the tale of the Black Flame?"

"No. We... He..." she stopped, frowning.

"The Black Flame is born from and feeds on those emotions that feed anger. It burns until you command it not to. I created it from my anger and grief while I sat deep in the Depths of the Dreaming, and I have now passed it to you."

"What is it exactly? I felt myself wield fire as any dragon would until that last moment. At that moment, there was power; magic. That is not the way of a dragon's flame. We use fire without such power requirements or restrictions."

"An Empath Nihility, a true Empath, is the only one who could wield the Black Flame. The power you felt was your own magic. What has happened to you, Nihility the Harbinger?" Pax asked quietly.

She looked up at Pax, and tears filled her eyes. "Nothing," she mumbled.

"Nihility," Pax said with a sigh. "I was an Empath like you. I know we did not grow the same. The Council of Elders would do whatever I said without question in my time. Their lack of action and conviction to change Petrall angered me. Beyond that, I did not have to suffer them. My pain was from grief, so much grief from war and losing so many. Laz and Iros were the last of what I had. I needed to deal with those emotions. Grief will consume you if you allow it for any other being on Sathea. For the Empath, the threat of it swallowing you is much greater," Pax said.

"It is not grief," she said.

Pax looked at her a moment. "You do not have control of

the Black Flame yet. It can be controlled, but it can only be done by one who truly understands the emotions that fuel it. Understands them and wields them. Understanding emotions are what we Weavers do, all Weavers. It is how we can aid and understand the dreamer. Mastering those emotions, learning to wield them like we would our own flame is what we as Empaths do. We do not look to eradicate their existence like Watchers. We do not look to balance and control them as Walkers do either. We seek to become one with those emotions. Empaths can find a deeper level of understanding of emotions than others. We understand that rage may mask sadness, or joy can mask anger."

"Master Terg saved me."

"At least you did not say he tried to seduce you," Pax said, chuckling.

She smiled, but it did not feel genuine. "Ergodi would restrain me, Ivylth would hurt me, and Pimo would heal me, so no one knew what she had done. It went on for years until Master Terg found me."

"He kept his promise to me then," Pax said, reaching down and nuzzling her. "To protect the one like me if she ever hatched on the peak again."

"You were close?"

"Very close," Pax said with a smile. "He was the one dragon who I could truly be myself without judgment and fear."

"He was your mate then?"

"Only in his dreams," Pax said, making her laugh. "He was my best friend. I had a mate, two in fact. One I shared my heart of hearts with, Iros; and one I did not, Verganeau."

"There is a forest that has that name."

"As there should be! I named it!" Pax said with pride.

"Destined holds my heart of hearts, and I hold his. Sia is my dragon."

"What of the other? Endrir,"

"He belongs to Destined," she said sadly.

"We will come back to that lesson, youngling. When you are ready. For now, the Black Flame."

"I understand emotions, more than I want to sometimes," she said.

"Your understanding is not the barrier we have to your use of the flame, Nihility. It is what you hide from even yourself, and it is her," Pax said, looking at the orb holding Ana. "She is an anomaly even to me. Half demon and half Warida; somehow, she amplified your feelings of anger, and it pulled her forward. You must learn more about her and her abilities."

"I am not in the mood to speak to her right now," she said.

"Find the mood, dragoness!" Pax snapped.

She flinched. "Yes, Lady Pax."

"Nihility, I know she was cruel, unnecessarily cruel. I suspect it was because of me. You suffered her anger towards me."

"But Lady Pa…"

"I am not excusing her behavior in the slightest youngling. That dragoness will pay if it is the last thing I do. However, right now, she is not my concern; you are. I would have you wield the flame better than even I did. I would have you stand in the face of anyone who seeks to harm you, not in fear, but knowing that you are their demise. That you are dragoness!" Pax said sternly. She nodded as her tears fell. "But first, you must deal with the other in your mind."

"Yes, Lady Pax," she said, sniffling.

"Exercise caution, Nihility. You are host to two separate conscious beings for the moment. I lack the power to do more than amplify your abilities. Perhaps because they are so like my own. The Black Flame burns any and everything in its path until there is nothing left but ash. The strength of the flame is directly related to your feelings. Ana is either tied to those feelings or drawn to them. When it is not fully expressed, the flame can turn upon you, as it almost did before I placed my barrier back on her. Your body grew hot enough to smolder the ground. I do not know what Ana's presence does to you, and that is something you must determine whether or not you are in the mood."

She was embarrassed. She was so drawn in her own feelings she did not factor in the demon in her mind. If Ana were feeding off her anger, she could unwittingly cause devastation. She was Empath, emotions flowed through her continuously, and not all of them were her own. She sat, trying to think it through.

"You said that kindness may prove useful with her. Maybe you should explore that first. Learn who and what she is," Pax said.

Nihility felt Pax pull her consciousness back. She knew Pax was still there, but it was faint. She moved over to Ana in the darkened orb. "Ana, I would speak with you," she said after she lowered the barrier. Ana's breathing was still ragged, but it seemed she was trying to calm herself. "I do not know if it will work for you, but I can help ease the pain if you need."

Ana stared at her. She could feel her fear and struggle. Ana must have seen something in her eyes because her demeanor changed, and she nodded her head. She touched the orb, and the barrier fell. A faint blue glow surrounded Ana as she hummed softly. Ana's shoulders slumped. She fell to her knees with a look of shock on her face.

"It is the magic of the Dreaming," Ana said, barely above a whisper.

"Aye, I am a Weaver."

Ana looked up at her with tears in her eyes. "My kind uses a spell similar to this, but not for the purpose you did. It is how the dreamer is lured deeper into the deep dreams."

"Aye. It is where I got the idea to use it for another purpose. The basis of the spell is to bring calm."

"I did not know you could do such a thing."

"I am a Weaver. I am tied to the Dreaming as much as the Warida."

"Why do you help me?" Ana asked, frowning.

"Why not? Ana, neither of us wanted this to happen, but from what little I understand, you and I are stuck with each other until the Black Flame finishes its task. I do not understand why, but that does not stop me from showing you compassion or concern."

Ana touched her hand to her chest. "It burns here," she whispered.

"It is where the flame lies."

"Compassion is not a thing my kind understand," Ana said. "It is not something I have experienced."

"Demons or Warida?"

"Are we not the same to you?"

"No, Ana, you are not the same. You may be a demon to the dreamers you haunt as Warida, but you are not just a demon. You are both."

"You were strong. Stronger than I expected. I was frightened," Ana said, looking away.

"I will take that as a compliment. A dragoness prides herself on her fierceness. However, that is not all that I am," she said.

"No. It is not. You say things I have never understood. Compassion, concern, and love are not common emotions to my people. Warida knows fear, but all emotions are simply food, fuel to sustain life, and give power. Demons deal in only chaos."

"That leaves you in an awkward place. I thought Warida feed on all emotions, and the purer, the better. I would think that your prison would be an everlasting meal for you," she said. "I have seen them kill those consumed by their dreams of lust and love."

"You are an interesting Weaver," Ana said with a laugh. It was an oddly guttural sound. "You know much of the Warida, but you are right. I am in an awkward place, as you say. I cannot feast as my mother's kind would on every emotion, only some, but I feel them all. The only reason your prison is a perfect trap for me is not because of the emotions you use but because of you.

A Weaver who protects these emotions," Ana said, pointing at the ring that floated around her. "The emotions you hold outside of this, however, are a temptation. The flame grew from here," she said, pointing at her chest.

They sat in silence as she thought over Ana's words. Her own emotions were always sacred to her. They were hers and hers alone.

"The one you call Destined has troubled sleep," Ana said, breaking their silence.

She lowered her head and looked at Ana closely. "How would you know that?"

"I can see through your eyes when you do not occupy that space."

"What space?"

"This space."

"You mean when I am sleeping?"

"Yes, but only deep sleep like now. During deep sleep, you do not occupy this space. You are here instead. It allows me to see what occurs on the outside. I am sure it is the same for the Grand Lady. Who is the other?" Ana asked quickly.

She did not respond right away. She was processing what Ana had said. It was dangerous for her to have that kind of access if she was incapacitated. She had exhausted herself before. It was the only time she truly slept; Weavers did not sleep. Sleep only came if the Weaver exhausted themselves from the overuse of their magic. Even then, it was not actual sleep. They hovered in the branches of Aconi, the Great Tree of the Dreaming, resting. She would need to be careful wielding the Black Flame and using her powers.

"What other?"

"The one who walks in shadows."

"He is mi… He is a friend."

"He is troubled. Deeply troubled, and in danger," Ana said.

She felt a flash of anger from Ana. "Ana, can you explain to me how you came to me?"

"It was out of necessity. You were near, and I could not take Destined. He was too strong. If I had touched him, I would have been nothing. I was burning. I still burn. I had hoped to stop the pain by taking another. You were stronger than I perceived. I misjudged because you did not sense me until I tried to push forward. Your focus was Destined."

"Why did you come?"

"Freedom. I had hoped to use you to escape, but I traded one prison for another. However, this one suits me better. I am safe here."

"Ana, are you ready to tell me your real name?"

"Not yet, Weaver. Maybe next time we speak. I grow tired now."

Nihility did not let the brush off bother her; she could feel Ana's fatigue. Instead, she nodded and place the barrier back but did not darken the surrounding orb. Reminding herself that, despite her discomfort, kindness was better, she left Ana in peace.

"Lady Pa…" she said before a scream ripped her out of her thoughts and broke her heart. She tried to wake herself to help him. "Destined!" she shouted. She felt her body jerk, but nothing more.

"He dreams, youngling."

"He does not dream like others, Lady Pax! He visits his fondest memories, ones that bring him peace. That was not the scream of a memory! He is afraid."

"Then it is a vision, Nihility. Regardless, you cannot help him. It is useless for you to try. Your body is not ready to wake," Pax said.

Pax was right. Her body felt sluggish. It needed rest, even if her mind did not. She heard him speaking to her. "It was just a bad dream. I am going to go for a bit of air, my love. I will return before you wake," he said. She felt no comfort from his words. He saw something that upset him, and he wanted her comfort.

"He needs me, Pax," she said, pleading.

"You need rest, Nihility Harbinger. Let the other look after him."

"Endrir," she whispered. He must still be with them. If he was, then Destined would be safe. Endrir would make sure nothing happens to him. "Why can she access my mind and body? I am not comfortable with that at all. What happens if I fall unconscious again?"

"It will not happen again, Nihility. You do not need to worry about that. She was able because you and I were occupied at the Courtyard of the Moon. Your channeling me provided her space. It will not be an issue again," Pax said.

"You do not trust her."

"No. My trust is earned and not easily given. It is a lesson I learned a long time ago. I do not expect you to be the same."

"Lady Pax, something provides her nourishment."

"Aye. Ana is not as weak as she was before."

"I noticed when I used the spell to bring her inner calm. I also reinforced the barrier you used to hold the Black Flame with my own," she said, laying down in front of Pax.

"How?"

"It is a Weaver barrier, well, the base of it is. You layered it with other spells, but at its core, it is a Weaver barrier like the one we use to imprison those who take too much from the dreamer in the Dreaming. I changed it," she explained. Pax stared at her long enough to make her shift uncomfortably. "Did I do something wrong?" she asked, looking away.

"Stop cowering to me, Nihility Harbinger. I will not harm you, and you are dragoness. Hold yourself, even in your own mind, as such," Pax said. She raised her head to look at Pax. "You are a gifted Weaver, perhaps more than I realized, despite Bendre's words telling me as much. Not even some of my brightest, like Ygi, could have seen the core of my magic," Pax said. She did not know how to respond. She was unaccustomed to praise. "You are more than capable of controlling the Black Flame. Maybe even better than I did. However, you cannot hold her with a barrier forever. Time wears magic like a river can wear a rock. You will need to expel her."

"I do not know, Lady Pax. She has no desire to leave. She said she traded one prison for another. I do not know what she means by that, but I do not think I have to spend much energy trying to find out either. I do not even think I have to worry about expelling her. She still burns."

"Hence my dilemma. Ana cannot stay with you forever, nor can I. When she goes, I believe I will as well. The seal I left to hide the door will disappear too. My intentions with my spell have gone far off course of what I had planned."

"What was your intention, Lady Pax? I would know in case we need it again. That door will not fade away with you."

Pax lowered her head and studied her for a long time. "Looking at you, I do not know if it is time's way of being cruel or kind, Nihility."

"What?"

"I am afraid for you. I have been since I saw you in that place. Not because you are weak, but because you are strong. I will tell you, but I require a promise that you do not repeat my mistakes. Do what you did with the barrier and modify," Pax said.

"I promise Lady Pax."

"I gave myself up that day in that space while Terg stood beside me. I cursed us both that day. I cursed him into carrying the secret of what I had done. For myself, I became the weapon my twin could wield. Should something happen to his life barrier, extinguishing what remained of him, my spell would trigger. I would do to them, as they had tried to do to Laz; latch on and take over. I designed the barrier that you sensed in Ana to hold the demon who came through Laz's life barrier while I made my attack. However, I did not word it for any demon. I warded myself into my brother's spell work so that it would trigger if one that was as strong as the one inside my twin's mind came through. I sealed what remained of myself and the Black Flame in that life barrier," Pax said.

"Lady Pax," she said, crying.

"Why are you sad, Nihility?"

"You sealed away your entire being, mind, body, and soul. That is what you are telling me. That is why you wanted me to promise not to do the same. You sealed yourself away!" she said with tears streaming down her snout. "They all lied to me! Those that remember you, Lady Ygi, and…they lied! You did not die peacefully on the edge of Xtyia Forest! You do not linger in the Dreaming! You died in the Between! You were who I aspired to be! Those stories were all I had to cope with all the misery I endured!"

Pax hummed loudly, cutting off her cries. "Then their words were not lies, youngling. They gave you hope, and if that is what I left behind, then I am filled with joy," Pax said, smiling at her. "Yes, I died in the Between some great many years after my brother. Do not fear; I lived a full long life in his honor and that of my mate. You are a testament to my work, just as those two dragons are, and it fills me with pride. That day, as I stood beside Terg, I divided what remained to me into the two most powerful emotions I could, love and hate. My love for Laz and everything he was. Love for my kind. Love for everything I had done. Hate for what Laz never got to experience. Hate for those that took my Iros from me. Hate for being left without them. I bottled that hate into the Black Flame, and I sealed it away."

"But Xtyia Forest!"

"It was an image, youngling. I projected my image from the Dreaming and placed it in a meadow. There was no forest there before, but it was just an image, nothing more. I wanted to be seen so no one would think to look where Laz did not want them to go."

"Then why did Iros leave a guard for the Between?"

"What guard?" Pax asked, frowning. She looked away. "Nihility."

"It is nothing, Lady Pax," she mumbled.

"Nihility Harbinger, I would know what the foolish dragon I shared my heart with has done. What guard?"

"Sia," she paused. "Sia the Mindbreaker is a Watcher, and he guards the Between."

"The name is familiar, but I cannot grasp the dragon it belongs to. Would I know him?"

"Aye," she said. An image flickered behind her as a beautiful, giant, orange, and yellow dragon appeared. His colors blended over his entire body except for a white patch around his right eye and his yellow horns and spine. A scar ran from above his eye to his snout.

"The Sightstealer's twin! The Twin Suns!" Pax exclaimed. "Oh, Iros, you damn fool! He lost his twin in the War of the Dreaming! He is your dragon!?"

"Aye."

"He is a Watcher, but he walks as Destined does?"

"Aye. Sia the Mindbreaker, Watcher of the Between. No one knows. Well, no one but I, Uzzod, Terg, Ygi, Bendre, and Jaydum, but we are family."

Pax hummed happily and looked down at her as the image faded. "He is a handsome dragon, Nihility. You have good taste in dragons, young one."

"Thank you," she said, embarrassed.

"The Twin Suns," Pax said with a chuckle. "A unique set of twins. They would lie together, and the color of their scales would match. It was beautiful. Where he was the orange of the setting sun, she was a beautiful yellow of it rising high in the sky."

"Lady Livy the Sightstealer. She lingers in the Pool of Spirits."

"She does not linger youngling. She thrives. We all have a purpose in the Dreaming when our time is done. Controlling the Pool of Spirits is the domain of the Sightstealer. I trained her myself beside Ygi. What a pair those two were!"

"They still are. When Ygi needs her in the Dreaming, Lady Livy is there. Lady Pax?"

"Aye."

"Is that how you are with me? Are you like Lady Livy? You are no demon."

"No, I am not here by choice, Nihility. Something went wrong with my spell. Something that was not as powerful as the demon that held my brother but as powerful crossed that barrier. We were twins. I knew the feel of the demon because of the link I shared with Laz. Something that had the feel of that demon came through."

"That makes no sense, Lady Pax."

"I know. I have been trying to figure out what went wrong when I arrived inside your mind. Ana," Pax said, nodding at the orb, "had to have come through with whatever triggered the door, to begin with. Whatever it was, it could avoid the Black Flame or deflect it onto her. My love bound her as it should have, but I believe, through luck, she got to you at the same time I tried to invade her. Instead, we both wound up here."

"She said she did not go to Destined because he was too powerful. If what you say is correct, Pax, it means that the one who betrayed Ana is the demon inside of Destined."

"And a powerful demon," Pax said.

"I need to speak with him," she said, thinking of his face and those moments where there seemed to be someone else looking through his eyes.

"You can when you wake. For now, your lessons must continue," Pax said, smiling. She sat up attentively, looking at the great dragoness before her. "Now you said something interesting, and I would hear more. You said you meant to produce my image in flames for the council. Is that something dragons can do now?"

"It is just a trick I picked up, Lady Pax. I can make things from my flame. Well, it works with dream fire too. I can make images from the flames and other things."

"Are they merely images, or do they move on their own?" Pax asked, frowning.

"They do as I wish. I have used it against the Warida when they trespass too close to the grove. I send an image in dream fire of the one the tales said you burned. His image walks among them, sending the call for them to return to their homes."

"Interesting," Pax said. "And you can do so on Sathea as well with your Dragonfire?"

"Yes. Animals, plants, short-lifers, and other things. It is how I dance the flames with the Daughters of Ote, but it is a little different."

"Explain, youngling."

"The Daughters are not much different from us, Lady Pax. Dragonesses stand above dragons on our peak, as the daughters stand above the sons of Ote. They even test their men as we do our dragons, but they do so by fire. I..." she stopped, embarrassed.

"You what young, vibrant dragoness?" Pax asked with a smirk.

"The first time I danced the flames, I made them come alive. If the one I dance for truly wants me, the flames will change to show me that," Nihility said sheepishly.

"Lady Shi was said to do something like that. Lady Ygi told me of it when she was around your age. She said the flames called to their men as Shi danced."

"Aye. It is like that, except I am not a Daughter of Ote. I am a dragoness. My flames are different."

"You are an Empath. You fuel the flames with their

emotions," Pax said. She nodded. "That is an extraordinary thing, Nihility Harbinger. Not even I can do that with fire."

"But you created the Black Flame!"

"That I did. Do you believe that your only powers are that you are an Empath, Nihility?"

She thought about Pax's question for a minute. "Yes. Everything I can do with my magic stems from being an Empath."

"That is correct, but there is more to an Empath than merely feeling, youngling. We do not differ from any other dragon on Petrall. Destined may use his mind to fight, but you use emotions."

"Well, I can channel my feelings through my hands when I am in my borrowed form, but beyond that, I have never used my powers for anything else," she said, frowning.

"You used them to bring forth the Black Flame. You have used them to create images in fire by your own words," Pax said.

"The Black Flame is because of you and her," she said, nodding at Ana. "And I told you those are merely tricks."

"When your body is rested, I would have you show me this trick," Pax said. "Do you feel up to explaining to me the nature of your relationship with that other dragon? The one you called Endrir."

She groaned. "We hatched together. Destined and I did, Endrir was trapped, but we saved him from his egg. I love him, and I know he loves me, but he did not pursue me. He," she stopped, frowning. "He found Destined instead."

"They are mated then?" Pax asked.

"They love each other deeply. I feel it every time I am around them. They do not realize I know."

"Because they forget their dragoness is an Empath," Pax said, chuckling. "Why do you not tell them you know?"

"Because I should not have to. Destined tries. I mean, he does not hide it, but he does. I know it is Endrir who does not wish me to know. I picked Destined when they danced for my heart, Lady Pax. I had to, but Endrir does not understand that. He does not see me. Neither of them does," she said, sighing. "I am just the dragoness between them."

CHAPTER THIRTY-ONE

He was back in the inner sanctum of the Tower of the Order of Walkers. It was dark, unnaturally dark. All the alcoves lining the inside of the tower where Walkers would lie to enter the Between were empty. Something was wrong, shadows moved when they should not, and he could feel his heart racing. It was then he realized he was in his short life form. He tried to shift and could not.

"Farseer," a female voice said. "Come to me."

The room changed around him. The sanctum changed into a place he did not know.

"You will not leave here, Farseer. You will suffer the fate that you have imposed upon my son. So as done unto him, I do unto you," a male voice said.

The voice froze him in fear. It was all around him, inside of him, setting his nerves on edge. Suddenly a light appeared. It latched on to him and wrapped itself around him. He could not move. He needed to move! He had to move! "Nihility!" he shouted. "Nihility!" He needed her. He needed the safety of her. He did not want to see the being that voice belonged to. "Nihility!"

"You will be my prisoner for eternities to come. You will walk the place you call the Between at my command, and you will show me the future," it said.

Two eyes appeared in the darkness. Destined screamed.

The scream followed him as he woke. He tried to move and could not. Panic gripped him as he thrashed, believing he was still trapped. Nihility's subtle shift caused him to gather and control himself. He was tangled in Endrir's cloak. He sighed with relief as he unwrapped himself.

The moon was still high in the sky. He had not slept long. He had visions in his sleep before, but they were never so vivid, so terrifying. He shivered and stood up. He needed to walk and clear his head. He was afraid, more afraid than he ever had been before. It was not a feeling he was accustomed to. He placed a hand on her snout.

"It was just a bad dream. I am going for a bit of air, my love. I will return before you wake," he told her. He did not know why he spoke to her; he was sure she was still sleeping. Although, right now, he would have given anything to lay with her for his own comfort.

A slight breeze was almost chilly, making his flesh feel free and alive. He had a nervous energy that made him jittery. He was trying to run from what he saw. He knew he was, just as he knew he could not. He walked with no actual destination in mind. He did not want to think. Thinking led back to those eyes.

He heard the steady flow of water over rocks. He remembered the river that flowed through the forest and made his way there. It was a peaceful place. He believed it was the very reason the three of them thrived here. They studied together, practiced together, and tested one another here. The last thought made him giggle. He vividly remembered spending three days with an extra tail because Endrir lost focus. He looked around for a moment. He could not shift if Endrir was hunting; it would disturb the wildlife. He removed his clothes, throwing them over the rocks, and slipped into the water.

He did not know why he picked this place, but he knew there was a reason. There was always a reason that guided one's actions. The trick was having the awareness to know. The only time he became clouded about his actions and motivations was with Nihility. His dragoness had the uncanny ability to turn him into a complete fool. He loved her for it and always felt alive around her.

He heard something being pulled across the grass and turned, startled by the sound, as Endrir came through the opening in the trees. He seemed just as surprised to see him. He stood for a moment with a blank look. He had a streak of blood where he had wiped his cheek. The trinket he made for him hung from his neck, laying against his bare chest.

"I did not realize you were awake. I came to clean these before I took them back to the cave," Endrir said, nodding his head at the four jerboas he had taken down.

"Yes, I," he paused. He did not want to say something childish like he had a nightmare. "I just needed a quick rest," he finished.

Endrir gave him a look. "Could have fooled me, Destined. You were out before I could even leave."

"You know how it is for me. I feel as if all I do is sleep."

Endrir laughed. "That's because all you do is sleep."

He was grinning like a fool. It felt good to have Endrir here. He ignited a spark in him that Nihility did not. He pulled himself out of the water and stood on the rocks. Endrir stared at him for a long moment before moving to the stream. He tossed the jerboa in a pile.

"Have you been working on your combat in that form?" Endrir asked.

He had gleamed Endrir's thoughts at that moment. They made him blush. Combat was not what the Watcher thought about. He grabbed his pants and quickly put them on, trying to hide his excitement. "Not as much as you have adamantly told me I should be," he said.

He moved to help Endrir. Years ago, Endrir had taught him how the short lifers prepared the animals they killed. Nihility took to it quickly, explaining that it was not unlike what some dreaming kind did as well. Endrir handed him a knife, and he stripped the hide from one jerboa. He could feel Endrir's eyes on him. "It was just an unsettling vision."

"Uh-huh. You should have Nihility help you sleep when she wakes. You look as if you could use it."

"You can tell in this form?"

"Aye. It is the eyes. They do not lie. Well, they do not lie to those that notice such things. I am always amazed by the number of short lifers that never realize what I truly am," Endrir said, laughing.

"Are there any that do? I would think in a city that large, someone would notice something."

"Exactly the opposite. In my time, I have only come across maybe four that have. Some short-lifers cannot say what, but they realize I am not one of them. Those who are more in tune with the land are always those who respect the Great Balance. Like a Daughter of Ote I met last year. Her name is Lyric. She knew but could not place me. She actually helped me pick out a gift for the Weaver."

"What did you say her name was?"

"Lyric. She stands as a guard to Lady Farmark of Tresai," Endrir said. "Why are you interested? She is attractive but odd."

"Endrir, keep that information to yourself," he said calmly. "I mean, do not bring it up in front of her." He knew if Nihility found out Lyric was in Tresai, nothing would stop her from trying to go, and then the hurt would begin again.

"Why?"

"Just do not. Treat it as you do the elf you took me to see."

"That never happened, Farseer," Endrir said.

"Exactly," he said, grinning. "You think they would be okay with the presence of a dragon given the others that traverse the cities as well."

"Those others are like them. They can find the similarities enough to be tolerant."

"Tolerant? Odd choice of words."

"No, I mean exactly that. It is tolerance, not acceptance. Short lifers in the cities can be cruel, Destined. I have taken you to enough places that you have seen some of their behavior toward each other. Most dream folks do not linger in the cities, only the dark ones and those like me. It is as if they can feel something I cannot."

"Speak to Nihility about it. Maybe she has an idea on why?"

"But not Lyric?" Endrir asked with a grin as Destined sorted through the herbs and leaves he had returned with.

"Not funny, Endrir. Please say nothing to her. She knows Lyric well. You will do nothing but cause her pain," he said.

"I did not realize," Endrir said, frowning. "But that means there is a story there!"

"Not mine to tell, Watcher."

"I knew you were going to say that. I did. I only hoped," Endrir said, laughing. "It is good to see that you have not let what I brought back to you wither and decay."

He placed the meat in the middle of large brown leaves called Neem and laid sprigs of a brown plant called Scoke on top before rolling it closed. They would cook the meat inside the leaves to eat in this form or raw if they were dragons. The Neem and Scoke helped their digestion and the fire in their bellies. They were staples in a dragon's diet.

"We spend more time than we probably should in these forms. It allows us some privacy."

"Up here it would, down below and beyond they would not. You know all this already. Some of your mannerisms are still odd. Does Nihility still do that head tilt thing when she is reading someone?" Endrir asked, smiling.

"You know she does. I do not see it changing either."

"You would not ask her to. You love when she does it."

"And you don't?" he asked, nudging him.

"Have you been feeding her properly? When I passed her on the Great Path, she was hungry, Destined."

He groaned and rolled his eyes. "I feed Nihility."

"Then why was she hungry? For that matter, why are you hungry?"

"I eat! They bring me food at the Order. She hunts for herself mostly, and she is always hungry!"

"Destined, it is our duty to feed her," Endrir said with a sigh.

"Then you should return more often, instead of running off like you do not have mates," he said with a tone. He instantly regretted it. "Endrir, I did not mean that. I am sorry, my treasure."

Endrir raised a hand to still him. "I understand, Farseer. I earned it rightfully. I was gone too long. I know you think I declined the position as Lead Watcher because of you, but it had nothing to do with you. You made the decision harder. Did you know that?"

This is not what he wanted. He was still a bit hurt Endrir chose to be away rather than on Petrall with him. He felt abandoned. The day Endrir declined Shegur's invitation to ascend to her place, it was as if Endrir delivered a blow to his heart. He did not want to bring up sore topics when they were finally together.

"No, I did not know that", Destined continued. "You said no, and I just figured I was no longer enough for you. I thought Nihility and I had pushed you away. That I pushed you away."

Endrir nudged him in the side. "You did not push me away, Destined. I would never abandon you. We made sure of that the moment we exchanged our heart of hearts," Endrir said, grinning. "You are my mate."

"Then it was Nihility," he said, frowning. "Endrir, she loves you. You do not need to run from her."

Endrir nodded. "It is what it is, Destined," he said as he washed up in the stream. "I have accepted it."

He rolled his eyes. He had accepted nothing when it came to Nihility. He held part of his heart. He could feel the pain he felt any time Endrir was around her. "So why did you say no?" he asked as he washed up beside him.

"A few reasons. Mostly the Council of Elders. I can't be around them, Destined. I can't just stand by and watch them disrespect Nihility as you do," Endrir said. He moved to interject, but Endrir silenced him with a wave. "I know why you do. What is that thing you say about heads?"

"Let a cool head lead," he said.

"I do not have one of those," Endrir said, laughing. "Especially with her. That is also a problem because I know her. If you said something, she would rip you to shreds for making her appear weak and in need of protection. Nihility is difficult, Destined, at least not for me. I envy you in that. You two are always easy together."

"Sometimes."

"Most of the time," Endrir corrected. "You two have a natural sync."

"It is not natural, Endrir. She and I talk a lot. In talking, we learn about each other."

"Regardless, the leaders of the three callings must be balanced. They must remain in harmony. Yes, we three have that harmony, but I will not be used by the council to be a middle ground between the two of you. I cannot choose, and I will not choose. If they forced me to choose, I would always choose the two of you over Petrall. It cannot be that way," Endrir said, looking out into the trees.

"You and Nihility make me question myself. You two see clearer than I do regardless of how many visions I receive."

"It is not that we see clearly," Endrir said as he stood. "It is love and a bond that I will not have broken by those that would have left me to die alone. It has already been strained enough."

Endrir had an odd look in his eyes. Destined caught an image of that short-life female again. He stood and placed his hands on the side of Endrir's face. "Not strained, just distant. I am always here," he said, kissing him lightly. "And so is she."

Endrir nodded. "We should get these back to the cave. I have plans for you," Endrir said with a grin.

"Oh," Destined said, grinning. "Does it involve moaning, stroking, and heavy breathing?"

"The sun is out in all his glory, I see," Endrir said, rolling his eyes.

"It has been a very long time, Endrir! Two years!"

"Does Nihility know?"

"No. I mean, I haven't told her, and I haven't asked. She's an Empath. I am sure she's sensed something."

"Destined," Endrir whined.

"It was not my idea to keep it from her. That was yours. Are you saying I can tell her? Because I would rather she know."

"No!"

"Well, what are you worried about?"

"She is right there!" Endrir hissed.

"She has exhausted herself. We have hours before she wakes."

"What?! How do you even know that?" Endrir asked.

"It has happened before," he said with a shrug.

"Story now!" Endrir said.

"No story, my treasure. Nihility," he paused, searching for the right words. "Nihility can be insatiable when she really is in the mood. Unfortunately, I cannot always keep up with her appetite."

Endrir narrowed his eyes at him, "what did you do?"

"I opened the cage. Just a crack," Destined said, holding his fingers apart. "Nihility said she could feel me and was really into it, and well, she exhausted herself."

"Wait," Endrir said, rolling his eyes. "You opened the fucking cage so you could last longer with her in bed? For Sathea's sake, Farseer."

"Did you expect me to let her down?" he asked, frowning.

"No, but it throws your whole keeping the cage theory out of whack," Endrir said, crossing his arms over his chest.

"That is where you are wrong."

"Really? How so?"

"She exhausted herself with just a crack. Imagine what would happen if the cage was not there."

"I'd wager she'd be a very happy dragoness," Endrir said, shaking his head. "I mean, I am a happy dragon when I get the Farseer. It does not matter anyway. I had something else in mind."

"Ouch," he said, making a face.

"I can't deal with her right here, Destined! Do not start. This lack of fear you have of her wrath is unhealthy for the both of us," Endrir mumbled.

"Fine, fine. I will wait," Destined said, laughing as he gathered the meat. "And Endrir, I have no reason to fear Nihility, and neither do you; about anything."

Nihility was still asleep when he stored their meat in the cave. "I love you," he whispered to her before he went back out again. He was excited. Endrir was planning something. He felt much better than when he woke. Spending time with Endrir always put him in a better mood. The Watcher made him feel like he could take on the world. The sun would rise in a few hours, but they had the moonlight to play for now.

Endrir stood bare-chested, holding two long sticks. He groaned. The Watcher stoked a fire in him that Nihility could not match. "Training time, Farseer!" Endrir shouted as he tossed him a stick. "Just use your magic to make it an accurate replica of your staff. We have no time for wood carving like your monks."

"No need, I have mine," he said, laughing.

"I see no staff. What tricks have you learned now?"

"Not me, Nihility. What is it you told us when you

introduced us to the weapons they use? That visible weapons make them nervous?"

"Aye, some of them, yes. Enough that they do ridiculous shit. It is why Watchers assigned to those areas are trained to cloak their weapons. She changed it, didn't she?" Endrir asked, shaking his head.

"Of course she did. I believe it was something to the effect of 'Destined Farseer we may use their forms, but we are always dragons, so act like one!'"

Endrir had to stifle his giggles. "Fire, you are asking for it. Show me what she has done."

He grinned and conjured his staff in his hands. "Meaning we are always armed in this form, no need to cloak when you can conjure them. Nihility got the idea from all those clothes she collects."

"Wait. What? She has more clothing now?"

"So much more," he said, groaning.

"I am so screwed," Endrir said.

"We covered this, and you said, 'I can't deal with her right here,'" he said, mocking Endrir's voice.

"I do not sound like that!"

"Forgive me. I have trouble with the excessive whine you carry. It has that slight touch of fear I can't match," Destined said, trying not to laugh.

"We will see who is whining when I am done with you," Endrir said, dropping the stick and pulling out his own weapon, a great long sword that would have required a natural short-lifer two hands to wield. Endrir only needed one. The blade shined in the fading moonlight. The hilt was decorated with a single purple gem at the center, while was the rest was covered in black leather. He held a matching one that he used when he was reckless. "Be sure your barrier remains intact, Farseer," he said with a grin.

He nodded. Endrir charged him, reigning down a flurry of blows. He blocked most of them, but Endrir was much faster than he was. In fact, he had not done this in far too long. After a few exchanges and a few welts, Endrir called a halt and showed him new motions and techniques with his staff. "Endrir, I might have embellished a bit when I said I was practicing," he said, rubbing a spot on his leg.

"I already knew that, but this is the only way I can pay you back for running your mouth," Endrir said. "You must not think that you cannot charge into battle, Destined. We have talked about this. You favor defense, but that does not mean you cannot still be offensive. What you lack in speed physically, you must make up for mentally. It would help if you opened that cage of yours."

"Do not start Endrir."

Endrir shrugged. "Just saying, Destined the Divided, the Farseer holds the power you need, and apparently the stamina."

"Yeah, I know exactly what you are saying. I do not want to hear it. The cage is there for a reason."

"Does she know yet?"

"No," he said.

"But you berate me about telling her about us," Endrir shrugged.

"Because she won't care!" he snapped. "She's going to be more upset that we did not tell her!"

"And she will care about the cage?" Endrir asked.

"Yes! Now leave it alone!"

"Alright, Farseer," Endrir said.

"Do you want me to use spells? My magic is must faster."

"I would have you defend yourself with whatever means you must. If that means spell work, then so be it. In this form, treat your spells as you would your fire."

"I thought the point was to fight as they do, Endrir!? My magic will give me away quickly!" he said, shocked.

Endrir gave him a look. "Things are not as they once were

when I took you off Petrall last, Destined. They learn things faster with each passing day."

"What?"

"I will explain later to the both of you. For now, use your magic as you will. Protect yourself from me as you would in battle. My barrier will sustain."

When Endrir charged a second time, instead of using his staff to block the attack, he placed it before him. The blue gem glowed. Endrir's blows were buffeted back. His eyes pulsed in time with the jewel on his staff. The Watcher jumped back as ice struck at his feet.

"How was that, Watcher?" he asked, smiling.

"Fantastic!" Endrir said delightedly. He had conjured swords made of ice instead of his staff to defend against Endrir's blows. "You are much faster with magic. Let's go again. I will not hold back this time."

They always shared what they learned. Endrir could not walk without aid, but his mental defenses were more robust than his courtesy of the lessons Master Sia had given him. Endrir helped them choose and perfect their short life forms. Endrir taught him to fight, and he took him down below to watch and learn. Endrir taught him how short-lifers shared themselves and did their dance of love and lust differently than dragons. He told Nihility of that trip because she did not come. It terrified him she would be angry, but she laughed at him and asked if he learned anything. He had, and he honed his skills on both her and Endrir. He was the Farseer, and he was greedy.

CHAPTER THIRTY-TWO

She woke just before dawn to the sound of fighting. She remained still, looking around while listening to the clash of weapons. She smelled fresh meat and herbs. Her belly growled loudly, making her groan. She realized where she was and knew Endrir and Destined were probably sparring. She shifted forms and watched them from the cave. Destined was rusty. His duties kept him far too busy to train, and he refused to with her. She trained often. She found it relaxing. She did so with the dryads in the Dreaming, the Daughters of Ote whose fighting style she used, or alone. She preferred her twin blades, but she was also proficient with a bow and hand-to-hand combat.

"He teaches you the ways of those below. The ones not connected to the Dreaming," Pax said.

"Aye. Endrir brings the knowledge back. He went to the council years ago and asked them to note the weaponry and other innovations the short lifers used, but they ignored him."

"Have they changed that much?"

"Aye. Short-lifer dreams tell us much, but you know it may not show the reality of the change, but what they hope for."

"Why did the council not heed his words?"

"They, meaning Ergodi, believed that the short lifers no longer believed in dragons, so why should we as dragons bother with them. He thinks we will always be safe on Petrall where short lifers cannot reach. Endrir was not so sure."

"You do not seem sure either," Pax said.

"Because I am not. I agree with Endrir. The nomads hold on strongly to their history and their ties to the land, but the city dwellers do not. They move further and further away from Sathea in favor of tools they believe make their lives easier. For a species of short-lives, they advance quickly. Even their weapons have become more destructive. They are learning to wield magic as well."

"I only knew of Ote's daughters. What are the others like?"

"Varied in their beliefs, attitudes, colors, skills, and knowledge just as we are. They are all different, though. I am not sure how it was when you were alive, Lady Pax, but now you cannot go far from Petrall without seeing a short-lifer. They fish the Durming Sea and hunt the forests at the base of Petrall."

"They had not come so far in my time. Destined's form seems familiar, but the other I have never seen one like him."

She laughed. "It is Destined's clothing, I am sure. He dresses as those at the Order of Zal do," she said.

"It still exists then?"

"Aye. The Order of Zal has grown in number, but they still live their peaceful life at the base of Petrall. As for Endrir, he looks like those that dwell in the cities. They are flamboyant, like the Fairy Folk of Wom."

"They do not notice him?" Pax asked.

"Nay, but short lifers are not the most observant species, Lady Pax. Honestly, they are lucky we do not eat them," she said, laughing.

"Spoken like a true student of Terg the Redeemer."

"He says he does not hunt them because they stink. It is really because he has a sensitive belly," Nihility said, grinning. She could feel Pax's mirth and hear her laughter. She started gathering wood for a fire; she was hungry.

"Nihility, do you weave the dreams of those other short lifers?"

"Sometimes. Mostly it is the Daughters of Ote and the Order of Zal, the ones who are the Sons of Ote."

"Have you ever seen anything strange in their dreams? Like a serpent?" Pax asked.

She stopped and looked up at the sky, thinking. "No, I have not seen a serpent. At least, I do not think I have. I saw one in the dream sand the Daughters use, though. It was surrounding Destined. It made me afraid; I mean, the image did."

"The image or the serpent itself?"

"Both. It made me feel like I could be consumed by it, and so could Destined. That is the only reason I was in the Between. Do you know what it meant, Lady Pax? I did not have time to ask Vivian what meaning they give serpents in dreams."

"No, but I would have you talk to Master Bendre about it when you return," Pax said.

"I will, but first food!" she said happily.

"Eat dragoness. You still have growing to do," Pax said, laughing.

"Do you think I will be as big as you?" she asked.

"I think slightly bigger, youngling. It is in the way your scales lay across your chest. You still have an overlap. That means that you have many more years ahead of you to grow before you hit the time of your fullness for a dragoness, but you must eat properly!"

"Not a problem. I love food more than anything else on Sathea," she said as she smelled the meat and groaned.

"So did I, youngling," Pax said, giggling. "And I can smell it through you. Oh, that smells wonderful!"

The sun was rising. They knew she was awake by the smell of roasting meat and herbs coming from the cave. "I think that means it is time for a break, Farseer," Endrir said smiling.

"Agreed!" Destined said. "I am starving."

He had given Destined a vigorous workout after he urged him to use his magic to fight. He felt invigorated and famished. They walked back to the cave with smiles on their faces. "She weaves dreams, and she can cook! I am in love!" Endrir shouted. She looked him in the eyes for a long moment before he kissed her cheek. "Hello beautiful," he whispered.

Destined walked up behind her and wrapped his arms around her waist. He kissed her neck. "I am glad you are okay."

"I am, but I am starving."

"Destined," he said.

"You're home now. You feed her," Destined said as he grabbed a bundle of leaves from the fire. He tossed it back and forth until Nihility handed him a plate.

"Gladly," he said, grabbing a plate and preparing it for Nihility.

"Thank you, Endrir," she said. The sound of his name from her lips made him shiver.

"Are you okay, Nihility?" he asked.

"Yes, I am now."

"Are you going to tell us what happened?" he asked. Nihility studied him, making him squirm under her gaze. She always made him feel exposed to her.

"I think we will all be telling stories today and filing in the space. For now, we eat," Nihility said.

He had to keep himself from panicking. "Oh, I love stories," he said over-enthusiastically.

She smiled at him, "forever the fledgling, Endrir."

"Someone has to keep you two from taking yourselves too seriously."

"Judging by the look of you, I believe the only one of us prone to taking themselves too seriously is you," she said, nodding at his form.

"I will have you know the female short lifers love this form! And some males too!" he said with confidence. Destined choked, making Nihility laugh.

"Are you okay, Destined," she asked with a smirk.

"He hasn't been feeding you, has he?" he asked her.

"I feed her, damn it!" Destined said around a mouthful of food.

"He feeds me, but I am dragoness, and I am growing. You

were gone too long this last time," Nihility said earnestly. "It has been almost two years. I have missed you."

He blushed and looked down with a smile on his face. "Told you," Destined said over their link.

"I am sorry, beautiful," he said.

"Are things below changing that much it keeps you from us for so long?" she asked.

He nodded. "Aye. They are finding more materials for building and, of course, making weapons. They seem to be heading towards a period of growth again. Religion is a business for them."

"Religion?" she asked.

"What they have called their beliefs in those seven deities I told you of."

She made a face. "What about the Great Balance?"

"They do not care if it does not aid them, Nihility," he said.

"That is not how the Great Balance works. You must accept the good with the bad as well. What are they expecting, happiness every day?" she scoffed.

"That is exactly what they expect," he said with a tone. Nihility looked at him sharply. "They have no patience to wait through the bad for the good."

"What have they done, Endrir? I do not see it all in their dreams."

"Temples are being erected and used for meeting places to worship the Gods of Bishamyr. They are also aligning themselves in strange ways. Can you believe the family that rules Tresai, the Farmarks, is trying to create an alliance with Wom?"

"Solara would never!" she hissed.

"The Queen of Wom will do as they advise her is best for her people, Nihility. They stand in a delicate position now with the Farmarks trying to encroach on the forest the Queen has been using for her people."

"Afersera is protected land! It is for those that are not the

Fairy Folk of fair skin. The ones that remain close to the old ways!" she said, shocked. "I will need to speak to Solara. She still does not know how to lead after all these years."

"You should report this to the council," Destined said.

"What the fuck for?" Nihility said, exasperated.

"Nihility!" Destined said, shocked, making him laugh. She rolled her eyes at Destined.

"I did not even bother to report any of it to them. I left my findings with Olvess. They do not find interest in anything beyond Petrall," he said.

"Those old two would, Endrir. You should at least tell them," Destined said.

"I am not telling Uzzod anything. I will speak to Britir, but not until I get the drink he likes."

"The drink you forgot," Destined said, laughing.

"That too," he said, laughing.

"All of them should listen to the both of you," Nihility said.

"It did not seem like they were doing much listening to me at the circle, my love," Destined said bitterly.

"That is because they, and by 'they' I mean Ergodi, prefers when you are his perfect puppet, that is not a puppet. When you bring them grandeur, they applaud you and take credit. You bring them news of a threat, and they become bumbling fools," she hissed. They both looked at her, shocked. He could feel her anger, which only happened when she was truly upset about something. "I am sorry," she said with a sigh. "I must not let them bother me as much as they do."

"You would not be you if they did not," he said. "You would be the Farseer, and I do not think you would look half as good bald," he said, sending them into more fits of laughter.

CHAPTER THIRTY-THREE

They filled their bellies with jerboa and their hearts with tales of the memories they shared in their little place below the Jagged Cliffs. She took Endrir's hand as they walked out of the cave and into the sunshine of the day. Destined raced ahead of them, finding a spot right before the forest where a large patch of the Pewhas she loved bloomed and sat down. She sat with her legs crossed as Endrir laid down beside her. She moved, placing his head in her lap to play with his hair.

"I missed you," she whispered. Endrir looked up at her with the violet eyes she loved and smiled. He touched her hand softly with his and then laced them over his chest.

"We have not done this so long. I think it has been at least a thousand years," Destined said as he plucked the surrounding flowers.

"Destined must you pick them?" she asked with a sigh.

"Just a few, my love," he said, fiddling with them in his hands.

"What are you doing," she said, wincing. She could feel the pain Sathea felt with each flower he plucked from the land.

"Patience, my dragoness. Patience," Destined said.

Endrir touched her hand. "Do not focus on the pain of them being pulled from Sathea. I think she will allow his actions," he said, smiling at her.

"Destined, what do you know of demons that we do not?" she asked absently. The smile died on Endrir's face. He sat up and moved from her. Ana's words came back to her. "Troubled. Deeply troubled and in danger."

Destined finished with the flowers and moved over and placed the crown he had woven with them on her head. "I know what a Walker should, Nihility," he said, smiling at her. "You look beautiful."

"You heard my question, Destined," she said.

"I am not ignoring you, my love! I did not want the moment ruined by other things just yet. It is a beautiful morning, you are a beautiful dragoness, and we are finally back together again. I have ruined enough moments I should not have lately."

"I am not angry about that anymore. I was not angry, to begin with. I was hurt because you are a fool," she said, rolling her eyes at him. She reached for Endrir, and he flinched. "Endrir?" she said, frowning.

"What I know is mostly conjecture," Destined shouted.

"Wha…" she said.

"Do you want me to tell you or not, dragoness?" Destined asked, interrupting her.

"Destined Farseer, watch your tone," she said, glaring at him. "Continue," she said, "but tread carefully." He grinned. She felt his arousal. "Destined," she said, sighing heavily.

"That is your fault, Nihility. You know I cannot handle when you get forceful," he said, still grinning. "I will behave, at least until I answer your question. After that, I make no promises," he said, chuckling. She nodded for him to go on. "There is really no place where you can find all the information. I do not know what they truly are or what they can do. The only thing I know for certain is how to tell if you are in the presence of one," he said.

"How?" Endrir asked.

"A vile green aura that exudes danger. Not surrounding them like any other creature, but a part of them, if that makes sense, Watcher."

"A physical manifestation you can see without magic?" Endrir asked.

"Aye. I think it is the eyes," Destined said.

"That is all you know, Destined. What good does that do?" she asked, frowning.

"I did not say that is all I knew. I said that there is no place where you can find all the information," he said. "I have found other things, pieces of things."

"Destined, you know it annoys me when you speak in circles. Just say what it is, you know, fool, before I set you on fire," she snapped.

"They, demons, have been around far longer than our histories say. I do not know where they come from or where they exist. I only know that they have been here in some form or another."

"Jerboa shit. We would have noticed," she said, making a face. "Tell him, Endrir," she said, looking at him.

"I think he is right, Nihility," Endrir said. He was frowning and looking at Destined.

"I think we have not noticed because something has forced us to forget, Nihility; conditioned us to forget. Our lives are long, and in a long life, forgetfulness is easy," Destined said.

"And you say that you have noticed?" she asked Destined.

"The Watcher has, and it started with them. The first of them became obsessed with the history of dragons and demons. I do not know what prompted his questions, but I know he sought the answers. Not just trivial answers either. He wanted to know what happens to the spirits of those before us."

"They go to the Dreaming," she said, making a face. "We all know that."

"Not all of them Nihility. I mean, they pass through, yes, but what then? Do all of them touch the Dreaming or just some? Do you know what happens to those spirits?"

"They feed the River Serpent Hynro, Destined! He decides their fate. I have told you this."

"Aye, but do they all, or just those touched by the Dreaming? The Dreaming is the domain of Weavers and Dreamfolk,

Nihility. As you said, Hynro passes judgment on their spirits. They pass on, their work fulfilled becoming one with the Dreaming, or are consumed at judgment, but where do the others go if they do not linger in the Dreaming like Weavers? Where do those that pass on down below go? Where do those that are kin to the Dreamfolk but not the Dreaming go? These are the questions that dragon asked," Destined said.

"Who?"

"Laz of the Between," Destined said.

"What?" she asked, shocked.

"Now is the time to listen, youngling," she heard Pax say in her mind.

"Laz was a twin. We all know the stories, yes?" Destined asked. She and Endrir both nodded.

"Laz of the Between was the twin to Lady Pax of the Depths. Together, they were named the Twin Stars of Petrall for their marks on their chest. After them, there were only two sets of twins hatched and given titles of grandeur on Petrall, the Twin Suns of Petrall, Livy Sightstealer, and her unnamed twin I have never found, and the Twin Moons of Petrall, both whose names I have also never found," Endrir said.

She looked shocked. "You study them?" she asked.

"Aye," he mumbled. "They are named for how they appeared or their talents. At least that is what I found."

"Endrir is right. Twins for our kind are omens of bounty, prosperity, and change. Did you know that Laz and Lady Pax were the first two twins born on the peak that both were not Weavers?" Destined asked. She shook her head. "Change," he said, smiling. "Laz was no Weaver, not because he was male, of course. Male Weavers are rare, but they exist. Laz did not have a link to the Dreaming, but Pax did. Laz did not show the same emotional range as his sister. In fact, from what I have gathered, he was the very opposite to Lady Pax in most respects. Where she was warm and full of life, he was quiet, withdrawn, and to some even cold."

"That is not true," she said. They both looked at her expectantly. "She was the same. Being an Empath made it seem like they were different. Laz was like her, but with only certain dragons, and she was like him, but only with certain dragons."

Destined smiled at her. "I did not think about the effect of her being an Empath would have on her personality."

"Then she was like you," Endrir said, looking at her. "Complex," he finished.

"I am n…"

"You are, my love," Destined said, interrupting her. "We do not mean it as a slight. It is a compliment. It makes you…" he paused, thinking.

"Beautiful," Endrir finished.

"Aye! Beautiful!" Destined said excitedly. She rolled her eyes to hide her embarrassment.

"Do you know what Laz's abilities were, Farseer?" Endrir asked.

"He was a master of memories, Watcher!" Destined said, grinning. "He did not have visions as I do, but he had a vision. He could access and see the memories of others. Nothing can be hidden in your deepest memories. Together with his twin, they could take those memories and make great illusions!"

"Why are you so excited, Farseer?"

"Because they misnamed Laz of the Between, Endrir," Destined said, lounging back on his hands. "I believe on purpose to save our kind from the demon he found. To teach us to tread carefully in a place where he locked that demon away. Laz of the Between should have been named Laz the Watcher, as in First Leader of Watcher Hold."

Endrir laughed. She was frowning and waiting on Lady Pax to negate what Destined had said, but the old dragoness was silent. "They had powers together?" she asked

"All twins do, Nihility," Endrir said. "They each have powers of their own, but together they transform into something different."

"Something powerful!" Destined said, waving his hands.

"How do you know he was a Watcher?" she asked.

"Why are you not shocked that I said he was?" Destined asked her with a wink.

"You have taken both Endrir and myself into that place. I do not think it is hard for any dragon to access it if they have the mind to do so. The mind is infinite. Power comes in controlling it."

Destined rolled his eyes. "You sound like Master Sia," he said with a groan.

"Nihility! He does not know about him!" Pax hissed in her mind.

"Because he chooses not to know. I have not hidden it, but I do not call attention to it either," she said, explaining quickly.

"But you are right," Destined continued. "Laz was everything the Hold now stands for. He spoke with those below the peaks, Nihility! He watched them and learned about them. He created a form of himself to outwardly project, so he could move among them. During his time, they were not afraid to speak to us. They had respect for what we are. They paid homage to our kind as keepers of the Great Balance. They knew dragons!"

"Why cover up what he had done? It is a feat! It is extraordinary! Do you know what it would mean to move in the cities, and they know we are dragons among them?!" Endrir said excitedly.

"I do not know Endrir, but I know that if that was the case now, it would do nothing but give us the power we do not need," Destined said.

"How so?" Endrir asked. "They would be a little less reckless knowing there could be dragons lurking to reign them in."

"Exactly what you just said. It would give us as dragons too much power," Destined said.

"We should not control them, but exist with them, Endrir," she said. "I do not wield power over the Daughters of Ote. They respect me because I respect them and their beliefs."

"That is easier for both of you to say. You do not know the chaos those in the city cause. What they lack is fear that there will be repercussions for their actions."

"Fear does not allow room for growth and change Endrir the Broken," she snapped. "You know this. Why would you say something so dangerous?!" He did not answer her. He looked down at his hands with a frown. She sighed, realizing he had closed his emotions to her. "What did Laz find out about demons, Destined?" she asked.

"He met one, Nihility, but I do not know when exactly. I believe it had to have been some time during the War of the Dreaming. I believe he knew what it was and took the burden on himself to protect Sathea from it."

"How did you come by all this, Destined?" she asked.

"His own words, Nihility," he said.

"Where did he write these things? Why were they not left in a memory orb as we use? Lady Pax left many of those," she asked. Endrir gave her a look.

"Patience Endrir," Destined said, noticing his confusion. "Nihility, he left a journal of sorts in the way those below keep them. You know, like Endrir does while he is gone. It was left with the Order of Zal."

"You went to get it?" she asked, looking at Destined. He nodded. "And you keep a journal?" she said, looking at Endrir. He nodded. "I want to read it."

"It is personal, Nihility," Endrir said, looking away.

"I meant the one Laz left, Endrir," she said with a tone.

"I do not have it with me. I hid it," Destined said.

"You are such the dragon with your stash of books and trinkets, Destined Farseer," she said, rolling her eyes.

"You have little room to talk, dragoness, with your collection of clothes."

"I do not hear you complaining when I wear them," she said with a smile. "Now tell me what the journal said."

"I need to reread it myself, Nihility. After what I have learned with the missing Walkers, I need to put it into context. However, I believe Laz was in the Between. Not just his mind but his entire body. I believed he explored it in such a way while carrying the demon inside him for a long time. I asked you earlier about where we go when we experience death, and where do the spirits of those not attached to the Dreaming go? They go to the Between. Laz found the place for lost spirits."

"You do not believe he found it," Endrir said, blinking.

"You do not need to truth-see my words, Endrir the Broken. I would have just said had you asked," Destined said, giving him a look. "No, I do not believe he found it. I think the demon he held took him there. I think the demon came from there. There is an entrance somewhere here on Sathea. I do not care how Laz found it; I care why. Why did the demon take him there? Why did Laz go? Laz did not say. I know he accessed that demon's memories, and he saw the Between was important, but not why."

"What does this have to do with what you spoke to the council about?" Endrir asked. "You were both hiding something from them."

Destined looked at her, and she nodded. "Endrir, do you remember those stories Ergodi used to tell me about the door that would lead to utopia for dragon kind?"

"The Lost Door. What was the name they gave it?" Endrir asked. "Gyalliagor Tomb!" he said, recalling the name. "Gyalliagor Tomb where the lost door stands that hides the serpent's coils and dragon kind's salvation. Now that is a story full of jerboa shit," he said, shaking his head. He stopped and looked up at Destined. "Wait. You found it!?"

"That is not what I found; if it is, the story is exactly what you said, jerboa shit. What I found was Laz, Endrir."

"I am not following, Farseer."

"Laz made himself into a living barrier. I think he picked a place in the Between like the story of Gyalliagor's Tomb, maybe even the basis for it. I do not know. I saw him, and I saw them."

"Demons?" Endrir asked.

"Aye. A host of them so thick it would cover the entirety of Petrall Mountain range."

"You believe this is the reason the Walkers have gone missing in the Between?" Endrir asked.

"No," Destined said. She glanced at him. "I think the missing Walkers reeks of foul play among our own kind. The same thing you sensed about them at the meeting. Nihility went in after me, Endrir, but I found a door. Just a plain door like you would see on the homes of the short lifers. Beyond it was darkness. Deep in the darkness was a bright light. The light was Laz."

She looked at Endrir and tilted her head. She felt his shock turn to fear before he composed himself. She narrowed her eyes at him. "Endrir?"

"Nihility, it can wait a moment," Destined said. She looked at him and frowned. "I promise it can wait. Endrir, Nihility and I weren't meant to be there. Something happened that was not in line with a plan we have not seen. I have no proof of it, just what Nihility would call a feeling. The council, they feel off."

"They lied, well, Ergodi did. So did Ivylth," Endrir said. "I do not know what about. I only know they were hiding something in their words."

"I sent Tuzys to the Healing Circle with Master Sia before the meeting to check on Mica. Tuzys said when Master Sia touched Mica's mind, there was nothing there."

"What do you mean, nothing? You said Ellot's mind was destroyed, not Mica's," Endrir asked.

"Even in death, our minds will leave images. Sometimes it is the last thought we had or the last thing we saw. Mostly it is things that are dear to our hearts, but there is always something. Even if it is faint and unreadable, it is there. It is like when you gaze into the sun for too long, and it leaves a mark on your eyes. Mica had no mark. Master Sia said it was there. He could sense the trace of it, but someone had erased it."

"Someone tampered with Mica's mind?" she asked. "Who could do such a thing?" Destined gave her a look. "Well, I know they are capable of it, Destined, but why would they?"

"To hide something they have done," he said.

"You said Laz accessed the demon's memories. Did he learn anything else?" she asked, changing the subject. She had her demon to deal with. The council could wait.

"Nihility, the council," Endrir said.

"They can wait, Endrir. The demons are a more immediate concern."

"How so? I would think the council plotting behind Destined's back is an immediate concern."

"She is right, Endrir. We have more pressing concerns than the council right now. Yes, Nihility, Laz accessed the demon's memories, but he made little sense in his writings about it. He was not even sure if they were called demons. They have another name, but the demon told him that names have power. It seems they can make themselves forgettable or unnoticeable to others. He also speaks of their number, which I saw for myself. There are more than can be counted, and of that number, there were seven great demons that could destroy everything we hold dear on Sathea if they ever escaped."

"Escaped? Is that the word he used?" Endrir asked.

"Aye. Escaped."

"So are they trapped somewhere then?"

"Aye, but that is not a reason to rest easy. Laz made it seem like they are trapped but only need aid to leave that place. Not all of them, though, just the seven."

"Did he tell you more about them? How they look? Their abilities? What they want?" Endrir asked.

"No."

"Then what am I supposed to go on, Destined? I cannot watch if I do not know what I am to watch for," Endrir said.

"You stand where I stand, Endrir," Destined said. "I urged the council to do something about the fallen Walkers because they are empty of mind-body. They can easily become paths for others to travel out of the Between. They did not agree to do any more than provide Ellot with a return since he was the only one I could supply proof for. I am to devise a plan to find the others and keep the Between safe."

"How did Ellot get to that place, Destined?" she asked.

"Someone had to have led them there, Nihility."

"Someone you cannot see?" she asked.

"Aye. I do not know why, though. I just see the word 'betrayer.' It is always random. I have had visions of that door I found for months, but I do not know," he said, shaking his head. "They were odd visions."

"Odd how?"

"Like I saw it, and it was not me, but it was. The visions were always the same. I would approach the door. The only difference was the last time, the door was open, but I heard a voice yell at me to turn back."

"Endrir," she said calmly.

Endrir looked as if he would be sick. "Destined, Nihility," he said, looking. "I need to tell you something, but can it wait until after you tell me what has happened, please?"

"You hide from those you claim to love, Watcher. I disregarded the emotions coming from you in waves, even though some of them are upsetting for you to have right now. I want to know what you know, and I want to know now," she said calmly.

"Nihility, please hear me and feel what I feel now. I ask you on all that I am, have been, and would hope to be to you, please let me speak last," Endrir pleaded.

"Fear, sadness, and confusion. You will not leave here without explaining yourself, Endrir the Broken. You have been gone far too long. I am not who I once was, nor what you have known. I have grown, I have changed, and I have suffered. You will stay and explain, or I will rip the truth from you," she said with a tremor in her voice. Tears stung her eyes as she felt his jealousy and anger towards her.

"I will not leave," he mumbled.

"Nihility, I think we all have something to add here. Not just Endrir," Destined said. "Why don't you tell him what happened to you in the Between?"

"I would speak to Destined first, youngling. It will not take long," Pax said before she could respond.

"She would speak to you, Destined. She says it will not take long," she said.

"Are you sure?"

"Yes, but do not overwhelm me like last time. I will need to keep eyes on this one," she said, looking at Endrir.

"I made a promise, Weaver. I would hold it. Do not belittle me like a fledgling, Nihility!" Endrir hissed. "I understand you are angry with me, but at least wait until you have a proper reason. You will need more than the emotions you read but have no context for."

"Careful Watcher, you have misplaced your honeyed tongue."

Destined groaned. "Enough, you two!" he shouted. "Nihility, he is right. You do not know what bothers him. No, I will not pry. Endrir deserves more than that from both of us. Endrir," he said, sighing and rolling his eyes, "control yourself with our dragoness. You fucking know better, Watcher," he said. She looked down at the ground, frustrated. Endrir wiped the tears from his eyes. "Now I have a suggestion. Nihility, can you block the other for a moment while I speak with the Grand Lady? I think Endrir would do well to join me."

She closed her eyes for a moment and blocked Ana's presence in her mind. "It's done. You talk to her first. Then you may bring him," she said with a tone.

"Fair enough," Destined said, taking her hand and closing his eyes.

"Welcome back, youngling, and this time under better circumstances," she said.

Destined smiled sheepishly and rubbed his head with his hand. "Forgive my rudeness of our first encounter, Lady Pax. I was unsure of the truth."

"Enough of that. We cannot speak long. I have other things that need my attention, so let us speak plainly and quickly this time," Pax said. He nodded. "Do you know how to rid yourself of your demon?"

Destined winced. "Nihility knows then?"

"Of course she knows, youngling. She is your dragoness. Now, do you know?" she said.

"No, I do not, Lady Pax. He is not like the spirits I have met that have attacked me in that place. I think it is because he is not a spirit at all, but something else."

"I was worried about that. Nihility cannot rid herself of hers either, but I believe that is my doing more than her inability."

"The Black Flame," Destined said.

"Aye. It is hers. I believe I will linger until the power of the Black Flame is hers completely, but that is not the only reason I asked to speak to you. The door you saw now burns with my mark. It will act as another barrier to that space, but it will not hold as long as the life barrier Laz created. The walls of that space will thin, Destined."

"Thin? Why does that sound familiar?"

"You have my brother's journal, Destined, but there are more. I will have Nihility give them to you soon. What you need to know now is that the wound you saw, the one you tried to heal, was where I placed my seal. Whatever came through the barrier made the one there," she nodded at the demon, "recipient of my ward causing me to be here now instead of my intended place. Whatever came through with her was not one of the Seven Great Demons but, some variation of one the Seven."

Destined looked confused for a moment, then his face changed, from confusion to terror. "Lady Pax, could the offspring of one of the Seven have triggered your warding?"

"I supposed they would have the making of one of the Seven, but not be powerful enough to be their equal if they are a youngling. This is not what I expected," Pax said absently.

"I will look into it, Lady Pax," Destined said.

"That is not all youngling. A life barrier is difficult to break. Laz lingered in a half-state. It did not differ from those lost to the Dreaming. Those that even Weavers cannot wake. I tied us together. He was not Weaver, but he was because of our bond. To break that barrier, it would take two to do what they have done. Two to make, two to break," she said. Destined's shock rippled through. "What is wrong, Destined?"

"Those words, Lady Pax. I heard them in my mind after, well after Nihility left. I thought they were part of a vision. Sometimes I only hear words and phrases."

"Those were the words I spoke to another the day I reunited myself with my twin Destined. Perhaps you merely heard the past."

"Perhaps," he said, frowning.

"Bring the Watcher, youngling. I would meet him."

"Aye, Lady Pax. I will return in just a moment," Destined said, bowing.

Destined opened his eyes. He knew Nihility sensed his fear. He could tell by the way her head tilted at him and the slight frown on her face. "Destined?" she asked quietly.

"Can you wait a moment, my love? I am okay for now, I promise," he said. She nodded. "Endrir, take my hand, please, and do not let go. If you need motivation not to do so, just remember that you upset not only your dragoness but an Empath as well. Not really the emotions you want to become lost in," Destined said with a weak smile.

"In that case, let me hold you like a long-lost lover," Endrir said with a hollow laugh and closed his eyes.

The sound of a dragoness's hums greeted them. "Hello, young Watcher. My, you are glorious to behold. Your scales shine," she said with a smile. "You have coloring like those that hatched, and I called the first brood of Watchers. My Iros did not have such scales, but it did not take away his beauty. He was a lovely purple, like you, and gold that glittered."

Destined nudged Endrir and laughed. "Oh, he of the slick tongue has finally seen something to keep him quiet!"

"Lady," Endrir said. He stopped and cleared his throat. "Grand Lady Pax of the Depths, Mother of Watchers," he said, bowing deeply.

She hummed loudly. "He is much more respectful than you, Destined," she said.

Destined grinned at her. "My Lady, this is Endrir the Broken," Destined said. He looked at Endrir, and the smile died on his face when he saw Endrir's tears.

"Come youngling," Pax said. "I would say something for

your ears alone." Endrir walked forward, and she lowered her head down, so she was level with him. "Place your hand on my snout," she said.

"I cannot do that, Grand Lady! To touch a dragoness as grand as you in the presence of my dragoness is…" Endrir said, shocked.

"It is fine, youngling. I am sure Nihility will allow it," she said, smiling at him. He reached out a shaky hand and touched her lightly.

"I can see in your shadow your true form. I can see that and more. You hold secrets, young Watcher, but you must not keep them from those that love you," she whispered. She saw the image of Destined and Nihility clearly in his mind. "She loves you as much as she loves him, Endrir the Broken. I think you know that. What has happened to you, I do not know, but I know it troubles you deeply."

A face appeared as she spoke to him. She hissed and felt his shock and fear. "Grand Lady," he whispered.

"Be still, youngling. I see. I do not understand, but I see. You must speak to Nihility about this and soon. The Dreaming has come for you when it should not be possible. Go and be strong. All will be well," she said.

He removed his hand and wiped his eyes. "Thank you, Mother of Watchers."

"A pleasure, youngling. Now go. You both know that Weaver is not known for her patience," she said with a giggle.

Destined nodded and bowed. Endrir did the same. Then they were gone. She looked over at the darkened corner of Nihility's mind to the orb that held Ana. "What games are you playing demon," she said to herself.

"It happened when I went to get Destined from the Between. It was easier to show you than to tell you. I hold her spirit. When I took hold of her, I also took hold of the Black Flame," she said. Endrir nodded. She still sensed confusion and fear from him, but there was also a feeling of relief. "I think she is beautiful."

"Aye, she is. More than I ever imagined from the stories, but still, she has nothing on you," Endrir said, smiling at her.

"And his tongue returns!" Destined shouted.

"So, it was not a Weaver spell at the circle. You actually channeled Lady Pax and the Black Flame," Endrir said.

"Aye."

"There is another tethered to Pax somehow. She lurks at the edges of you. Who is she? I did not see her," he asked.

She looked at Destined. "I will explain that later. As for channeling Lady Pax, I had to, so they would listen to Destined."

"I am not so sure you were successful in that. Shegur still questions," Endrir said.

She sighed and rolled her eyes. "When does that one not question? She claims to see the truth but cannot read you, her most prized Watcher," she said. Endrir looked at her, shocked. "Do not look so surprised, Endrir. Who would know you better than I, save for Destined?"

CHAPTER THIRTY-FOUR

"Endrir."

"Aye."

"Are you going to stay on Petrall?" she asked, as they walked hand in hand to gather water for the tea she often brewed for them and more branches for a fire. Destined had gone back to the cave to get more food for her.

"I was thinking about it, but I am not sure if I can."

"Are things that bad in Tresai?" she asked.

"No, well, nothing that another Watcher can't handle. It is not Tresai that keeps me from here."

"Then what?" she asked.

He did not answer her, only squeezing her hand gently before helping her collect water. They gathered branches in silence on their way back. Destined was smiling when they returned and helped them start a fire. She watched Endrir as he sat away from her with his back against a tree. She could tell he was in his own thoughts, but there were so many emotions coming from him that made little sense.

"Endrir, I think it is time that you tell us what troubles you," Destined said.

Endrir sighed. "I have known you two my entire life. If it was not for you two, I would not exist," he said, looking at his hands. "Nihility, while you slept, I asked Destined to tell me what really happened when both of you found my egg. I do not know why I asked, but I did. Destined could only show me his memories of what happened. If it is okay, before I begin, I would like to have yours."

She frowned and looked at Destined. There was a knot in the pit of her stomach. "Is Endrir leaving us?" she asked Destined over their link.

"I do not think so, but I am not sure what he is thinking, Nihility. He closed himself to me," Destined said.

She moved and sat down in front of him on her knees with her legs tucked beneath her. She produced a memory orb and let it hang above her open palms in her lap. "What would you have me tell you?" she asked.

"You dreamed and heard my call, did you not? I would hear of it."

The orb changed. Nihility was sitting in the corner of the nursery and crying. "I do not dream, Endrir. I am Weaver. I exist in the Dreaming. I heard you in your dreams. You were the first thread I ever saw, the first I ever touched. You were my first, but I had no clue at the time that's what it was. I could see your dreams. Egg dreams are interesting because all you do is sleep. In our egg, weavers form our links and travel the upper levels of the Dreaming as if it is a game. We fly in and out of the dreams of others just like ourselves. I," she paused. "I was shaken from that game and into your thread. I thought you were mad. Sometimes you would call for help, others you would speak to your twin. It was distressing to hear and see through your eyes but not find you. It was heartbreaking to feel your pain. Destined helped, though," she said, smiling.

The orb shifted, and she sat before his egg with her snout pressed against it. "What are you doing?" Endrir asked.

"She was taking…" Destined said before she shook her head.

"Words of comfort. That we would free you both," she said.

"Nihility," Destined said. She looked back at him and smiled, but it was sad. She did not want Endrir to know that what she had really done was take his pain away from him. She had consumed the last of his pain and grief for the loss of his twin.

"What is wrong?" Endrir asked.

"Nothing, Endrir. He just can't let me tell my story," she said, laughing. "I sent a Weaver spell through your egg. I did not know such a thing was possible until I overheard Ivylth speaking with the Matron. I sent you the deep sleep. You did not wake for days after we got you to the Matron. I stayed with you until you did," she said. The orb was changing again, but she waved it away quickly.

He sat back with an odd look on his face. "Nihility, could you show me what she looked like?"

Her head snapped up quickly. "Endrir, I cannot show you what is not mine. I saw her through your eyes in your dreams. Do you not remember how she looked to you?" she asked him gently. She could see tears in his eyes.

"No. I only see the tree that grows on the far side of the nursery. You know the one," Endrir said.

"Do you wish to see?" she asked.

"Nihility, that is enough! You cannot do that!" Destined said.

"Be still, Destined Farseer. I would astound you at the things I have learned to do with dreams," she said.

"But it is a memory, not a dream!" he said. "Besides, you told me tampering with memories is forbidden, Nihility Harbinger!"

"I am not tampering with his memories, Destined Farseer. It is his memory, yes, but it is also a dream. Because he was in his egg, it means they are special dreams. I can help him see those dreams. Dreams I touched," she said, giving him a look.

"What do you mean, Nihility?" Endrir asked.

"You will know if a Weaver has touched your dreams, Endrir. It is subtle, but for you, a Watcher, you would know. If you wake to a smell that triggers a memory from your youth, for example."

"Or if you see something in a dream that should not be?" he asked

"Sometimes, if the dreamer is lucid, they can glimpse the Weaver. A shadow, or a face that you cannot quite make out. Those who are truly in touch with their dream will see the Weaver clearly, but not. Like if you had a dream of Destined, but instead of Destined, you saw me even though your mind knows I should be Destined."

"I did not know that is how the weaving works," Endrir said, frowning.

"It is an effect of the weaving. I can pull your memory easily, but I have never done it so precisely as to pull a certain image from a dream."

"I trust you," Endrir said, staring at her.

She averted her gaze, embarrassed. She loved his eyes; she always had. "You must sit still and focus on your sister. Do not waver your thoughts, or I cannot find the dream. Focus on her and how you feel about her, your strongest emotion. Do as I say, or you could have nightmares for the next year. Nightmares bring the Deep Dwellers from the bottom of the Depths, Endrir."

"Well, that's comforting," he said, making a face.

She placed her hands on the sides of his head. In her mind, Pax was giving her instruction. "Nihility, I know you can do this. Weavers do so in other ways; however, pulling an image is delicate work. It was a skill special to me and another dragoness. You must be precise in your actions."

"Yes, Lady Pax."

"Pull the Dreaming behind you just a little. When you see the light of it, focus on his wavelength. Let him lead you to the dream memory," Pax instructed.

Weavers did not need to sleep to enter the Dreaming. It was a constant for them as the sun and the moons of Sathea. They walked around and lived their lives with a piece of themselves permanently attached to the Dreaming. She touched her link, drawing herself to the surface of it. She saw the thoughts of those who slept flow into the Dreaming. Long strands of bright colors feeding the sky. She looked above those to see the colorful clouds of the thoughts of those awake who provide the Dreaming with their emotions and hopes, those they called the great thinkers.

Every dream had a color of whom it was associated with, the

Aura of Individuality. She looked for Endrir's iridescent purple. She spotted it easily in the grouping of those threads she held as Weaver. Even in the Dreaming, he shimmered. She floated along with his thoughts. He was feeling a longing for his womb mate.

"I have it, Lady Pax."

"Be precise, youngling. Find the image of Endrir's sister and draw it to you. Very precise Nihility or you will cause him renewed grief for her."

She knew exactly what Pax meant. She did not want to pull an image of his sister at her passing. She wanted one from before. He never felt pain from her death; she had siphoned that from him the moment it happened. The only pain he ever felt from the loss of his half was grief. Even then, she eased it without taking it away. He needed to grieve, to move past it, but she did not want him to suffer. She found the image she was looking for. There she was, a beautiful lavender dragoness close to hatching. Their chests touched, and her tail was wrapped around the leg of her brother. She pulled it into a rain-drop-shaped dream holder when she had the memory.

"Very good Nihility! Now pull the dream holder into yourself from the Dreaming. You can transfer it from outside the Dreaming now since the two of you share a link," Pax said.

"Thank you for this, Lady Pax," she said, opening her eyes. She removed her hands from Endrir's head. He took a deep breath as if he had been holding it for some time. "I am going to transfer the memory to you now. You will not forget again. Lean forward."

"Do I get a kiss?" he asked playfully.

"Only if you behave yourself," she said. She leaned in, and their foreheads touched. A slight glow formed, and then just as fast disappeared. She pulled back and saw he was crying; his hair hung in his face. She moved it away and kissed him. She lingered longer than she meant to, feeling her blood rise. Then she saw a short-life female's image and pulled away quickly.

"Thank you, Nihility," he said, wiping his tears.

"You are going to be renamed Endrir the Weepy if you do not stop," she said, teasing him. Her heart was breaking in two.

"I just need a moment," he said.

She moved away from Endrir quickly. Destined took her hand and squeezed, glancing at her as she wiped her tears away. Destined pulled her to him. "I have lost him," she whispered in his ear. Destined pulled back from her with a shocked look on his face.

"You saw her," he said over their link. She nodded. He sighed. "Endrir," Destined said. She touched his hand lightly.

"Who is she?" she asked.

"What?" Endrir asked, shocked. "Who?"

"If the emotions are powerful enough, I can see the image of what invokes them, Endrir," she said. She wanted to leave. "I saw her when I kissed you. The short lifer. Who is she?"

"Nihility, it is not like that!" Endrir said quickly with panic in his eyes.

"Empath," she said, looking up at him, struggling not to cry. "I am an Empath."

"I know! It is not like that, Nihility! Please understand."

"Understand what? That you love her? I do not need to understand it. I felt it," she said, standing up. Destined grabbed her hand tightly. "Destined, I need to go, please," she said, looking at him.

"No, my love. Let him explain."

"Destined, please!" she shouted. "I do not want to hear this."

"It is not like that, Nihility! I swear! I…" Endrir paused, shaking his head. "I don't know what it is. I think I opened a door that was not meant to be opened. I think she has something to do with it."

"What door?" Destined asked, shocked. "What door, Watcher!"

"I do not know, Destined!"

"I saw no door. I saw her," she said.

"Please, just let me explain," Endrir said.

She sat down again. "Fine. Let's get it over with, so I can leave."

Endrir looked at them and sighed. "Where do I begin?"

"The beginning is a good place to start, Watcher," Destined said, frowning.

"I was trying to get away from Petrall. It hurt to be here. It still does. I wanted to get away from the expectations I believed you had of me. I no longer wanted to feel like I owed you a debt for saving me," he said. She gave him a look coated in fire. "Before you move to disembowel me, Weaver, I know you did not believe those things, but I did. Somewhere deep down, I did."

"Why did you ask me to tell you of that day?" Destined asked. "Twenty-thousand years, and you have never asked. Why now?"

"I don't know, honestly. I have been dreading coming back, even though I did not hesitate when I heard Nihility call to me. I feel like we are broken like our bond has been broken. I know you do not understand, but I broke it. I wanted to know the truth before I lost the chance. I didn't need to ask before because the stories I heard from others were enough. I didn't realize that what those stories left out was how much both of you cared."

"That hurts, Endrir, and you know why," Destined said.

She looked at them both and frowned. She knew they had secrets. At least they believed they had secrets. She knew they loved each other deeply. It did not bother her. In fact, it suited her just fine because it meant that if she were not around, they had each other. They had each other when she had no one. When she had no home to run to from the pain they caused her sometimes, they had each other. "You were gone for almost two years, Endrir. What happened? What...what did I do?"

"You did nothing, Nihility!" he shouted. He closed his eyes

and took a deep breath. "That fight I had with Destined, do you remember it?"

"Aye. It was silly on both of your parts," she said.

"Aye. You and I went for a flight after you told us to stop. It was just the two of us because Destined was angry. I took you to that area off the base of the mountain where that tiny village was. We sat and watched those that lived there."

"I remember Endrir."

"You asked me how they handle such short lives after we watched a mother placing her lifeless child in the ground in the way they do. I told you I did not know, but in truth, I knew. They live, Nihility. They just live. Same as we do. They do not know their years are short because they know nothing else. They do not realize others live far longer lives than they do. Some fear death, some fear life, but regardless they live."

"That is not living, Endrir. That is merely existing," she said.

"Regardless, I left you that night and decided I would live too. Not as a dragon, but as they do. I watched, but I also indulged in their lives as I have not done before. I drank and shared their meals. I listened to their stores and what they believe in," he paused and looked down at the ground. "I loved as they love," he mumbled.

Rage blinded her. She was up and in his face in seconds. She heard Destined's gasp of surprise and the look of resignation on Endrir's face. "You are a dragon! You do not love as they love! Our bond goes deeper than the flesh they share and their empty promises, and it always will!" she screamed at him with tears in her eyes.

"Sometimes their love goes deeper than flesh, Nihility!" he shouted at her. "You are so blind. It is my duty to watch and to learn. It is yours to feel! Just as you would die protecting Destined, some would do the same for those they care for; mothers, fathers, sisters, brothers, lovers. Not all of them Nihility, but some. Enough that it makes watching them not so hopeless. In all the bad and death, love exists, and it is beautiful," he snapped.

"Endrir," Destined said calmly.

"No Destined! Her anger with me clouds my words. She will not hear me!" he yelled.

She turned and walked away. She was angry and hurt. She felt the sting of it in her chest all over again. It was always Endrir that brought pain. "Damn it," she swore, angry at herself for allowing it to happen again when she said she would not. Destined took hold of her hand as she passed.

"Endrir," Destined said again softly. He was looking at her. She could see him from the corner of her eye. "She is angry because you have hurt her. Twenty-thousand years, and you still do not see that she would give her life for more than just me, but for you as well," he said. He sighed and moved in front of her. He wiped her tears away and kissed her forehead.

"I want to go, Destined. I need to go, please," she whispered as he wiped her tears away.

"Nihility, my love, do not cry, please. Will you stay for me, my dragoness? I do not want to say it doesn't matter because I know it does to you, but I think he's done more than fall in love with this female in his mind," he said.

"For you," she said, sitting back down with her back to Endrir.

"Go on, Endrir. I would hear the rest of it," Destined said.

"Because I am not screwed enough, Farseer?" Endrir snapped.

"That's enough, Endrir. You made the mess, do not take it out on me," Destined said calmly.

"I met a female from down below. Her name was Ena. I fell in love with her, and I killed her. I watched the life force drain from her body," he said, fighting tears.

"Good. Saved me some work," she said under her breath.

Destined covered his laughter with a cough. "Tell me about

her, Endrir," he said. She looked at him like he had lost his mind to madness. He grinned at her and winked.

"I did not know what I was doing or what it could mean. I met her in Tresai. There was nothing uncommon about my meeting her. I meet many short lifers down below, but she was different. She was crying at the grave of her lost twin. We spoke at length for many days. She told me of her twin and the emptiness she felt left in her. It was like she was just what I needed, someone who understood me and how I felt."

"For Sathea's sake. I am an Empath. Am I the only fucking dragoness on this peak that knows what that means?" she asked, exasperated.

"Nihility! Your language, dragoness!" Destined said, trying to keep himself from laughing.

She turned, glaring at Endrir. "I know the emptiness you feel better than you do, you half-wit dragon!"

"Nihility, let him finish, my love. I know; I am pushing my luck. Trust me, I can feel the heat from the flames already. I can!" Destined said when she looked at him. "I can even hear Tuzys telling me how charred my bones are!"

"Go on then, fool," she said with a sigh, trying to fight the need to smile.

"I felt relief and hope. Here was someone I was not bound to. Here was someone that could understand my empty feeling because she had experienced it too. Although the circumstances were different, it was the same. She was beautiful too," Endrir said with a smile. Destined cringed and glanced at her. "She had long black hair that she kept in a single braid down her back. She was tall and had intoxicating green eyes. She would speak my name, and it was as if my entire body were on fire."

"Endrir, perhaps that is too much information," Destined said absently. He was watching her. Her head was tilted, but she was tense. The feeling that something was wrong was thick in the air.

She remained silent, reading Endrir's emotions. Something was off; even his color was wrong. They were muddled when they should not have been. She had a feeling and needed to think it through. Pax was silent in her mind, listening. "Go on, Endrir," she said in a faraway voice.

"I fell in love, and I did the things they do when they are in love. We shared our hopes, our dreams, and our flesh. Then I told her the truth of what I am," he finished quietly.

"They are not to know what we can do! Our sightings and stories you Watchers tell are what keep Petrall and us safe! What have you done, Endrir?!" Destined said in shock.

"I wish I could say that was the worst of it, Destined, but it is not," Endrir said. Destined groaned. "She had her own secrets. She told me that she could fill the emptiness of her missing twin because she could commune with her spirit. I have seen them do such things, although I do not understand them. I know they find relief in it. She told me she could help me find my sister's spirit even though she was a dragon. She said she could perform two different rituals. One would allow me to speak to my sister but not see her. The other required that I sleep, and in that sleep, I could see and speak with my half."

She turned to look at Endrir. She was struggling to keep her anger under control. She had lost Endrir to Destined first. Now she had lost him to some creature from the Dreaming. She did not know how much more she could take of him degrading her as dragoness. "Did it work," she asked in a calm voice. She felt Destined pushing at their link, trying to speak to her, but she blocked him out.

"I do not know. I cannot remember any of it. I only remember a door," Endrir said.

"What did the door look like?" Destined asked.

"No different from any door on any short life home."

"What happened with Ena, Endrir?" she asked.

"Nihility, don't you think you've heard enough?" Destined asked.

"Not even close, Farseer," she hissed. She knew he felt the rage in her words. He flinched and moved out of reflex.

Endrir sighed. "I cannot get any deeper than I already am, can I?" he asked.

"Actually, I think you can, Endrir," Destined said, looking at her with shock on his face.

"She came to me sometime later and said she was with child. As you know, their bellies grow large, and they carry their children for months as they grow inside them. I was shocked and did not even stop to think if such a thing was possible. Her belly grew and in a shorter amount of time than the other short-life females. I figured it was because I am a dragon. When she said her time was on her, I watched her birth, not one but two. The first was a lifeless one of short-life like her. He was shrunken and shriveled; his life force gone. The other was a dragon egg, but it was much smaller than normal."

"How on Sathea? Endrir, that is not possible," Destined said.

"I do not know, Farseer!"

"What happened to Ena?" she asked again.

"Nihility, is that all you care about?! Did you not hear him?" Destined said.

"Shut your mouth, Destined Farseer," she said with her teeth clenched. "He doesn't throw you away when I call or discard you for some fucking adventure, so just shut your mouth."

"She died Nihility! Is that what you want to hear? She died! The color left her eyes, and her body shriveled like the first child. I buried them both months ago. I hid the egg. It did not hatch, but it grew. When you called me back here, I brought it back with me and hid it where we hatched."

"Of course you did," she said. "Is there anything else, Endrir? Dreams perhaps?" she asked.

"Aye, after her death, I was plagued with strange dreams. Dreams of…" he stopped. "Dreams of things I do not wish to think about. It has become so bad that I have not slept to keep them away. I have had dreams of dark rooms with white light. I have had dreams of a door I know I should not open. I have had dreams of…" he stopped again.

She watched his face go slack when he tried to speak. A glazed look came over his eyes as if he was deep in thought. She stood, and her rage swirled around her. Destined stood up quickly and stepped in front of her. "Nihility," he said.

She stepped around him quickly. She was in front of Endrir as he stood before Destined could turn. He needed a reminder that he was a dragon, and she was dragoness. She needed to shock him from whatever held him. She punched him, drawing blood from his lip. She hit him two more times in quick succession. With each blow, she sent shock waves of her emotions through him. She allowed her feelings to say the things she could not find words for. She hit him one more time, driving him to his knees, where he stayed. She stood over him, barely out of breath. She took his chin in her hand and lifted it. There was a faint glow as she healed the damage she caused.

"I did not think to know a bigger fool than the one I gave my heart of hearts too. Destined is a fool, yes, but he is a fool for me. When he is not thinking of my safety, welfare, or heart, he is the most agile Walker Petrall has ever had. I never considered you a fool, Endrir. I never even took pity on you, but perhaps I should have. In my eyes and in my heart, you were strong, stronger than Destined," she said.

"Nihility," Destined said.

"Your sister shielding you from that collapse made you strong, Endrir. She poured all the life force she had left for the tiny thing she was into you. She did it to protect you, but you sold her memory for cheap tricks and fed a monster. Believe me, Endrir, Ena was indeed a monster. Maybe not the same monsters

I have told you tales about, but a monster. I do not know what you have done or the consequences of it. I do not even understand why you did it because, as your dragoness, your explanation is lacking."

She was crying and trying to keep her composure. She took Endrir's face in both of her hands. He looked up at her with wide eyes. "That was not love you felt from that creature. It was not even close. I would know because," she paused and sighed. "You could have sought comfort in the wings of one who would have welcomed you, your loneliness, and your pain and still loved you. Someone who would have loved you more because it was what you needed. It is what I need. I am not blind to your feelings, Endrir. I never have been," she whispered.

He stood but would not look up at her. "Look at me, Watcher," she said. He shook his head slightly.

"I can't," he whispered. "I can't."

His shame washed over her, almost taking her breath away. "Endrir, look at me, please," she said, placing her hands on the side of his face.

"I don't know what is happening to me, Nihility," he said, sobbing. "I thought I loved her, I feel it, but I know it can't be true. It can't be. How can it when I felt as I did when you called to me?" he asked with his voice breaking.

"I will always love you, Endrir, always," she said, moving the hair from his face. "Pull yourself together now." She kissed him lightly, letting her fingers trail over his lips. Then hugged him tightly.

CHAPTER THIRTY-FIVE

"We should go back to the cave," Destined said, looking around.

Endrir nodded and doused the remains of their fire, methodically covering the traces of their presence. Destined took her hand and led her back to the cave. "Destined, you are too rough," she said, pulling away from him.

"Come in, Nihility, please," he said, waiting for Endrir.

"What is wrong with you?" she asked. "Are you angry about Endrir? You are the one constantly telling me to accept him."

"I do not care about that, Nihility. You could have had him right there if you wanted, and I would have welcomed the show."

"Destined!" she said with a giggle.

"He opened the fucking door!" he hissed at her.

"I figured as much the moment he said he dreamed of it," she said, shrugging as she walked deeper into the cave.

As soon as Endrir entered, he ran his hands around the entrance of the cave placing barriers. He put barriers to alert them if someone came near and prevent anyone from seeing inside. It would appear as if the rock face was solid instead of the cave entrance.

"Why are you suddenly so paranoid?" she asked him.

"Why are you not?" he snapped. She gave him a look.

"Careful, Farseer. She will beat you bloody, then heal you, so you are tip-top for the next time," Endrir said with a weak laugh.

"You are lucky that is all you got, Watcher," she said, rolling her eyes. "Destined, what is wrong!? Your emotions are all over the place."

"I think we are in more danger than we have ever been in before. The threat was there, yes, but this," he shook his head, "this is big. Perhaps too big." He was thinking and talking. He started pacing. He was missing something; he could feel it. "Nihility, can you remember what you saw when you entered that space? I want to see how you saw the barrier."

She produced her memory orb. It floated right in front of him. He squinted, trying to see, and she giggled. "Here, fool," she said as it expanded in size.

"Did you know Laz created these? I wonder how he did not harm his eyes looking at such small images. Show me how you did that later, my love," he said, rambling and distracted. The barrier appeared as he remembered it. It floated in a sea of black. The wound already existed. He walked away and began pacing again. "I wish it could see it before the wound when the Twin Stars of Petrall were together. There is something there. I can feel it," he said, agitated.

"Destined," Nihility said over his ranting.

"Yes, my…" the words died on his lips. Endrir stood looking at the orb with the same glazed look on his face. "Endrir?"

"He will not respond, Destined. A creature from the Dreaming has touched our Watcher."

"What?!"

"Be still. Endrir is in no immediate danger. However, why don't we see what we can while I have the trance triggered," she said. She touched the side of Endrir's head. Her memory orb changed; instead of her memory, it was Endrir's.

"Nihility!" Destined gasped.

"I see," she said calmly. Endrir was in the dead space, walking towards the barrier in darkness. The door stood open behind him. Destined watched, waiting for the orb to bring forth the picture of the barrier. As the light came into view, it was not Laz but Destined. "Well, that is strange," she said.

"Nihility, why am I there? Why am I there?!" Destined shouted. He looked at the orb and saw the eyes from his vision, and he screamed.

"Destined, are you okay?" Endrir asked as if he had missed

nothing in the last few minutes.

"My light," Nihility said, rushing to him.

"The eyes! The same eyes!" he cried out.

"What eyes Destined?" she asked. He shook his head. He could not answer. "Destined, you must tell me if you want me to help. Is it the other?" she asked. He shook his head no, and then he stopped. He kissed her as if she had won a prize. "I do not think now is the proper time for that," she said.

"You wonderful, beautiful, brilliant dragoness!" he said smiling. He kissed her again. "Hidden from me," he whispered to her. She looked at him, confused. She had given him the piece that was bothering him inadvertently. Endrir was hidden from him, just as he was hidden from the demon he held prisoner. "Endrir," he said calmly. "What have you done to prevent me from seeing any part of you?"

Nihility groaned. "Fools. I am surrounded by foolish dragons," she mumbled, walking away. Endrir moved and then seemed to think better of it and simply sat down on the ground.

"You told her more than just about you being a dragon, Watcher. You told her everything. And by everything, I mean everything! You told her of me and my abilities!" Destined said. His voice was like steel.

"Aye. I," Endrir stopped and shook his head. "I don't know why!"

"Did you not find it odd that she would be so curious about me, but not her?" he asked, pointing at Nihility. "She is our dragoness, female, the same as this Ena."

"Watch yourself, Farseer! I am nothing like that creature," Nihility hissed.

"Of course not, my love! I definitely know the difference even if the Watcher does not," he said, winking at her. "My point is Endrir, even if you did just tell her the story of you, it cannot be told without her, so why, Endrir the Broken, did you not watch?!" he scolded. He was not shouting, but his words had force. "Did your feelings for me not make you question? Am I not your…" he stopped and sighed. "Did the rival in you not question why she would be so interested in me, another dragon? Specifically, me, who you harbor some jealousy for?"

Endrir recoiled as if he had struck him. "I am not jealous of you!" he shouted.

"You talked too much and listened too little, and the worst part is you did not see Watcher! That damn dream did not end in some bright light. You saw me! You have always seen me! Now tell me how you hide from me?"

"I did nothing of the sort, Destined! All I did was tell her of you and the council. She wanted to know what it was like living here on Petrall. She was curious about how we dragons have lived so long among them, and no one ever knew."

"What do you mean, he is hidden from you?" Nihility asked.

"I cannot see him in my visions. It happens sometimes, so I thought little of it. I think it is because we are so close. However, with him being gone for so long, I should not struggle as I have. But I realized I was not struggling, Nihility. My visions, I have seen him, but I did not see him."

"You were watching the Watcher," she said with a grin on her face.

"Aye! It did not occur to me until he said what his dreams were. I watched Endrir but could not see him because I looked through his eyes. Why are you smiling, Weaver?"

"I am waiting for you to put it together, my light. You take your lessons well from your Weaver, unlike someone else I know."

"Did you sense anything from him just then with the orb?"

"Only confusion, fear, and a few others that I have constantly sensed since his return."

"How long were you allowing yourself to be led to your sister in your dreams, Endrir?" he asked.

"Almost a year. It was not right away," Endrir answered with a sigh.

"You said you began having dreams after Ena died. Where the dreams always the same?"

"Yes. I mean no. Sometimes they changed. The ending is always the same. I wake up screaming."

"Do you hear anything in them? Voices, perhaps? Screaming?" he asked. Endrir nodded. "If what he says is correct, they started about the same time my Walkers went missing in the Between."

"The catalyst was her apparent death," Nihility said, nodding.

"Correct. I sent them in, to begin with, because the appearance of another dragon frightened a youngling training under Master Sia. Master Sia found nothing, so I dismissed it. Sometimes the young ones do not have a strong handle on their minds. Spirits in the Between cannot take on their physical forms or the forms of anything else."

"What changed?" she asked him. She still had a smile on her face. She caressed him with her fingertips, and he shivered, feeling her desire.

"Behave my dragoness, at least for now," he said. "Nothing changed. It just kept occurring. Master Sia was frustrated, and so was I, so I sent the others in to investigate. They did not return. I mean, that did not raise the alarm because it did not occur with every Walker sent into the Between. It appeared random."

"Does it appear random now?" she asked.

"The weaker pairs. It was always the weaker pairs until Mica and Ellot!" he exclaimed. "Obviously, Endrir is part of this," he said. His eyes went wide. "Two to make, two to break!" he said. "Nihility, we were not expected! He was!"

"What?"

"Why is it always about you, Walker? Must you be everyone's revered dragon? I am sick of it!" Endrir shouted.

"Nihility, my love, what are those creatures you told me

about a long time ago that live in the Depths of the Dreaming. You know the ones that feed on one's greatest desire?" he asked, grinning at her.

"You and your stoic responses and perfection. They treat you as if you are a god among us all because you are a Walker of the Between!" Endrir continued shouting.

"Endrir, if you do not shut your trap, I am going to have your tongue," Nihility said.

"Nihility, the name my love. That creature has him."

"It is a Warida, Destined, but do not think that because one has him, I will not use it as an excuse to silence the fool."

"I would think nothing of the sort, my love. I just thought that perhaps you could show your new fool some compassion."

"I would have shown him compassion had he paid attention the day I told you both of the dangers lurking in the Depths and how to spot their kind. No, not this fool. This one walks right into the arms of one and shares himself with it!"

"How long have you known, Nihility?!" he asked, shocked.

"Not long enough. I did not know what I sensed until he spoke earlier. I disregarded the feelings I felt from him when I saw him on the Great Path, but Endrir…Endrir is always hard to read."

"You let him continue on without questioning him? You always question me when my emotions change, or there is something odd," he said, feigning hurt.

"Why wouldn't I? He was gone a long time, Destined. I do not even know who that damn dragon is right now," she said, glaring at Endrir.

"My love, I know things are complicated between the two of you, but they do not need to be."

"Destined the Farseer, Great White Hope of Petrall. The one to save us all, the rest of us just shit beneath you!" Endrir said.

"They are not complicated, Destined!" she shouted. "Endrir, will you shut up!" His eyes went wide as Endrir stopped screaming and looked at Nihility. He could feel the rage between them. It felt like when another dragoness challenged her. Endrir looked as if he was ready to attack her at any moment, but she did not move. "Try me, Watcher," she said with a tone that spoke of fire. "Right now, I would welcome the chance to put you on your ass properly."

Endrir blinked rapidly but did not move. "Nihility, why did he stop?" Destined asked.

"I am dragoness!" she said. "His anger is not directed at me; he sees me as only a rival because of that thing that had its claws in him."

"What?!" he asked, shocked. "Nihility…"

"I do not care, Destined. Just as I did not care about his erratic emotions. I never know with the two of you, anyway. For all I know, it could have been another prank where you toyed with his mind. It wouldn't be the first time. Like when he smelled like the bushes at the base of the mountain for a week, the ones that smell like sick jerboa shit. Or when you had an extra horn for a month. More welcome home gags. No, I did not care to investigate Endrir the Broken's feelings."

"Our downfall will be the fact that you know every foolish thing we have ever done," he said, laughing.

"Why are you laughing? There is nothing funny here!" Endrir started again with his tirade against Destined.

"We can't talk to him like this, Nihility. Can you stop it?"

"Why should I? This is the most entertaining thing I have seen in a while. He really does not care of your grandstanding, oh great Walker of Petrall. Besides, he may even have a point or two," she said with a smirk.

"Nihility!"

"If he gets himself killed challenging me, it is your fault," she said, moving to Endrir.

"What? Wait," he said.

"Too late, Great Farseer," she said, coming to stand in front of Endrir. His eyes were full of rage as his fingers flexed into balled fists. He would fight if she provoked him. "Endrir, you will be still, or I will make you be still Watcher." Endrir took a step towards her, and she smiled. Destined saw nothing but danger in it. Endrir nodded and relaxed. She reached up and touched the sides of his head. "See that foul bitch you fancy and only her," she said. Her hands glowed a furious red. It sounded like Endrir's flesh was burning, but he was in no pain. He blinked a few times, and she let go.

"What was I saying?" Endrir asked.

"You were saying what an ass the Farseer is," she responded, walking away.

"Hilarious Nihility," he said.

"I found it highly amusing. Just as I will this next part," she said, looking over her shoulder as she walked to the back of the cave.

Endrir grabbed his head and cried out in pain. "What is wrong with my head?" he asked, grimacing.

"Nihility, what is wrong? Help him!" he shouted.

She spread out one of the woven grass pallets they had used many years ago. "I already have. Twice, in fact. Once to remove the glamor he was under when I smashed his face in, and a second time when I removed the emotions, she left behind. My work is done," she said, stretching out on the pallet and placing her hands behind her head.

"My love…"

"I can do nothing else for him, Destined. The severe pain will pass in a moment, but the spell was placed deeply. His head will pain him until I can remove it completely," she said.

He moved over to Endrir and kneeled to comfort him. He pulled him to his chest as Endrir cried in agony. "It is okay, Endrir. I am here," he whispered to him. "You said it would only be a moment, Nihility," he said, wincing.

"Normally, this only happens in the Dreaming, while the

one under the spell is asleep. He must experience my work while awake. It is interesting to watch," she said absently.

"You also said they only take you while you sleep," he said.

"He was asleep. He allowed himself to be placed in a type of sleep. You heard the fool's tale. That is not my concern," she said.

"What is then?"

"Destined, stop with your protective shit for him before you find yourself in a worse place than he currently sits," she snapped. "He will be fine. My concern is the how," she said, sitting up.

"Are you still angry with him?"

"Wouldn't you be angry?" she asked, giving him a look. "Yes, act shocked. Feign hurt, Destined. The fact is, he has never placed you beneath anything else. You are the pinnacle. I am just the dragoness."

"Nihility, you are not just the dragoness. You are our dragoness," he said.

She rolled her eyes. "Endrir, are you better now? Does the pain still overwhelm you?" she asked.

He sat still for a moment, cradling his head while he leaned against Destined. "No. It only throbs, but it is not unbearable. Can you tell me what just happened? I feel like I have been asleep too long."

"Your head pains you because you were a fool who ignored the teachings of your Weaver," she said.

"Endrir, what happened?" he asked softly.

"I got angry at you. I do not know why, but I did. They were my feelings, but I could not find a reason. I was just angry."

"It is okay. Those feelings were already there. If what I remember from our Weaver is correct, they were just heightened," he said.

"Correct," Nihility said. "At least someone listens to me."

"You know I wish you no ill will. There is no way that I can," Endrir said, looking up at him with sad eyes. It broke his heart.

"I know, Endrir, but I would be a fool to think you did not

have some ill feelings deep down. After all, look where life has taken us. Not to mention loving the same dragoness has a funny way of creating those types of feelings," he said.

"Aye," Endrir said.

"But we both know she chooses for herself. No one makes her do anything," he whispered, making Endrir laugh.

"I upset her," Endrir whispered.

"She loves you," he said, grinning at him. "It will be okay. I promise."

CHAPTER THIRTY-SIX

Destined brought Endrir water and food, encouraging him to eat. They spoke in whispers she could barely hear. She knew they talked about her by the glances they both made in her direction. She sat on the grass pallet, watching them. "You were right. They do not realize you know they love each other as more than friends," Pax said in her mind.

"No, they forget I am an Empath. They forget I am dragoness," she said with a tone.

She felt Pax's hesitation before she spoke. "How long have they been in such a way?" Pax asked quietly.

"I think it has been ten-thousand years. At least that is when I noticed it."

"But you have only been Destined's mate for how long?" Pax asked.

"Three thousand years," she said with a sigh.

"There should not be such secrets between the three of you, youngling."

"Lady Ygi was right; you are always the teacher," she said with a smirk.

"How else will a dragoness learn? We must give lessons when they are needed," Pax said, making her chuckle.

"There shouldn't be, Lady Pax, but we all have secrets or questions not asked."

"Nihility, you are correct. It is a Warida, but I have never seen one outside of the Dreaming. They cannot leave. They exist there alone," Pax said.

"I know, Lady Pax," she said, taking a deep breath. She needed to put her anger aside and focus on helping Endrir.

"Nihility, do you have any idea who the creature is that did this to him? You said they have clans. Perhaps one of those that live there knows," Destined asked, pulling her from her thoughts.

"No, unfortunately, I must know more about this Ena," she said, making a face like she had something she did not like on her tongue.

"Is that really necessary, my love?" Destined asked.

"A creature from the Dreaming touched him here on Sathea, Destined. Yes, it is necessary."

"It is fine, Destined," Endrir said, moving away. "What would you like to know, Weaver?"

"You said you knew her from Tresai. Had you spoken with her before? Did you know of her or her twin?" she asked.

"I never spoke with her before that day, and I do not think I had ever seen her either. Tresai is large, Nihility. The city could house the three of us with room to spare. I cannot remember all of their faces, but I can say that I never spoke to her before."

"How is your head?" she asked.

"The water helped. I am tired, though," Endrir said.

"And your stance, does it still function properly?"

"Aye."

"I need you to use it for clarity. I want to make sure what you remember is exact, not what you feel needs to be said."

"I will not lie to you, Nihility," he said with a tone.

"But you would try to spare my feelings, Watcher," she snapped. He looked at her, shocked.

Endrir was a Watcher, but being a Watcher was more than the color of scales and the magic of changing forms. Their minds were different from other dragons. They could store information from their lifetimes with precise detail. A Watcher who used the Watcher Stance could remember and recount even the smallest detail. Their eyes would glaze over as their minds collected information. In that stance, they became detached fact givers and receivers.

"I can access it without pain," he said, looking away.

"Good. What do you remember the first time you noticed Ena?"

He sat up, and his eyes glazed over, appearing a darker violet than usual. His voice was monotone as he answered. "I saw her at the death yard where they keep their dead. She was sitting on a stone seat, crying. She walked me to the stone marker they used to show where their dead lie. It was her sister's," Endrir said. He frowned, coming out of the stance. "I cannot remember the name on the stone."

"Can you recall how Ena looked that day or any day after?" she asked. "Not the basic details like her eyes and her hair, Endrir, but things like what her mannerisms were, or what she wore?"

"She was wearing a green dress in the style the city females' favor. Long black hair, braided, and green eyes," he said, slipping back into his stance.

"What about the day you shared her flesh for the first time?" she asked.

He flinched. "What?" he asked, coming out of his stance.

"The day you shared her flesh for the first time, Endrir. It is not a moment you would forget. I have not forgotten my first time, and I am no Watcher," she said, rolling her eyes.

"Who was that with?" Destined asked with a grin.

"Not you," she answered.

"Ouch!"

"Oh, you meant you. I am sorry. Well, it was quick, so the details escape me," she said, grinning at Destined.

"My ego is shattered!" Destined said, clutching his chest.

"Endrir, an answer, please," she said.

"Green dress. Black hair. Green eyes."

"And the day of her death?" she asked. He sat for a moment with his eyes closed. She saw the frown appear on his face and the lines on his forehead deepen. He looked at her. "Green dress, black hair, and green eyes," she answered for him. "Do you have recollections of conversations you two shared?"

"Aye. They are intact and detailed, as are our physical moments. Any attempt to recall just a mental picture of Ena results in the same image. It is like when you stare into the light too long, and the image remains after when I access my stance."

"Was she present when you attempted to speak with your sister?"

He nodded. "Just the two of us."

"When you slept, did you dream on your own, or did she give you something?" she asked.

He groaned. "Every time I think I might just be done screwing myself over with you, I am right back where I started," he said. "Ena gave me a potion until her passing. Now anytime I sleep, I have the other dream," he said.

"Other dream?" Destined asked.

"Wait, Destined, I will explain soon," she said, nodding at him. "Can you recall the taste of the potion, Watcher, since you were fool enough to drink it," she paused and sighed, "repeatedly." He sat with his eyes closed for a long time before opening them and shaking his head.

She sat, thinking for a moment. "Control your emotions, the both of you. I am trying to concentrate," she said absently. The Warida did not need a potion to lure the dreamer, but that is because the dreamer was already asleep. If one was to somehow operate outside of the Dreaming, they would need a potion to send the dreamer to sleep to work their magic, but she could not think of any substance that would affect Endrir's mind. He was not like other Watchers. He is a student of the Poisoned Four. Taught to withstand the effects of most poisons and plants that would induce sleep. "Had to come from the Dreaming then," she said to herself. "Endrir, did she ask you what you desired the most?"

"Aye," he said, looking at her in a way that made her pause. She realized why she had not triggered his anger as Destined had, only his jealousy.

"Your answer was not your sister," she whispered. He nodded as a tear slipped from his eye.

"Have my memories been tampered with?" he asked.

"No. There is no way that could happen. You are Watcher and would have noticed. This is subtle, intricate work; done with a delicate hand. Something I have only seen from inside the Dreaming," she said, tilting her head. "From the Beauty of the Depths," she said, frowning.

"Who is this Beauty of the Depths, Nihility?" Pax asked in her mind.

"A myth. I never found the creature they call such, but it could do as this one has done to Endrir to dreamers and those in the Dreaming. However, all their victims were unharmed, unlike Endrir has been, and never the same victim twice. They would always leave the dreamer something else to dream of."

"Interesting," Pax said. "Did you ask Terg about them?"

"No. I never had the chance," she said, frowning.

"What other dream, Nihility?" Destined asked, interrupting her thoughts again.

"Destined must you keep interrupting me," she snapped. He looked shocked, then grinned at her.

"Sorry, my love. I should have known you would consult with the dragoness you admired."

Pax hummed in her mind at his words, and she looked away, embarrassed. "Ass," she mumbled.

"I do not dream of my sister anymore," Endrir said.

"You will now, Endrir. Just as you used to. I have given you back what it took. She needed something to fuel her work, and she used the dreams of your twin. However, you are not completely mended," she said. "I will deal with that later."

"What do you dream of then?" Destined asked.

"He dreams of the door, Destined. Before, while Ena worked her magic, he dreamed of his greatest desire," she said.

Endrir's fear, confusion, and shame were thick. "Control yourself, Endrir," she said. He nodded.

"But he saw me," Destined said.

"Aye, but that was not the truth, Destined. Endrir saw the barrier, but you are linked to him. You were his mind's way of warning him to turn back."

"Did you always see me at the end, Endrir?"

"Aye, until recently. Now I see something else," Endrir said, shivering.

"Do not push, Destined. I would not have those things lingering in Endrir's mind right now," she said, laying down.

He nodded at her. "Nihility, Endrir did not lead those Walkers into the dead space. He may have been the reason they went in, but he was not how they found that place."

"I know," she said. "That means we have another problem to add to our growing list."

"What is that?" Endrir asked.

"We have Walkers who are still missing in the Between, and you seem to be the catalyst for providing a distraction for their absences. They were searching for you, Endrir." Destined said.

"But that does not explain who led them to the dead space or who has done this to Endrir. However, I believe they are connected somehow."

"Why do you say that, my love?"

"A feeling," she said, closing her eyes.

"The council?" Endrir asked.

"The council is not capable of what was done to Endrir," she said in a dreamy voice. "But that does not absolve them from a hand in the missing Walkers. Regardless of my feelings, Destined Farseer, the fact is Ergodi and Kuri have access and knowledge."

"I know," Destined said. "I believe they are up to something, but I cannot be sure of what. They are hiding something from me. Ergodi was not even alarmed when I said something consumed Ellot's mind-body. He was more concerned with where I found him."

"I know they are hiding something. It was in their words," Endrir said. "But it was not just Kuri and Ergodi. It was Ivylth too."

"What about Pimo?" Nihility asked.

"She did not show any signs of falseness until you spoke. It was not her words, but her body language Nihility. The same as she has always been since you rescued Ivylth," Endrir said, looking at her with a frown. "Destined, what is wrong with Nihility?"

"Nothing. Our Weaver is in the Dreaming," Destined said. Her eyes were closed as she lay there with her hands behind her head. Her breathing had slowed considerably. The deep black lines on her body moved and swirled.

"Her markings are moving, Farseer."

"Another thing that has changed while you were gone. Nihility maintains footing on Sathea and the Dreaming."

"It is disturbing," Endrir said, watching her.

"I can hear you, Watcher," she said, sitting up. "Keep an eye on the council. Destined, I encourage you to speak with Master Sia about what is going on. Ergodi and Kuri avoid him. Why?" she asked.

"I don't know, Nihility. I have never asked. You know how Master Sia is. He is always angry."

"Only with you," Endrir said, laughing.

She rolled her eyes. "He is firm with you, unlike everyone else. Speak with him, please."

"Aye," he said, pouting.

"As for Endrir, whoever did this to him would have had to bargain with a creature I believed to be a myth. I do not know if Ena is this creature or how she would have contacted you on Sathea. I also do not know what spell she could have used to create that egg. How would she have known to seek you specifically? Most creatures from the Dreaming fear dragons and would know us on sight. She had to have known what you were the minute she met you. Were you having nightmares before you met her?"

"No. I was fine," Endrir said. She tilted her head, feeling his embarrassment. "What do you mean, physical contact? I met her."

"Aye, and that is the problem. I told you Ena appears to be a Warida, Endrir. Do you not remember what I told you about them?" He shook his head. She sighed. "Dream feeders, Endrir. However, I have not met one that could physically manifest themselves on Sathea to work their magic to feed. They require the dreamer to be in the deepest of sleep. That is why I said it sounds like the one I have heard of from those that live in the Dreaming but have never found myself. The problem is, that creature, whether real or myth, harmed none of those it fed upon."

Destined stood up and started pacing again. "Someone had to have known about Endrir before. Known enough to know where he was and for how long. They had to gather emotions, memories, and circumstances about him. Someone watched the Watcher," he said.

"Not possible," Endrir said. "I would have known. I am a Watcher!"

"A Watcher who bedded a monster without question," she mumbled.

Destined rolled his eyes at her and sighed. "You said things have been changing rapidly down below. Perhaps you were distracted by the new magic they are using," Destined said.

"What new magic?" she interrupted.

"They do more than heal the sick and pull the elements now. They are studying in more formal ways," Endrir said.

"That is not new. That is natural growth. I have seen as much from some of their dreams. What is new?"

"I cannot tell you with absolute fact Nihility because I have not seen it for myself. I was going to investigate before I met her," he said, looking down at his hands.

"Good to see you have not forgotten you had a duty. Now humor me with the tales you have heard," Nihility said, sitting up attentively. "I would know. Drinkers are on the move and other nastier things that can move between Sathea and the Dreaming."

"They say that there are those they are calling necromancers wielding death magic. Magic that takes life or uses the dead to do its work," Endrir said, making a face. "Ghastly tales of those that have known someone that died, but then saw the individual walking around at night with the stink of death on them. One tale was that a dead short lifer who had his life taken by another returned and destroyed his killer with flame."

"Do you know how they do it?" Destined asked.

"For Sathea's sake, Farseer, no, I don't. I don't think I want to know either. Dead things should stay that way. Imagine if every foe I fell got right back up."

"Most of them would have trouble doing so without limbs, Endrir," she said, trying not to laugh at the look on his face.

"And now you get her started," Endrir said, rubbing the side of his head with both hands. "The stories are all different. Some say it's the ground they bury the dead in. Others say it uses an object that once belonged to them. I am tired, and my head hurts."

She stood. "Then it is time you slept properly. I need you rested and at your best to deal with the spell and the egg. You too, Destined. I will keep watch. We can head back up at sunrise."

"I will sleep later. I have something to do first," Destined said. "Tend to Endrir." He moved to the wall near the cave entrance and sat down.

She took Endrir's hand and moved him over to the pallet

she was lying on. He laid down on his side, and she laid down beside him to see his face. He would not look at her. "Endrir."

"I know you are mad at me," he mumbled.

"I am not mad," she said, moving the hair from his face.

"I just want to sleep and forget this all happened," he said, closing his eyes. Nihility leaned forward and kissed him. He groaned and tried to fall into the kiss with her, but she pulled away. "Nihi..." she put her fingers to his lips.

"Sleep. We can talk about it later," Nihility said. She leaned over him and whispered in his ear, "As you sleep, I lie awake. As you dream, I weave." Her words were laced with the sleep spell Weavers used. "Rest well, Endrir the Broken, dream of me."

CHAPTER THIRTY-SEVEN

He settled down across the cave near the entrance. He wanted to give them privacy without leaving. The relationship between Nihility and Endrir was always chaotic. He never knew if it would end in happiness, anger, or hurt. He blamed himself for it. She chose him to share her heart of hearts, but it was his fault the dance began. He lied to them both, but he could never bring himself to tell her the truth. He was afraid she would walk away from him, and that fear was enough to seal his lips forever.

There was also the secret he kept about the relationship he shared with Endrir. They were mated. He did not think Nihility would care, but Endrir had sworn him to not tell her, and he obliged. He knew why. Endrir believed it would ruin any dream he had of holding Nihility for himself. He struggled with it, his need of her. Destined felt it deep down all the time since he had exchanged his heart of hearts with Endrir. An ache for her he could not sedate or distract Endrir from.

He sat in his meditative pose with his legs crossed and his back straight. Nihility walked over to him and smiled. "He snores in this form too," she said, making him giggle. He watched her project an orb from her hand as her marks moved. It moved to Endrir and floated over his head. A second followed and stopped above his own where he sat. She took a few steps outside the cave. Both orbs pulsed black for a few seconds then changed colors; one shimmered purple, the one above him a yellowish-white.

She walked back to him and crouched down in front of him to speak to him quietly. The Watcher snored, but he would be up in a second if he thought something was wrong. "I will record your thoughts, and if you sleep, your dreams."

"But Nihility, you are not supposed to," he whispered.

"I know, but I also know what it is you are about to do,

Destined. I must weigh the rules of Weaver against the promise to protect my dragon. The dragoness will always win. I cannot stop you, and I cannot go with you," she said, glancing up at the orb, "It will alert me if you find yourself in danger. You only need to focus and call for me. Do you understand?" He nodded, and she kissed him. His hands went to the side of her face, wanting more of her before she pulled away. "I love you. Be safe," she paused, "Be the dragon I know you are," she said.

His heart throbbed like it wanted to burst from his chest with love for her. The orb blazed white, and she grinned at him. "I love you, Nihility," he whispered. He watched her walk out of the cave. She would watch over him while he confronted his demon.

As a dragon, he only needed to close his eyes to find the flow of his own thoughts. In this form, it was harder for him because he could not sense himself completely, but he did not want to shift. He needed the safety of the cave. He resettled himself in his pose. Nihility's kiss had woken a part of him he did not require at the moment. He put his hands loosely in his lap and relaxed from his head to his feet. He steadied his breathing. It was hard not to match the steady breathing of Endrir while he slept.

Everyone accessed their consciousness differently, some easier than others. Nihility seemed to just place herself there. It always amazed him at how easy it was for her. He asked Master Sia why she could do it so quickly, and he said it was because she spent so much time in her own thoughts. Endrir did not have to do any work; it was like opening a locked door when he accessed his inner mind because of his Watcher Stance. He was not like them; he needed to concentrate. There were always too many other thoughts that intruded on his mind to make his ability empty his mind and find his own flow easy.

It was made more difficult because he had locked a part of himself away in a forest in his mind. The dragon, Endrir called the Farseer, lurked in that forest, held back by a tangle of thick trees. Endrir and Master Sia called it a cage. Destined considered it a safeguard for himself and everyone around him. He struggled with controlling all the power at his disposal. Once before, he lost control and hurt others, innocents. It was something he refused to let happen again. It also kept Ergodi from knowing precisely what he was capable of. He loathed being called Destined the Divided, but it was an apt title. He was divided; he had done it to himself. It was another secret he was keeping from Nihility. He frowned, uncomfortable with the thought, and forced himself to relax again.

His mind was always the same. He was in grassland that led to a pool of water. The pool had various paths of rushing water running from it deeper into his mind. All of them were paths of thought. Even standing at the mouth where all his thoughts formed, he could not count them all, but he could be consumed by them.

There was a forest to one side. Only a single path led there, made of purple and white stones. The trees were thick, creating darkness within. He heard the low growl and sighed. He pushed at the trees, forcing them back from him. Anytime Endrir was around, the forest crept closer to the pool in his mind. Regardless of how he divided himself, the Farseer always sought his freedom; he pursued his treasure.

He turned his attention back to the pool. As he grew, he had learned to merge more minor thoughts into larger ones. It was a constant task, and why he meditated often. He looked over to one of the larger legs. It was vast, fast, and the water jet black. It was all his thoughts of Nihility. He wanted to dive in, especially after that kiss, but he could not. He was searching for the white water of his mind. That was the line that took him deep into his own consciousness. His breathing slowed, almost as if he was asleep. He moved towards the pool of water, and a small raft appeared.

He got the idea from watching a group of short-life fishers in a river below.

Fishing fascinated him. All the fishers he had watched seemed so at peace with themselves. It was not rushed like chasing prey through the forest or plucking them from open grassland. He did not enjoy killing, but something removed its horror in fishing. He stepped onto the raft and let the current carry him down the path. He floated until the river ended at a platform. He climbed up and opened the solid white door that waited at the top of a short set of steps. When he entered, he was hit with his emotions for Nihility. This is where he kept his feelings for her, the part they shared in their heart of hearts. It created a warmth that empowered him. The dark grey orb was in the center of the room. It might as well have been a giant stone hovering off the floor.

The beast would not get free. Despite its efforts, it could not break the barrier. Its greed had allowed it to be caught in a perfect trap. He had read its thoughts the moment it touched his mind. It wanted to feast on more Walkers, and with Destined, it was in a place of ecstasy until it realized something trapped it. Then the greed that consumed it turned to fury. He had sealed it inside the orb since, but it was clever. Instead of continuing to rage, it tested its confines, looking for cracks. The moment he felt it, he reinforced its prison.

He approached and paused. He had to suppress his feelings quickly. A large part of him felt shame that this demon took him so easily. It was a violation to him he could not scrub clean. He turned his head as he heard the growling from the forest. He sighed and dropped the barrier enough to speak to the demon within.

"Hello, demon. I see you stopped your wailing," Destined said, smiling.

"Let me out!" it screamed.

"You know that will not happen," he said, laughing.

"I said let me out now, dragon!"

"Commands will get you nowhere, demon. Try please," Destined said with a smile. "Courtesy should not be overlooked," Destined said as he waved his hand and conjured a chair made of wood. It was the kind the Order of Zal used. He sat in it backward with his arms resting across the back. He conjured one inside the orb. "You should calm yourself. Have a seat and relax. We should talk."

"I have nothing to say to filth such as you," it said.

He was receiving waves of incoherent thoughts. He realized the demon was, in fact, a male of their kind, and it really believed itself above him. "Filth, you were so eager to take over. Filth you were eager to feast on. The filth that made you his prisoner? Is that the filth you mean?" he asked. The demon paced before he resigned himself and sat stiffly in the chair. "Well, at least you are capable of more than just shouting. I was worried for a moment." The demon looked at him with fury in his eyes. "I will not insult your intelligence, well any more than I already have anyway, and I would appreciate if you would not insult mine. Can we agree to those terms?" he asked.

"Aye," the demon said.

"Good. How about a question-and-answer session to break the ice then?"

"Sure," the demon said, relaxing back in the chair. The demon's entire demeanor changed quickly, but Destined did not let the demon know he was shocked by the change.

"Obviously, you know I am a dragon, even though both times you have encountered me, I was in this form," he said, pointing to himself. "How did you know?"

"I could tell from your mind. That form does not hide the truth of who and what you are from one such as me. Regardless of what form you see yourself in, I will always see the truth of you in your mind."

"Did you kill Ellot?"

"Who is that?"

"The one before I arrived."

The demon tilted its head up. "There were only two before you. Neither perished by my hands," he answered.

"The hands of someone else, then?"

"Perhaps," the demon said.

He got excited by the game he was about to play. The demon was answering each question directly and without detail. He would need to keep him talking. Details always came from those who did not guard their tongues. "How is it you know of dragons?"

"We have always known of your kind."

"I am flattered then. We have had little talk of demons among my kind," Destined said. He saw the demon's eyes flare briefly. "The only mention of demons in the histories is how the great Laz defeated one of your kind and sealed it away in a prison of emptiness so long ago no one really remembers if it is true. I am afraid your kind are nothing more than tales told to young dragons to keep them in their nests at night."

"He was not great. He was merely lucky. He created an obstacle, that is all. One that we obviously overcame," the demon said.

"How do you consider his victory luck? He created a barrier that kept you away. You may have captured him, but it was only a small piece of the glory that was the dragon Laz." The demon's eyes went wide for a second, and he shifted in his chair.

"It was luck that the one who inhabited him did not foresee his plan. He was not that great. If he was, why would he have wasted his efforts to create a barrier that could be crossed?"

"Or perhaps it was a warning to not attempt to cross. I guess it all depends on the side of the barrier you stand on," Destined said. The demon sat, reflecting. Destined had kept himself still, even though his excitement was ripe. The demon had done precisely what he wanted him to. He needed an unrestricted view of the barrier, and now he had both sides. The demon had forgotten he could visualize its thoughts. "Who is Ena?"

The demon's face lit up as he smiled. "A perfect tool and an even better distraction."

"Who is she to you?" he asked.

"Nothing."

"Who came through the barrier with you?"

"Many," the demon said, grinning.

"Come now!" he said, laughing. "Let us not pretend and give empty answers. I do not mean those bottom feeders I felt in that dead space. The ones who hid in fear of the mention of my name. I am sure you heard the whispers, 'the Farseer comes.' I came, and they hid. I want to know how many came through that matter."

"We all matter, dragon!" the demon said with anger in his voice. "Even those you call, what was it? 'Bottom feeders', have a purpose."

"What would that be?"

The demon shrugged. "Do you not have a purpose? Do you not exist for a reason? What is your purpose?"

"You felt my purpose the moment you attached yourself to my heart's desire."

The demon looked at him, confused. "I do not understand what you mean."

"Is it you lack understanding? Are you capable of what you feel surrounding you?" he asked. "Touch the walls of your new home and see."

The demon made a face of disgust. "I have no need for this emotion. It has no purpose."

"Once again, it depends on where you are standing," he said, spreading his arms.

The demon scoffed, "what do you intend to do with me?"

He did not answer right away. He did not know. "I have not decided yet," he replied.

The demon jumped up from the chair, sending it crashing to the floor as he pounded on the orb. He hissed in pain as the orb burned his fists. "You will not keep me here like some animal in a cage! Either kill me, which I do not believe you are capable of or release me now!"

"Free yourself," Destined said calmly.

"I cannot! You hold me here!"

He sighed. He was extremely patient by nature, but even his patience had limits. He also had a distaste for the rudeness of strangers. It was the one thing he found repulsive about some short lifers, and especially the Fairy Folk.

A growl in the distance made the demon turn towards the door and frown. "What was that?" it asked.

"I had hoped we could have a conversation, a civilized conversation, but it seems I was mistaken. I will not tolerate demands. As you are not here as an invited guest, I expect better behavior. It was your own foolishness that landed you where you are, so do not think you are some mighty creature. If you could best me, you would have done so."

"I miscalculated!"

"You were overcome with greed!" he said, emphasizing the last word. "You were overcome with greed and blind to your own limitations. This happens when you think too highly of yourself. You find a force that you cannot match."

"I was not even looking for you, so do not get too full of yourself, dragon," the demon spat.

He caught a clear image of Ellot and Mica, but that was not all. He saw Endrir. His treasure. The growls in the distance turned to hisses of anger. He saw the demon flinch at the sound as it echoed through his mind. "Who were you looking for?"

The demon closed his eyes and took a breath. He turned and picked up the chair and sat back down. "That simple bitch had one job. Lead one so that her other could break the barrier with their magic, magic special to them. It did not go as planned. I do not know why he was trusted or why his bitch spawn was trusted. I warned them they should have taken the other, but they did not listen. I saw the treachery in her mind. Then that damn dragon ran in fear, fucking coward that one was. I do hope he was not one of your best."

"Not even close," he said with a smirk.

"We saw the trap too late. I could deflect it but used up too much power doing so. You were there. You were the only choice I had."

Destined frowned as he saw the image of a creature that looked demon, but not like the demon he held. He could not tell if he saw the same female or two as he saw two images in different attire. The demon's response had raised a host of questions, but before he could ask, the demon spoke again, interrupting his thoughts.

"I have answered your question. I would have one of my own," the demon said.

"Go ahead," he said, nodding.

"Who is the one I see when I touch this?" the demon asked, pointing to the orb. "The one I have glimpsed through your eyes."

"She is mine," he replied casually. He did not know where this line of questioning was going, but he would follow it if it allowed him to ask more questions of his own.

"You possess her?" the demon asked.

He was so shocked and put off by the question; he started laughing hysterically. He waved his hands at the demon to show he meant no offense and tried to collect himself. "No one possesses that one," he said with a giggle. "My whole tail just clinched from the thought of it," he said, sending himself giggling again.

"Then how do you control her?" the demon asked.

The question made him giggle harder. "Is that a serious question?" he asked, wiping the tears from his eyes.

"Aye."

"I do not control her. The thought has never crossed my mind. I think if it had, I would spontaneously erupt into flames," Destined said, snickering. "Do you control the females of your kind?"

"Aye. Females do our bidding. The one with me was mine before the trap took her."

Destined had to compose himself, but he realized the one he spoke of must be inside Nihility. "Do you mourn her?"

"Why would I do that?" the demon asked, making a face.

"Because you cared for her," he said, giving the demon an odd look.

"She was entertaining and filled a need. She held no other meaning for me. However, I would understand the meaning of the one in black," the demon said.

"Her meaning is simple. Danger. Danger to you or anyone else who tries to harm her."

"You protect what you do not possess?" the demon asked.

"Do you?" he asked.

"A question to answer a question," the demon said, laughing. "I suppose you can say I did. I kept her for myself. It is not unheard of for us to do, but it is rare."

"The danger is not from me," he said, smiling. "The danger is her. She is dragoness!"

The demon sat back, expressionless. "We were looking for those that travel that place, but in pairs only," the demon said.

"For what purpose?" he asked.

"To find the one that would be two to open the way."

At first, he was confused, Endrir was no Walker, and he would never be in the Between with a pair. Then it occurred to him, they needed him to find the space. He remembered what it was about the door he had seen. It was not his memory, but that of Lady Pax; 'two to make, two to break.' The words she spoke to another he could not place before she sealed herself to her brother's barrier. He turned his attention back to the demon. He needed one more thing from it. "I would have your name, please," he said.

The demon chuckled. "You have heard the tales of my kind Destined the Farseer!" he said. "You have heard the stories of the Lesser; that names have power."

"I have, but I will say I did not know what it meant."

"They have the power to bind, the power to hold, the power to banish, and even control. With a name, one can be seen and unseen."

"You mean it ties the essence of who that being is into their name?" he asked.

"Something like that, Farseer. Does your name have meaning?" the demon asked.

"Aye, to the one who gave it to me. However, I do not believe that their will defines who I am," he said, thinking of Ergodi.

The demon nodded. "A Lesser will conceal their name as you do the one in black from me," he said with a sly grin. "For those like myself, however, there is no such limitation. You will need more than a name to harm me, Destined the Farseer, Long Walker of the Between, and Seer of Past and Future; much more than a name. So, you may have my name freely, without lies or trickery, only because you asked."

"It is that easy then?" he asked.

"Aye. You have shown me the value of this word 'please.' I am Malolon."

He could not see any image when Malolon spoke his name. However, he felt the power behind it. He knew the moment he heard it; it would be more problematic than he expected to rid himself of the demon. "Pleased to meet you, Malolon. Although I wish we did not have the pleasure of knowing one another in this way."

"I agree, Farseer. However, I think you and I will speak again before this is all over. In fact, I think we will both come to know each other very well," Malolon said. "I am sure I have given you enough to set your mind to work."

"Aye," he said, rising. He nodded at Malolon. The demon had moved the chair and stretched out on the floor. He placed his barriers back on the orb and turned for the door. He stopped and looked back at the darkened orb.

Something bothered him. He walked out, and he could hear Malolon laughing. He felt like he was missing something. He knew his mind. It usually meant he was indeed missing something obvious when that feeling occurred. Until he found out what and why he needed to be cautious, especially with Nihility. Malolon seemed far too eager to know about her. It made him uncomfortable. Before he willed himself away, Destined did something he felt necessary; he locked the door. It was the eyes.

CHAPTER THIRTY-EIGHT

"As you sleep, I lie awake. As you dream, I weave," Endrir heard Nihility say with her lips lightly against his ear. He tensed, then felt himself grow lighter.

"Nihility," he said, jerking awake, but he was not in the cave. He was back in his home in Tresai. The smells of the city invaded his nose as he watched the flicker of the candles dance across the wood ceiling. He was lying on the room floor in his home where he used to think. His house was modest, not the largest in Tresai by outward appearance, but once inside, you realized your eyes had tricked your mind.

This was the room he created with Nihility in mind. He had done so on impulse. There was no furniture; only soft cushions littered the floor with large woven mats the nomads used for sleep. Recesses in the walls held candles the locals made from wax and flowers. It made the room smell almost like her. "Nihility," he whispered to himself as he laid in the middle of the room in his borrowed form in nothing but his pants.

"Aye," her soft voice answered.

He sat up quickly and gasped. Nihility stood across from him, wearing one of the long shirts he used to attend the city short lifers' formal events. It hovered above her upper thigh, teasing more. The candlelight flickered across her face, lighting up the deep brown of her eyes. "Is this real? Are you really here?" he asked.

"I am always with you, Endrir," she said, making her way to him. She laid down beside him and touched his arm. He laid back down on his side, facing her. "I missed you," she said, moving the hair from his face and tucking it behind his ear. "Endrir."

The sound of his name from her lips made his whole body tingle. He kissed her as he moved on top of her, straddling one of her legs. He ran his hand up the side of her leg, feeling her skin's softness. He pressed himself against her, trying to ease the ache he felt for her. "Nihility," he murmured as he kissed her neck. "Oh, Nihility."

She moaned as he let his fingers caress the soft place between her legs. He felt the wetness of her. "You are all I ever wanted in a dragoness," he whispered to her. "My Nihility." He moved his hand faster, listening to her moans of pleasure as he buried himself in her neck, taking in the smell of her. He felt her press against him squeezing his hand, and moved to see her face. She looked at him not with the beautiful brown eyes he had known all his life but green. He recoiled from her, moving away quickly.

"Endrir."

"You are not her!" he shouted. "You are not my Nihility!"

"I am all you desire," she said. "You welcomed me in."

"Lies!" he screamed, covering his ears and closing his eyes.

"Two to make, two to break," she whispered next to his ear, making him gasp and open his eyes quickly. He was in darkness. He turned, searching for a way out. He saw a faint light in the distance.

"My Sun," he said, running towards the light that felt like Destined. When he drew close enough to see, he saw him standing there with open arms. He rushed to embrace him. "Destined! Something has happened."

"Aye," Destined said as a tear rolled down his cheek.

He frowned as Destined's face changed to one he did not recognize. "Watcher of Watchers," the stranger whispered, "the Demilune calls to you. Embrace the shadow. Beware the Serpent!"

"Who are you?" he asked, backing away. "You are not my Sun!" he shouted, turning to run when a giant jade serpent appeared tightly coiled. Its head loomed before him, large enough to consume him even as a dragon. It lunged at him in the darkness with its jaws wide. He flinched and crossed his arms over his face, waiting for the feel of its jaws.

Then there was nothing. Endrir uncovered his face to find himself once again in the room of his home. He turned his head to look and saw Ena. "Endrir," she said, but it was like an echo. He turned his head away from her, but there was Nihility on the other side; rage filled her eyes.

"No!" he shouted, sitting up quickly. Right in front of his eyes was the egg he helped create.

"Look here, my treasure. Look here and rest," the Farseer's voice said. He looked past the egg and saw Destined standing in the darkness creating his own brilliant light.

"Help me, my Sun," he cried. "Please help me."

CHAPTER THIRTY-NINE

He opened his eyes and let himself adjust to being back in the confines of the cave and out of his mind. He looked over at Endrir. The Watcher slept, but it seemed troubled. He moved over to him and touched his shoulder. "Find me, my treasure. Find me and rest easy," he whispered to him. He kissed him on the side of his head and went to the cave entrance. He projected his thoughts toward Nihility, letting the orb do its work. She appeared before him out of the darkness.

"Will you not sleep?" she asked as she brought the orb to her palm and led him outside.

"No, my love," he said. His body felt fine. Meditation always had a way of rejuvenating him. His mind was tired, but sleep never cured him of that.

"Do you wish to keep this?" she asked, holding out the orb. "I only used it in case you needed me."

"No. I need you to keep it. Especially if it does what else I think it does."

"What do you mean?" she asked, tilting her head.

"It records emotions as well, doesn't it?" he asked.

"Aye. You know my magic knows no other way."

"Then I would like you to keep it for me. Do not access it yet," Destined said, placing his hand over the orb in hers. "I would speak to you first." She nodded, but he could tell by the slight frown on her face she was not comfortable. He kissed her forehead where the lines of her worry appeared. "If there was anyone I would trust with my thoughts, aspirations, ambitions, and fears, it is you, Nihility Harbinger. You, who knows me better than anyone on Sathea."

"I do not want this to linger in my hands regardless, Destined. Thoughts and emotions are not to be taken lightly. I already stepped beyond where I am allowed by recording it. You know I am forbidden from touching your thread."

"I know, my love, and I thank you for taking the chance on me."

"That is an odd thing to say, Destined. I took no chance with you. I love you. There is no chance in that."

"There was for me. There was a chance you would not want to love me."

She scrunched her face up in a way that he found absolutely charming. "I would have cared for you regardless, Destined Farseer. You are the dragon who kisses my tears away, even when they are not mine."

He grinned like a fool. "Did Endrir give you trouble? He thrashes in his sleep."

"No. Endrir's sleep is troubled because the magic still holds him. Lady Pax is going to help me rid him of it, but she said she had to prepare first."

"You cannot create a better dream for him?" he said, looking back.

"No. I would have Endrir have whatever dreams would come that he cannot seem to speak of or remember clearly."

"Nihility," he said, frowning.

"Destined, do not start with your worry over the Watcher. He is safe. I would know if he was not."

"Why did you not know someone had tampered with his dreams?"

"I don't weave his dreams, but I know nothing has touched his thread."

"Why not? He is not like me," Destined asked.

"Because I can't, Destined," she said with an attitude.

"What have you been doing?" he asked, leading her to a group of rocks where they could sit. He helped her up and then stood between her legs.

"Storing energy. I have been away from the Dreaming too long."

Unlike himself or Endrir, she needed to keep contact with the Dreaming. Even her Empath abilities were tied to it. She equated it to a fish in water when he asked her about it. The Dreaming was her pool, and she must not stray too far from it. He wrapped his arms around her and put his head on her chest while she rubbed his back.

"Did you rest enough, Nihility?" he asked. He could smell the Dreaming lingering on her skin. He kissed her chest lightly.

"Destined?"

"Hmm," he answered, rubbing her lower back and moving his face across her chest. He loved the smell of her. Thoughts of feeling her against him invaded his mind. The place she sat put her in the perfect position for her to wrap her legs around him, making him grin with delight.

"What has caused that?" she asked.

"I desire you all the time, Nihility," he said, kissing her neck. He felt the urge to have her strongly. The dragon wanted his dragoness.

She took his head in her hands and moved it so she could see him. She ran her fingers over his lips. "Would you like me to create your dream space?"

"Why? I have the real thing right here?" he asked, pulling her towards him and kissing her.

"Destined," she said with a slight moan.

"Would you deny me, my dragoness? Would you deny me even though you feel my desire for you?" he whispered in her ear. He unlaced her shorts slowly as he kissed her neck. He could feel her breathing change. She moved her hands to help him slide them off. "I want you, my love," he said.

"Hurry," she said, freeing him from his own pants. She wrapped her legs around him, and he pushed inside of her slowly, relishing the feel of her around him. She grabbed on to him tightly, squeezing him with her thighs. "Destined," she moaned. He did not know what had come over him. All he knew was that he wanted her badly. He held her hips as he pushed in deeper, moaning as he found his rhythm. She bit at his neck right below his ear and clawed his back. "More, my light. Please don't stop," she moaned.

He grabbed on to her tighter and quickened his pace with her moans. She leaned her head back as she moaned his name. He felt the warmth of her wash over him and sighed, leaning into her as he released from the sensation. She rubbed the back of his head. "I am sorry, my love. I do not know what came over me," he breathed, kissing her shoulder.

"I thought you said you wanted me," she said, biting at his ear. He groaned. She squeezed him, looking for more.

"I have left you unfilled," he pouted.

"I do not feel unfilled my light," she said with a wicked grin.

"How do you feel?"

"Like a greedy dragoness. You should clean up the mess you made, Destined."

"It is the polite thing to do, isn't it," he said, kissing her quickly.

"Courtesy is important," she said as she leaned back, and he kissed down her chest. The minute his tongue slipped inside her, she moaned loudly. The beast in the cage groaned in pleasure with her.

"Did I do something wrong, Nihility?" he asked as he sat on the rocks, watching her dress.

"No, my light," she said, coming to him and wrapping her arms around him. She laid her head on his chest. "I worry about Endrir."

"I am worried too, Nihility," he said, kissing the top of her head.

"We are drowning in problems right now. There is little room to move, and I am afraid to make a decision that may harm one of us. Destined, what Endrir has done with that creature, and that egg…" she said, stopping herself.

"I know, my love, I know," he said, rubbing her back. "I am sorry he hurt you. I hope you know that."

"It is not your place to apologize for him, Destined. He must stand on his own as a dragon."

"I know Nihility, but…I do not know how else to help him right now."

"I have a feeling, Destined."

"Good or bad?" he asked.

She sighed. Destined was one of the few that believed her feelings meant something. It was not because she was a prophet or anything of that nature. He believed them because he knew where they came from. Sathea spoke to her through them.

"Bad, Destined. Really bad."

"I was hoping you would say something that would put me more at ease, my love. Like when you tell me, Endrir will come home safe."

"I am sorry. I did not want to burden you."

"Burden me? With what?" he asked, frowning.

"I have had the feeling for a while. Since Endrir left."

"Nihility!"

"I did not know what it meant, Destined. I did not want to tell you for obvious reasons. You two were fighting, and I was afraid Endrir would not come back, but now…"

"What made the feeling stronger, Nihility?"

"When I came to get you from that place," she whispered. "I saw something when I was with the Daughters. Vivian…" She stopped.

"Talk to me, my love," he said, cupping her face in his hands. "I am here. I am listening."

"She threw the dream sand Destined, but she was asleep! I

saw you in the image, but a jade serpent surrounded you. It made me feel…small."

"Small? I do not understand," he said, frowning.

"I felt like whatever it was or is I could not save you from. Not fear, but small; weak."

"I did not see a serpent in that space, Nihility. I have seen nothing like that in the Between. I mean, some things are lurking in there, but they have no form. They hold meaning to the things they see in the dream sand, yes?"

"Aye," she said.

"Maybe you should contact Vivian and see if she can tell you."

"Maybe," she said. Destined hugged her tightly.

"I am failing at protecting the both of you," he said. Nihility tensed against him. "I know you do not think I am, but not being able to see what comes feels like I am failing. I spoke with the demon I trapped inside of my mind."

"About that," she said, pulling away from him. "Why did you not tell me?"

"Because I did not want to be set on fire, my love," he said, thoughtfully.

"Get rid of him."

"I…I can't," Destined said, wincing.

"Destined."

"I can't, my love. He is not what I expected. He is strong, cunning, and dangerous."

"He cannot be that strong. He could not overpower you."

"No, but…"

"But what, Destined Farseer?" she said.

"He feels like he is almost an equal in power to me, or he has the potential to be equal. We play a game," he said. Nihility groaned. "Not like that, my love! I just have to watch every word. He told me his name."

"They lie better than a Watcher. The one in me lies, or at

least tells half-truths. She has given me her name, but not her complete name."

"I do not believe this one lies," he said. Nihility stepped back and put her hands on her hips. There was a frown on her face as she eyed him carefully. "You saw a glimpse of him before, I know, but I assure you, my love, my dragoness, it is me."

"Then why would you say something so foolish?" she snapped.

"I am your fool, my love," he said, laughing as the thought of possessing her popped into his mind.

"I do not know why you are laughing. There is nothing funny here, Destined. I swear I should be more like Ygi and punish the both of you when you forget who is the dragoness around here! Maybe bathing in flames will bring you to your senses."

"Nihility, it is me," he said, trying to sober himself. "If it were not, your orb would have alerted you. That is why you gave it to me!"

"Aye," she said, looking at him suspiciously. "Explain yourself. Why do you trust the words of a demon who sought to take you over?"

"I was going to, my love. I got distracted by your eternal beauty," he said, coming to her.

"Your laments are still shit," she said, trying to hide her smile.

"He was gone for two years. I have no one to steal from," he said, pressing his forehead to hers. "I only laughed because he is misguided in how a dragoness behaves."

"Who? Endrir?"

"The demon," he said.

"Same difference," she said, rolling her eyes.

"Nihility, be nice, my love. He does not love that short-lifer. He loves you. You said yourself he was under a spell."

"He shared himself with her Destined. The desire to do so had to be there before," she said sadly.

"Will you forgive him for me? I do not like when you two are at odds with one another."

"Tell me why you trust the demon's words."

He sighed. "I was going to see if you had spoken to Lady Pax about this yet," he said, hugging her.

"We have a little, but not while you were speaking to that demon you hold. I was watching you and storing power. Pax and I both agreed it was more important I have my full concentration on that."

"Do you need more time?"

"No, I am fine now," she said.

"How much longer do you believe Endrir will sleep?"

She shrugged. "I do not know. Are we keeping secrets from each other now, or are you after more of me?"

"No, and yes," he said, grinning. "I do not want to explain all over again if he interrupts."

She rolled her eyes, "speak, dragon."

"You must work on your patience, my love," he said, laughing. She gave him a look, and he spread his hands in surrender. "No fire, please! I spoke with Malolon, and he…"

"Who?" she asked, cutting him off.

"Malolon," he repeated. She shook her head as if she was being annoyed by something. "Can you truly not hear his name?"

"No. Every time you say what it is you are saying, my head fills with buzzing as if I walked into a nest of insects."

"Interesting. Can you say the name of your demon for me?"

"I do not believe it will be the same since she did not give me her true name, but she said her name was (buzzing)."

"What is it?"

"(buzzing)."

"I hear buzzing when you say her name. He told me names have power over demons less than himself. The power to hold, banish, bind, and control. He said demons will hide their names if those things can affect them. However, with him, I would need more than his name. Perhaps your demon does not."

"Why do you believe what he says?"

"Well, my love, to some extent, we have proved the truth of his words. We cannot share their names. You said your demon would not tell you her full name, but she has given you a piece. I think we are going to use all of our abilities to determine if what they say is the full truth."

"How so? What can I do? I know why Endrir would be useful, he can see the truth, but I am only an Empath."

"You are much more than just an Empath, Nihility Harbinger," he said, rolling his eyes. "However, your ability to sense emotions may prove useful. That is why I wanted you to keep my orb."

"Tell me what you want me to do," she said. Destined hesitated, and she frowned. "Destined, tell me."

"You must promise me you will not make this a priority, Nihility. I want you to take it as just another task that you can do."

"Destined, tell me what is going on."

"I think you can sense the emotions I felt when I heard and said the demon's name. I need you to try because it may be the key to ridding myself of him."

"Tell me now what you need!" she said with wide eyes.

"Nihility, please remember that this is not our only task," he pleaded. "The council lingers, and then there is Endrir."

"Destined, I can help you and do whatever else needs to be done. Helping you may very well be the key to helping myself. Love aside, the thing we need the most is the one who can sense what is coming clear of mind," Nihility said. "The only fool between us is you. Do not doubt my ability to love you with my entire being and do what needs to be done again. I am your dragoness."

"Yes, my love," he said, smiling.

"Now, what do you need from me?"

"There is a moment recorded on the orb where he told me his name. I think I said it pleased me to meet him and used his name. I need to know what emotions you can sense during both moments."

"I will need a moment. Before I shift through the contents of your orb, I need to know if there is anything else I should look for. This is taxing work, and it would be best to get it all now, considering I have to shift through Endrir's dreams as well. I have to find the creature that did that to him."

"Aye," he said, ashamed of himself for thinking her incapable. "He gave me a clear view of the barrier through his eyes. I just need to know if you see anything. And he speaks of another female; her image entered my mind. It is there. It was after I asked if he knew Ena," he said, looking away from her.

She touched his face and turned him to face her. "I love you, Destined the Farseer," she said before releasing him. She moved away and sat down on the ground in the position he loved. She sat with her knees tucked under her, back straight, and her hands loose in her lap. The orb she used to record him hovered before her as she closed her eyes. He shifted to a dragon and laid down to wait.

He did not know how long he dozed. He was startled by a strange shift around him. Nihility lay on the ground when he opened his eyes, eyes open, mumbling something he did not understand. He reached forward and touched her lightly with his snout. She stopped mumbling and blinked. Her eyes were alive with flame. She stood and walked over to him, placing her small hands on either side of his eye.

"See what I see, Farseer," she said in a faraway voice. "What only my eyes can see, I share with you. Burn it in your memory. Once it is shared, the fire will begin to cool. Fan the flames through the past, so the message burns bright in the future. You shall be the keeper of what should be closed. I remain the keeper of what burns."

He could not move. He kept his eye locked on hers, mesmerized by the flames. They spiraled in her eyes, shifting colors of orange, red, white, and yellow. Then she spoke. He could hear her voice and countless voices behind her. Their voices echoed and harmonized together in a smooth cadence that was almost a song.

"Oh, the prophet of white, are you near? You have led the broken here. The barrier of life created from the heart of one, but the soul of two lay forgotten. The one who would be two walks through a dream, and the door becomes a reality. The one who would be two, the two who would be one, twin souls set free. Guardian of the Between, beware the Serpent! Summon the Harbinger!" she said.

He felt as if he was on fire as she spoke. Once she was done, she collapsed back to her knees. He blinked and was thrust into a vision. He could see Laz in battle with a demon that was monstrous. He saw Laz in the space alone. He saw Laz as his soul, and the soul of Pax was poured into the creation of the barrier. He felt himself burning, and he heard the demon scream in anger. He was feeling Laz's pain as if it was his own. It was a pain so great he did not know if he could bear it. Just when he thought he would have to rip himself apart to get away from it, it stopped. He opened his eyes and shifted forms. He ran to Nihility and scooped her up into his arms. He carried her into the cave where Endrir was just stirring.

"What has happened?" Endrir asked. He was rubbing his eyes. "Destined, what is going on?"

"Be quiet, Endrir, please. Just for a moment," he said. He set her down gently and placed her head in his lap. He placed both hands on her temples and closed his eyes. "Nihility, my love, come back. Where you are right now, you cannot stay. It is not a place for you. Come back," he said. When she did not move, he touched their mental link. "Endrir, open your link with her, please. I need you to call her to you."

Endrir nodded and moved over to them. He took one of her hands in his. "I need you, Nihility. I need your warmth, and…and I need your love. Please come back to me."

She gasped, and her eyes flew open. She looked at Destined with large brown eyes. "Destined! Destined! The fire was glorious!" she exclaimed, sitting up and turning herself to face him. "It was glorious. The most beautiful flames I have ever seen! Alive. Painful. Destined, what was that?!"

He touched her face and frowned. "I am sorry. I should not have asked you to look at my memories. That is not a place you should go."

"I touch your memories all the time," she said, frowning. "What was that?" she asked.

"It is the place of seeing my love. It is where the River of Time flows, and the Fire of Life exists. It is beautiful, but it is also dangerous to those without sight. You can become lost in flames," he explained.

"Well, I do not know how I got there, but it does not change the fact that it was one of the most magnificent things I have ever seen. You see that all the time? How did I get there? One minute I was examining the demon's memory of the door, and then the next, I was staring at flames. A great fire," she said. Her words were quick and full of excitement.

"I should have exercised better care, my love," he said softly. "You will need rest after that."

"Are you serious, fool?!" she said, rising. "I feel alive. Rejuvenated! I have not felt this good since I rolled around in the grass with this one," she said, pointing at Endrir.

"She is not herself, Destined," Endrir said as a matter of fact. He was watching her, unblinking.

"I know, Endrir." Her thoughts were racing so fast he could not keep up. "My love, did you touch the flame you saw?"

"Aye!" she said as her face lit up with glee. Then her brow creased. "I am not sure why I did, though. Something whispered to me to do it. Whispered something about a promise of a gift. You know I adore presents," she said, making a face Destined would have found charming in another situation.

"I know you do, my love," he said, smiling at her. "Do you know what the gift was?"

"The Gift of Flame! That is what the whisper said. What is the Gift of Flame? Why does your eye look like that Destined?" She turned and collected the orb that still hung over Endrir's head. "We will need to speak about what is recorded here, Watcher. We also need to talk about how we feel about one another. That kiss, that day in the grass, the way it made me feel!" she said, looking at him with a grin. "I would have taken you there if it were not for your foolishness!"

"She is definitely not herself," Endrir said, blinking in shock.

"Nihility, you must stop. I need to know what you collected from my orb, my love."

"I can do both, Destined," she said, exasperated. "Stop underestimating me. I am dragoness!"

"I know you are, my love. However, Endrir and I are merely dragons, and we cannot keep up with the glory that is our dragoness at the moment. How about we take them one at a time?" he said.

"She is like a bird when it does not want to be caged, or a butterfly darting through flowers," Endrir said, shaking his head.

"Watch and remember, Endrir," he said as he pulled her to sit with him. He could feel her annoyance with him. "Tell me what you learned, my love."

"I accessed the parts concerning the demon first. What I felt was jumbled. The demon is," Nihility paused, choosing her words with care. "The demon is linear and dark. When he spoke his name, I could still not understand it. Only that sound. However, the word itself disturbed your inner balance."

"What demon?" Endrir asked.

"Destined is holding a demon prisoner," she said, looking at Endrir. "You should not hide things from your lover, Destined the Farseer," she said with a tone.

"What?" Endrir said, shocked. "Nihility, we are…"

"That one has grown too comfortable lying to my face. The Broken Watcher is going to find himself on fire if he keeps it up," she said, looking back at him.

"I know, my love. Endrir, I will explain later. For now, listen, please," he said. "Nihility, there are emotions around the demon?"

"Aye, everything has an emotional base Destined, you know that. Fear will surround the bird as we walk past or elation at the feel of the sun. Even now, you surround yourself in fear and excitement, where Endrir has none because the Watcher watches again," she said.

"Can you tell me what surrounds the demon?" he asked.

"Love, lust, excitement, and happiness," she said, touching his face with her fingers tips. She had a grin on her face. "That is his prison. All the things my dragon feels for me," she said with pride. "Around him, it is not so distinguishable. His colors are blurred by pain and fear. It was not until he said his name that the pain and fear were pushed aside. In their place, two surged forward, greed and excitement."

He frowned, trying to recall what Malolon looked like at that moment. "Was there anything else, my love?"

"Aye. I have rarely seen it, but when the demon spoke his name, the color around his face changed with the words. The colors for selfishness, indulgence, and lust appeared."

"What does that mean, Nihility?" he asked.

"The feelings it invoked in you, Destined, felt familiar yet odd because you feel the same, but not in the same way," she said.

"I am not selfish or indulgent, Nihility," he said, making a face.

"Lies you do not even believe, Destined," she said, giggling.

"My dragon is selfish, my dragon is greedy, my dragon is full of lust and pride. Even a forest cannot hide him from me," she said.

"Farseer," Endrir said.

"Shut up, Endrir!" he hissed at him.

"Silly dragons, with your silly secrets," she said, giggling at them both. "Destined, you can control your emotions. However, you are not like Endrir, who hides them; you balance them carefully. You protect them. You must exercise caution. He brings them forth."

"What do you mean?"

"He is not an Empath, but a perversion of one. When you said his name, it was like a spell. I could see where the feelings the two of you share merged, but his were stronger. I believe the exchanging of his name bound the two of you together through those emotions, but only because you hold them. That is why I say you must exercise caution. Emotions are a dangerous weapon to wield."

"I locked the door where he is trapped," he said.

"When you return, and I know you will because you must; you cannot keep that place locked away. You cannot lock away your dragoness," Nihility said, grinning at him. "When you return, carry a box of the strongest your mind can imagine. Place those emotions as you feel them in the box, Destined. When you leave, lock the box, not the door."

"For what purpose? You cannot contain emotions, Nihility Harbinger. They will just find a way out or overrun me. You have taught me that much."

She leaned forward, so they were almost touching. "The box is as big, deep, and strong as you need it to be," she said, tapping Destined's head. "The purpose is your protection and preservation. The result is a weapon at your disposal."

"Weapon? Why would I use what would strengthen him?"

"You do not listen!" she said, agitated. "I told you those feelings felt familiar to you. They are not foreign to any of us.

However, you do not indulge in them negatively as this demon seems to. His name did not bind them to you as he interprets them. Only the base emotion, the raw emotion, was. When you spoke his name, the emotions it amplified were the ones you have experienced; lust, indulgence, and greed. Imagine those amplified to extreme levels with no receptor for when you are sated; that is this demon."

"You said he was not an Empath, though," he said.

"He isn't. He cannot do as I do. He must use what is already there. I can create those emotions whether you want to feel them or not. Those feelings you experience can be turned by him, but they can be used by you as well; they are yours."

"Like Britir," Endrir said in a monotone.

"Aye! He can only use those emotions he has experienced personally when he uses them against others. It is an illusion, but it is grounded in reality," she said. "I do not know if it is a way to defeat him, but it never hurts to prepare. I need to investigate something first because something changed when you called him greedy. I do not know what, but something did."

"Thank you, my love. Is there anything else?" he asked.

"Aye, but before I tell you, let me impress upon you the importance of the box, Destined. This is not a case of balancing the good and the bad to keep centered as you do when you walk. This is the difference between sanity and madness. If you value who you are and everything you stand for, you must build the box and lock it. Build and lock it as if your life depended on it. Lock it like my life depended on it because it very well may," she said.

The look on her face unnerved him. She was more serious than he had ever seen her. The desire Malolon had to find out about her nagged at his mind. "Build and lock," he whispered.

"As for the door, it cannot really help you. I am having trouble recalling the details. I mean, I remember seeing it, but then I saw flames. Brilliant red, yellow, white, and orange flames," she said, growing excited again. "Sometimes the colors would overlap, but mostly they stood apart. Then I remember being called to them. A voice whispered to me, calling me to the warmth of the flames. I was afraid. I felt like I was being taken over. I was afraid of losing who I was. The fear did not abate until I saw a place where all the flames touched. Where they touched, they created a flame of pure black."

He gasped in shock. Nihility had read the flames to find a place for herself. It was no different than when he had a prophecy. She had described with accuracy the way he felt in those moments. The flames pulled at him, and the only place he could touch to receive the prophecy was where the fire touched and created a white flame.

"I felt compelled to place my hand on that spot in the flames. When I did, the pain was almost unbearable. The flames shifted from black to white and black again. The pain made me wish I could sever my hand. Then it was gone. I heard my dragons calling me to them, and I woke up here," she said.

"Nihility, what you experienced was the Gift of Flame. You read the flames like a prophet to find the place of your giving. The flames give you the gift of a prophecy. Can you remember the words you spoke to me?"

"No. I don't even remember speaking."

"You did. You passed the prophecy to me. A prophecy I was meant to receive but did not probably because," Destined stopped and sighed. "I had one in my sleep that frightened me badly, and fear clouds the mind. I am not a receptor to what I should be right now. The flame has marked you as it has marked me," he said, turning over his hand and hers. They now had identical black marks on their palms in the shape of a dragon's eye encased in flames.

"Why me, and what is wrong with your eye, Destined? The coloring is all wrong in one of them."

He stood up and paced. He was missing something again.

This time he felt like the time he had for figuring it out was passing quickly. "Farseer," Endrir said.

"Do not start, Endrir. I am trying to think."

"I am not starting, and do not speak to me that way," Endrir snapped. "Why don't you just show her what happened. It is the past now, after all. Do as I do with the Mind's Eye and share the memory. When you are done, please explain to me why you have a fucking demon trapped inside your mind," Endrir said, exasperated.

He stopped pacing and looked at Endrir. "The past," he said. Suddenly it made sense. He remembered her words, 'fan the flames through the past, so the message burns bright in the future.' "Endrir the Broken, what would I ever do without you?" he said smiling.

"Apparently, allow demons to crawl up inside you," Endrir mumbled.

"Nihility, come outside, my love," he said, rolling his eyes at Endrir.

"Where are we going? Somewhere romantic, I hope. I have plenty of energy, Destined. Did you bring a book?" she asked.

He faltered in his steps and shook his head. "If only," he said. "Your fool forgot a step, and we do not have much time left. However, after, I will be more than willing to fetch a book and watch. I must give the message back to you, or it will be lost forever. Could you please shift for me, my dragoness?" he asked.

She shifted. "What is this all about, Destined?"

"There are some things I cannot see Nihility. They are hidden because they are fixed in time and have no chosen paths. Then others concern me. I believe this is both of those, and my fear has blinded me to it. I pulled away before I was supposed to because I was afraid, but I have pushed away because I was not meant to see. However, whatever forces out there that control prophecies have demanded that I see it and have found a way for me to do so. It concerns us both, my dragoness. I cannot say how until the circle is complete. I must pass the flame back to you. From black to white to black again," he said. He lay down in front of her and nodded to lie beside him.

"I do not want to," she mumbled. "I am afraid."

"I am here with you, my love. You share my heart, and I yours. Whatever it is, we will deal with it together," he said. She nodded and laid down. "You must not blink. Withstand the pain and see. Most importantly, my dragoness, remember," he said as they locked eyes.

CHAPTER FORTY

Destined blinked as she did. He had almost failed to complete the circle. The flames were the end and the beginning where all things met. "Is it done?" Endrir asked. "You two were strange for a while as if you were here, but not here. At one point, I swear I could see right through you. You have never done that when you have a vision."

"It is done," he said. He was concerned by what he saw, but he could feel Nihility's sadness.

"What happened?" Endrir asked.

He shifted and walked to her. He touched the side of her snout and kissed it. "I will explain everything inside, Endrir. We should give our dragoness a minute to follow," he said. He looked into her big brown eyes and smiled. "In this life and beyond we are bound Nihility. But I will wait for you beyond the end of forever, my love. I have no choice, you know. You are the only reason I soar," he said before he walked to Endrir.

"What is wrong with her?" Endrir asked.

"She received a prophecy, Endrir. One meant for her and me, it seems. One that tells of what is happening now."

"She is not a prophet, Destined," Endrir said, frowning.

"No, she is not. That is why she was given the Gift of Flame. It fortifies, strengthens, and rejuvenates the prophet so they can endure the Pain of Prophecy."

"That is why she behaved as she did when she woke."

"Aye," he said with a chuckle. "Seems it gave Nihility the ability to speak without fear too. My visions come from the River of Time that flows beneath the flames. When I receive a full prophetic vision, it burns because it is a vision given directly from the flames."

"Those that you lose control of yourself?"

"Aye. When I have those, they leave me incapacitated from the pain. They are the visions that are monumental or foretell of some significant change."

"Why did you not receive it directly, and what is this talk of your demon?" Endrir asked.

"You know, Endrir the Broken, we are both fools for that dragoness," he said with a laugh. "I mean, look at us. We have excelled beyond expectations for both of our callings, but that dragoness out there is our weakness. However, she is also our strength. Do not forget that, Endrir."

"Destined, what has happened?"

He could not bring himself to tell him yet. "Do you remember when we began our competition for Nihility's heart?"

"Biggest two fools on Petrall," Endrir said, laughing.

"I looked into the River of Time for an answer on who would win her heart," he said. "Instead, the flame took hold of me."

"I know you did," Endrir said with a shrug.

"What? How?"

"Oh, please, Destined. Just because you are incapacitated by the flames does not mean you cannot speak," Endrir said, laughing. "It is okay, Farseer. I do not think you changed the course of our future. Nothing can make that dragoness do what she does not wish to do," he said, giving Destined back his own words from earlier. "Things are as they are meant to be."

"I lied, Endrir, and I feel guilty about it. I have caused you pain. I did not realize you knew."

"I knew and have known. Rest easy, my sun. I hold you no ill will for it. I never have. Regardless of what you did and the lie you told, the choice was always hers."

"I had a vision in my sleep."

"Thought you said you only need a short rest," Endrir said, nudging him.

"I know, but I did not want to sound like a hatchling. It scared me badly. That fear made me shut down. The Flames of

Prophecy sought me out through her. I do not know what she saw, but I know what I saw. I can only assume they overlap at some point. Let her deal with what it is she now must carry with her."

"You won't tell me, will you?"

"No. Not right now," Destined said, looking down at the ground.

Endrir looked out at the dragoness hidden in the darkness. "Will she be okay?"

"Aye. I think Nihility just needs time. While we wait, why don't I humor you with another tale? The tale of the Great White Hope of Petrall, and his battle with a crafty demon," he said laughing.

"Finally!" Endrir exclaimed as they walked into the cave together.

CHAPTER FORTY-ONE

The fire in Destined's eye shifted and blazed. His normal hazel eyes changed. Three separate bands of color circled around the black pupil mesmerizing her. Then it changed. She was standing before a great dragon that was both white and gold. He looked at her with sad blue eyes and shattered.

Behind him, she saw a sea of demons who stood on a barren land of red soil and green fire. There was more than she could have ever imagined. They stretched for as far as her eye could see. She could see their savagery and disregard for one another. They were taking the bodies of their own kind as they screamed. She saw them kill each other with reckless abandon. She saw them feasting on things she could not describe. It was madness. It was chaos.

She looked up at a series of black rocks that rose above the crowd and saw seven bright colors. She did not know how, but she knew they were the seven great demons when she saw them. There was one who held the colors of them all. It was larger and more prominent than the surrounding six. In front of it, on a pedestal of stone, was a bright sky blue crystal. When she looked at it, it sparked first gold, then white. Then she saw the eyes peering out at her from inside of it, and she wanted to roar in outrage and pain.

The barrier slammed into place, blocking her vision. She heard voices speaking all at once. Countless voices all saying the same thing, calling to her. "Harbinger! Harbinger! Harbinger! Into the heart of the Dreaming, you will carry the hopes of all. Feel and fight. Bring forth the light to balance the dark. Bring forth balance to carry the chaos. Find the heart of Aerrad! Carry the Viceroy to the serpent's demise!" they cried.

She blinked and gazed into Destined's hazel eyes. The color

in them swirled as if unsure where to settle. Her heart broke with a sadness she did not think possible. She watched him walk back to Endrir at the cave, but she could not bring herself to follow. She let the tears fall from her eyes as she watched the stars light up the night sky.

"Nihility," Pax's soft voice called.

"Hello, Lady Pax."

"I am sorry to intrude, youngling, but I did not want you to fall too far into despair out there alone."

"I must get used to sadness again at some point," she said with a sigh.

"What has happened? Your emotions were erratic, and then for a while, I lost touch with you completely."

"Destined says I have received a prophecy."

"You are not a prophet, youngling."

"I know, but it seems to have happened, anyway. Destined can explain better than I can. I was examining Destined's memories, and that is when it happened."

"You are not to touch the memories of a prophet Nihility," Pax said. She made a noise to protest when Pax spoke over her. "However, he is your mate, and I believe you are wise enough to know better than to tamper with them. What has upset you about what you saw?"

"I saw Laz, Lady Pax."

"Nihility, I know it was upsetting to see him that way. You have now been touched by three sets of twins in your young life. Twins are special, though, so that makes you special. You know, I never felt my entire self after he was gone. It was like a piece of my existence was in constant torment," Pax said. She looked up at Pax and quickly looked away as she cried again. "What does that look mean, Nihility?"

"I believe that is exactly what you were feeling, Lady Pax. You were feeling the constant torture and torment of Laz. It is a fate that awaits Destined," she said through her tears.

"Calm yourself, youngling. Explain to me what you saw of Lazarus."

She took a deep breath and then another. "I was in that space, but there was no barrier, just Laz. Then he shattered, and I saw multitudes of demons; so many demons they could cover Sathea. I saw them doing things, such abhorrent things, Lady Pax. I saw the Seven."

"Did you see Lazarus again?" Pax asked.

"Lady Pax, I am not sure you want to know or if I should even tell you. You have grieved enough. I feel like this is cruel."

"My sweet youngling, what a gift to Petrall you are. A Weaver of extraordinary skill. A natural Empath that can use her abilities in a way, and with such skill that I never achieved, I would have given anything to make you my protégé so many years ago. Not that Ygi and Livy were not excellent students mind you, but they were not like me. You have all my fire but an openness that I could never grasp. Time is cruel even in the simplest ways, and sometimes what seems like cruelty is a blessing. Take this as a lesson I give you now from one Empath to another. You will find it applies in other situations as well. Some wounds never heal. Sometimes the flesh may knit, but beneath is a weak spot, easily damaged. You simply learn to manage the pain."

She nodded, understanding what Pax meant. "I saw the barrier, and I saw Laz."

"You realized already he gave himself to create that life barrier, Nihility."

"No, Lady Pax. I saw Laz trapped in a crystal. The part of himself attached to that demon left a taint around him. Your twin was trapped in that crystal, on a pedestal of stone, and surrounded by the Seven. Lines of energy came from the crystal and attached to the Seven. They were torturing him and feeding on him!" she said, crying again. "I saw his eyes and the look of sadness they held as he faded away. Then it was no longer Laz trapped in that crystal, Lady Pax. It was Destined! My Destined! Trapped and being tortured by those things! Surrounded by demons, all hungry for him!"

Pax looked shocked. "Nihility, did you receive the Gift of Flame?"

"Aye, so Destined believes. Destined said the prophecy was meant for us both. Although, I do not know why it would be necessary for me to see such a thing concerning my heartmate."

"Perhaps that was your warning, but the actual message was something else. Did you see anything else?"

"No, just voices calling to me. How do you know of the flame, Lady Pax? I have never heard of such a thing."

"You have, youngling, just not by that name, I am sure. The Gift of Flame exists at the heart of the River of Time. It is an ever-burning flame that is the point where past, present, and future meet. The river itself flows in the Dreaming," Pax said.

"You mean the Utos River? The one controlled by the serpent Hynro?"

"Aye, that is the one. You know the Dreaming is where the prophecy exists once the prophet has received it. It goes to the one area that we as Weavers may not go—a forest hidden from our sight. Prophecies are guarded fiercely. Even as Weavers, we cannot see the dreams of the prophet. It is why you may grant Destined sleep, but never weave his dreams," Pax said.

"I grant him safe space, dream space. He rests peacefully there. Sometimes his visions leave him unable to protect himself. He worries about those that circle around him," Nihility said.

"Dream space?" Pax asked. "You have said this to him before. What is it?"

She frowned. "I make space in the Dreaming for him," she said, frowning. "I tether a piece of the Dreaming to my Weaver crystal. It is like a barrier, but I control what happens in that space."

Pax chuckled. "You are full of talents, little Weaver! You do as another dragoness I once knew did, but she used it to create grand illusions. At my side, we could rend our foes to nothing by feeling the horror she had placed in that space."

"I thought all Weavers could do it," she said, frowning.

"No youngling. Creating space in the Dreaming is an ability that I have only seen twice in my time. An ability I did not have. We will come back to that, Nihility Harbinger. First, I want to know something else. How did you know it was the Seven you saw?"

"Well, I," she stopped herself and reflected on what she saw. She really did not know, but she did. "I could feel it was them. Yes, I saw them, and I could feel it was them in seeing them. They were larger and tough to ignore. I know you are going to laugh at me, but I could feel it."

"Why on Sathea would I laugh. What you said makes perfect sense to me," Pax said, puffing smoke.

"Sorry, Lady Pax. Normally I have to fight to be understood when I say things like that," she said, laughing at herself.

"We are Empaths. We cannot help that the rest of Sathea does not understand us. Now explain the feeling, youngling."

She shivered at the thought. "The feeling was dark, almost like I had touched the bottom reaches of negative emotions and was experiencing them all at once," she said, shaking her head. "I just felt like I knew it was them and that they could sense me. Not see me, but sense me. The worst was the hunger I felt from them for Destined when the crystal changed. They were overjoyed, like a hungry beast on the edge of starvation who finally finds a meal that will sustain it for some time. They desired the crystal."

"Desired in a way that would signify that it was of some great importance? As if it were perhaps a key to something?"

"Aye, but to what I do not know."

"And you are sure there were seven and the crystal?" Pax asked.

She took time to think back to what she saw, even though

she did not want to. "Yes, I am sure. They were very distinctive in their size and the color of their emotions compared to the others. There were others near them that had a similar color."

"So you can see the color of emotions," Pax said, smiling at her. "You do not use the ability."

She looked away, ashamed. "Aye."

Pax huffed. "How far into the Depths of the Dreaming have you been, Nihility Harbinger? Did you drink from the Well?"

She was confused. Pax was elated but annoyed at the same time. "What well? I do not know exactly how far I have been. It changes."

"Far enough that the land turns black as our scales, but what grows is a vibrant and lush green you do not often see on Sathea?" Pax asked. "Far enough to see great pillars of gold sand that bear the image of a serpent woven around itself, where sand runs and water flows, perhaps?"

"Aye," she said, frowning.

"You can read the physical manifestation of emotions, their color, as you say."

"Aye, Lady Pax. I have for many years now. What well?"

"In a moment, Nihility Harbinger," Pax said. Her tone was forceful. "They would not have kept an Empath of your caliber in the nursery to rot, not with my memory living on in the Dreaming, but from what I have gathered, you were the last to leave."

"Aye."

"Why?" Pax asked. There was anger in her tone.

She took a deep breath and then another. "Ergodi and Ivylth demanded I remain. Ivylth would come and retrieve me for lessons, but they were not lessons. They were merely a way for her to hurt me without eyes upon her. She would scrape me with her claws, remove scales, tear away the flesh underneath, break bones, or bash me against the rocks. Pimo would heal me, and they would begin again. Ergodi was there to make sure I remained still and did not fight back."

"How long, Nihility?" Pax asked.

"Three thousand years."

"Years you should have spent in freedom as a new dragoness on Petrall. Why did it stop?" Pax asked.

"Master Terg saved me."

"But not for three thousand years. Where was Terghelm during all of this? How was this allowed to go on for three thousand years?" Pax asked.

"He does not live on Petrall. From what Ygi says, he had not for many years, so he did not know. That day, like many others, Ivylth made me eat the Dreamflowers that grow outside Weaver Circle, but I could not. I knew agony would come if I did, but it did not stop her from hitting me," she said, shaking her head. "I do not remember much. I remember the pain, and I remember Master Terg. He arrived and took me to Lady Ygi and Master Bendre."

"But he did not punish Ivylth?"

"I asked him not to. I was okay as long as it stopped, and it did. From that moment on, I was under the care of Lady Ygi and Master Bendre. Master Terg remained on the peak for a while but eventually left again. I was okay because I had them, and I had those of the Dreaming that cared for me."

"Lady Ygi did not tell you about the Well of Infinite Emotions that lies in the deepest part of the Depths of the Dreaming?" Pax asked.

"No, Lady Pax, but that is not her fault," she said quietly. "She was…"

"Trying to keep you safe," Pax finished smiling at her. "I hold no fault with Ygi, Nihility. She did a wonderful job helping you become the dragoness you are. I am proud of her and you. However, you found the Well on your own, and I would know how."

"Ivylth forbid the Weavers from traveling into the Depths. She told us that going that far was not our way," she said, looking away.

Pax narrowed her eyes as she looked at her; a smile played on her face. "But you dared the venture, anyway?"

"Aye."

Pax's laughter and happiness crashed around her. "You do not fear her," Pax said, laughing. "Your lack of fear makes her angry. Not to mention you are a brilliant Weaver that wields more power than she has!"

"No, I never feared her. Ergodi was the one I feared because he did things in my mind. Ivylth just doesn't like me. She never did, but she did not hate me until after I ventured into the Depths."

"Enlighten me, youngling. In the process, I am sure we can teach you of the Well you have obviously seen," Pax said, composing herself.

"But what is the Well of Infinite Emotions?" she asked.

"This is why she does not like you, Nihility. You are inquisitive of things that are rightfully yours to know, unlike Ivylth," Pax said, reaching over and nuzzling her. "The Well of Infinite Emotions is a place in the deepest part of the Depths. It is guarded by a creature that values its existence above all else. He has a sworn duty to protect the Well and its contents. Those that approach the well and seek to drink must do two things. First, they must not question the Dreaming to seek answers. Their desire to drink must be only to achieve greater control over emotions to aid the Dreaming. Second, they must answer his questions. If anyone should seek to drink for power or to further their own goals, the protector will attack. If they cannot answer his questions and do not heed his warnings to leave, he will attack."

She gasped, and her eyes went wide. "Is the well not a well

like they use below, but an actual pool of water? Water the color of my scales?"

"Yes! Yes, youngling! So, you have drunk from the well!" Pax said excitedly.

"No, Lady Pax. I dove in."

"What on Sathea... You swam the Well of Infinite Emotions?! Why on Petrall would you do such a thing? Why would the protector allow it?"

"When I found it, I was searching for Ivylth. She was gone for too long in the Dreaming. After following her link, I found someone had injured the Protector when I arrived. I provided what little healing I could. As a thank you, he told me that the one I was seeking was in the pool. He said that she had come to drink but could not answer his questions. Instead of leaving, she attacked him and tried to drink from the pool, anyway."

"He allowed you access to the pool as gratitude?" Pax asked.

"Nay," she said, laughing. "He asked me if I wanted to drink from the pool as well. He behaved like Ivylth had not just committed a transgression against him, actually. I told him I was only seeking Ivylth as she was Lead Weaver of Weaver Circle. He told me I could pass if I answered his questions, but I would need more than correct answers to retrieve her. When I asked him why he told me she was in the arms of the Nightmare."

"You answered his questions then, untrained and unprepared," Pax said.

"Aye. I thought it was going to be something I did not understand. But the Protector does as the children of the Daughters of Ote do as they grow. They play word games to test their mind. Questions posed as a play on words or riddles."

"How time flows around us, even when we are gone," Pax said absently. "Tell me what happened after you answered his questions correctly."

"He stepped aside, but before I passed him, he told me that if I was to drink from the pool, my powers would grow. If I recovered Ivylth from the Nightmare that holds her, I would see, his heart would be mine, and the Dreaming would rejoice."

"Interesting," Pax said. "Go on, youngling. I would know the fate of Ivylth the Trickster."

"I retrieved her from the pool, Lady Pax. I brought her back. She was never the same after, though. Ergodi decided she should ascend to Elder along with Lady Pimo. I took her spot as Lead Weaver of Weaver Circle. Ergodi was not pleased, but Master Bendre insisted, and when Master Bendre insists upon something, you must listen," she said.

"Bendre can be very persuasive when he wants to be," Pax said, chuckling. "How many years were you when you ascended to Lead Weaver, Nihility?"

She looked away, embarrassed. "Almost eight thousand years to the sky."

Pax hummed. "Bendre is wise. He placed you there because you are capable, Nihility. Do not be embarrassed by your accomplishments. You could not have done better at the Well, even if you had been properly trained. I am sure Ygi knew this as well. Now, as for Ivylth the Trickster, I must apologize to you."

"What? You have nothing to apologize for, Lady Pax."

"But I do, youngling. My behavior towards Ivylth is why she did what she has done to you. I was never fond of her. She was off in a way that I could never articulate. I am sure she knew it. I paid little attention to her until I lost Iros, but that was because I believed she had a hand in his death. That, however, is neither here nor there. What is important is that I say I am sorry that you had to endure so much because of her. I promise before I leave you, I will make sure she pays for all that she has done."

"I do not understand why Ivylth was even there. They questioned her in front of Petrall, and her answers were lies. She said she searched for a Weaver's soul and simply lost her way. Master Bendre said it was jerboa shit," she said.

"Because it is, and Ghost would know," Pax said. "Ivylth was a youngling before my passing. She and Pimo were under my wing at one point in their lives. What she has done is a disservice to you and to Weaver Circle."

"How so? I mean, I know what she did to me, but I do not see how it affects Weaver Circle."

"Weavers are the oldest of the three Great Callings of Petrall. As Weavers, we have a constant link to the Dreaming. We cannot control it. It is a part of us, like breathing flame," Pax said. "Some of us must work to understand and cross our emotions into others to soothe, control, and aid their dreams. It is how we get our name. We weave our link with the Dreaming to dreamers using emotions. Our position does not give us much room for questions and answers. We, as Weavers, only seek understanding. Do you know why?"

"Through emotions, you discover the true heart of any being on Sathea," she said.

"Aye. Weavers, like you and I, are natural emotional receptors. The empath is the name they give us. Not only do we have to work at understanding emotions, but we must work at not being consumed by them. We have very little room for our own emotions. To some, we are cold, indifferent, or secretive; but the truth is, we work through our own feelings quickly to make way for the weight of others. Their pain becomes our pain, and their happiness is our happiness. We face great danger as Weavers. The emotional weight of others can be binding if we do not learn to separate and compartmentalize quickly. That weight can be a dangerous thing to our wellbeing and ability to weave."

"When we take on too much of their emotions and carry them as our own," she said.

Pax nodded. "The Empath, more than any other Weaver, is more susceptible to the madness of the dreamer. The Well of Infinite Emotions heightens our empathic abilities, allowing us to stand above the dreamer's emotions. To observe, not absorb."

"Lady Pax, you mean their emotions, right? Observe them, but do not become one with them."

"Aye. The Well of Infinite Emotions grants you the ability to see them, not just feel them. For me, I could detect positive and negative emotional markers. I can see the trails of color-like after effects within the Dreaming. I also learned to store my own emotions, creating the Black Flame. I did those things with just a sip from the pool, Nihility. You swam in the pool. I do not doubt it has affected you in ways you did not realize because you did not know what you had done. The Well of Infinite Emotions gives us a means to control, sense, and create emotional weapons. We become warriors."

"How old is the Protector of the Well? He seemed wise, but he had no emotions I could detect. Being near him was the first time I truly felt silence."

"I do not know. I know the Protector existed without a name for as long as the Dreaming has existed, much like Hynro."

"He has a name. It is Zisevral. He told me his name when I returned a short time after."

"He granted you a boon for your kindness! He has existed without a name for as long as I have known about him. I am not sure if even Gilliphae knows his name," Pax said, laughing. "Now, since I have you in better spirits, I would like you to show me that trick you can do with fire."

"What?" she said, shocked.

"I can see through your eyes. Show me what you can do, youngling," Pax said, sitting up.

"You want to give me a lesson now?" she asked, making a face.

"Do you not want it, youngling? It is a once-in-a-lifetime chance to train with the Great Pax of the Depths!" Pax said with a smirk.

"Of course I do!" she said excitedly.

"Then show me this trick. I would see what you can do."

CHAPTER FORTY-TWO

Nihility opened her eyes and saw the grass before her. Darkness surrounded her as the Maiden and Mother Moon held the sky. A glow emanated from the cave where Destined and Endrir had started a fire, but they did not disturb her. They sat at the mouth of the cave watching. She took a deep breath and then carefully let ten small fireballs flow from her jaws. They hovered for a moment before transforming into small creatures of flame with long tails that hopped in the grass before her.

"In my day, those were called Glits," Pax said.

"They still are, Lady Pax. They only come out at night in the meadowlands."

"Good definition in the flames. I could tell immediately what they were. Can you do anything larger?"

"Aye," she said, embarrassed.

"Why are you embarrassed, Lady Nihility? This is a wonderful talent."

She sighed. "I have done it using dream fire to conjure your image in the Dreaming," she said.

Pax laughed and hummed happily. "I would see this image of myself."

"Lady Pax, it is embarrassing. It was not even accurate. I only had my imagination based on what Masters Bendre and Jaydum told me."

"But you have the real thing at your disposal now. I would see it. This is better than any lament a dragon could do," Pax said.

She closed her eyes and focused on the details of Lady Pax as she really was. She opened her jaws, spouting flames that coalesced into an image of Lady Pax. "I know it is not perfect..."

"Hush, youngling. It is fantastic. Now, you have done my

image in Dragonfire. I can see the detail. However, the color is wrong."

"I cannot change the color of my flames. I mean, I can use the green of dream fire, but that is all."

"You can if you use the proper emotion. What you have done here is the same as what I did with the Black Flame, Nihility. The difference is you do it naturally."

"It is a trick!"

"That is no trick. Look at my image, Nihility. That is not the correct color of Dragonfire. Do you see the amount of pink and red in the flames? I can see the aura through your eyes. That image was made from adoration and love, youngling," Pax said, humming again.

"I have never done anything like that before," she said in awe.

"Lies and jerboa shit, as a friend of mine used to say," Pax said, chuckling. "You said you have done so when you dance the flames. Now I would like to see my true visage. I could craft emotional illusions. Did you know that? They would act like the real thing and even feel the same. Let me see if you can do the same with your fire."

"But the Black Flame…"

"You will require it. I am a black dragoness, after all. I mean, you must keep the red of my spines. It glitters so nicely, but the black is necessary. I am not pink, Nihility," Pax said with a huff, making her laugh.

"I do not want what happened before to happen again."

"Then do not touch your genuine anger. Save that for when you need a weapon. Observe the anger and then use it. Think of the times Destined has made you angry. It was not genuine anger but annoyance with his foolishness. Use it to draw forth the Black Flame."

"You would have me use the variations of anger?"

"Exactly. If you can see the color of emotions, then you can wield the Black Flame."

She concentrated on the image of Lady Pax that hovered over the grass. She thought of how hurt and annoyed she was when Destined acted as if he did not trust her. She gradually blew flames. They turned black, creating a perfect replica of Lady Pax as they touched the image. She tilted her head, feeling for a moment until she realized what she was missing. She thought of the happiness and the feel of the Dreaming and spout two more small waves of flame that changed the tail spikes and horns on Pax's tail and head, making them glow in white flame.

"Well done, Nihility Harbinger! Well done!" Pax said, delighted. "Now, all you have to do is will the flame away, no different from when you let those emotions go."

She closed her eyes and took a slow, deep breath, relaxing. When she opened her eyes, the image of Pax was gone. "I did it!" she said, rising and trashing her tail.

"You did indeed, youngling."

"Oh," she said, falling back down to the ground in a faint.

"That is the cost of the Black Flame, and I believe any flame you create using those types of emotions. At first, I did not understand why it left me drained. Do you know why?"

"Because those emotions manifest themselves physically, and those like anger and hate are harsh on the body."

"Correct. You must use it with caution. Even a small amount of Black Flame will leave you drained. While you rest a moment, I would have you listen," Pax said.

"Aye."

"Why do you believe you held no other abilities?" Pax asked.

"I am an Empath like you. That is my ability."

"But not your only ability, Nihility. I was not just an Empath. I was also an illusionist who could glimmer thoughts. At the side of my twin, we could manipulate memories, making them believe something other than what actually occurred. We could wipe their dreams away with ease."

"I can't do anything like that. My mind is not capable," Nihility said.

"What about Endrir?" Pax asked. "He is a Watcher, but what can he do as a dragon?"

"Wind. He can harness it. I have seen him cut down trees with precision."

"And Destined?" Pax asked. "He is more than just a prophet."

"His mind is formidable. He can conjure, read minds, and move objects. He can do things with the cold too, but he rarely does. He says it requires too much concentration."

Pax made a noise. "I would have you think of the Weavers you know. They all have abilities beyond their link to the Dreaming. Abilities that sometimes, like Ygi, are lethal."

"Aye, but I cannot do any of those things. I feel. I feel everything, even Sathea."

"Incorrect, Lady Nihility," Pax said. "You create dream space, control emotions, and manipulate fire."

She frowned. None of those things seemed special to her. Others had extraordinary abilities that made them notable. Master Bendre could manipulate and control shadows.

"You are the dragoness to half of the Twin Suns of Petrall," Pax said.

"Aye."

"I do not remember much of Sia after Livy died in the War."

"Iros sent him to Emberwood Thicket. He remained there for years, training. He said he returned shortly before Iros died."

"I remember him, but from his younger days. He and his twin set fire to Weaver Circle," Pax said.

"He never told me that!" she said, laughing.

"Oh yes. They were practicing, according to the jerboa shit

Livy fed me. Those two were notorious for their games and pranks."

"He is not playful like that," she said, frowning.

"I am sure the loss of his half had something to do with that, Nihility. I remember him as spontaneous. Livy was the one with the schemes, but he always went along."

"He is spontaneous. He always surprised me."

"The reason I remember the fire is because we could not douse the flames of the Twin Suns. Ygi and Ben were able to carry Livy to the Dreaming with Bysi's help. They dropped her in the pool of water she now controls. However, her twin required something more. Iros burned himself badly, trying to help that little dragon. In the end, it was a quirky dragon named Cimbu who smothered the flames."

"Rising Dragons," she whispered.

"That is what those two came to call it. Flames that would ignite when they connected mind, body, and soul. They even had a phrase to help them channel the power," Pax said.

"I see you," she said.

"Aye! Have you touched those flames, Nihility? Have you touched the flames that could burn the tough hide of a dragon instantly?"

She looked at Pax with tears in her eyes and nodded. "I helped him extinguish them," she said, thinking of when he saved her using those flames. The night the drinkers came. The night she fell madly in love with Sia the Mindbreaker.

"Because you, Nihility Harbinger, are an Empath that can control fire. All fire," Pax said.

She felt the warmth of embarrassment. "I struggle with seeing my abilities."

"Being an Empath is consuming and tiresome. Feeling all the time is exhausting. Everyone expecting you to know how they feel is exhausting. Everyone forgetting how you feel is exhausting," Pax said.

"Aye! Exactly!" she said. Pax had given words to her exact feelings about her powers.

"But you must not let it consume you. Fight against it if you must. Be the fire manipulator and then the Empath if it helps," Pax said.

"Lady Pax?"

"Yes, youngling."

"You said the Well of Infinite Emotions gives the Empath the means to control, sense, and create emotional weapons, right, but how?"

"Yes. First, there is control. We can observe the emotions without taking them on, but it has its limits. Multiple beings in a space all feeling will still overwhelm you. However, you can observe on a smaller scale without taking them on yourself. You observe Destined and Endrir's emotions with ease. Then you can see the images attached to those emotions. They do not even have to be powerful emotions, just focused ones with practice. You will work on that from now on and see their color. You must become faster with your assessments," Pax said.

"Yes, Lady Pax."

"Next, there are sensing emotions," Pax said, sitting up. Here all I say to you is well done, Nihility the Harbinger. Well done! Continue being as perceptive as you are. You will see that your sense grows faster the more you practice finding the color and images of emotions."

"Thank you, Lady Pax," she said, humming loudly.

"Last is emotional weapons," Pax said. She lowered her head to see her closely. "Show me what you hide about your fire. I sensed more while you crafted the image of me. There was a pull of something wild. The same I felt at the Courtyard of the Moon."

"I cannot control those two!" she exclaimed.

"Who?" Pax asked. She went quiet, afraid to answer. "Nihility?" Pax called.

"You will see," she sighed as she recalled the memory.

"Nihility! Nihility! Where are you?" Sia called. There was panic in his voice. "Nihility, my little dragoness, answer me, please!"

"I am here, Sia," she said from the floor in the hidden space of the alcove they now shared. She could feel his magic as he shifted and entered. He was handsome in his simple Greenbark linens, soft green cloth pants, and brown hooded tunic. His dark brown hair was tied messily on top of his head, his bright amber eyes showed worry.

"Ygi said Ben was hurt," he said as he entered. "What happened?" he stopped. "What on Sathea…"

"I hurt him," she whispered as her tears fell.

"Nihility, what are those?" he asked, nodding at the tiny creatures that sat at her feet. Two beasts of pure fire sat before her. Both had a shimmering thin black chain around their neck.

"I hurt Master Bendre, Sia!" she wailed.

The color of the fire around the beasts changed to a deep blue as she cried. He walked over to her slowly. The beasts were tense and alert. He sat down beside her and took her hand. "Ben is fine. Even Ygi said so. Their worry, my worry, is for you. Can you tell me what happened?" he asked.

She looked at him, trying to control herself. He wiped her tears away and kissed her forehead. "Master Bendre was trying to get me to imbue my fire with my emotions. I told him it was impossible, but he insisted I could."

"He was giving you a lesson then. Were you able to?" Sia asked.

"At first, yes. Master Bendre told me to think of things and my feelings about them."

"Like what, my little dragoness?"

"Like you."

"Oh, like me," he said with a smirk. "What happened when you thought of your old dragon?"

She scoffed at him and rolled her eyes. "You are not old, Sia," she said as he smiled at her.

"I am old," he said, touching her face.

"I have told you, Sia Mindbreaker, you are perfect for me." The two beasts at her feet glowed orange and yellow.

"How did Ben get hurt?" he asked her gently.

She frowned, and her lips trembled as her eyes filled with tears. Both beasts went deep blue. "Master Bendre made me think of things I do not wish to think of."

Sia nodded. "Is that when they appeared?"

"Aye, Master Bendre tried to touch one, and it burned him!" she said, crying again.

"Hush now, my little dragoness," he said, squeezing her hand. He reached out a hand to touch one, and she grabbed it.

"Don't. I do not want you to get hurt," Nihility said.

"I am not afraid, my little dragoness," he said.

"Sia…" she whined.

"Trust me," he said. Nihility nodded but gripped his hand tight. He reached out with his other, holding it under the beast's snout, allowing it to smell him. The beast lowered its head and sniffed Sia's hand. He closed his eyes as they made contact.

"Sia," she said, alarmed.

"I am okay, Nihility," he said, opening his eyes and looking at her in shock. "My little dragoness, they are you."

"What?"

"They are you, Nihility. You have created life from fire," he said.

"I do not understand," she said.

"We need to find a home. I think it is time. You have been here with me long enough. There is little room for you to grow as you need here," he said, looking around the alcove. "They will need space as well."

"Sia, what are you talking about?!"

"Our future," he said, grinning at her. "You need to give them names, Nihility. They long for your acceptance. This one here is female, and the other is male."

"They hurt Master Bendre!" she snapped.

"Nay, they did not. They do not know their purpose, only your feelings and your will. They are young and wild, like a hatchling. Ben touched living emotional fire, Nihility. He is lucky all he got was a little burn. You'd think he was a student of Iros the Blender doing something so foolish."

"Sia, I cannot keep them!" she shouted. They growled at her feet. She looked at them and then quickly at Sia.

"They respond to you," he said softly. "Care for them as you care for a new flame."

"Why is this happening to me?" she whined. Both of the beasts lamented with her.

He sighed and turned to face her. He took both of her hands in his. "Whatever you have experienced in your young life has been traumatic, Nihility. What you endured in the Dreaming saving Ivylth was traumatic, and I know some things have happened before," he said. She moved to speak, and he pressed his fingers to her lips. "No, do not tell me. I do not want to know. The only way I will listen is if you, my little dragoness, feel deep in your heart that you would share that information with me. I do not say that to disregard your feelings. I say that because I know myself. I am fine living my years not knowing who caused you that kind of pain. It is hard enough to keep myself from burning those two fools you are bonded to when they bruise your heart."

"Do you know what they are?" she asked.

"Emotions that have been given life through fire. Whatever your mind refuses to deal with has manifested in these two here, but like all things Nihility, you can allow it to consume and destroy you, or strengthen and build you."

"I created them?" she asked.

"Aye, you did."

"So they are real."

"Very real. Their minds think, and they feel on their own, but they also feel what you feel. Go ahead, see if you can sense their feelings," Sia said, nodding at them.

She looked at them and closed her eyes. "Hunger, fear, and curiosity," she said. "Sia, I can't have them here on Petrall!"

"Ah yes, that is why I said we need a new home," he said, smiling at her. "I also think you should stay here with me for a bit while we get it sorted out. That means no Weaver Circle. You can enter the Dreaming from here, and I will keep watch."

"Destined and Endrir will come looking for me," she said.

"Nay. The Farseer has gone with Endrir on one of his assignments. They will be gone for a couple of weeks at least."

"I'm actually relieved they are gone for once," she said, taking a deep breath. "I do not have it in me to deal with Destined's endless questions about these two right now when I barely understand myself."

"The questions will come, but I would have you train with me in the meantime. I want to teach you a few things the mind is capable of. It will help you with them. I also want them to be properly trained. They are not lesser beasts, Nihility."

"But Sia."

"My little dragoness, you have two lives that now exist because of you. There are no longer any buts about this. You must care for them," Sia said. Nihility nodded. "Now I want to try something because, in their current state, they are not entirely manageable. They will set something on fire. Can you close your eyes and think of something that brings you peace all the time? Visualize every detail of it." She did as he asked. "Do you have it?" he asked.

"Aye."

"Now think of nothing but the feeling of peace it gives you," he said. The beasts were no longer covered in flame. Before them, sat two little creatures that resembled wolves he had only seen in Emberwood Thicket, home of the Greenbarks. They had long black fur and bright eyes that shifted colors, red, orange, and yellow, like living fire. The chain sat around their necks and continued to shimmer like her scales when she entered the Dreaming. They whined and made tiny growling noises. Her eyes opened, and she gasped.

"Oh, oh, oh," she said, scooping them up and pulling them to her chest. "You are adorable!" she squealed. They licked her face and squirmed in her arms. One escaped her grasp and crawled into Sia's lap.

"This is the male," he said, holding him. "He has quite the opinion of his surroundings and himself."

"This one is hungry," she said, giggling as the little pup nuzzled her. "They need food, Sia."

"Aye," he said as he examined the male pup closely. "Nihility?"

"Yes," she answered through giggles as the female climbed over her.

"Why do they look like this?" he asked.

"What do you mean?" she asked, scrunching her face in a way he loved.

"Their form," he said, nodding at them.

"I don't know, Sia," she said with a shrug.

"Have you been looking through my books, my little dragoness?" he asked with a smirk.

"Aye," she said, looking away. Sia touched her face gently so she would look at him. "I didn't mean to pry, but you draw beautiful pictures."

"You are not prying, Nihility. You are learning," he said. He kissed her forehead. "They resemble creatures that no longer exist on Sathea. The descendants of those extinct creatures are the Curcal. The wolf packs of Sathea."

"The ones that guard the special places of the Dreaming?" she asked.

"Aye."

"Do you think it is wrong they look the way they do?" she asked, frowning.

"Nay. I think you have given Sathea back a magnificent gift it lost once. Now I must feed the three of you. I want you to remain here with them while I get something."

"Master Bendre, Sia," she whispered.

"I will check on him as well. I will not be gone long, my little dragoness. Think of names for them. Suitable names! I want to hear nothing that sounds like it came from Destined the Farseer! None of that shit he spews like mind fire beasts or wonder pups," he said, rising. The memory faded with the sound of her giggles.

"Bendre tried to teach you how to create the Black Flame," Pax said. "He knew."

"He never said, Lady Pax, but just now, I realized it myself."

"What of those beasts, Nihility?"

"I raised them beside Sia. They roam free in the Dreaming at Great Mother's request, but when I need them, they come no matter where I am. Once they were happy, but they have not been in three thousand years. Now they are just angry at me."

"Jerboa shit. They are the key to your use of the Black Flame. I felt it when I saw them in that memory," Pax said.

"Lady Pax…"

"Nihility, do you understand what he tried to help you do?"

"Deal with the emotions I avoid."

"Aye. I did not avoid my feelings, Nihility. I turned it into a weapon. Bendre saw that and knew you could do it too. Now I see you did more than I could. You gave them life."

"They are monsters," she whispered.

"Aren't we all, Nihility?"

"What?!"

"There is a beast inside us all. Our experiences, lives, and pain we suffer throughout create and mold that beast. Where some lash out, others do not. Some let their beast consume them; others do not. You have experienced savagery that had no rhyme or reason, Nihility. You did not understand why they hated you; only that they did. You did not understand why they took such pleasure in your pain, but you recognized it for what it was, their monster. No being on Sathea could withstand so much as you and still be as vibrant as you are. The mind copes for you. It created the beasts of fire for you. What I saw when I gazed upon what lay beneath the fire was the same I see in you, a sweetness like a cool breeze on a hot day. Love when your heart longs for it," Pax said.

She was silent, absorbing what Pax said. "You think I could wield the Black Flame through them?"

"I believe it would not hurt to try," Pax said. "Great Mother saw something in them as well. She has named them guardians, has she not?"

"Aye. Hounds of the Dreaming, Shadow Wraiths, and Hounds of the Harbinger depending on who you are speaking to," she said. She felt a sense of pride in their titles.

"You are afraid they will not obey you if he is not at your side," Pax said.

"Yes. They love Sia as much as I do."

"Then they will be fine, just as you are now," Pax said. "Call to them, Nihility."

She took a deep breath and let it out slowly. "Afisan. Adhul. Will you come to me?" she asked.

The air before her shimmered. You could hear the rattle of chains on the wind. Two enormous beasts covered in thick black fur appeared. Their eyes glowed like a dying fire. They were much larger than any normal wolf. They had grown much from those small pups that cuddled with her at night. Once they hit the max of their growth, she could ride them in her short life form. If they stood on their hind legs, they towered over her. They swung their heads from side to side and shook themselves. They sniffed the air. They howled loud enough it made her scales tingle. They made their way to her and laid down before her.

"I am sorry I have not called you in so long," she said. Afisan huffed at her and turned her head away. "I miss him too. You can feel it, like a piece of us is missing, but what am I to do?" she asked. Adhul moved away and made his way to the cave entrance where Endrir and Destined stood. He sniffed them both, then growled low in his throat.

"I need you," she said loud enough for him to hear. "The both of you. I want us to do as we used to with my fire, but..." she stopped.

Adhul had come back and stood before her. He tilted his head, "but what, Nihility?" he said in his rough voice.

"Oh, my Sathea! They speak!" Pax said, astonished.

"But I would have your promise you will not lose yourselves," she said, lowering her head to the ground.

"Then do not lose yourself," Adhul said. He was never the one to bite his tongue with her.

"Adhul, do not start with me," she snapped.

"I only state facts. The fact is, our loss of control is your own. Do not burden us with your own shortfalls," Adhul said, yawning.

"You do not have to be so damn cruel, Adhul!" she snapped.

"Enough, Adhul. She has called us because she needs us. That is enough for me. I miss her too. I will not have your mouth drive her away again," Afisan said. "Nihility?"

"Aye."

"I do not wish to be without him. I will not suffer his absence any longer," Afisan said.

"I hear you, Afisan."

"Good. Then what would you have us do?" Afisan asked.

"Black Flame," she said. They both whined and stepped

back. "I am afraid too," she whispered, "but we must be strong and remember what he taught us."

They both stood attentively. "Nihility, remember what I said. Do not touch your true anger," Pax said.

"They only respond to the truth of my feelings, Lady Pax. Petty squabbles and simple feelings are not enough for these two. They much have the truth of it," she said.

She closed her eyes. The sound of chains filled the air once again. Adhul caught fire, first a dark blue, then black. He growled as his eyes rolled white. Afisan dug her claws into the ground and whined. Adhul paced around her. He howled and snarled. He shook his head like he struggled to control himself. She released the fire, and he collapsed to the ground, panting.

"Try something else, Nihility. That one does not work on me," Afisan said. She closed her eyes and thought of the pain she had experienced at the hands of Ivylth. Afisan's fire bloomed a pale grey as she growled and barked.

"Try to channel both emotions, Nihility," Pax instructed.

She took a deep breath and pulled forth her anger and her pain. Both hounds caught fire. They flared a bright red before the flame went black. Their chains sparked as clouds rolled in overhead. There was a charge in the air that she could feel under her scales. The rumbling began, growing much like growls of the hounds. The charge filled the air around them, raising the hair on the hounds. Heat rose around them, causing the air to shimmer. Adhul and Afisan turned their heads to the sky and howled. Lightning struck the ground between them, and she felt it latch to the chains around the hounds, linking them together. It arced between them as they pawed the ground. Where they touched, the ground smoldered. She felt it wanting to jump free from her grasp and quickly released it. Adhul and Afisan settled down on the ground, panting.

"Do you both know nothing else but my hurt and anger?" she asked

Adhul flared orange and yellow and huffed at her. "None of your self-pity, Nihility. You know well that we are capable of more. That flame is," Adhul stopped and tilted his head, "dark," he finished.

"And deep," Afisan said as she flared a pure white flame.

"Why just him?" she asked. Afisan shook herself, and the flame changed from white to purple, tinged in grey and black. She looked away.

"Because you cannot deal with the feelings of the other yet. The one who stinks of Warida magic, and something else," Afisan said.

"Death," Adhul said. "That is all he is going to smell like if he keeps it up."

"That is enough, Adhul," she said, sighing.

"He needs a dream space with me, Nihility. Make it happen. He will come out a much better dragon for you," Adhul said.

"Or humping your leg too, Adhul," Afisan said with a huff.

"Hey!" she said.

"I will not apologize for the truth," Afisan said, rolling her eyes.

"They know your heart, youngling," Pax said with amusement.

"Aye, they always have," she said, looking over at Destined and Endrir.

"We will need to practice those flames if you mean to use them, Nihility," Adhul said. "I must keep my mind while they hold, but it is a struggle."

"Is it the same for you, Afisan?" she asked.

"No, my head is clear, but to move is painful," Afisan explained. "However, we felt the power when you used them both. We felt the surge again."

"Aye," she said, looking at Destined and Endrir. She could feel their shock.

"Go on. We will remain here and stand guard. You must go to the Dreaming and rest before we can do anything more."

"You cannot remain on the peak!" she said quickly.

"We don't want to. We stay to guard you, Harbinger," Afisan said. "However, I would much rather be home," she said, getting up and walking towards the river. "Come, Adhul, I am hungry. There is game in these woods."

"You just ate!"

"That was hours ago. Come now."

Pax sighed deeply. "Never have I had a moment in all my years where my life made sense. Until now, that is. I was named the Herald by Gilliphae herself; she said I was a symbol of change in the Dreaming and Sathea. The problem is, I never saw myself that way. I never saw myself as one who controlled fate or bent to its will. I was a Weaver, bending the Dreaming to my will. I was an Empath that made other's control themselves around me. I never humbled myself before anyone or anything on Sathea. I thrust myself into that place to reunite with my twin with little thought for anything else but myself. I cared little for what I left behind, what tasks I left incomplete. Here I am now, the Herald, a shade in the mind of another. Another who is a symbol of all my failures and forgotten tasks," Pax said.

"But Lady Pax..."

"Nay, youngling, now is the time you should listen. Nihility if I were alive the day you were hatched, I would have called you the Harbinger as well. Not for the reasons Petrall did, but because it is a title that speaks to the truth of who you are. You are the Harbinger of Sathea's wrath. That is what the lightning is, her wrath. Wild and free. The storm comes, and you see Sathea's tears fall upon the land, but sometimes the storm brings her fury. Sometimes it brings forth her wrath in the fire that blazes from the sky, igniting anything it touches. Raw, indiscriminate fury that has been gifted to you to wield. The Empath that feels Sathea all around her. The Empath who can hear her words in those feelings."

"Could you not feel Sathea, Lady Pax?"

"Nay. I refused to. I turned my back on all of it, Nihility, and I did so willingly. I did not embrace Sathea as she opened her arms to me. I turned my back on her for my own kind. Here you are on this peak, but you mimic the forms of those I did not try to know. You speak to those I did not even attempt to speak to, but I shared their space. I was nowhere near the Empath or dragoness you are, Nihility Harbinger, and I am humbled to be here with you now. I am humbled to see a flame I brought forth in grief, held so gracefully by one who has endured far more than I ever did in all my years," Pax said with a mixture of pride and sadness.

"I am not afraid of the storm when it comes, but I know the danger it brings," she said, looking up into the sky. The clouds had disappeared, leaving only bright stars in the clear sky. "I am the reason the lightning no longer leaves the Apex. It was the first time Ivylth took me for one of her so-called lessons. She pushed too hard, and I fought back. The storms came and never left. I do not think anyone on Petrall even realizes."

"Is that why she made you consume the dream flowers that grown around the circle?" Pax asked. "To keep you from wielding all of your magic on Sathea."

"Aye. Ivylth would force me to eat the flowers and take me away from the peak. After the Apex, she was never alone. Ergodi and Pimo were always with her."

"Nihility, the Black Flame is yours now. I could do no more with it but create it. Of course, I was never a dragoness who had the patience for finer control. Not when a fire burns so nicely," Pax said with a chuckle. "You can not only control and manipulate the fire, but I believe you can use it to channel the lightning, to control it. Despite the Hounds of the Harbinger, I think you should work on crafting a weapon that suits you. One you can wield as not only dragoness but in your borrowed form as well."

"What is wrong with the Black Flame?"

"Nothing, but it can be more. It wants to be more. The wild feeling I felt was the lightning and those hounds. You called it, Nihility."

"I cannot control it," she said, frowning.

"You must try. The Black Flame is fire, yes, but in you, it knows it can do as all fire wishes to. It knows it can grow, and it can change. Nihility lightning is frightening, it is free, and it is wild, just as you are. It is carried by clouds of the storm, but the clouds cannot control it. Where it touches, fire blooms. Watching that display of power showed me the truth of who you are, Nihility Harbinger. You are wild. You long to be free, but the world's emotions carry you. When you release those feelings that burden you, your feelings, and your wrath is potent. It is the lightning."

"Sia tried to teach me how to wield it, but he said the fire was his domain."

"I only knew one dragon that could wield the lightning," Pax said.

"Uzzod," she mumbled, looking at Endrir.

"Aye," Pax said. "Think of how you would wield the flame in battle. Refine it as you did my seal, Nihility. It is your task given to you by me. Show me what you can do when you choose to confront the darkness." Pax said.

"Does this mean you will leave me now?"

"You heard Adhul; he wants to find the place of control, and I would help," Pax said. Nihility sighed with relief. "I do not know how much time we have Nihility, but I promise you we will make the best of what we do. You…"

"Lady Pax?" she said frightened. It felt like the old dragoness had vanished from her mind. "Lady Pax!?"

"I am here, Nihility."

"Are you okay?"

"Aye, I think so. Did you feel anything just now?" Pax asked.

"It felt like you faded away for a moment," she said frowning. "Are you sure you're okay?"

"Aye. As I was saying, you need to rest. There is another task I need you to perform to help Endrir."

"What is it?" she asked hopefully.

"After you have rested, Nihility. Besides, your dragons seek you out," Pax said. She turned her head and looked at the cave. Both of them were standing at the entrance watching her. "See to them, but before you go, did Destined say anything about helping you rid yourself of that one?" Pax asked, nodding at Ana.

Her anger flared for a moment before she quickly pushed it away. "What I saw requires an explanation from her, but I will not question her until I see what lies in Endrir's dreams first. Then she will answer all my questions without lies or hesitation. If she does not, then I believe she will no longer find herself in the haven she believes my mind to be," she said, rising and shifting.

She made her way to the cave entrance and smiled at them both. "You are hungry," Endrir said, looking down at the ground.

"Aye. I am and tired as well. I will need to go to the Dreaming and recharge."

"I did not hunt enough to feed you as dragoness," he said.

"I will stay in this form. I can touch the Dreaming in it as well. Destined did that for me," she said, smiling at him. She kissed Destined on the cheek as he embraced her.

"That was better than anything I could do with my mind. Pax looked exactly as she does. I told you that your fire was a part of your magic," Destined said.

"I will not say you were right," she said, smirking at him.

"I'll take it anyway," he said, chuckling. "Are you sure you are okay, my love? I have not seen those two with you in a very long time," he said.

"I will be. We all will be. Our light will see us through," Nihility said, winking at him.

"Lightning, my love?" Destined asked, giving her a look. She looked away from him. "Hey, do not do that! I am not upset. I am shocked," he said, grinning. "See what I did there?"

"You are such a fool," Endrir said, rolling his eyes and groaning at Destined's joke.

"No more short lifer books for you, Destined," she said, giggling.

"Seriously, it is a rare gift, Nihility. Only Uzzod does it as far as I know."

"Nay. He rides it. He cannot summon it from nothingness. He must set the stage for it or encounter it naturally," Endrir said. "You called it to you."

"I cannot control it, Endrir," she mumbled.

"Perhaps we could help you figure out how," Destined said, nudging Endrir.

"Of course!" Endrir said. "I mean, I have spent enough time with Uzzod being zapped by it, anyway."

She giggled. "Not now. I am tired and hungry. Come, we could all use a rest," she said, leading them into the cave.

"I should keep watch," Endrir said.

"Nay. Afisan and Adhul will when they return. Nothing will harm us this night."

"What are they?" Endrir asked.

"Hounds of the Harbinger. The Shadow Wraiths of the Dreaming," Destined said. "Don't piss them off, Watcher. Especially that one that came to smell you."

"Now, I'm worried."

"They will not harm you," she said.

"Unless you piss him off. Do not sugarcoat it, Nihility!" Destined said. "Adhul has a temper like a dragoness!"

"You got bit, didn't you, Farseer," Endrir said, trying not to laugh.

"He is just protective," she said, laughing. "He warned you."

"He did no such thing!" Destined said, narrowing his eyes.

"A growl is a warning, Destined," she said, giggling.

"How the fuck was I supposed to know? One minute I was minding my business, and the next I was staring at teeth."

"Jerboa shit!" she said.

"What did he do, Nihility?" Endrir asked.

"He tried to touch Afisan's mind without permission. Adhul is protective."

Endrir looked at Destined and burst out laughing. "The Great White Fool of Petrall strikes again!" he said.

"Fly off, Watcher!" Destined said, smiling.

She composed herself and hugged Destined. "We can head up to Petrall before the sun makes its way over the peak. With the light of a new day, we can find a better way through what we face, and we will do so together. Endrir will remain until we do."

"Of course I will," Endrir said.

"It has been a long time since Petrall has held the three of us," Destined said.

"Somehow, I think that is all the advantage we need," she said.

CHAPTER FORTY-THREE

"She called the lightning," he said, sniffing a scorched patch of grass.

"Pax must be helping her. It is not like Nihility to play with that power. It frightens her."

"She is not frightened. She understands what it truly is. She understands the destruction she can wield."

"She would have control of it by now if it wasn't for her sorry excuse for a dragon, Mindbreaker."

"Come on, Ygi. I told you I would make it right. Besides, she has control. It's the darkness she runs from," he said as he turned his head toward the smell of the hounds.

"Hello, you two," Ygi said, smiling as Adhul and Afisan came out of the darkness to greet her. "It is good to see you here."

Adhul tilted his head and moved to Sia. He shifted and embraced him. "I missed you too, little pup," he said. "No love for me, Afisan?" he asked as she stared at him. She growled low in her throat.

"Even I know what that means," Ygi said, chuckling.

"Hush, Ygi," he said, rolling his eyes. He sighed and looked at Afisan as she laid down before him. "I will make it right somehow, Afisan. I'm trying."

"Who do they think they are keeping out with this kind of magic?" Ygi asked.

Adhul grunted beside her. "The Watcher stinks, and the Farseer is still the Farseer," Adhul said.

"At least someone shares my views on those two," Ygi said. "Seriously, did you train them at all, Sia?" she asked as he removed the Farseer's protection ward. "Novices!" she hissed as several small black beetles made their way around the entrance to the cave. They would alert her if anyone other than those three came in or out of the cave.

"Those who have no business here. Besides, you are cheating, Ygi. Your bugs give you an advantage, and you know it. Destined's work would have been sufficient for the likes of Ergodi, and that is who he is cautious of."

"Rightfully so, fucking coward he is," she said with a hiss.

"Your language, dragoness. Where did your mouth learn such vulgarities?" Sia asked with a smirk.

"From your twin, Mindbreaker. Along with a few other things," she said, grinning and wagging her tongue at him.

"I walked into that one," he said, shaking his head.

"Every time, Sia. It is why I love you. However, you should've trained those two to protect themselves against us as well. You never know what may lurk."

"They are not fledglings anymore, Ygi. They must find their own way."

"One is never too old to learn, Sia Mindbreaker. Nihility never stops learning. She will know that we have been here the moment she returns from the Dreaming, and that is not because the hounds will tell her."

"I know," he said, watching her as she lay on her back in between Endrir and Destined. She had her head turned towards Destined as his hand rested on her belly. Endrir lay curled close beside her.

"This cave is much too small for them now. Why would Endrir and Destined bring her here?"

"Because it is the safest place they know," he said, heading into the cave. He took the Farseer's cloak and draped it over Nihility. She did not like to be cold. He left a small piece of scroll rolled up and tied with the stem of the yellow flowers Terg would always give her by her head. He stopped himself from caressing her cheek. He touched his chest with a finger, then his chin, pointed at her, and spread both his hands apart, signing, "I miss you very much." He made his way back to Ygi.

"I did not know she could do that, Ygi," he said, watching her shimmer as she touched the Dreaming.

"Aye, the Farseer tethered that form of hers. He is useful, even if he is foolish. Bendre helped them," she said, rolling her eyes.

"But you like him more than you do the Watcher," he said, laughing.

"He reminds me of another dragon I know; perhaps that is why," she said.

He rolled his eyes and sighed, "You mean a dragoness you know."

"He has her fire. You did spend a week bright red because of her," she said with a giggle.

"I do not need reminding of my sister's pranks. And it was pink, Ygi. I was fucking pink!"

"A beautiful reddish-pink," she retorted. "Come on, little brother of my heart. Ben and Jay will want to know she is well."

"I will be right behind you. I just...I need a moment," Sia said.

"Take your time. I will be up top," Ygi said, moving away and taking flight.

He watched her. Thousands of years at his side, and she was still as beautiful as the day she first came to him. "Be safe, my little dragoness," he whispered. "Adhul, Afisan, do not leave until she returns. She needs you too," he said.

"I want to go home," Afisan said. He knew those words were not just hers, but Nihility's as well. Afisan spoke only the truth of Nihility's heart, while Adhul spoke that which lurked in her mind. Still, hearing them made his throat close, and tears fill his eyes.

"I know," he said, shifting and taking flight.

CHAPTER FORTY-FOUR

Jezzar slithered down the foggy pathways of the Rem flicking her tongue as she went. She had to send for more of herself than usual after her run-in with the dragon who cut her sight with his leaf magic. It was something she was loath to do, but not unable. While her real body remained locked away, she had learned to project her aura and her power with it. She never drew this much power because she had to remain cautious. Dragons, like the one who attacked her, those aligned with Magnus and his Greenbarks, were dangerous. She did not realize that was what he was until it was too late. He hid well all these years. He knew this place well, but not as well as she did.

They called it the Between. She snorted at the thought, but she expected no less from dragons without the gift of weaving. This place was a Rem. It was the same as the place the Weavers waited in the threads of the Dreaming while the dreamer came into their dreams. Weavers that did not have her power, anyway. She was the first Weaver. Jezzar Brightflame. First Weaver to consume the dream essence of the Great Tree Aconi. The Rem in any dream bent to her will. This place was no different. It was a blank slate where she could impose her will.

She found it by accident. She was the guardian of a prophet's thread. Even though that prophet was her twin sister, she held her duty with honor. When Rona would fall into her visions, she would guard her and guide her back from the flames. She kept the many trees she planted with her visions in the Prophet's Grove deep in the Dreaming. It was during one of Rona's moments when she noticed her twin would touch a place of emptiness. A place called Apathy. A place that mirrored Sathea, but there was peace. There were no emotions to bombard her. There was only silence. She latched on to it and began coming to get away from Rona and her infernal erratic emotions. She built her home here when Rona betrayed her. Surrounding Apathy in a Rem of its own. Its mimicry of Sathea became her dream, her wish. Then her dragon imprisoned her beyond its limits when he felt she had lost her way. Now she could only spread her aura through it and watch it change.

Jezzar turned her head slightly. She could smell the bronze dragon so full of himself, and the sycophant red behind him. They were calling her. Their urgent whispers of "mother" echoed along the Rem. She had no desire for them. Not now. She may need them later, but she wanted to allow them to bring her the remaining two souls she required to solidify her hold on Petrall. If they failed, she would have theirs. They did not know their lineage, but she could see it. Brood of Rona Brightscales, and descendants of her nine faithful dragons who helped destroy the life she once had.

She led them away from her, changing the landscape with a thought. The others who were slowly making their way through the fog searching for the tower in Apathy, where she took in lost souls, cringed, and cried out as she passed, sensing the anger in her at the thought of her traitorous twin, Rona. She stopped before the door the Farseer had so boldly entered. She grazed the mark left by the weak Weaver with her nose, placing her own over it.

How low had Gilliphae fallen in her absence? She had seen the Weaver many times with the Farseer. At first, she was delighted another Weaver had found their way to her. Then she realized the wretched Weaver did not even notice her. Excitement turned to rage. The Weaver did not differ from the others who had forgotten the Grand dragoness, Jezzar Brightflame. The Grand Weaver, who held the Dreaming on her wings and filled Sathea with life. She was the Mother of All, not Rona! She entered the space, allowing her rage to pulse out before her.

"The Serpent! The Serpent who will devour us all is real! It's real! The Seven of Bishamyr lied to us!" a voice screeched in the darkness.

"Cower and be silent you pitiful creatures!" she hissed. Bright blue-green flames erupted around the room, freezing all the Lessers in place. "There are more of you than I realized," she said, surveying the room. "Enough to lead me to believe your pathetic king might be afraid of something," she said playfully. She could taste their fear on her tongue. It tempted her to consume them all, but she needed them to remain for her plan to work.

The Farseer would return here, and when he did, she would have him. A budding power she wanted to herself. A power to open the barrier to her prison, and a new mate to replace the descendants of Rona Brightscales with her own.

However, she had a problem to deal with first. The Farseer carried one of the Seven's children out of the Rem. She could not have the Seven interfering with her plans. She had lost her dragon many years ago. It was his magic, aided by the Great Tree Magnus, that kept her body sealed away. She had another mate, however. One who never lost his love for her, Quenrum. He was the betrayer of his kind. Even now, he showed his devotion to her. He worked to rebuild the gate to allow her passage. A gate the Farseer could use to open the door.

Soon she would have everything again. The Farseer, Quenrum, and the egg he had used his magic to create for her. The last made her chuckle. Rona left behind a useless brood of dragons, who raised more useless dragons. They did not even realize a demon was walking among them. Those that did welcomed him with open wings for their own gain. They were all just as foolish as Rona.

She moved around the Farseer's ward and nodded her head in approval. He was a clever dragon and strong. She made her way to the fallen twin dragon. "I told Quenrum it was a mistake to take you. You were too strong for him to dominate. Especially when he is not at his full strength," she said, standing before the barrier. "Pity he did not listen to me."

The barrier glowed. "You go no further, false serpent!" a deep voice commanded.

She turned her head away until the light dimmed. "Aren't you an interesting pair?" she said, observing the dragon that had emerged from the barrier. A dragon, both black and white, loomed in front of her. On its chest was a red star. "You've merged yourselves into one being. You must have been close."

"Turn away, Jezzar Brightflame," the dragon said. "It spoke with both their voices.

She paused a moment, reading them. "You've bonded yourselves in your love for one another. How sweet you are, Lazarus the Gold and Paxtiya the Red. Yes, I know you both. I have seen you."

The dragon lunged at her, jaws snapping. She dodged, coiling herself around them and pinning their wings to their sides.

"Why are you so angry?" she asked, feigning shock.

"Fallen Weaver! Threat to Sathea!" they hissed, struggling against her.

"I am Sathea!" she shouted, gripping them tighter.

"Dark Memory," the twin dragons whispered.

Jezzar recoiled, releasing them as memories of her fight with Rona flooded her mind. Rona appeared before her and attacked. Claws raked down her back. Teeth ripped at her tail. She lashed out, striking Rona repeatedly with her fangs. Rona released her and backed away slowly.

"Infinite Pain," the twins said.

She was forced back into the fight again. She hissed in rage, trying to push the memory away.

"We are the Twin Stars of Petrall. Sworn defenders of the Great Balance. The shining lights of Sathea," the twins said as a light erupted from the star on their chest, striking Jezzar in the eyes.

Jezzar hissed as excruciating pain enveloped her, forcing her to make herself small by coiling tightly. The agony was terrible. She wanted nothing more than to make it go away. Suddenly, the pain eased. She lifted her head enough to see the dragon falter for just a moment. She struck quickly, lodging her fangs deep into the twin's neck. Their cries of pain filled the room. She wrapped herself around them and called for the fire of her name, Brightflame. Pure red flames sprang forth.

"Your light fades, Twin Stars, but I will not let it be for nothing. You put up a worthy fight. Now, I will ease your suffering. After all, that is what a mother does," she said as she opened her jaws wide and devoured the dragon whole.

Belly full and her rage sedated, she looked in on the thin space where the barrier once stood. She could see the land of the demons, Bishamyr. She could see the Seven in full view. Their king sitting upon his throne of black stone, while the other six stood on either side of him. The crystal once holding Lazarus, was now empty.

"Jezzar!" the king shouted, pointing his black claw at her.

"So, you can see me," she said. Her jaws widened in a smile. "Stay away from Sathea."

"I will have your heart, beast!" the demon king shouted.

"Or I will devour yours," she said. "The Betrayer says hello and farewell."

The room shook and her eyes glowed as she pulled at the Rem. She closed the space on the screams of rage from the demon horde, leaving a rock wall in its place. She placed her mark upon it, the great serpent, where the Twin Stars once laid. Her belly rumbled loudly.

"Settle younglings. Settle and rest. Mother is here," she said as she slithered away. Her flames holding the Lessers dissipated as she crossed the threshold. "Do not leave," she said, looking back. "You are needed."

EPILOGUE

Terg placed his hand on the trunk of the old tree growing between the rocks. It creaked and groaned before creating an entrance. The Ciel flowers glowed faintly along the walls. He began saving his memories shortly after he realized the truth of what he had done. He had released the demon on Sathea again, and woke the sleeping dragoness, Jezzar. He sighed heavily.

He was avoiding going to see Magnus. He needed time to get his thoughts together. He needed time to figure out if he was ready to deal with Jezzar and the madness she would unleash on Sathea. He winced as the image of when he first found Nihility jumped into his mind. It had been happening since Ygi called to him. Nihility was heavy on his mind. More so than Pax. He was worried for the little dragoness who captured his heart so long ago. He conjured an empty flower and poured the memory at the front of his mind into it.

"Where are we?" Nihility asked as Terg landed. "There is water here!" she said. She was perched on his back, taking in everything around her.

"That is the Durming Sea, little one. We are below Petrall. Weaver Circle is above us through the clouds. This is the home of those I said would care for you," he said.

"They live here?! It is beautiful! The water is so blue! Look how far it goes!"

"Aye, but you must be cautious of it until you grow a little bigger," he said as he walked through the grass towards Ygi and Bendre's cave. "Lady Ygi finds peace here, and Ben..." he stopped, shocked at what he saw.

"What dragoness has finally roused you from your cave?" a large blue and black dragon asked through gritted teeth.

"Bendre," he said as he watched him try to mend his wounds. There was a gash on his side, and his back leg was broken. They were the same wounds he had seen on Nihility hours before.

"Ygi is not here, Terg, and I am afraid I cannot entertain you right now," Bendre said. He sent his magic to mend Bendre's broken leg, making him sigh with relief. "I did not ask for your help."

"You never have to, Ghost," he said as the gash closed itself.

Bendre huffed smoke. "Ygi is not here. She…" he said as his words died. "Nihility," Bendre whispered.

"You made him feel better," she said, sitting between his feet. "He was in a lot of pain."

"Aye," he said, sitting himself down. "Do you know who he is?"

"Bendre the Ghosteater!" she said confidently.

"And you are Nihility the Harbinger, the beautiful black dragoness of Petrall," Bendre said, composing himself.

She hummed loudly. "The Matron says you are one of the most powerful dragons on Petrall. She says you and Jaydum the Soulbreaker are special. I learned all about you!"

"Did she say that about me?" Terg asked, nuzzling her.

"She said you were a lecherous dragon, but I do not know what that means," Nihility said.

"The most accurate description of you I have ever heard," Bendre said, laughing.

He huffed smoke. "It means I am powerful."

"Sure does," Bendre said, chuckling. "Lecherously powerful."

"Fly off, Ghost," he said, trying not to laugh. "I want her to stay here with you and Ygi."

"What?" Bendre asked. His shock was evident.

"Ygi can teach her. Take her to the circle and have her linked to the crystal," he said.

"Terg, I can't," Bendre said, wincing as he stood. "If I could, I would have done so well before now."

"Why on Sathea not?" he asked.

"Otunte no longer holds Weaver Circle, Terg. She has not since shortly after Nihility's hatching."

"My hearing must be going," he said, shaking his head.

"You heard him just fine, Terg. You would know if you did not linger in that damn forest wallowing in grief," Ygi said as she landed next to Bendre. "I did not find her, Ben, but her cries have stopped. Are you okay?"

"Ygi, love bug, look," Bendre said, nodding towards him.

"Sweet Sathea, you found her!" she gasped as she spotted Nihility.

Nihility tugged on his beard. "She is the one I saw," she whispered. "The one like the sunset."

Ygi smiled at her with tears in her eyes. "I was looking for you. Do you remember me, young dragoness?"

Nihility nodded. "You were sad. Are you still sad?"

"I always carry some sadness with me, youngling, but right now, I am happy."

"I like happy. It feels nice. You feel nice," Nihility said. Ygi hummed at her words.

"I was asking Ben if she could stay here with the two of you," he said.

"That is her decision to make, Terg. She is dragoness!" Ygi huffed. "I am Ygi the Screecher, and a Weaver, like you. Would you like to stay here with me?" Ygi asked. Nihility looked at her but did not speak. "She will not come here, Nihility. She would not dare. This is my home. Trespassing here would cost her life."

"Do I have to decide right now?" Nihility asked.

"Nay," he said before Ygi could respond.

"Terg!" Ygi hissed.

"She is afraid, Ygi!" he snapped.

"I am not afraid!" Nihility said. "I…I just want to be sure."

"Sure of what, little dragoness?" Bendre asked.

"That this is the place I should be," she said, looking up towards the peak.

Bendre chuckled. "Are you worried the Matron will miss you?"

"I know she will. It is just that… Destined and Endrir," she whispered.

Terg looked at Ygi and frowned. "The one they have named the Farseer is a prophet, but Sia named him Destined as Cimbu desired. Ergodi keeps him close," Ygi answered. "The one she called Endrir lost his twin at hatching. She and Nihility saved him from a worse fate. He is under the care of those four that the Grand Lady claimed."

"A Watcher and a Walker?" he asked.

"Aye, with a Weaver between them," Ygi said.

"You do not need to worry about Destined and Endrir, Nihility," Bendre said. "You need to worry about yourself for a while. You have done your part in saving Endrir, but now you must save yourself."

Nihility nodded but did not move. "Will you stay with me for a little longer?" she asked Terg.

"Aye. I will stay until you are ready."

"Terg," Ygi said with a sigh.

"Ygi, please," he said.

"Terg the Redeemer! We had a fucking agreement, dragon! Remember, you do not leave without sending me a message. I did not know where you were. Someone disturbed the forest, and I smelled blood!" Jaydum said as he landed next to him.

"Jay, wait," he said.

"Don't even try to sweet talk me, dragon! I should set you on fire for making me worry!" Jaydum shouted.

Nihility moved and stood between him and Jaydum. She

hissed and shot a small ball of fire. "You do not talk to him like that!" she shouted. Jaydum took a step back and looked down in shock.

"Who are you, little dragoness?" Jaydum asked.

"I am Nihility the Harbinger, and Terg is my dragon!" she snapped.

"For Sathea's sake, Terg!" Ygi hissed.

"Ygi, wait," he stammered. "It's not like that!"

"What if I told you he is my dragon, little dragoness?"

"But you are a dragon," Nihility said with a confused look.

"I am. Do you think that means I cannot love another dragon?" Jaydum asked.

Nihility sat for a moment with her head tilted to the side. "No. I felt you care and worry for him," she said. She looked back at him, "you should not make him worry like that. It makes him afraid."

"You felt..." Jaydum said as he looked at him, shocked.

"I had to come back, Jaydum," he said, nodding at Nihility.

Nihility moved and sniffed Jaydum. "You smell like the Matron," she said, rubbing her snout against his leg. "It's a nice smell. You are even warm like her."

"I'm keeping this one," Jaydum said, nudging Nihility with his snout and making her giggle.

"You have Frety and Apryl to worry about," Ygi said. Nihility moved over to Ygi, smelling her. When she smelled Bendre, she hummed loudly. "Ben, do I have competition for your heart?" Ygi asked playfully.

"Perhaps," Bendre said, smirking. He made space for Nihility as she laid herself down between his front legs and groomed her scales.

"I think Ghost just stole your dragoness, Terg," Jaydum said.

"That's a first," he said, making a face.

"Jerboa shit," Ygi said, chuckling. "Do you know what it means to be Weaver, Nihility?" Ygi asked her.

"The Matron gives me lessons. She showed me how to weave dreams, but only the hatchlings," Nihility said.

"She has taken you to the dream nest?" Terg said, shocked.

"Aye, but she said I was not to tell Ivylth."

"Jes…" Ygi started and stopped, looking at Jaydum, "the Matron is wise and saw something in you. I am sorry I could not come to retrieve you, Nihility."

"She said Ivylth would not let you, and it was better if I stayed with her. She feels strange sometimes," Nihility said.

"Strange how youngling?" Ygi asked.

"Sometimes, she feels more than just love. Sometimes she feels sad. When she does, she speaks to me differently, but it is always gone quickly," Nihility explained.

"That is a power you have," Bendre said. She looked up at him. "You are an Empath."

"Ivylth says they are fragile," she mumbled.

"Ivylth is fucking fragile," Jaydum snapped. "Fucking dragoness makes my ass itch."

"Be still, Jay," Bendre said. "You are not fragile, Nihility."

"I feel fragile and helpless," she said, looking out into the water.

"I do not doubt that, but I believe it is only because you are young. Can you tell me when you felt something for the first time?" Bendre asked.

"I have always felt things," she said, frowning. "I felt them when I came out of my egg, but also before."

"Tell me about before," Bendre said gently.

"I felt the others. They followed me through the darkness along the blue path. I led them through while Endrir's sister watched behind. She said she would be the shadow that followed to make sure we made it safe. I…" she stopped. "I do not want to talk about this anymore."

"That is fine, little one. You do not have to," Bendre said, giving him a look.

"Even before she left her egg? You cannot be serious, Ghost," he said in awe. Ben nodded at him. "She traveled Perpetual Night!"

"What's Perpetual Night?" Nihility asked.

"That is the name of the blue path you walked, little Weaver," Jaydum said. "It is a path controlled by Bendre and me."

"Is that bad?" she asked.

"It is extraordinary," Jaydum said. "You are an extraordinary Weaver."

"Well, Nihility, it seems you have a thirst for knowledge, and I have finally been granted my wish to have you under my wing. That is, if you want to stay," Ygi said.

"You will teach me?"

"Aye, but only if you want. The bond between dragonesses should not be forced. There must be harmony between the young dragoness and the elder she learns from. I felt that harmony in the nursery. Did you feel the same?" Ygi asked.

"You felt warm and made my scales tingle, but..." Nihility stopped looking over at Terg.

"You cannot remain under the wing of Terg the Redeemer, Nihility," Ygi said.

"Why not?" he said with a wink.

"Terg, for Sathea's sake, be serious," Ygi said, exasperated.

He grinned at her. "Nihility, I would have you grow strong with Ygi, but I will always be here if you need me."

"But you said I was your dragoness. You do not just leave your dragoness," Nihility said with fire.

"Really, Terg!" Ygi hissed.

"Hush Ygi bug," he said, smiling at her. He moved over to Nihility and Bendre. "You are my dragoness, but you must grow to stand beside me, not hide under me," he said, flicking her lightly with his tongue. She hummed loudly.

"If Lady Pax was here, she would have your hide, Terg," Ygi said.

"But she is not," he said, trying to suppress a shiver as Nihility sniffed him.

"The Matron has mentioned her name. She said I was like her, but who is she?" Nihility asked.

"The only dragoness that ever existed that could scare Terg the all-powerful Redeemer," Bendre said, laughing.

"I was not afraid of her!" he said, hiding his grin.

"I would hear more of her," Nihility said, sitting up attentively.

"Then Ygi will be the best teacher for you," Bendre said. "She was a student of the Grand Lady."

"Really?!"

"Aye. I learned much from Lady Pax, and since that is what you wish to learn, it will be your first lesson while our dragons hunt for us. After I have your belly full, I will teach you how to make sure your lazy old dragon cares for you properly," Ygi said. "Ben, she will need double. She has not had enough to eat in a while."

Nihility looked up at Bendre, "are you my dragon too?" she asked.

"Aye, for as long as you need me to be," Bendre said, nuzzling her and making her hum. "Will you stay with Ygi while I hunt for the both of you?"

Nihility nodded. "Can you see the Matron too? She will worry if I do not return soon. She always worries when they take me."

"Ben and I will let her know you are safe," he said.

"I will go with you, Terg," Jaydum said.

"Are you sure, Jay?" he asked.

"Aye. It is time."

He released the memory into an orb and tucked it safely into one of the empty spaces in the wall of his cave. It would bloom into a flower soon. He walked out of the cave, the tree closing behind him. He readied himself to shift to his true self and stopped as a great white dragon stood before him.

"Lazarus?"

"Memento Mori, my handsome dragon," Lazarus said.

Tears filled his eyes, "Memento vivere, my loving dragon," he responded just as he always had in their late-night whispers while Bysi, the mate they shared, was away.

"She remains, Terghelm, and you must prepare," Lazarus said as he faded away.

He brought his hand to his chest, absently rubbing the spot where his heart ached faintly. Laz was gone.

About Kenla Nelson

Kenla Nelson is a West Texas native currently located in Central Texas. Before moving back to Texas, she spent twenty years traveling and studying. She graduated with a dual B.A.S. from Bradley University in Peoria, Illinois. Kenla then moved to Washington, D.C., where she attended Howard University School of Law '05. She has lived in Japan, Virginia, Alaska, New York, North Carolina and is back in Texas. If she isn't writing, she spends her time playing video games, chasing her children, watching anime, or being buried in books, models, and legos. Dragon's Breath: Black Flame is her debut novel. You can follow her on her website at www.harbingersrest.com for updates.

Also from Dreamsphere Books

An Angel Among Dogs
Charli Mac

Bethany is dead. It was horrible and violent, but it's over now. And she's still here, kind of, floating aimlessly in a vast nothingness, a mind without a body.

Kai Strand is First Hound. It's a heavy responsibility, trying to ensure the survival of his race against the men who have always seen them as second-class citizens. After his Hounds are instrumental in winning a battle for valuable new land, he is astonished when Price Faron offers him an unbelievable reward: a chance to stand before the Ether at the Solar Convexion—the first in a hundred and fifty years—and see if he is lucky enough to call forth a spirit to bind.

A strange doorway opens before Bethany, pulling her through. Is it the real world or something else? On the other side, she finds a riot of noise and confusion…and a handsome man whose tortured expression called to her through the portal. She clings to him as he whisks her away into the night.

This may not have been the wisest decision because it seems there's been a case of mistaken identities of epic proportion: he and his companions, Hounds, they call themselves, think she's an angel. A sacred being with all sorts of powers. Ha.

Available now in paperback and ebook

Also from Dreamsphere Books

Realms of Valeron
Alison Cybe

When Roka joined the Realms of Valeron, he was a fledgling elven cleric with only a minor healing spell and a dingy brown robe to his name. But that was just fine, since it was the hottest fantasy MMORPG, with over a million players, and Roka could not resist the allure of this rich, bright fantasy world, eccentric NPCs, and ravenous monsters.

And best of all, he met his friends—a wild and eccentric band of misfits who would change his life forever!

Join Roka and his newfound guild as they face devastating Razor-Squirrels, confront the Labyrinths of Ancient Storylines, and rush to max level in order to take part in end-game content (while probably not reading any of the quest text as they go!). But the real treasure that they find isn't the Bejewelled Anklets of Monster-Commanding or even the mythical Pointy Stick—it's the friendship they make along the way.

Enter the Realms of Valeron, a tale of high humor and eager adventuring like nothing before!

Available now in paperback and ebook

Also from Dreamsphere Books

Immortal Whispers
Kon Blacke

The Whispering Monks have foretold change to the world, and it's fast approaching. They also speak of the mortals who'll be involved.

Hereward, a lord knight who only worships the steel at his side, as the mad magician Ealdræd has taken away everyone he had ever loved. Wymond, an oblate determined to find his true self, even if it means turning away from everything he has ever known. Beornræd, a powerful magician who fears to love again after the cruelties of his past. Kieron, a stable hand with dragon blood flowing through his veins and is the rightful heir to a realm of unimaginable beauty.

All four will travel their own paths, to destroy their pasts and rebuild their future, as they thwart the evil plans of Ealdræd and his conduit, the immortal Abbot Hosho.

The whisperings continue through epic battles, both on the ground and in the sky.

The whisperings shall continue beyond the aftermath.

As it has been foretold.

Available now in paperback and ebook